Prophecies and Promises

by

Alana Lorens

Prophecies and Promises

Cover Art by *Jennifer Greeff.*

The Wild Rose Press, Inc.
PO Box 708
Adams Basin, NY 14410-0708
Visit us at www.thewildrosepress.com

Publishing History
First Edition, 2022
Trade Paperback ISBN 978-1-5092-4144-6
Digital ISBN 978-1-5092-4145-3

Published in the United States of America

Dedication

To those who embody the spirit of adventure—may
they never stop taking us on wonderful journeys

Acknowledgments:

With most grateful thanks to my Pennwriters Fellowship of the Quill folks—Todd, Christie, Fritze, Uncle Dave, Aimee, Johanna, Kara, Janyce and Janet (E.T.), Jennie, Carm, Amy, Kathy, Terry and Dan-O; and the folk from MVP—Janet, Ellen, Naima, Doris, Monica and Maggie. Who would have thought that your love and support would be the best thing to come out of COVID? Without you—and our fabulous ZOOM meetings—this book would not have happened.

~

Gratitude also to Margie Lawson, whose teachings helped improve and support this work.

~

And as always, thanks to my editor Ally Robertson and publisher, The Wild Rose Press, for letting me tell my stories in the best way possible.

He nodded. "An old Cuban woman taught me one evening as we sat around a fire at a rebel camp, drums beating in the distance, smoke in the air. She leaned close to me and took my hand, just as I'm holding yours now, and told me my future, showing me how the lines of my palm intersected and moved apart." He examined her face, more serious. "I never believed a word until now."

Tamsyn was thoroughly intrigued, her curious streak in high gear. "What did she say?"

"She told me a time would come when a young woman would rescue me. That woman, she said, would be…" He stared at her, intently watching her face.

His deep gaze hypnotized her. She could almost smell the camp smoke, so taken was she. "Would be what?"

"Would be—" He shook his head. "It's not important. Something about love."

Tamsyn pulled her hand back sharply. "I'm sure it had nothing to do with me, then." She turned and walked away in the direction of her carriage. But she lost one of her sandals in a sudden rush of water and stepped hard onto white coral rock. "Ow!"

"Allow me," he said behind her. Before she could argue, he scooped her up in his arms. As she protested, he replied, "I told you I was in your debt. Please permit me to repay you." Ashton's boots easily traversed the rocks, his arms strong around her. He smelled of salt water and the ocean breeze, and she felt gentleness within him as he carried her.

Chapter One

Shadows. She pushed her way through darkness and the strong standing roots of the banyan trees. Vines hung low, catching her arms, her hair. Hurry! Don't let him catch you! Her heart beat like Clara's tambourine on a Friday night. The moon shone overhead, and she caught movement as he emerged from the shadows. She slipped inside the gate to her father's courtyard and slammed it closed behind her. The man stepped forward and—

"Missy Tamsyn! Time for you to be wakin' now." Clara yanked the curtains open, their weight swaying her thin fourteen-year-old frame. The sun shone in, bright already even though it couldn't be more than seven a.m. The tropic breeze whispered through the palm fronds outside her open window, birds filled the air with their songs, and the rattle and bump of carriage wheels rolled on the rocky street below.

All these Tamsyn took in without opening her eyes. She was safe in her bed. But she would have preferred to sleep just a few more seconds. This dream was one she'd had more than once in recent days, and she'd never been able to stay asleep long enough to determine the identity of the man who pursued her.

But I will before this dream goes away. I will.

She stretched lazily under her white, lace-trimmed sheets. Squinting through the heavy mosquito netting to

1

see the timepiece on the small wooden table beside her, she fervently wished she could fold the covering away. But malaria was a constant threat in 1897 Key West. After her mother, Ellen, had succumbed to the tropical disease three years before, Papa had sworn he'd not lose anyone else. There was no arguing with him.

Well, then, there never was. Papa was...Papa.

And I'll be eighteen in a few months. Mistress of my own fate.

"Come on now, missy. You know Marse Angus be awaitin' you before too long."

"I'm coming, Clara. I'm coming."

She wrestled her way out from under the mosquito netting and set the books she'd been reading the night before on the bedside table. She stretched, allowing the girl to help shift the dark-blue dressing gown onto Tamsyn's shoulders. A bowl of water and a soft cloth awaited her on her bureau, and she took a moment to wash her face and hands.

The port whistle blew, signaling the arrival of a ship. She ran to the window, looking out toward Mallory Square.

Six tall ships anchored in the harbor there, sails furled, and just beyond them, another maneuvered into the docks. Though she squinted her eyes, the ship was too far out to identify the flags against the clear, blue sky.

The whistle began a rush of activity across the town, as it always did. Boys abandoned their sticks and hoops on the narrow sidewalk out front to run down to the docks. Housewives bustled into their morning coaches on the street out front, each followed by an entourage of servants, both dark- and light-skinned, to help make their purchases at dockside.

Tamsyn leaned on the sill, enjoying the gently scented breeze. It was warm already, hot where the sun fell on her extended hand. She must be the luckiest girl in the world to live in such a bright-painted heaven, their own yard a feast of tropical, flowering plants, thanks to the legacy left by her mother's gentle hand. In front grew broad-leafed crotons in speckled green, sharp, pointed snake's tongue, and a huge fire-flowered poinciana tree that shaded Tamsyn's window. A small flock of green Amazon parrots landed, chattering, on the yellow tabebuia and then, bickering among themselves, flew off to chase the sea breeze.

The port whistle blew again, drawing her attention back to priorities. Whose ship was it? Perhaps there would be some new silks on board—she'd been waiting ages for the new Sunday dress Papa had promised her. Miss Pearl had agreed to make her one as soon as Tamsyn chose the materials. No doubt, someone would have brought fresh fruits from the North, apples and oranges. There might be wonderful boxes of something unexpected, depending on where the ship had come from. Tamsyn grinned. Those were the best. She loved surprises and was always open to the unforeseen.

Life was too brief to be rigid.

Her musings were cut short as Clara prodded her. "Missy Tamsyn, aren't you dressed yet?" The dark-skinned girl clanked the dishes on the tray she'd brought, so hard the water spilled out the spout of the teapot. "Him say he going down to the dock right quick!"

Clara poured her a cup of tea and shoved it into her reluctant hands. Tamsyn sipped the cooling brew as directed.

"Because of the new ship's arrival?" Tamsyn thrilled with curiosity. It might be one of the Winslows' ships coming in to dock. Thatcher Winslow would be there, supervising the unloading of cargo. Maybe they could steal a moment alone together—shocking in the midmorning open air. The thought of being so naughty made her smile. "Very well, I'll get dressed. I expect he'll want the carriage ready, too. So ask the men."

The maid's big dark eyes filled with gratitude. "Yes'm." She rushed out as quickly as she had come, bare brown feet slapping the wooden stairs as she descended.

Choosing a cool cotton shirtwaist ensemble, a white blouse with tiny pearl buttons and a soft pink skirt, Tamsyn dressed quickly, finishing the tea as she intentionally set herself to look appealing. She brushed her hair thoroughly before winding the majority of it into a knot at the back of her head. Small tendrils curled in the humidity along the nape of her neck and her forehead. As they stirred in the small breeze coming in the window, she recalled the lips of Thatcher Winslow brushing the back of her neck lightly, tickling just as the hair did now. She shivered with remembered delight. *Stop daydreaming, Tam, and hurry!*

The sound of neighbors exchanging greetings floated through the open front window as she hurried downstairs in soft, buttoned, brown leather boots. Papa was in his office giving orders to his chief clerk, his Scottish burr unusually evident, showing he was agitated.

Tamsyn slipped on past, not ready to deal with Papa's moods just yet. Instead, she went to the kitchen to have Juba make her some breakfast. Someone would have served her at the huge dining table if she'd wished it, but even when her mother had been alive, Tamsyn had preferred the warm and lively kitchen to the formal dining room.

A bright yellow scarf wrapped around her head to cover her hair, the rotund cook scolded her, waving a large metal spoon for emphasis. "You been layin' abed half a day!" A large pile of cut vegetables sat in front of her on a well-worn board. She held bread over the fire on a long-handled fork until it was browned and gave it to Tamsyn with a hot, sweet cup of tea.

One of the girls laid a clean cloth on the stool so Tamsyn wouldn't soil her skirt. "I have done no such thing," Tamsyn said, smiling at the familiar exchange as she took in the busy tasks of the morning kitchen in the MacKiernan house. New curtains hung in the high window this morning, an island print of red and black. Her charge delivered, Clara returned to kneading dough on a side table, flour white against her brown skin.

"Him been at it since dawn," Juba whispered conspiratorially, jerking her head back toward the office.

"What's the matter?" Tamsyn asked in the same tone. Longtime familiarity with the servants' lilting Bahamian and Jamaican speech allowed her to understand more than she let on, especially now that she was nearly grown. But no one was afraid to speak even their native language in her presence—she kept their secrets. She learned a lot from those who seemed to hear everything.

"Spongin' boats fulla holes at daybreak!" Juba said.

No wonder her father was upset. Sponging was one of the two main industries on the island, and Angus MacKiernan had a good business, sending his men out in small boats to grab the marine animals off the bottom with long-handled hooks. Natural sponges were in high demand around the world, used in hospitals to cleanse wounds since they were more sanitary and shed no lint to cause infection. The flat-tabled warehouses her father owned employed a dozen people to dry, sort, and trim the sponges. "Do they know who did it?"

Juba shrugged her wide shoulders. "More toast?"

Tamsyn shook her head. If she knew her father, he'd be in a rare temper. *Best to get finished quickly and report for duty, sharp as any soldier!* It also made her twice as determined to escape the house today. She brushed crumbs from the front of her blouse. "Well, it's eight o'clock. Time to face the music." With a deep breath, she stood up.

The sympathetic eyes of the servants met hers, and the balding, dark-skinned houseman, Old James, smiled his toothless grin as he walked in the back door. "Carriage be ready soon. But Marse Angus be forgettin' 'bout boats and problems when he see your pretty face."

Tamsyn blushed. "Old James, you are a charming devil!" she said. She brushed her worn skirt down, standing tall as if she was balancing a book on her head, an exercise her mother had strictly enforced. Then she went to the office.

She waited around the corner, leaning forward just until she could see, feeling a coward for letting her father's two clerks take the brunt of his displeasure. *But I have nothing to do with sponging sabotage. I'll take criticism for the things that are my own fault, when it's due.*

Her father's slight frame nearly quivered with intensity. "Then post ten men at the harbor by night!" he yelled. "We willna have this happen again, or you'll be looking for other positions. Is that understood?"

The men nodded, pained expressions on their faces. Tamsyn felt sympathy for them. Her hot-tempered father's skin was a ruddy color now, as it always flushed when he was furious. With a bit of a smile, she remembered her amazement once she noticed that he turned red all the way up to his desperately receding hairline.

When Angus didn't speak for another several moments, the senior clerk, Timothy, looked up cautiously. "Is that all, sir?"

"Yes, yes, get to it!" He slammed a book on the desk. All of them, Tamsyn included, twitched at the sudden noise. The clerks took the opportunity to make their escape, with an apologetic glance for Tamsyn as they passed.

Tamsyn stepped in quietly and crossed to her small secretary desk. She got out the thick book of accounts, her mother's before her, and lifted her feathered pen before glancing in her father's direction. "I'm sorry about the boats."

"Can ye believe some scalawag has scuttled them again? How's a man to make an honest living?" His voice steadily rose, then nearly cracked.

"Papa, you'll make yourself sick," she said.

He looked at her with a discouraged eye. "You shouldna worry about me. Let's total these financials. Then I'm going down to the harbor to examine the scene of the crime. Those no-account constables are likely to miss valuable clues, I expect."

"Does that mean we'll finish in time that I may go out today, Papa?" She was still amazed that the catastrophe had actually worked to her benefit. "The flagship came in this morning. The lending library in Jacksonville is supposed to send books this month, and I'd dearly love something new on the sciences. And…Miss Pearl said she would make me a new dress when the silks came in."

The gray-haired man stared down at his beloved books. His ink came out in a huge blot, and he reached for the sand to dry it up. "Damnation!" he muttered. "A *new* dress? Didn't ye just have a new dress made up?"

"Aye, Papa, but that was nearly eight months ago, and that was for parties. Remember, you're the one who said now that I was nearly of age, I had to start being 'seen' before I became an old maid." She twisted her face into a pretty pout, playing on his love for her.

He finally smiled. "Nay, you'll never be an old maid, my dear. As a matter of fact, I've noticed young Winslow spending quite a bit of time here." He winked, and she was thrilled he'd become aware of Thatcher's attention, too. She could tell when her papa was pleased. Her Scottish father had taught her the value of money and had given her every opportunity of education, diction lessons, and what wardrobe and frillies he could so that she could be seen as equal to even the daughters of the best families on the island of eighteen thousand residents.

"Mr. Winslow has been kind," she said, a soft smile tickling her lips. *Mr. Winslow has been increasingly forward—even fresh.* That was what she wanted to say. But her father would be scandalized.

"Mr. Winslow stands to inherit a booming business and quite a bit of money," Angus said thoughtfully. "I'd never have to worry about you going hungry or having to take in laundry."

He shook his head and looked at Tamsyn soberly, wagging a finger at her. "We had nothing when we came to America. *Nothing.*"

She glazed over, having heard the story a hundred times before, how they had come from Edinburgh, first to New York, welcomed by the huge Lady Liberty. Her parents had lived in a dirty tenement, Papa working in a factory and dear Mamma handwashing other people's laundry by candlelight. After that, Angus had promised his wife and his one-year-old daughter, Tamsyn, a better life, and they'd traveled by boat to Key West in 1880, where sponging, cigar making, and most importantly, shipwrecking were ways to turn a quick profit.

After that dire pronouncement, her father got up and paced, still agitated about the crime to his boats. Sensing her father's mind was not really on his work, Tamsyn managed to cajole him into putting the books away early.

"Right you are. I have no time to wait for you and all your folderols. I must go straightaway." He shrugged on his day coat.

Just as well. Traveling with one's father was no way to attract certain young men's attention. "I may take the carriage, then?"

"You take Old James with you, and one of the gals." He reached for his hat. "Remember, you're a young lady!" He marched out the door, bellowing for

Timothy to accompany him.

"Yes, Papa," she said, exasperated. He admonished her exactly the same. Every time. *But it never seems to keep me from getting into trouble.*

At the dock, she was pleased to discover new silks had arrived, and she chose two of her favorites and had them sent to Miss Pearl. Disappointment found her, though, because Thatcher Winslow was nowhere to be found. Probably working in some dark warehouse, Tamsyn thought sadly, locked away from the sun. His absence didn't diminish her good spirits one whit. She knew he'd come by the house to see her later, as he often did, more often than Papa even knew. Now she was free to escape to the other side of the island, to her ocean.

****

Tamsyn stood ankle-deep in the warm coastal water and raised her face to the sun. Even in October, the rays still shone with summer-hot intensity, causing beads of perspiration to form along her forehead under her pink hatband. *Curse the sun, anyway, but it was too hot for a hat.* "Clara?" she called. She untied the ribbon holding the wide-brimmed hat and removed it. "Put this in the carriage, would you?"

The young girl's dark eyes opened wide. Clara herself wore a broad Bahama hat made from woven palm fronds. "Missy Tamsyn, Juba beat me if you come back sunburnt again." She wrapped her hands together behind her back.

Tamsyn sighed. "I know. It's not seemly for a young woman to have anything but the palest skin, and we *must* protect it at all times." She made a disgusted face. "Balderdash. The sun feels wonderful, and what happens in the next half hour isn't going to make any difference to the rest of my life."

Her bare toes wriggled in her light woven sandals, which protected her feet from sea urchins or other hazards. Though her sleeves were to her elbows, she'd cut off one of her old skirts to a shocking knee-length just for her frequent excursions to the ocean. She'd changed quickly and modestly, with Clara's help, once they'd arrived. Of course, Angus knew nothing about this scandalous revealing of her ankles and shins. It was another of the silent conspiracies between herself and the servants.

But Tamsyn loved the sun reflecting off the bay, the smell of the salt air, the small creatures that inhabited the shallow waters. She felt at home there, gazing out upon the horizon as the waves rippled onshore. Angus never asked where Juba got the fresh seafood, and Tamsyn didn't volunteer. "Besides, do you think Juba would approve of my outfit?"

Clara shook her head violently. "You won't tell her, Missy Tamsyn?"

Tamsyn smiled. "We won't stay long. I didn't know we'd find crabs here. Get the nets, and we'll catch enough for Juba to feed us all. Then she'll be too busy to scold either of us."

The girl quickly complied, hitching up her own gray skirt. The two of them darted after sidestepping crabs, dumping them into a large bucket full of seawater. Clara also found some clams and other shellfish, which she added to their catch. They'd have a delicious feast that night, with the fresh produce from the ship and Juba's spicy crabs.

Seagulls glided overhead in midafternoon,

raucously challenging the salty breezes which bore them, their white bodies a sharp contrast to the blue, cloudless sky. Other birds in the distance cried out in answer. One cry was louder and more urgent than the rest. Tamsyn suddenly realized it was a human, not a bird, a sound filled with anguish. She looked at Clara, who'd obviously guessed the same. Whoever was making that noise was in a great deal of pain. Tamsyn passed the handle of her bucket to the girl. "Store this in the carriage. I'm going to see what's happened."

"Missy Tamsyn, don't you be runnin' off dere," Clara warned timidly, but it was too late.

Tamsyn moved lightly around the coral rocks in the direction of the voice. Listening, she heard the cries turn to pained moans, and she hurried onward. Coming around a particularly big rock, she ran headlong into the grumbling victim, knocking him off his feet into the water. He splashed and shook a fist in her direction. "Damnation, watch where you're going, girl."

Tamsyn stared at the man sitting nearly twelve inches deep in the water. His hair was black as a crow's feathers, curling around his shoulders, with brilliant brown eyes set deep. His clothing was simple and dark, and she noticed with a little thrill of fear that he had a knife tucked in his belt and another in his boot.

When she didn't speak, he grinned. "I apologize for disturbing you," he said in an amused baritone, a voice that seemed to resonate within her. "If you've finished examining me, I could really use some help." He held out his right hand.

Tamsyn impulsively pulled him to his feet. She noticed blood on his left hand. "What happened here?" She automatically reached for the injured limb, her mother's well-taught nursing skills at the ready. A sea urchin spine was embedded in his index finger, which was already red and swelling by the minute. "Oh," she gasped. "That." She'd once had a similar encounter and knew how painful it could be.

"*That*." He winced as she tilted and twisted his hand for a better look. His palms were rough and calloused, but his nails were clean, she noted idly as she contemplated his wound. His hands dripped seawater and were warm, and at least half again as big as her own.

Mindful of the other end of the spine, Tamsyn fumbled in her pocket for the pliers she'd brought to snap open shellfish. "This will hurt," she said softly. Before he could stop her, she grasped the spine with the pliers and pulled it out. His roar of pain frightened her, and she backed away out of arm's reach, eyes wide.

He repeatedly gasped and squeezed his finger, letting the blood and poison drip out, finally rinsing it in the salt water, provoking a string of curses. Amazed at his repertoire, she finally giggled.

"You think it's funny, do you?" the man asked. He looked ruefully at his hand, apparently satisfied with her treatment. "You're probably right. Man versus urchin means urchin wins."

He smiled, and his deeply tanned face changed from brooding mask to engaging charmer. His eyes sparkled, bringing a surge of vitality to his face. He was young and handsome, and Tamsyn found she could hardly take her eyes off him. "Thank you, ma'am." He bowed low.

Now that she had tended to his injury and the crisis had passed, Tamsyn realized with dismay she was talking to a strange man—had touched him, caressed his hand—*did I do that?* She had to admit she entertained an instant attraction which she tried to discount. Her gaze went to the knives again. "You're most welcome." She blushed, suddenly conscious of her inappropriate dress. She looked down at her feet, trying to generate a polite way to excuse herself. "I should go," she said, inching away.

"Not so fast!" He stepped forward quickly to take her hand. "I don't even know your name."

She experienced a flash of panic but realized at the same time he wasn't holding her tightly enough that she couldn't escape. Despite the knives, the stranger seemed relatively harmless. Something in his eyes appealed to her, and she felt she could trust him. "Nor I yours, sir," she said with a touch of her usual sass.

He dropped her hand and his jaw simultaneously. "Where are my manners?" He shook his head. "Drake Ashton, at your service." He bowed again, then sank to one knee in the water. "Since you have saved me from the evil creatures of this ocean, I am now in your debt. Tell me how I can repay you; your wish is my command."

Astonished at his flowery pledge, Tamsyn's first reaction was to laugh. *What an unusual fellow.* "You're getting wet."

He chuckled. "I am, indeed. Let's go up on shore." He held out his hand, and she let him help her from the water, then found him reluctant to release her again.

"My hand?" she reminded him.

"What about it?" He looked down and then acted as if he just realized he hadn't let go. "Oh, yes." He turned her hand over and gazed at the palm. "Hmmm."

He traced several of the lines with an uninjured finger.

"What do you mean?" she asked with interest. "Can you read palms?"

He nodded. "An old Cuban woman taught me one evening as we sat around a fire at a rebel camp, drums beating in the distance, smoke in the air. She leaned close to me and took my hand, just as I'm holding yours now, and told me my future, showing me how the lines of my palm intersected and moved apart." He examined her face, more serious. "I never believed a word until now."

Tamsyn was thoroughly intrigued, her curious streak in high gear. "What did she say?"

"She told me a time would come when a young woman would rescue me. That woman, she said, would be…" He stared at her, intently watching her face.

His deep gaze hypnotized her. She could almost smell the camp smoke, so taken was she. "Would be what?"

"Would be—" He shook his head. "It's not important. Something about love."

Tamsyn pulled her hand back sharply. "I'm sure it had nothing to do with me, then." She turned and walked away in the direction of her carriage. But she lost one of her sandals in a sudden rush of water and stepped hard onto white coral rock. "Ow!"

"Allow me," he said behind her. Before she could argue, he scooped her up in his arms. As she protested, he replied, "I told you I was in your debt. Please permit me to repay you." Ashton's boots easily traversed the rocks, his arms strong around her. He smelled of salt water and the ocean breeze, and she felt gentleness within him as he carried her. He deposited her next to the carriage, before the startled eyes of Clara and Old James, and inclined his head briefly to each of them.

"Your mistress has just saved me from my own stupidity." He held out his finger. Clara winced at the blood, and Old James took a step back, uncertainty written on his face.

She finally found her tongue. "Mr. Ashton was kind enough to help me across the rocks. I shall have to retrieve my sandal."

Clara scrambled to catch the offending shoe before the wave took it out to sea.

Tamsyn noted the amused light sparkling again in his eyes and spoke up, hoping to deflect his attention from herself. "Do you have something to wrap that in?" She fumbled in her bag for a handkerchief. The only one she had was one of her early attempts at needlework, her initials roughly sewn into a corner. She hated to give it to him, this souvenir of her wasted lessons, but she had nothing else.

He took it from her with thanks and wrapped it around his wound. "You are too kind."

She turned back to see his amusement hadn't abated. The rogue even had the nerve to wink. It irritated her. "I think we've taken up enough of your time. Good day, Mr. Ashton."

He reached for her hand and kissed it lightly, lips hot against her skin. A chill ran through her in response. "The pleasure has been mine," he said. "You still haven't told me your name."

"This hasn't been a proper introduction," she said primly. Perhaps it was true that Key West was more European than American, its international populace drawing heavily from the Caribbean, but young ladies were held to certain codes of conduct anywhere. As much as Tamsyn liked him, she was coming to see how scandalous her behavior had been in the heat of the moment.

He nodded. "Then I promise you we shall have one. Until then, milady." He bowed and walked away.

"Who be that man?" Old James demanded suspiciously, invisible feathers ruffling like a rooster protecting his territory.

"I don't know," Tamsyn replied, thinking of how strong Drake Ashton's arms had felt as he carried her. He'd smelled so good. Thatcher often drenched himself in cologne, which overwhelmed her. She much preferred Ashton's fresh natural scent.

"I don't think Marse Angus like you associatin' wit him." The old man scowled, and Tamsyn had to smile.

"You're probably right, Old James. Now, please turn your back while I change into my town clothes." She stepped behind the carriage, and Clara helped her drop her proper skirt over the one she wore, then slip off the wet one from underneath.

As she changed, she revisited the encounter in her mind, amazed that she had plunged into her acquaintance with Mr. Ashton without hesitation. She'd reacted to his injury without seeing him as a stranger, but as an injured thing, like a kitten or a bird with a broken wing.

When she climbed up into the carriage, she spied a couple of men in brightly colored shirts waiting behind a sand dune farther down the shore, carrying a large chest between them. *I never noticed them. What kind of men are those? I'm sure I never saw them around the dock.* They looked a little unsavory, and as her patient joined them, he turned back and saluted her.

They all laughed as if sharing some private joke, then climbed into and launched a small boat into the water. Drake Ashton, she noticed, kept his eye on her as the other two began to row. Her eyes followed their direction off the beach, and for the first time, Tamsyn noticed the sailing ship well offshore, sails furled while at anchor.

So he was a part of a crew...more likely captain, as the others were doing the manual labor. What kind of ship was that? Remembering the touch of his rough hand on hers, she watched as the rowboat grew smaller and smaller, heading straight for the ship across the rolling breakers. She felt the instant attraction between them reverberate through her like an electrical spark. And his companions? *Those men had looked like...pirates!* she realized with a gasp.

"What is it, missy?" Old James asked, without turning around.

"Nothing. Some cold water just splashed on me from this crab bucket," she said. If she told either of her companions they'd seen pirates at the cove, she'd never be permitted to come again. She caught Clara's speculative eye on her, but Clara glanced away with a tiny smile.

"He be a fine lookin' man," Clara said, just loud enough for Tamsyn to hear.

Tamsyn smiled. "Yes, he is."

As Old James found the main road and urged the horse briskly forward to take their catch home, her mind returned to the way he'd studied her palm, and his prediction. He said he'd be rescued by a woman who'd be...something? Tamsyn had the feeling he had meant to say more, but stopped before he said the words.

Pish-tosh! she scolded herself. She didn't know the man, and she didn't ever expect to see him again, despite his promise to make her a proper introduction.

Besides, Thatcher Winslow would soon be asking her father for permission to marry her. That was where she needed to concentrate her efforts. She had to make sure it happened. Then all her dreams would come true.

Chapter Two

Drake Ashton held the wooden sides of the small boat as it bounced up and down, rocking hard over the waves near shore. *Now there was a metaphor for life— whenever you're close to the land, you ride rough.*

Life seemed simpler out at sea on his ship, the *Raven*, where a full cargo hold waited, bound for a rebel sanctuary in Matanzas, Cuba. The ship was all his: a three-masted vessel, square-rigged on the foremast and mainmast, and lateen-rigged on the mizzenmast.

God above appreciated that the ship wasn't new. Galleons came on at the turn of the last century, so she might have been eighty years old or more, but it made him no less fond of the rough old girl. The newer warships were being retrofitted with steam power as an alternative. He'd also seen some fitted with steel armor along the hulls for extra protection.

I'd have to sell a lot of guns for that.

Yet despite the bouncy journey back to his ship, he didn't regret his excursion to the beach. He'd gone to pick up a chest of ammunition to add to his cache, but he'd discovered something much more interesting: his nameless nurse. What an appealing woman-child she was. She couldn't be much older than eighteen.

Something in her touch, in her eyes… That smile permeated his heart with its sweetness. He couldn't stop puzzling over her. Even if she wasn't obviously an upper-class brat, she did possess the trappings of it. What lower-class woman would travel with two servants and a carriage? She'd barely flinched at the sight of his blood. She'd boldly held his hand and rescued him from his own clumsy accident.

Drake closed his eyes and thought back to his first look at her, standing over him as he had sat in the shallow water. The sun had shone full on her face, grazing her skin with a pink glow. Green eyes, so serious, so wide and beautiful, searching his face for clues to his injury. Dark hair carelessly pulled up into a knot, loose ends escaping in all directions, softening her outline. *Delightful.*

Evidently a girl of means, yet none of the usual prissiness or disdain for those of other social caste graced her lips. Instead, she had a sharp tongue and a wicked sense of humor which revealed her inner fire.

He was determined to see her again, even at the risk of encountering such a tongue. In fact, he'd promised her he would. And a proper introduction. *Now, how are you going to manage that, Captain? How can I discover who she is? More importantly, how can someone like me interject myself into a society where proper introductions are made?*

He chuckled at his own sense of romantic derring-do. *I've got my work laid out for me this time.*

As the dinghy came alongside the *Raven*, the wooden side bumped repeatedly into the larger ship, so everyone had to watch their fingers. The crew overhead dropped a rope ladder down the side. He boldly grabbed hold with both hands and hauled himself up the ten meters to the main deck.

At the top of the ladder, strong arms reached to lift him over the edge. His booted feet landed with a thump on the deck. Before he got his balance, his gaze was already scanning for his first mate, Samuel Johnston. No time to think about the girl now. Time for ship's business.

"Samuel? Where do we stand?" he yelled. He waited and watched as the crew lifted a round net holding the chest with the precious ammunition and then the skiff. The crew he'd landed with climbed over the edge too, having come up the ladder after the cargo was secured.

The first mate had current control of the ship's wheel and stretched his tall, spare body to its length as he was summoned, weary from his time on watch. He held his tongue until Drake joined him on the quarterdeck.

"So," Samuel said, "while we prepare for possible mayhem and death, you take time to play at the shore with pretty ladies?" He stroked his russet sideburns and cocked an inquiring eyebrow.

Drake frowned. "How'd you hear about that already?" He glanced around, suspicious, and caught the guilty expression from one of the men overhead, staffing the crow's nest with his long spyglass. "Makes no matter. We received the ammunition. That's why we went."

He surveyed the deck. The barrels of provisions they'd picked up in the Carolinas had now been set at even distance from one another around the length of the bow. "The weapons and ammunition we got for the Cuban rebels?"

"Safely stashed belowdecks, hidden as best we can.

Shouldn't no inspector spy us out unless they're really searching."

Drake nodded with approval. He often carried multiple layers of cargo, the top rack being innocuous items of standard trade—candles, rope, sundry supplies, which could be sold in any port of the Caribbean. Any cursory examination would overlook the real cargo. So Drake and his crew would avoid a potential date with the hangman.

"Guess I'd rather hear about the woman," Samuel said with a chuckle. When Drake's gaze proved hard as steel, Samuel fell back into line. "The men have prepared the guns since you left the ship. Everything's been taken apart, polished, and reassembled, and the munitions for each gunport piled in a tall basket."

"Good. Although I'm not expecting trouble this run. The Spaniards are complacent. After all, they believe they control Cuba. There are always, of course, a few pockets of rebellion," he said with a devilish grin.

"Which will make us a handsome profit," Samuel finished.

"Which will, indeed," Drake agreed. His clothes, dried in the wind, were beginning to itch him with flaking sand and salt. *I should change before we set sail.* He took a last look around, satisfied his hybrid crew, half American, half Cuban, were fulfilling their various duties. They were his connection to the rebels on the island of Cuba, which was struggling to throw off the oppressive Spanish rule.

At last the American press was beginning to circulate stories of the atrocities committed by the Spaniards on the Cuban natives. Having lost Florida and struggling to maintain foreign possessions thousands of miles across the Atlantic, Spain desperately tightened its hold on the populace. But every miscarriage of justice, every forced closing of a business, every abduction of wives or children, just led to the birth of another rebel.

It was the same battle England had fought with its colonies a century earlier. The more tyrannical the government, the more citizens were willing to take up arms and fight it. All he had to do was provide the arms to the right people so that, when the time came, the people would be ready.

While he was pleased he would make money from his dealings, he'd come to know the men of Matanzas and the other small villages they supplied well enough to believe in their cause.

Mateo, the squat, crippled boy who took care of the captain's space, slipped from the cabin as Drake arrived. "I thought you might want a clean shirt," he said with a smile.

Drake tousled his hair. "What would I do without you, boy?" Already unbuttoning his encrusted clothing, he went in and closed the door behind him.

The cabin was Spartan and spotless, as Mateo normally maintained it. It was the largest cabin on the ship, as befitted the captain, and one of three private rooms. There was no frivolous decoration—just a bed with plain sheets, a nightstand, dresser, table, and two chairs. He opened the small port, noting the breeze had picked up since he'd left shore. *About time to sail southward.*

He changed quickly, hanging his wet things on hooks near the door. Sailing south meant meeting the *Blackbird,* his brother Frederic's ship. Together, they'd make the Matanzas run.

He and Freddie had grown up together on their own after their parents died from malaria when Drake was just seventeen. Freddie had been fourteen then; he was twenty-two now and thought himself as invincible as he was good-looking. But Drake had done his best, mentoring him in the salvage business so many Keys sailors used to feed themselves and their families. He'd taught Freddie everything he knew about sailing, and that was a great deal.

Freddie had actually become a master, in some things, and acted much bolder than Drake himself. His arrogance was a concern for both Drake and for Frederic's primarily Afro-Cuban crew, but his headstrong rush into danger often led to success. It was hard to scold him when he dropped a valuable salvage treasure on the worn wooden deck.

"I always keep one eye close on the game," Frederic had confessed after one particularly memorable sweep off the Cuban island the previous year. He'd met up with Drake after Freddie had pulled two heavy wooden chests of Spanish gold from the depths, the light *Blackbird* sailing away before the Spanish *Bellona* could catch up to them. Freddie had sat cross-legged before the smaller of the two chests on the floor of Frederic's cabin, running his hands through the gold and jewels. The coins had been so shiny, so cold and heavy.

"You think they'll come after you?" Drake had asked.

Frederic laughed. "Of course they will. The Spaniards have a code of honor. They will never let this bad blood rest, now that we have embarrassed them."

Drake had been amazed. Frederic had come to be larger than life. He took bigger risks, lived harder, played rougher than anyone he knew. "So now you're a hunted man?"

"At least someone wants *me*." His brother finished his mug of cool red wine with a rogue's grin. "Now, when are you finally going to get married and settle down?"

Drake frowned. "I'm fine as I am. I've got responsibilities, no time for that. What would I do, leave a wife behind onshore, visit twice a year, make her a widow as this war comes full-on?" He shook his head. "Taking care of you is a full-time occupation, thanks."

"Don't worry about me. I'm staying one step ahead. Maybe more. Without spice, what's life, Drake?"

The run that followed was one that left life lessons. They'd sailed to most of the islands in the Caribbean, and it seemed to Drake that Freddie had kept a woman in every port. It was part of his persona, and he bragged among the men, who cheered him like a hero. The two brothers had sailed separate paths four months before to gather the equipment and cargo the rebels needed. In the next few days, they would compare catches in Cuba.

Drake's eye was often focused for news of the Spanish. Freddie wasn't wrong. The captain of the *Bellona* would be after him, nursing that injury to his ego. If anything happened to his brother... Ten thousand dead Spaniards would not bring Freddie back to his worn leather chair, sharing well-polished tales of wild bravery.

Now that the Spanish were causing trouble in the Caribbean as the United States patrolled the seas, there was talk of war between the Spanish and American fleets as well. Drake thought it an excellent time to be an active player in the politics of the Caribbean. He intended to be part of any move to vanquish the Spaniards and to help whomever shared that goal. Better to get the Spanish out of these waters altogether before they took the life of someone who mattered to him.

Then we can both go home.

They had a land-based home their parents had left them, a small, one-story house with the broad, west-facing porch, built of wood and coral rock, on the leeward side of Islamorada. Drake hadn't done much to it since they'd inherited the place. He and Freddie spent most of the time on their respective ships. Either or both used it as a base, though, and somewhere to go to ground when the sea was too dangerous—whether weather, enemies, or even the law.

While he had no intention to marry, it would be sweet to have someone there waiting for him upon his return, with a pot hanging over the fire and soft blankets on the bed...

Business! Freddie's voice snapped in Drake's mind. *You have no business getting involved with a landlubber. Not at this particular moment.*

He let the hem of his shirt hang loose and returned to the deck. The bosun directed the men in their tasks, and from what Drake could see, all had put their backs into the effort to scour the ship while they'd been anchored. *I've got good men and a solid ship. I don't need more than that.*

Samuel stepped aside to let his captain put hands on the heavy wooden wheel that guided the ship. "Any other business here?"

"Not at present." Drake winked.

"Ah, so ye haven't abandoned the lass altogether?" Samuel chuckled.

Rather than answer, Drake called out, "Raise the anchor!"

The call echoed from man to man, to the crew member who controlled the second great wheel that would haul the iron anchor from the sands below. The crew strove hard to lift the thousand-pound weight that held them still when need be. In these shallow waters just outside the reef, the anchor was solid enough to secure them.

While some of the waters inside the reef were only six to eight meters in depth, the ninety-three miles between Key West and Cuba boasted depths of three thousand meters or more.

If only we had some solid underwater marine vessels, we could find such treasure. Who knew how many ships of all nationalities had gone down in storms or under attack?

Freddie had expressed some interest in such a venture, but thank the stars, he'd never discovered a proper vehicle. *Else he'd be giving me another reason for worry.*

"Set the sails!"

As before, the cry passed through the crew. Two dozen men shimmied up ropes to release the ties that held the furled sails, and their heavy canvas bulk crashed down into place and was tied off. The sails immediately picked up the wind, and the *Raven* began to turn.

"Southward bound, friends! We've a mission to accomplish!"

The flapping of the sails coincided with the crew bursting into song, as they always did at the start of a sail. They chose a well-worn sea shanty that they'd sung many times.

Way, haul away, we'll haul away the bowlin;
Way, haul away, we'll haul away, Joe…

The slow beat fitted itself perfectly to the tidying and securing of all the lines on the ship, as well as the other last-minute tasks that the *Raven* crew executed in rough synchrony of habit.

When I was just a little lad, or so me Mammi told me

Way, haul away, we'll haul away, Joe

Drake turned the wheel hand over hand, his breath catching with excitement. His heart beat in rapid rhythm. This was life for him. The spray of the sea, the bite of the wind, the sounds of the ocean as they passed.

That if I didn't kiss the girls, me lips would grow all moldy

Way, haul away, we'll haul away, Joe

"Dolphin sight!" called the boy in the crow's nest. He pointed just right of the bow out ahead of the ship. A pair of dolphins gracefully leapt out of the water in tandem, seeming to dance and celebrate the *Raven*'s launch.

The crew cheered. "Now that's good luck for the journey, ain't it, lads!" Samuel clapped his hands. "I think that calls for a tankard of ale, don't you?"

That brought an even greater affirmation. Samuel organized the tapping of a large, sloshing barrel, and the men stopped by one at a time to fill a mug and toast their success.

When the men had wet their throats, Drake released control of the wheel to the second mate and strolled across the deck to the forecastle, soaking in the atmosphere and the sheer joy of the ship flying across the water. Soon he'd be with Freddie again, and they'd share the stories from their time apart.

And I'll wager he hears all about the young woman on the beach.

Maybe he'll let it lie and treat her like one of his own shore wives. No need to discuss it further.

But something told Drake she would be significant to his future, more than he'd care to admit.

It wasn't that Drake didn't care for women; to the contrary, he found them appealing and wonderful. He had been introduced to the arts of love before he left his teens by an older woman in Jamaica. By her gentle touch, he'd learned much about pleasing a woman and what pleased a man. Her memory, carefully cherished—and perhaps embellished—over time, had contributed to his image of the woman he sought to make his life's partner. Though not rich or educated, she had been a lady in every sense of the word.

It was gentility he first looked for in any woman. He could always find a girl interested in a quick tumble and was not unaware of his own good looks. But before he made any permanent commitment, he wanted to find a woman with a sense of her own worth, someone refined and of delicate sensibilities, but strong enough to be interesting…

And I'm definitely interested.

I've got all the way to Matanzas and back to figure

out how I can put myself in the young lady's path again.

He reached into his pants pocket and took out the handkerchief she'd given him. Holding it to his nose, he gave a quick sniff. *A faint scent of lavender.* His eyes widened as he found a clue. *Initials. TM. Now I'm on the trail!*

Despite Drake's business dealings with some residents of the booming town of Key West, he didn't know many of the gentry there. *Not my sort of people.* But he had connections on the island the Spanish called Cayo Hueso. He'd find her again.

He had to know if the Cuban magic woman's prediction was true—that he would be rescued by a woman who he would come to love more than life itself, a woman prophesied to give up her life for him.

Chapter Three

Tamsyn's mysterious meeting with the suspected pirate on the Key West beach fled to the back of her mind during the next several weeks, filled with the excitement of the New Year's Masquerade Ball. It was the most important event of the Key West winter social season, and Tamsyn had been invited for the first time.

She had no delusions that she had secured the invitation on her own. Surely it came by way of Thatcher Winslow's personal request. *If he wants to squire me to such an affair, that says something about his interest. Doesn't it?*

Thrilled that her love life had escalated in the direction of her dreams, she visited the small garret where Miss Pearl did her magic. In a room in the second floor of a Bahamian-style home on Catherine Street, the space served as shop, work area, and bedroom of the wizened seamstress. No curtains hung at the windows, giving the room a full measure of sunlight every day so Miss Pearl could create in comfort.

"Come in, come in!" the woman cried when Tamsyn knocked. Miss Pearl threw the door open, greeting her with a wide smile. Tamsyn didn't care if the other woman's grin had gaps or if her hands were sometimes swollen and red from an arthritic affliction. Miss Pearl always welcomed her and seemed glad for the company.

"I cannot wait to see what you have fashioned for the ball," Tamsyn said, once seated in the satin-cushioned customer's chair. Miss Pearl stayed on her feet, abuzz in motion, flitting from one muslin-draped hanger to another, to her small sewing machine and back. Despite her age, she radiated energy.

Of the two lengths of silk Tamsyn had chosen at boatside the week before, she and Miss Pearl had agreed to put the periwinkle blue aside for now and make the New Year's dress from pale-pink silk. While most women in New York and Boston were wearing the Wasp Waist dress style with a low, square neckline, Miss Pearl had suggested a dress cut more modestly around the neck, with an Empire waist and narrowly cut floor-length skirt. Tamsyn trusted Miss Pearl, for she had always felt beautiful in any creation from that tiny studio.

"Come, dear, let's try this on you."

What followed was a bit of a struggle, as the room was small, Miss Pearl's back quite hunched with age, and her arms not as flexible as they once were. Tamsyn had left Clara outside with the carriage, as there was hardly enough room for the two women. But with patience, some vigorous contortions, and good humor, the dress eventually got onto her body.

Miss Pearl had faced her away from the mirror, so she had to wait to see herself, although the soft billows of the dress in front were certainly appealing. "Take these ribbons, love." Miss Pearl handed her three matching pink lengths two feet long. "You can weave them in your hair or use them to tie your cameo around your neck."

"Thank you." Tamsyn's impatience to see the total effect drove her feet a-tapping.

"Here you are."

Miss Pearl turned her toward the mirror. Tamsyn was dazzled by the vision of herself as a young lady of means dressed to attend her first significant ball. Amazed at the transformation from her everyday appearance, she murmured, "It is the thought of my dear Thatcher that puts the pink in my cheeks, I am sure."

"Young Master Winslow is still courting you, miss?"

"He's escorting me to the ball. I've never been to the Pickhams' home. I have heard some remarkable descriptions, though. I understand they've just installed electric lighting throughout the home. It must be amazing."

She turned from side to side, trying to take in all the angles. *Perfect.* She had some soft ballerina slippers that would match exactly and be comfortable, too. "I love it, Miss Pearl."

The small woman beamed. "It's not quite finished, dear. But I can see what needs to be done now. Here, let's take it off and back to the hanger."

The two repeated their twisted dance, wriggling and pinning, repinning and inching the fabric over Tamsyn's head. When it was settled back under its muslin cover and Tamsyn restored to the everyday calico she'd worn before, Miss Pearl asked if she'd like a cup of tea.

Thinking of her other errands yet to be done, Tamsyn nearly refused, but the loneliness in the older woman's eyes finally decided her. "I'd like that, thank you."

Delighted, Miss Pearl retreated to her small fireplace, where a large pot hung over the fire. She scooped out enough water for her Wedgewood teapot and brought it, with two cups and the sugar bowl, to the small worktable. As hospitable as any fancy island hostess, she poured and stirred tea for them both, handing Tamsyn the cup.

"So tell me about Master Winslow," she asked. "I'd thought he was sweet on some of the other girls last season. Miss Pickham, particularly."

Tamsyn frowned. Catching her reflection in the mirror, she immediately erased that expression. Her mother would have scolded her for making an "ugly" face. "I may not be the first girl for whom he's expressed an attraction. But he has made his interest quite plain now. And I intend to return it." She sipped her tea, trying not to pout. She didn't like hearing anything that detracted from that dream of marriage.

Of course, there'd been whispers about their supposed alliance, considering the Winslows' shipping lines contained an entire fleet of ships, and they lived on Duval Street among the wealthiest Key West residents. Angus MacKiernan, by comparison, was known as a member of the "codfish aristocracy." His "fleet," such as it was, consisted of a number of small dinghies that scrabbled up sponges from the ocean floor, and a couple of dilapidated larger ships that salvaged wrecked boats for valuables.

But Key West wasn't Philadelphia or Boston, and such strict courting levels lacked enforcement. One hundred fifty miles from the mainland, much closer to the islands of the Bahamas and Cuba, life in the Keys allowed for relaxed rules. Without her mother to show her how to manage such a situation, Tamsyn had been left to her own whimsies. So, if she wanted Thatcher, and Thatcher wanted her, why shouldn't it be?

"I'm happy for you, then, miss. One of these days, perhaps I'll be sewing you a white gown?" She smiled and drank her tea.

"I hope and pray it will be so."

"Of course, miss." But the seamstress sounded less than confident.

After an uneasy silence, Tamsyn finished and set her cup down. "And the other silk? What do you envision for that one?"

The conversation turned to patterns and the examination of fashion plates from designers far and wide. They selected a day dress with a bell-shaped skirt and gigot sleeves to be finished by mid-February. That gave her a total of four dresses to be cycled through for succeeding events. Papa couldn't afford more. She'd be competing with the other young women whose fathers could buy them new styles from Paris for each and every affair.

If I am fortunate, my future will be settled long before the season is concluded. I will be Mrs. Thatcher Winslow, and my life will begin without further worries of competition.

On that note, she bade Miss Pearl good afternoon and headed out to complete her errands.

Feeling joyful and free, Tamsyn sent the carriage home and walked alone to La Africana, the Bahamian neighborhood along Thomas Street. The freshest vegetables were shipped in from farms farther north along the island chain, in places like Plantation Key, where sweet golden pineapples thrived, and Key limes and sapodillas were prized fruits for the table.

The bougainvilleas painted colorful coral and fuchsia splashes in front of the so-called "shotgun" houses of the transplanted Cuban cigar makers. She admired them as she passed. The simple, single-story buildings one room wide and three rooms deep were so called because a shotgun fired through the front door would pass straight on out the rear entry.

She enjoyed the birdsong, the green parrots, and red macaws as she walked, purposely taking the long way around town to clear her head of Miss Pearl's doubts. The heavy basket she carried for her purchases banged against her hip with each step.

Marking off the three palms that she had to pass before reaching Thomas Street, she noted the Christmas palm with its red and green pods, the coconut palm, tall and spare, with clusters of coconuts at its peak, and the traveler's palm with branches that fanned sideways as if pressed, always pointing to the north.

As she entered the Bahamian district, many of the shopkeepers called out, knowing she lived in the household where Juba, Clara, and the others were employed. Tamsyn had visited in their homes—without her father knowing, of course. Others from the upper end of Duval Street might worry about the "foreigners," but Tamsyn knew she'd be safe as she was in her own living room.

"Missy Tamsyn!" an old black man cried from his rickety wooden porch. "Got de fresh mangoes, juicy and sweet!"

"How be our Clara?" asked a woman hanging laundry along her balcony. "Tell her Auntie Lucy be missin' her."

"I will," Tamsyn said. She reached in her pocket for Juba's list: two chickens, spices, and mangoes and limes for chutney sauce. She had particularly wanted some Bahamian bread from a local baker.

Old Nilda was a dark, dark woman who had come from the Bahamas as a young girl, following in her mamma's footsteps, baking sweet Bahamian bread which she bartered for other foodstuffs and services. While the people of European stock preferred their ground white flour bread, the Cubans and other ethnic peoples loved the coconut-milk bread that Nilda made, and kept her in business.

"Good morning, Nilda." Tamsyn stepped gingerly on the wobbly wooden steps to Nilda's front door. The small shotgun house stood crookedly, held together with string and a prayer, but strong enough to shelter Nilda and her family.

"Good day, missy," the wrinkled woman said, rocking peacefully in her well-worn chair.

"Juba asks for three loaves of your bread."

The woman nodded sagely. "Juba's a good girl." She called into the house for the bread.

Tamsyn thought it odd that Nilda referred to Juba as a "girl," since Juba was nearly forty years old, with two grown sons of her own. But she paid over the household money Juba had given her. The bread was wrapped in brown paper and smelled wonderful. "Thank you, Nilda." She waved at the grandchild who had brought the bread outside.

"You enjoy dis good day de Lord has brought," Nilda called after her.

Tamsyn nodded, thinking her day had improved as

soon as she'd left her own house. She visited the old man who had mangoes, and purchased a few, then was tempted into buying a ripe pineapple as well. The chickens she had to buy at the meat market in town— Juba wasn't convinced her people had the most sanitary methods of killing the birds.

Fragrant frangipani, bright pink and white flowers lining the branches up to twenty blossoms on a stem, was her favorite; she snagged the end of a branch and picked some blooms to scent her room at home. In the summer, the royal poinciana flamed with orange-red flowers; in the fall, the African tulip tree burst into crimson splendor. Jacaranda added a touch of violet to the floral palette. In between, indigenous, thick green foliage captivated her eye.

As she walked down to the market, the basket grew heavier, and she decided she'd walk straight home after. Toward downtown, the streets filled up with passing carriages. Every once in a while, the occupants of a carriage would turn to stare at her as they went by, accompanied by a nudge of the elbow and a whispered comment. She frowned. It probably was unseemly for the future Mrs. Thatcher Winslow to go to the market alone, on foot, especially on Thomas Street. She could hear Edwina Winslow's cultured voice in her head: "But my dear, that's why you have servants."

Tamsyn couldn't imagine what she would do all day if she left everything to the servants. Of course, she didn't know how many servants Mrs. Winslow employed. The MacKiernans had their cook, Juba, Old James, perhaps really too old to be working at all, and a houseman who helped with the upkeep of the house and yard. Clara cleaned and helped Juba and Tamsyn with whatever was left to be done.

I suppose I could sit and struggle to learn piano or embroidery or some other perfectly useless skill.

For the first time, it occurred to her to wonder what her role might be as the future Mrs. Thatcher Winslow. Would she accompany him to his office during the day to keep his books as she kept her father's?

Not likely. Surely that wouldn't be good enough for a Winslow woman.

So…what would she become?

She wished her mother still lived so she could ask questions. Mamma had always been sensible. Would she have liked Thatcher? He was certainly the first person of his circle to notice Tamsyn. She struggled a moment with her own knowledge, even beyond what Miss Pearl had said, of his previous interests in girls. So what if he had been Miss Pickham's beau—now, he would take Tamsyn to the dance, right in front of that arrogant girl's nose.

Tamsyn imagined her mother's answer would be sensible as well: marry a man who can suitably provide, and the rest of one's life would be satisfying. It might not give her everything she wanted, but she'd be better off than she was now.

Can we really ask Fate for more than that?

Half an hour later, with her purchases complete, she walked home, basket now banging against her knee. *Why did I believe this was a good idea again? This feels more of a burden with each step.* "I can't wait to get home and take off these shoes," she muttered.

Finally arriving at the back gate to the courtyard, she swung the door open with a great sigh of relief. "Clara?" she called.

Thatcher Winslow stepped out from behind the door.

A shriek fought its way out of her throat, even though she tried to cut it off. What was he doing here now? "Thatcher," she gasped.

"Did I frighten you?" His eyes widened, and he seemed annoyed. "We always meet here in the shade."

"Missy Tamsyn?" Clara came running from the kitchen and stopped short when she saw Thatcher. "Oh. I din't know you had company."

"Neither did I." Tamsyn handed Clara the basket, then smoothed her hair with her hands. "I'll be in after a moment."

Clara nodded and disappeared inside.

Now that she'd had time to recover her composure, she extended her hand to her would-be suitor. "How lovely to see you."

He looked her up and down, wearing a disapproving frown. "Where have you been? You're sweating like a common wench."

She pulled back her damp hand. They lived in the islands; what did he expect? "I had some errands at the market."

"Why wouldn't you take a carriage? No lady would..." He trailed off.

She just stared, unsure how to reply. Perhaps "ladies" wouldn't, but "gentlemen" surely wouldn't say so right to their faces. She didn't want him to see her embarrassment, so she tried to keep a calm, loving expression. Finally she asked, "Is there something you wanted? Why wouldn't you go to the front door, where someone would have welcomed you inside for respite from the heat and offered you a cold drink while you waited?"

A flush crept across his cheeks, and he pulled at his collar. "Tamsyn, my love. Shall we begin again? I wanted to see you. To kiss you. I have been pining for your touch."

There. This was more what she had expected. She managed a smile. "Would you give me a moment to freshen myself?"

He nodded vigorously. "But of course. I shall wait here."

"You won't come in?"

Thatcher glanced anxiously at the door. "No. Return promptly, though. I haven't much time."

"I will." She hurried into the kitchen, mortified that he'd seen her in disarray. Did she have time to change her clothing? Probably not. She'd have to wash up the best she could.

Juba stepped aside from the faucet, allowing Tamsyn to fill a small bowl with cold water. She set the bowl on a nearby counter and splashed her face and neck, wiping them with a towel. "Clara, fetch me a comb, would you?"

While the girl ran upstairs, Tamsyn removed the pins and combs that held her hair in place and shook it loose to her shoulders.

"Why Mista Winslow come to de backyard?" Juba asked. "He hidin' from somet'ing?"

"I have no idea," Tamsyn said. She took the brush and comb from Clara's hands when she returned and quickly ran the brush first, then the comb through her hair. She wound it deftly into a knot and jammed some pins in to secure it. *This will have to do.*

Taking a deep breath to clear her anxiety, she

squared her shoulders and went at a more ladylike pace down the three steps into the courtyard.

When he saw her, he came right over and swept her into his arms. "There's my beautiful lady." He kissed her, then kissed her again, more insistently. "I've missed you."

"I only saw you two days ago," she said with a small laugh as she caressed his cheek. "I've been making plans for the ball. I went to see my dress at Miss Pearl's—it's beautiful. I hope you'll love it."

He grimaced. "I'm sure it's fine." He pulled her close again and kissed her, a little longer than she thought was proper. *But it feels good. And even if Papa would look out the window and see, he would likely not* totally *disapprove, if he wants me to marry Thatcher. I know he'd be proud of me for making a good match. Since he's done everything for me since Mamma died, I owe him my best effort.*

Thatcher's hand moved from her waist to her breast, squeezing it. Startled, she stepped away from him. She cleared her throat. The last thing she wanted to do was criticize him. But what sort of manners had he been taught? These touches would be for the bedroom, not the public courtyard. Hoping to distract him, she flailed for a new topic of conversation.

"Miss Pearl hinted that she would be happy to make a…a wedding dress as well."

Thatcher scowled. "Why is it that women cannot think about anything but marriage? You're all alike! A man has needs!" He paced in front of her. "You, of all girls. I'd thought a girl from the east side of Duval Street would be more grateful for the attention from a man like me."

The insult cut at Tamsyn's heart. What did he mean? That he only pursued her for carnal reasons? Ridiculous. He'd sent her poetry. He'd brought her flowers. He'd been ever so romantic. What had she done to inspire such contempt?

It was my appearance when I arrived. Unfit for the wife of a Winslow. I must make sure that does not happen again. Ever.

"I must go, Mr. Winslow. Good day."

Her cheeks burning, she turned and retreated into the house. She went straight up the stairs to her room, closed the door, then closed the curtains and had a good cry. Once that passed, she felt more like herself.

He has never actually asked for my hand in marriage. What if I have imagined his interest beyond looking for a companion to the ball? Truly, I must give him time to clear his head. He will certainly come around and realize he has misspoken. As he said, we should begin again.

And he should become accustomed to coming to the front door and formally courting me if he so chooses. No more sordid moments among the bougainvilleas.

Having made this decision, she again washed her face and hands and changed into an at-home dress and apron before returning to the kitchen to make sure Juba had all she needed to prepare dinner for that night.

Chapter Four

Having left Key West in midafternoon, the *Raven* arrived at Matanzas, on the north side of the Cuban island, just before dawn. While the city proper had been settled some two hundred years before, the cove where the rebels made their home lay east of the city, past the Bay of Matanzas.

One foot on the bowsprit, Drake watched from the arched bow as the ship neared the small tributary next to the camp. Freddie's *Blackbird* was moored just offshore, sails furled, rocking in the small waves. Fires burned low, as would be expected. Morning life in camp had begun, though. A full survey through his spyglass revealed the shadowy forms of women moving around those fires and children running loose.

"Drop anchor!" the first mate shouted.

The process of landing and debarkation commenced. Their precious supplies of guns and ammunition went ashore first, guarded by several crewmen. Drake had confidence they were reasonably safe here. While their passing sails could be spotted from the city, Havana was but thirty miles farther east. Anyone seeing their ship sail by the entrance to the bay would naturally assume they were Havana-bound, not building a rebel base outside the city to attack the Spanish.

By the time the ship was secured and the majority

of the crew ashore, the sun rose fully above the horizon. Drake came on the last transit boat. When he stepped on the sand, he stopped for one moment to give thanks to the sea gods for the safe crossing. Then he went looking for his brother.

He found Freddie and a dozen children in a field behind the camp, playing baseball. The young ones stood out in the field while Freddie stood at what must be home plate, batting balls out in all directions for them to catch and return. All of them were laughing and thoroughly enjoying the game.

"You've missed your vocation," Drake called. "You could have been a famous player."

"About time you sailed in." Freddie dropped the bat for the boys to use and ran to embrace him. They celebrated the arrival with manly punches to the other's shoulder and shaking each other until their teeth rattled. "We'd about given up on you, brother mine."

Drake frowned. "How long have you been ashore?"

"Let's get some breakfast, and we can talk."

They walked back to the fire, the woodsmoke awakening memories of former times spent on beaches across the Caribbean. Drake's arrival was greeted with hugs and kisses from the women and cheers from the men. He surveyed the small encampment, finding that several more tents had been added since he was last there. Two squat, brick buildings served as the main housing for the salvaged guns and ammunition and other supplies. Many of the families lived in tents or slept under the stars. Space had been cleared for the settlement, perhaps ten acres, by the first Cubans of their group; three more acres had been added since then. Most importantly, the stand of palms and brush that sat between the camp and the shore had been left intact and screened them from the casual observer sailing past.

Freddie said, "We've been here two—no, three days. Montez has been inland and back to trade a load of weapons we brought from the Yucatán for, shall we say, less volatile cargo." He grinned. "You've come fully loaded?"

"Would I disappoint you?"

The brothers took a seat near the largest fire, which the cooks had built up and furnished with a large spit, no doubt awaiting a pig or cow later in the day. Cassava and tostones with toasted bread and, of course, rum made their breakfast, then they were left to talk business.

Drake concentrated on filling his belly while Freddie rattled on about his supplies, the trouble he'd had with his men fighting among themselves at sea, and ending, of course, with the lurid tale of another woman's heart he'd broken when he had to leave her behind in Cancún.

"Women. More trouble than they're worth, wouldn't you say?" Freddie eyed him, mischief in his gaze.

He couldn't know already. He hadn't spoken to a man on my crew. Drake listened, face like a stone. *He's baiting me. Ha! I wasn't born yesterday.*

"For you, apparently." Drake shrugged and handed his empty bowl to one of the children passing by. The rum, he kept.

"This one, she was something special, though."

Was that a touch of regret in Freddie's voice? Had

one lady finally sunk a hook in his heart? Drake chuckled at the thought of his brother caught up permanently by a pretty face or a curvaceous body. He sipped the rum, enjoying its slow burn. "That's what you say about all of them, Fred."

"Hhhmph. Maybe." Brooding, Freddie toyed with the toast on his plate, then tore it into bits, tossing it into the air for low-flying seagulls to snap up. Their strident cries drew in others who swooped down, looking for an easy meal. "At any rate, Montez also made contact with some of the sugar plantation rebels. They're willing to join our cause when the time comes."

That raised Drake's eyebrow. "That's good news. We'll need all the support we can get if the Americans are still not ready to join the fight."

Drake had never personally had dealings with the plantation men, but he was well-versed in their history. Sugar plantations in Matanzas had known multiple slave rebellions, some begun on the plantations, and others fomented by outside agitators, including the infamous *La Escalera* conspiracy in the 1840s. Though mass executions and imprisonments had followed each of the incidents, those who survived grew stronger and even more determined to free themselves. The Spanish, at the moment, were a convenient target at which to aim these veteran warriors.

"Damned right it's good news. We're going to be invincible, I swear it." Freddie set his empty plate on the sand. Disappointed, the flock of gulls headed back to the bay. "Do we have a timetable to return to sea?"

Drake shook his head. *The only thing I have to do is determine how to find my lovely nurse back in Key West. A few extra days to set a strategy will not go amiss.*

"Then I say we spend the afternoon helping our *compadres* plan their attack, and spend the night drinking rum and chasing women, chuckaboo."

"Why should today be any different?" Drake broke into laughter, having predicted his brother's proclivities well before he'd spoken.

Freddie growled in mock irritation. "Your day will come, brother. Your day will come." He stood and stalked away, heading for the communal tent.

"I hope it comes soon," Drake said to himself once Freddie left. "Now, who do I know in Key West who can tell me the identity of 'TM'?"

****

By the time they were ready to sail a week later, the sailors for both ships had had their chances for time ashore, which boosted morale. Home-cooked meals remained much more popular than salted pork and hardtack, and the crews nearly ate the small settlement out of all their fresh food supplies. In return, they helped build another set of small huts for the women and children to stay in when it rained.

On the last evening, those men so inclined caught a basketful of fish. The cooks filleted the catch and wrapped them in banana leaves, spicing them with red peppers, ginger, and salt before baking them in the fire's embers. The result was an aromatic, flaky delight.

Drake sat with cabin boy Mateo and his mother, Leta. She was a shapely woman with large, dark eyes and a four-inch scar on her left cheek. Scuttlebutt said she'd been a *puta* in Havana until she conceived her son. When he was born with a clubfoot and the beginnings of scoliosis, she took that as a sign to give up her work. Now, she helped lead the fight to throw her former Spanish masters off their island.

"So, Mateo serves you well?" she asked quietly.

"He does." Drake grinned. "It took a while for him to develop his sea legs, but I believe he enjoys his life now."

"He's gotten taller, I'm sure of it." Delicate fingers picked at her food. "I appreciate you giving him this chance. We tried to find him something in the city, but…" She trailed off with a sad look. "One man scolded me and threw me out, telling me we were both cursed. It became too hard to bear."

Drake reached out to pat her shoulder. "Leta, you have no worries with this one. He works hard, and the men enjoy his youth and sense of humor. He will make you proud." He glanced over to the new building. "Meanwhile, you and the others continue to work hard to prepare for the revolution. Mateo will be proud of you, too."

"I can hear you," Mateo said, his voice tight with irritation.

"Good." Drake poked the boy in the ribs. "Then you'll know I've decided not to throw you to the sharks this week."

Mateo gave his captain his shy, crooked smile. "*Bueno.*"

Leta laughed softly. "Let me get you some more fish, Captain."

She stood before he could think to protest, then he decided he'd be glad of another helping. He urged Mateo to get one, too.

"You don't know how long it might be until we get another fresh meal, yes?"

"*Sí*, Captain!" The boy limped off after his mother.

Drake leaned back against the stump he'd chosen to prop himself up, took a long draft of rum, and closed his eyes, thinking of the glorious sail they'd have back to Florida on the morrow. He and Freddie had each set an agenda that involved their mysterious women, and he knew that quest would resonate in his dreams.

****

Drake gathered his men and ordered them aboard. The farewells of men and their wives, and men and their would-be wives, and the children, whom everyone cherished, took a while. Eventually they were ready to set sail. Samuel ordered the anchor lifted and the sails let down. The easterly winds filled the sails with a snap. He winked at Drake.

"We're on our way, Captain."

"Steady as she goes, my friend."

The *Blackbird* was taking a bit longer to get started. Puzzled, Drake took the spyglass from the hook on the mast and checked out the deck of his brother's ship. Nothing looked out of place—men scurrying, lines flying. Finally, the sails went up and a new little flag on the topmast, a red field with a black bird on it.

Arrogant little bastard. Bet he held that back just to rub my nose in it. It's a fine-looking symbol, though. I'll have to find one for myself when I get back to Key West.

The wind picked up and gave his ship a boost forward. The men sang from their hearts, bellowing the verses of *The Coast of High Barberee*. Drake had settled into that glorious feeling of being underway when his eye caught a different part of the picture. Freddie remained well behind him. Another ship sailed from the bay. As Drake watched, it unfurled the Spanish flag.

"Identify that ship!" Drake yelled.

Several men working high on the masts spied out the flags. "*Esta la Bellona, el Capitán!*"

Drake felt an invisible punch to the gut. They must have been lying in wait just inside the mouth of the bay. That ship's captain held the longtime grudge with Freddie after that stunt with the Spanish treasure chests. Did he realize that was the *Blackbird*? Did he—?

The *Bellona* came around and fired a barrage of cannons broadside at Freddie's ship. Their two ships sailed closer together than the *Raven* was to either of them. Through the spyglass, Drake saw wood splinter all along the port side.

"Get your guns loaded," he muttered, willing Freddie to return fire. But the *Bellona* fired again before he could. This time, Drake spotted men escaping overboard.

"Turn this ship 'round!" he cried. He rushed to the wheel, shoving Samuel aside to heave at the spokes himself with wrenching hand over hand pulls that pained his shoulders.

"Cut the sails!" Samuel shouted. To Drake, he said, "Captain, you'll never turn the ship with the favorable winds. All ye'll do is break your arms—"

"I've got to get back there, have to help him," Drake said, breathing hard. *I've always been there to look out for him. How could I have failed him this day?*

More sounds of cannon fire echoed across the water. His struggle to command his ship left him no hands to spy out the battle. "What's happening?" he roared.

"The *Blackbird*'s launched a volley at the Spaniard," Samuel said, nearly as breathless as his captain. "But they've taken a handful of shots low on the hull."

No, Freddie! No...

The ship had finally begun to respond to his steering demands, and she came around just in time for them to see the *Blackbird*'s aft deck burst into flames. She lurched to the starboard side, leaning at a forty-five-degree angle, the open gunports dangerously close to the water.

"They've launched some lifeboats, Captain." Samuel's voice trembled. "I'm sure your brother's aboard."

Drake guided the ship in the direction of the conflagration. "Prepare the men to rescue survivors."

But even as they watched, someone trimmed the *Blackbird*'s sails and turned the dying ship toward the *Bellona*. Whipping the sails up again took time, but eventually, it picked up speed and cruised directly for the aggressor.

Drake's men cheered. "He's taking 'em down, Captain! Hip hip hurray! Hip hip hurray!"

He didn't share the same enthusiasm. It was clear that they'd never get back in time to assist Freddie; the wind was against them. He had no doubt that Freddie himself stood astride the deck, steering the ship into certain death so he'd not die defeated.

The *Blackbird* took another round of fire, and the bow dipped into the water. Those in the dinghies paddled madly, trying their best to be out of the area when the two ships took their final breaths. It was too easy to get sucked under with them.

Drake's chest tightened, his heart hammering inside his ribs. A cold, numb feeling settled over him. He rallied his men and fought for every inch of water that separated the *Raven* from the other two ships, but it was all over when they arrived.

Both the *Bellona* and the *Blackbird* took on water, Freddie's bowsprit lodged amidships of the Spanish craft. Now that they could cross from one ship to the other, several sailors engaged in sword fight on the decks. The first dinghies arrived aside the *Raven* for rescue, and the sailors worked like a ragged machine to salvage both the men and craft.

They had just finished taking the boats aboard when a last gun barrage went out from the *Blackbird*. That gave the death blow to the Spanish ship, and it sank quickly. Those still alive swam out and waved to be picked up by the *Raven*. Those who hadn't survived floated, bloody, awaiting the sharks that would inevitably be drawn in.

The last two men from the *Blackbird* paddled awkwardly, dragging a third between them. When they'd been hauled aboard, they laid Freddie's body on the deck, carefully and with respect. "We're sorry, Captain," they murmured, then left him with his brother.

Drake hunkered down and studied what was left of Freddie. He'd taken multiple shots, one just below the shoulder, one in the center of his bowels. Another had skinned the right side of his head, leaving his skull bone exposed.

The evidence of the agonizing death tore at his heart. His own body filled with pain in the same places the blood had pooled in his brother's, as if he'd taken the shots himself. His eyes filled with tears and his mouth opened, but he could force no sound from his throat.

At least Freddie went out fighting. He would have wanted it no other way.

As Drake slowly stood up, his first impulse was to destroy the Spanish ship a second time. But they faced another peril.

"Captain! Best we move on," called Samuel, who stood on the forecastle, spyglass in hand. "We've caught some interest."

He pointed toward the bay, where other sails moved in their direction, no doubt curious captains wanting to see if this was the beginning of war.

"Captain, Spaniards call for rescue in the waters below. Shall we send them a ladder?"

Drake stared at his brother's body.

"Turn us about and sail for home. The Spaniards can drown."

****

Freddie was laid to rest in a shallow grave on their Islamorada property. Since the majority of the island was made of coral rock, there wasn't much "underground" for digging. Some pits in the coral were deeper than others, though, and Drake found one that would serve.

He dug and covered alone; he'd left the men on board. *Nothing they could do here anyway. I'm the one who has to say goodbye to the single constant in my life. We were two suns that rotated around each other, fed off each other, loved each other.*

What—or who—will draw me with its gravity now?

Chapter Five

All too soon, the anticipated night arrived.

Clara helped her dress, restringing her cameo with the new ribbon and helping her curl her hair into ringlets that cascaded from a clip at the back of her head. Her rough fingers caught on the delicate silk, and Tamsyn bit her lip, jealous that she didn't have her own lady's maid, as many of the other girls her age did, to help her prepare.

But I'm going to the ball, just the same. I have a new dress and a beau who cares about me. I don't need all the frills and folderol. Do I?

She shooed the servant away and studied her reflection. She poked and prodded and picked until she was satisfied she'd done all she could. She cleared her throat and closed her eyes, then stood straight and opened them again, taking in the full effect.

"A masterpiece," she said, half-joking and self-deprecatory.

"No, Missy Tamsyn, it is no lie. You look a queen in that dress," Clara said. "You float like a garden rose."

"Thank you. I hope Thatcher agrees."

Steeling her courage, she went to the stairs. She descended slowly, afraid she might trip over the hem of her skirt.

Her father waited at the bottom of the staircase. His

eyes narrowed as he studied her, then his expression faded into a smile. She wondered idly if he was pleased by how she looked or by the thought that his money had been well invested in the search for a husband.

When she reached the bottom step, she saw tears in his eyes. "If your mother could only see ye," he said.

She hugged him, and he actually returned the embrace. Tamsyn reveled in the rare display of affection. Whether it was just the part of her mother inside herself or in the form of a guardian angel, she could feel Ellen's comforting presence. But she believed that, on occasions like this, Ellen would have been pleased.

"Young Winslow's here," her father whispered in her ear. "This will be an important evening. Conduct yourself like a lady and make me proud."

"Yes, Papa."

"Let him in," Angus said. One of the housemen went to the door and opened it. Thatcher entered, resplendent in a black tailcoat and red satin vest. He greeted Angus, then he handed Tamsyn a rose in the exact shade of her dress.

"However did you know?" she asked, amazed and gratified. The flower gave off a tantalizing scent. She nipped the stem and skillfully tucked the flower into her topknot, checking her placement in the foyer's mirror, which was brilliant with a heavy, Spanish gold frame. A pair of rich antique swords hung crossed above the mirror. All were salvaged from wrecks in years gone by.

"Dear Tamsyn, every bit of information has its price," Thatcher whispered as she came close. "There's nothing money can't buy."

"Have a pleasant evening," her father said as he walked them to the door.

"Thank you, sir. I will take fine care of your daughter," Thatcher said. He took Tamsyn's arm and led her to his waiting carriage. They could easily have walked to the Pickham house, as it was only a number of blocks away, and the evening was mild, but Thatcher had declared the idea much too gauche. "We'll drive," he said. "It will make a more suitable entrance."

Once the door to the carriage closed, and they rolled away from the sight of Angus as he stood watching from the front step, Thatcher leaned over and stole a kiss.

Tamsyn smiled, still a little dazzled by the wondrous, romantic air of the entire evening. Thatcher apparently took her expression as encouragement. He pulled Tamsyn toward him, holding her neck with his hand, kissing her until she was breathless.

She was too shocked to think, overwhelmed by his passion. It was passion, wasn't it? He surrendered to his desire so often, once they were out of sight. But this was the first time they'd been utterly alone without a soul in shouting distance. As the carriage lurched over a stone in the road, Thatcher's grip slipped, and she managed to break apart from him. Her head snapped back, and the rose fell from her hairdo.

"Thatcher, please stop. I'll wrinkle my dress, and we've worked so very hard to make it just perfect."

"Oh, my darling," he said. "I can't help it. Your very presence excites me so. I just want to kiss you and hold you, and…" His gaze slid from her face down the front of her dress. "You have such sweet endowments, and I know soon you will let me share them." He dragged his eyes upward once again and sighed deeply, then took her hand and squeezed it. "Say you forgive me, won't you? If you weren't so delectable, I would be better able to control myself."

Tamsyn looked into his face in the dim light from the street and thought she saw contrition there. "You must not be so indiscreet. If someone were to see us—"

"They would think us madly in love. You do care for me, don't you, Tamsyn?"

"Of course I do, Thatcher. You and no one else, my love."

She straightened her skirt and took a deep breath. Was this what it meant to be a couple? Whenever they were apart, it seemed she thought about him all the time. He'd written ardent letters which she kept tied with a ribbon in a drawer, taking them out to read and reread. In company, he was a gentleman, speaking kindly to her, showing his thoughtfulness in a dozen ways. It wasn't until they were alone that his demeanor changed, the cultured, polished Thatcher displayed to the world being replaced by a demanding, spoiled child with carnal demands.

The shift in his personality and his insistence as he pressed himself on her made her uncomfortable, but she did her best to convince herself it must be a fault of her own. Perhaps she just didn't love Thatcher enough. He had grown into a social class different from hers; they might have different rules of conduct from the ones Ellen had instilled in her daughter…

Drake Ashton found no need to force himself on you, thought an unexpected voice in the back of her head, but she shushed it as the carriage rattled on. *I don't even know him. Thatcher is the man who's shown interest, and he can change my life as my true love. I must strive to love him better if I am to achieve this dream.*

Studying Thatcher's pouting silhouette against the carriage window, where the last coral tones of sunset lingered in the sky, Tamsyn brought a smile to her lips. *Time to put aside this unpleasantry.* "Thank you for inviting me to the ball."

He notably hesitated, then patted her hand. "It is my pleasure. I'm sure you will prove to be an asset to me this evening."

The carriage stopped, and as the driver opened the door, Thatcher leapt out so that he could assist Tamsyn himself. Just as she stepped out of the carriage, she noted the flower she'd worn, lying on the ground, pressed flat by the sole of Thatcher's shoe.

He didn't bother to notice.

All the windows were flung open in the large, white Pickham house, and the sounds of a waltz floated down along the tropical breeze along with the smell of orchids. The white gingerbread trim along the wide front porch of the house reflected a blaze of electric light from inside. Chinese lanterns were hung along its upper length, providing an air of festivity. Men in formal jackets gathered on the porch to smoke fat Cuban cigars, nodding to Thatcher as he and Tamsyn passed up the steps. Threads of conversation swirled after the pair like the pungent tobacco smoke.

"Only a matter of time, Wellingford. Those Papist Spaniards will continue to oppress the Cuban people until there's a revolt."

"The refugees come here in droves," complained another man. "Every day, there's some woman or guttersnipe knocking on the back door looking for work. More likely, they're bringing disease. The lot of them should be rounded up and sent back."

"It shall be war, gentlemen," a third voice with a heavy British accent stated unequivocally. "But we English beat the Spanish dogs once before, and we'll do it again."

Tamsyn was vaguely alarmed by the talk of war. Cuba was only ninety miles from her home, closer even than the mainland United States. Would the Spanish hostilities spread to their tiny island?

She wanted to hear more, but Thatcher apparently had no interest in such talk. His strong arm propelled her forward into the crowd.

The furniture had been cleared from the two huge front rooms of the Pickham house, and women in beautiful gowns danced with dashing men, amid huge potted palms and more lanterns. All wore brightly colored masks which covered half their faces. A servant near the door had a basket full of masks and handed her a pink one. Thatcher put on his, a brilliant blue which highlighted the color of his eyes, then helped her don hers. The feeling of the mask on her face gave Tamsyn a thrill, an awareness that the night had taken on an air both mysterious and fantastic.

"Dance with me?" Thatcher said. Without waiting for an answer, he led her down the length of the room, where they moved into the twirling crowd. Thatcher waltzed her stiffly around the floor, past a dizzying panorama of faces. She was breathless by the time the music ended, and Thatcher smiled.

"You look beautiful." He leaned forward to nearly kiss her, a bare brush of his lips against hers.

She turned her head away as several society women passed, flustered by their frowns in her direction. "We should greet our hosts," she said to discourage him from inappropriate public displays of affection.

Well, that's no way to get yourself married. Where's that devil-may-care attitude you had about kissing Thatcher in the open at the docks?

That bravado had definitely vanished in the vicinity of all the society's dames, with their glares of disapproval. Try as she might to pretend she didn't care, she had to admit that deep down, she did. Her mother had been quite determined that Tamsyn know the "rules" of local society. But learning rote lessons and putting them into practice had proved very different. Especially when others seemed to behave outside those confines with careless abandon.

Rules, rules! Back at my ocean, not a creature cares what I do or who I'm with...

Thatcher's lips pressed tightly together, and he looked away. "Of course."

He and Tamsyn made their way along the end of the dance floor to the salon, where the senior Pickhams sat in high-backed, perfectly upholstered chairs, greeting their guests. Tall, plain Mary Elizabeth Pickham, their eldest—and Tamsyn knew, very eligible—daughter, fidgeted behind them in her expensive, low-cut magenta dress, obviously waiting for their permission to dance. *She was the one Miss Pearl had mentioned. Did she still pine after Thatcher?*

"Mr. Winslow, you honor us by your presence," Lucinda Pickham cooed as he bowed over her hand. As the heavily made-up woman's gaze shifted to her,

Tamsyn noticed a certain distaste in the sharp blue eyes, then the longing in Mary Elizabeth's face as Thatcher smiled. "And this is?"

"Tamsyn MacKiernan," he said.

Tamsyn took the woman's limp extended hand, lowering her head so her reddened cheeks wouldn't be noticed. Mrs. Pickham certainly knew who she was or at least who her father was. The only reason for forcing a direct introduction must be to humiliate Tamsyn. "Mrs. Pickham," she said between gritted teeth.

"Charles Pickham." Her husband kissed her hand.

"Good evening, sir."

Mrs. Pickham rose to her feet and took Thatcher's arm. "Now, Thatcher, Mary Elizabeth has been hoping to dance with you. I trust you won't disappoint her." She drew him closer to her, and Mary Elizabeth pinkened at her mother's boldness. Thatcher inclined his head and flashed what could have been an apologetic look at Tamsyn.

"Of course. I would be no gentleman if I refused such a request from my hostess," he said amiably and took Mary Elizabeth's arm with a smile. They gracefully blended into the dancing guests.

Mrs. Pickham's satisfied expression as she watched them go made Tamsyn feel suddenly invisible. *Gentleman! Clearly, he is no gentleman to abandon the woman he brought to the ball. I should have known I would not really be welcome here!* She excused herself to the Pickhams and rushed away through the crowd, thinking only of escape, when she was brought to a halt by a tall man in a silver mask, who caught her hand as she passed.

"Always in a hurry, but never watching where

she's going," the man said in a familiar voice.

Tamsyn thought her heart would stop as the man's dark eyes met hers, amusement crinkling their corners. Did he remember her? Her current appearance was worlds apart from her dress at the cove. "Mr. Ashton?"

"You remember my name." Drake chuckled. "I regret we have yet to be properly introduced." He smiled broadly. "Are you free for the next dance?"

"I-I don't know—" She was confused, too many things turning in her mind at once. She looked for Thatcher and vaguely caught the bright bloom of Mary Elizabeth's dress in the middle of the floor.

"Come, now. Your gallant escort has abandoned you. The least you can do is show that zounderkite you don't give a fig." He held out his arm. "I think we should join him." He drew her onto the floor before she could protest.

As they danced, Tamsyn felt the difference between Thatcher's mechanical steps and *dancing*. The stranger flowed when he moved, and she found it easy to simply listen to the music and move where he directed, light in his hands. He didn't try to converse with her, but smiled at her constantly, bathing her in the warmth of his regard. Tamsyn thought she would like to ask him many things, and wondered if he had questions about her as well. At the same time, her nerves tingled pleasantly, knowing she was dancing with...a pirate? *Scandalous.*

As the dance concluded, he arranged their final turn to move them out onto a side porch where they were alone. He kept her hand as they moved apart after the dance. "So, we meet again. I discover my rescuer is a fair maiden who demonstrates great decorum—in the proper setting."

Tamsyn found him even more handsome in formal clothes, and showing great self-assurance, not at all the adventurer chasing sea creatures along the shore. "So do you," she answered at last.

"Yes," he agreed. "We did not meet under the most conventional of conditions." He studied her face in the moonlight. "Drake Ashton, again at your service."

Tamsyn felt compelled to reciprocate, his charm overcoming any questions of propriety. "Tamsyn MacKiernan." She examined his tawny face, the light of the porch lanterns combining with that of the moon to add interesting shadows to his cheekbones. "I had no idea you were part of Key West society, Mr. Ashton. The last companions I saw you with..." Her voice trailed off as his smile grew broader.

"Not exactly the cream of the aristocracy, those men. Very observant of you, Miss MacKiernan. I probably should not be here at all." He winked at her. "I was compelled to come in hopes I would find something I was particularly seeking."

Her breath caught with interest, though she covered it immediately.

He added, "A man may find a mask hides all sorts of secrets."

"Do you have secrets, then, Mr. Ashton?" Her quick mind and wit gave her the usual verbal advantage over most young men of her acquaintance. But she found Ashton as practiced as she.

He only nodded and smiled. "Don't we all, Miss MacKiernan?"

She smiled and turned to observe those on the dance floor. He moved a little closer, speaking close to her ear. "Your mask hides disappointments as well."

Did he read my mind? Jealousy passed over her in a wave as Thatcher and Mary Elizabeth passed, chatting with great animation. "Yes, I suppose it does."

"It's his loss," he said under his breath.

"I beg your pardon?"

"Miss MacKiernan, I should know that anyone who wields pliers as well as you has broadened her horizons a good bit, unlike most of these silly debutantes." He looked over the crowd. "Insipid bunch of frilly little girls."

Tamsyn agreed wholeheartedly. Watching the society misses and their moneyed beaux swirling around the hall, she felt more like an intruder. Ashton's presence was a calming influence, and she felt perfectly comfortable with him. But she remained uneasy with his familiarity, puzzled by her attraction to him even though they hardly knew each other. She had to give him—and herself—no encouragement to know each other better. "Perhaps you dislike them so because they rejected you first."

His eyes twinkled behind his mask. "She has barbs as vicious as those of her sea friends."

She retorted, "Many animals are dangerous if you do not know them well enough to perceive their attack."

"Indeed, Miss MacKiernan, indeed." His gaze seemed to pierce right through her.

Tamsyn, as much as she was trying to control her feelings, found his charisma overpowering, like the scent of white gardenias in a closed room. Ashton seemed years older than Thatcher, experienced, confident, with no need to impress her with money or stature, only sharing of himself. It was not a flattering comparison for the Key West heir.

As if drawn by the thought of his name, Thatcher burst onto the porch, face flushed and out of breath. "There you are!" He looked from one to the other of them, suspicion carved in the lines which crossed his forehead as his lips drew into a petulant frown. "What is happening here?"

"Nothing is 'happening,'" Ashton said, his baritone rising over Thatcher's sulky tenor. "Miss MacKiernan felt a bit faint after our dance, so we came out for some air."

Thatcher was immediately solicitous. He took Tamsyn's hands and pulled her to him possessively. "My darling?" He peered down into her face, but the strong emotion in his eyes felt not at all like love to her.

"Thatcher, do not concern yourself," she said quickly. His raised voice had drawn some attention from inside. She looked with alarm at both men, not wanting to be the cause of a spectacle at this, her first real society outing.

"She's right. Everything is fine, Mr. Winslow." Ashton bowed slightly and excused himself, returning to the main room with a mysterious smile.

As Ashton left them alone, Tamsyn was grateful for his thoughtfulness in averting potential trouble. She turned to reenter the room, but Thatcher's hand closed painfully on the arm that held his, squeezing until she gasped.

"So, Tamsyn, what were you doing out here with that man? Who is he?" An angry stranger looked out at her from Thatcher's eyes. "You're here with me. *Because* of me. You will not shame me in front of these good people. While you're with me, you're mine."

His tone worried her. What had happened to the gentle Thatcher of their courtship days? Or even more puzzling, the delicate boy who had always retreated from their children's play at the first sign of injury to watch from the window of his house?

That change in Thatcher Winslow had been what most impressed her when they'd reconnected six months earlier. The "sissy" side she'd always pitied had nearly vanished. He was bold now, bragged of his accomplishments, and never allowed others to dominate him in a conversation. In the few times she'd visited his parents' shipping business office, she'd been awed by the way he handled the employees, directing their work as the future owner should. She'd been proud of his progress, and she thought that pride had been what attracted him to seek her as companion thereafter. But that was a different man from the insecure one who stood before her, his wildly jealous look provoking fear.

Unsure how to react, Tamsyn tried to soothe him.

"Thatcher, I'm not harmed in any way, and I have not been indiscreet. Mr. Ashton and I were dancing. You were dancing with Miss Pickham. I-I didn't think there was any harm in it."

"No harm in dancing with that man?" Thatcher's focus was beyond her now. Tamsyn began to wonder if it might have been safer if Ashton had stayed. She forced herself not to look for him, to see if he had remained nearby, in order not to inflame Thatcher again.

"Please, Thatcher," she begged, her voice quivering despite her effort to be firm. She stood to lose much more than he if there was a scene. A Winslow would continue to be accepted; a male would continue to be accepted. But she was a woman, and not of the strict upper crust. The fault would fall to her no matter what the true facts were. She sighed and forced the apology. "I'm not used to these big parties, and...I was quite overcome by the press of the crowd." She smiled placatingly. "I'm sorry, love. I am. Shall we return?"

He searched her face for what seemed like an eternity. "You will learn how to behave when you are with me," Thatcher said, steel behind the words. After a visible effort to control himself, he finally relented, his hand gradually loosening its grip. "Yes, let's get some punch." His manner sharply reverted to that of kindly host, and Tamsyn was relieved. Speculative expressions appeared on several faces as they returned. She made sure she held Thatcher's arm just tightly enough to imply delighted harmony, not daring to meet the eyes she was sure were gawking at her.

Minutes passed. At the refreshment table, Thatcher handed her a crystal cup filled with sparkling rose-colored punch. Tamsyn stole a glance around and saw no one was even looking her way. The dance had resumed, and everyone had returned to whatever had fascinated them before Drake Ashton had spirited her from the room.

She was safe, and her plans were back on the path to a good match with a man she loved.

Avoiding the Mr. Hyde-like shift she'd seen in Thatcher's character, she took the moment to observe the variety of silks and satins used in the gowns worn by the women. The different shades of green, pink, red, and blue reminded Tamsyn of the colors of the parrots and other tropical wildlife which inhabited the island.

Mary Elizabeth Pickham's dress, for example, was

just the shade of summer bougainvillea blossoms. Tamsyn noticed that particular young lady still had her eye on Thatcher, and she moved closer to him, trying to stake her claim. *Why would the Pickhams allow Thatcher to invite me to their soiree if they were determined Mary Elizabeth should have him?* She sipped her punch, which was deliciously cool, spiced with ginger and lime.

Once again the warm lover, Thatcher leaned close and asked, "Are you enjoying yourself?"

"Oh, yes!" She smiled, hoping he would remain magnanimous. "Everyone looks so fine, and the music is lovely."

"It is an exceptional affair, but then most of them are," he said offhandedly. "The Pickhams have quite a reputation for excellent entertainment."

In the doorway across from the table where the punch was set out, Mrs. Pickham and another dowager, in dark-green voile, glared at her. Tamsyn turned her eyes to her escort, daring herself not to feel inferior. "And then supper?"

Thatcher laughed at her. "You are such a ninny. Of course they will have supper, probably a buffet such as you've never seen, with crab and shrimp and all sorts of exotic fruits..." He went on to tantalize her with description, but she half listened, hearing instead the undercurrent, his patronizing tone. With a thread of resentment, she accepted that Thatcher Winslow attended such parties as a routine matter, since his parents were wealthy and his presence welcome. Angus MacKiernan and his daughter were not part of that particular social circle. For Tamsyn, this was the party of a lifetime.

"Thatcher! Is that you, old man?"

Two young men, nearly identical in pressed black jackets, stepped up in front of Thatcher, and there was an exchange of handshakes and claps on the shoulder as they laughed and crowed.

"I hear you have a new vessel, Charlie," Thatcher said. "When can I get a look at it?"

"Come on down to the water, Winslow," demanded the shorter of the two. "She's a few blocks away, right at the pier."

"She's a beaut—she'll easily take the prize in the summer races," the other said sagely, puffing on his lit cigar.

Tamsyn had always disliked the smell of cigar smoke, even though cigar making was prevalent in the city, thanks to the influx of Cuban refugees. Now as a cloud of it descended in her face, it made her eyes water, and she began to cough.

Thatcher noticed her discomfort and apparently took advantage of it to escape. "All right, Geoffrey, I shall, but only for a moment. I shall return directly, Tamsyn," he said, with a warning glance. "Wait here."

The three of them slipped out a door in the back of the room.

Tamsyn clutched her crystal cup, suddenly feeling orphaned again. No one spoke to her. The girls her age chattered to each other, enjoying shared backgrounds and histories. These young women probably didn't sit of a morning with their fathers going over the household accounts, or darning their stockings, or styling their own hair. Tamsyn felt a bit envious and wished very hard she had a friend in the room.

Though she knew most of these girls casually, they

were not her friends. She didn't have close girlfriends with whom to share secrets and adventures. Norah Brennan, who'd lived next door since Tamsyn was twelve and whose bedroom window was directly across from Tamsyn's, was her only real confidante. On warm evenings, sometimes they'd both sit by their windows and talk. Norah, of course, wouldn't be invited to such a grand ball, either.

"Are those glass slippers uncomfortable?"

She turned at the amused words behind her to see Drake Ashton helping himself to the pink liquid in the punch bowl dotted with hibiscus blossoms. He held the ladle out to her, offering to refill her glass, which she accepted wordlessly. He sipped the drink and shuddered. "No one has spiked the punch," he said in a stage whisper.

"I should think not," she said primly. *Was the man never serious?* "And I think you'll find my slippers are not made of glass. That would hardly be practical." She looked quickly in the direction Thatcher had gone, hoping he wouldn't see Ashton near her. Because of the prior conflict, not because she found Ashton distasteful.

"I'm sorry," he said. "You had a look about you that reminded me of Cinderella, gazing about you as if you'd never seen such finery and frivolity. You don't belong in this setting, milady." He smiled, but there was compassion in his eyes. "I see you as part of a natural landscape, in the cove where we met, enjoying the susurration of the ocean's touch along the sand, not this stilted and artificial society talk."

"How do you presume to know me, sir?" she said with a tart bite. Inwardly, she marveled that he *did* know her, and well. She was in fact most comfortable as he'd first seen her, skirt hitched up to her knees, feet six inches deep in the water, a crab delicately crawling over her fingers, or marking a seagull's flight as it crossed the horizon.

His answer was a cocked eyebrow. *He knew!* Somehow, he knew she recognized herself in what he said. *How could he?* Tamsyn's heart raced, and suddenly she wanted to be at the cove, away from this crowd of strangers, back to her own life. *Mamma...* she thought. *What shall I do?* There was no answer.

Her hand trembled, and he took the cup from her before she spilled it. "Miss MacKiernan...Tamsyn," he said warmly. "Please forgive me if I've upset you. It was merely an observation on my part, perhaps drawing on the fact I feel out of place here myself." He leaned a little closer. "You know, I'd rather be on the water, breeze in my face as the sails are raised and the ship leaps ahead under the power of the wind." His smile was kind. "We cannot change our natures. We must be true to our own selves."

Unable to answer as he seemed to reach inside her soul, Tamsyn could do no more than nod, her throat fiery with boiling emotion. At last she had to turn away. She retrieved her cup, taking a deep breath to calm herself. "Thank you, but I believe this is mine."

He nodded. "So where is the intrepid Winslow now?"

She wondered at the rancor in his voice. "He went to look at a boat, I think."

He shook his head and smiled tightly. "In his absence, I will take it upon myself to escort you, then."

Tamsyn hesitated. She'd had a longing for Thatcher's love for months. Finally, he showed more than a passing interest. Now he did. *Well, at least to the extent that he would profess his love as long as she demonstrated her devotion by letting him have his way.* Then she met Drake Ashton, a man who simply looked into her soul and seemed to understand her without asking for anything in return. What was she to do?

As she hovered in indecision, he asked her to dance again. She glanced to the door, but Thatcher had not returned. *Surely Thatcher wouldn't expect me to stand here like a lump on a log all night. Or if he did, he was expecting the ridiculous.* "Very well. One dance," she said, a smile escaping.

They moved onto the floor as another waltz began to play. The expert dancer didn't want to let her go after that dance, or the second, or even the third. Finally, laughing, out of breath, she persuaded him to stop long enough to get another glass of punch. Her cheeks were hot, and she wanted to hold the cool crystal against them. Thatcher was still nowhere to be seen.

"You are a fine partner," he said for only her ears.

"I could say the same for you." She didn't look at him, aware of her warm feelings. "But then you'd get a swelled head. And I believe you are well-endowed in that area already."

"Stung again!" He chuckled. "I think I prefer the sea urchin."

"Perhaps you'll have the opportunity to encounter him once again."

Tamsyn was about to go on when she looked up and spotted Thatcher across the room, speaking with Mary Elizabeth Pickham.

Her again? What's going on here? Why is he so fixated on her?

She wondered if he even wanted to be with her at all. *Why would he bring me to the ball if...?* She watched, horrified, as the two began an argument that escalated until they were nearly shouting. Then Mary Elizabeth slapped him.

A collective gasp went up around the room. The music faltered and went silent. Thatcher looked around, frozen. His gaze fell on Tamsyn. She could see his mind calculating, in the twitches of his face. Squirming like a trapped rat, he clenched his fists. Then something came to him, because his eyes lit up. He took a step back and waved at the servants gathered by the door.

"Someone fetch Angus MacKiernan. Bring him now!"

Chapter Six

Drake found next to no joy in attending the New Year's ball, but he'd insisted on obtaining an invitation through back channels for two reasons. The main one had been to speak to his nameless nurse from the cove. It hadn't been difficult to discover her identity, not with the contacts he had in the community.

But his second reason was to take the pulse of the town regarding the Cuban situation. He'd heard the discussion of growing Spanish-American hostilities as he had arrived, and he wanted to hear more. He needed all the information he could gather in order to be prepared to fight the Spanish in the days and months to come. And fight them he would—it was the promise he'd made to his dead brother, a vow he would spend the rest of his days fulfilling.

After he'd buried Freddie, he used the intervening three weeks to search out news. It looked like the Americans were about to become involved in a war against the Spanish. Both here in Cuba, and in the Philippines, the two countries' interests had come up against each other. Financially, it would be difficult for Spain to maintain a war on two fronts, both so far from their homeland. Cuba was, at least, on America's doorstep.

He crossed to the open porch doors to smoke a cigar with those discussing the political situation.

Although none of them were likely to recognize him, especially with a mask, he was dressed in the right clothes and had the right inflection and accent to pass for one of them. None questioned him. As he had as much new information to share as any of them, he learned a great deal and taught them even more.

Despite his focus, however, he felt claustrophobic in the closely packed rooms.

All those years with the horizons as the barriers of his personal space had shaped his comfort zone to include open spaces with few people.

And even though he was happy to have found his mystery lady, he was astounded at her life choices. Thatcher Winslow, of all men! Ashton didn't know many people in Key West, but he recognized Thatcher, the pampered darling and heir of the Winslow shipping empire. The man would not be acquainted with him, of course, as he did not deign to notice those beyond his class.

Was that why Winslow continued to walk away from Tamsyn? He felt she was below him? That didn't make sense. If Winslow was seeking a match, he certainly had plenty to choose from.

Drake couldn't see how a man could leave Tamsyn for anyone else in this vapid social group, even for as long as a dance. In her pale pink gown, she was lovely. The pink half mask she wore just served to heighten her mystery. He felt sorry for her, the way she was being treated. *Another victim of society who needed protecting.*

He tired of the jingoism of the newspaper editor, who carried forth at great length on the subject of a possible war, and returned to have another dance with

Tamsyn when he found that Winslow had left her alone again. He didn't care if the man returned and saw them. He could thrash that man with one hand. *Maybe half one…*

Then the slap that effectively put a halt to the dance occurred. Drake had been in similar straits on several occasions, and he knew from those situations that slaps didn't occur without considerable passion being involved. So why was Winslow having a passionate encounter with their host's eldest daughter?

When Winslow bellowed for Tamsyn's father, the temperature in the room rose. Drake stood near her at that point, as they'd been engaged in conversation after their dance. She looked at him, questions in her eyes. He lifted his shoulders slightly and studied Winslow, trying to guess what he had in mind.

Winslow crossed the room with long strides. He took Tamsyn's arm and led her to the open staircase, marching up four steps where the two of them could be seen above the crowd. Tamsyn removed her mask, looking defeated. She surreptitiously tried to break away from Winslow—Drake saw her do it—but Thatcher refused to let her go.

The babble of discussion flew around the room as the partygoers tried to ferret out what Winslow was up to. The Pickham girl's face was scarlet with embarrassment. She'd gone to her parents immediately after their confrontation, and she stood uncomfortably behind them. Winslow wore a triumphant smile when looking in her direction.

Whatever the man was planning, that girl was squarely in the middle of it. And Tamsyn was tangential, at best.

He had a bad feeling about what was to come next. *And just like with Freddie, I stand here watching, helpless to do a damned thing about it.*

It took nearly half an hour for Angus MacKiernan to appear at the Pickhams' front door. He wore a clean, but obviously not new, day coat and a bewildered expression.

"Bring him in, bring him in!" Winslow called. "Right up here on the steps."

A buzz of conversation followed MacKiernan as he walked through the crowd. His gaze went to Tamsyn, who waited on the stairs with wide eyes, one hand picking at the silk of her dress.

"Mr. MacKiernan, we are sorry to disturb you at this time of night, but your presence is required. May I have your attention, everyone?" Winslow beckoned to the man to join them. When he had walked nervously up the stairs to Winslow's side, Winslow leaned close and whispered in his ear.

MacKiernan's eyes opened wide in shock, and he froze where he stood.

Winslow waited a moment, then rushed ahead. "I have an announcement to make. I will be marrying Tamsyn MacKiernan, Angus' daughter, as soon as the banns can be read. Angus has agreed and wishes us well."

Amid a fluttering of polite applause, Tamsyn leaned forward and eyed her father, panic taking over her countenance. From where Drake stood, it was clear to him that she'd had no inkling of this development. When had this attendance at a dance become the forerunner to an instant wedding?

When Miss Pickham had disagreed with Winslow.

This must be some sort of "punishment" for his wishes being thwarted. Indeed, Mrs. Pickham's scowl and tears on Mary Elizabeth's cheeks would indicate this was so. *So, Winslow had intended all along to marry Miss Pickham, and Tamsyn had just been an instrument of vengeance.*

It was all he could do to stop himself from climbing the steps and wiping the self-satisfied smirk off that man-boy's face. Such action would serve no purpose and would likely hurt Tamsyn further. He stared for a moment, then quietly turned and slipped out one of the French doors.

Drake moved quickly, blindly from the Pickhams' house toward the pier where the *Raven* awaited. *Her eyes!* He'd seen the confusion and reluctance as her eyes had sought out his across that room full of people. If he could have saved her at that moment—

What?

If you could have saved her, what? Could you have asked her to marry you instead? A man who lives on a ship at sea, raiding shipwrecks for a living? What could you possibly offer her? The chance to die under Spanish fire as you deliver guns to the rebels?

Of course not.

It was her life, and Tamsyn MacKiernan had apparently set her cap for Thatcher Winslow before Drake had entered it, despite his opinion of Winslow's treatment of her. She was engaged and would be married to another man. There was no reason he should do anything.

Besides, he had his ship, his crew. His cause helping the Cubans throw off the Spanish harness was a good life's work, and he owed the Spanish every misdeed he could muster in revenge for his brother's death. He had more on his plate than the surprise marriage of a pretty girl.

No matter how much she appealed to him.

Drake made his way to his moored ship, slowing down only once to shove a drunken and belligerent sailor out of his way. The drunk rolled off the dock and hit the two feet of water with a satisfying splash. He could only wish the sound belonged to the stone-weighted body of young Thatcher Winslow.

****

Later that night, miles away from the MacKiernan household, the *Raven* was becalmed on the sea, floating almost soundlessly except for the gentle lapping of waves along the keel. A full ocher moon hung overhead, reflecting across the water like a spotlight. Drake sat on the prow in the moonlight, staring in the direction of the southernmost Keys island, thinking of the woman he could not put from his mind.

He told himself a dozen times it would be better for him to return to his cabin and pick up the shreds of the plan he'd had—blending the remains of Freddie's men into his crew and deciding how to proceed, having lost Freddie and the *Blackbird*, with his ongoing mission to Matanzas.

His current problem was ready cash to buy the weapons he needed. But he'd heard rumor at the party that a large ship had wrecked near the Dry Tortugas, and it was said the unfortunate *Maeigwyn* may have been carrying gold fixtures for churches in New Orleans. *Certainly worth spying out.*

As for Tamsyn, he had made a promise to introduce himself properly, and he'd carried it out. But every attempt to leave it at that was thwarted by the persistent vision of Tamsyn laughing as he whirled her around the Pickhams' ball in a mad waltz, Tamsyn concerned and maternal as she held his wounded hand at the cove, or her bright eyes glittering with provocation as they played their introduction game. The woman had infiltrated his soul.

He shrugged tired shoulders, rubbing his weary forehead. The adrenaline had drained from his body, and even remembering the evening sapped him. He remembered the shock in her eyes as Thatcher Winslow announced the impending nuptials. *Could I be wrong?* The event could have been a surprise to her, the sudden appearance of Angus MacKiernan, the proclamation to the gathered people...and she was so much out of her element in that company. Small wonder she projected what he must have mistaken as fear or regret. Any other young woman in the room would have been ecstatic to marry so well; surely that Mary Elizabeth Pickham was green with envy...green as Tamsyn's sparkling eyes...

It would be better to be happy for her good fortune. She'd not want for anything material as the wife of Winslow—no doubt, a beautiful house and gardens, a fine carriage, a husband whose future was financially secure.

His own fortunes lay along a much different path.

If Drake were to be caught by the Spaniards, it wasn't likely he'd live to be tried for the crime back on the mainland. The Spanish were known for their quick tempers and sharp swords. The mercenary trade paid him well, for now, and if the buzzing rumors he'd heard on the Pickham veranda were true, war would come within the year. Guns were a prime commodity in time of war. He always carried rum when he returned from the islands, of course, and sugar and tropical fruits, to cover his real motives. He had not been interdicted yet. As young men often did, he played the odds and planned to beat them.

For the first time, however, that focus was shaken by thoughts of this woman.

What distinguished Tamsyn MacKiernan from the other women he'd met in a hundred different ports? Drake couldn't put his finger on it. He just knew she appealed to his heart in a way that possessed him. She held an intriguing blend of strength and vulnerability, stomach ironclad in the face of blood yet timid as a lost waif left alone in the midst of the ball. He wanted to know her better.

But she was to be married. Even if he had been able to marry her, even though he had a proper home with a hired woman to maintain it, it was nothing compared with the empire Winslow would command in a few years. Drake knew he had no business thinking Tamsyn might prefer a lonely pirate to the golden boy.

Damnation!

He tried to shove her from his mind, focusing instead on the next several days' sail to the Yucatán to finish the trading Freddie had planned to do after they left Matanzas. His brother had promised he would able to add to the rebels' stockpile of medicines, preserved foods, and ammunition on their return trip.

They had a plan to overthrow their hated Spanish rulers. They'd agreed on a timetable which needed to be met, as the supplies were hidden in the hills, awaiting the time when the rebels would have enough to move against the oppressors, whether alone or in league with the Americans. Drake could not let Freddie's words curl and burn and blow away in the wind. *This* was what needed his energy at the moment.

His boots heavy against the deck, he strode across the rough wood and passed down the stairs to his small cabin. Though no one bunked with him, it was obvious he was not alone in his room. Papers of all sizes were strewn across the tiny table and bed, bearing the likeness of Tamsyn MacKiernan in pencil, in charcoal, full-faced, in profile. He'd spent an entire day in his cabin, barking orders through the door, letting no one in to see his obsession.

Her memory appeared again, slowly, lightly, like a hint of frangipani on a summer breeze.

If she only hadn't been so changeable, a variegated butterfly with beauty of form as well as function, so different from most all others he'd known! Part wondering child, part young girl entering the big world, part nurturing woman...

But it was over now.

He had to let go of her, allow her to follow her life path even if it led away from his. He had other matters which were of greater importance to him.

But even as he put her from his mind, he was aggravated by the fact that Winslow seemed indifferent to Tamsyn's uniqueness, seeming to take her for granted, another of the rich boy's possessions, like one of his fine ships or a cherished pet. That seemed the greatest offense of all: that Tamsyn would fail to be appreciated for what she was.

Drake closed his eyes and completed his vow to turn his thoughts from her. As he did, the smell of woodsmoke entered his mind, and he recalled the

Cuban *obeah* woman holding his hand in the flickering light from the fire.

This woman, she'd said, *this woman of light, she will appear in your hour of need and help you. She will come to mean more to you than life itself.*

Words, only words. *Why am I so fixated on this? There is no such thing as magic. These expectations, like all desires and dreams, vanish into the air just like that smoke.*

Tormented by his loss of hope, he threw himself onto his bed, willing sleep to overcome him. Like many other parts of his fate in these days, his will simply laughed at him, leaving him staring at the cabin's ceiling until dawn.

Chapter Seven

Tamsyn wished she could melt into the floor.

What mischief was Thatcher up to? Calling for her father? Bringing the whole event to a halt? *And everyone is staring at me.*

She tried to slip away from him, but his grip was like a square knot. "What are you doing?" she asked quietly.

"You'll see."

"Thatcher—"

His smile never wavered, but his voice held the edge of a knife. "Be patient. You'll see."

Tamsyn was reluctant to look up, but from the corner of her eye, she spied Drake watching with disbelief. Following his gaze, she saw the crushed Miss Pickham. Something else was happening here, something below the surface. She couldn't quite grasp it.

Perhaps the fact he's causing a scene during her grand ball has embarrassed her.

Likely, it had discomfited one and all. The murmur of conversation carried an unpleasant air, a sharpness of waiting. But he could get away with a spectacle because he was a Winslow.

For all this time, I've had that dream—to be a Winslow, to be his wife. But if this is what it means... She glanced at his arrogant expression, that smile which she was really beginning to dislike. *Maybe I have set my hopes on the wrong dream.*

When Thatcher saw Angus, he immediately called him up to stand beside them on the grand staircase. Her father looked to her for some clue, but she had none to provide. Thatcher spoke to her father briefly, and her father gave her a puzzled, anxious look.

Thatcher cleared his throat. "I have an announcement. I will be marrying Tamsyn MacKiernan, Angus' daughter, as soon as the banns can be read. Angus has agreed and wishes us well."

What? When had he agreed? Just then? She eyed her father, panic filling her. He hadn't asked her. Didn't he have to ask her?

Thatcher let go of her wrist. "There. It's what you wanted, isn't it?" he said so only Tamsyn and her father could hear.

"I thought so," she said softly. *We must be true to our own selves...* Ashton's words echoed in her head. She'd started to have some real qualms about an alliance with Thatcher. *And now it was too late.*

"Then we shall be married as soon as everything may be arranged."

Satisfied with his *fait accompli*, he walked away, speaking to several of the society women coming forward to congratulate him.

Angus moved closer to Tamsyn. "Did you know about this? Why did you say naught to me?"

"I-I didn't know. He just...it happened so suddenly, Papa. He never said a thing." She flexed the fingers of the hand he'd held. Her wrist was red and sore.

" 'Tis what you wanted, girl."

Was that a question in his tone? At that moment, she wanted to shout a denial and run from the room.

"Maybe it's—I don't know what I want, Papa. I don't think I—" Or did she? She couldn't corral her thoughts as they raced past and past again. The guests were all watching her, talking about her. She was trapped.

Edwina and Kenton Winslow approached the bottom of the staircase. Edwina didn't speak, her lips pressed together, and her gaze only met Tamsyn's for a moment before looking away. Kenton, however, extended a hand with his congratulations to Angus.

He smiled. "My boy has always been one for acquiring beautiful things."

Tamsyn's chest pulled tight, and she reminded herself to keep breathing. A wild picture passed through her head, wondering whether she'd be displayed with the rest of Thatcher's trophies on a shelf somewhere.

"A toast!" someone called from the crowd.

"A toast!" came answering cries, and Thatcher came back to grab Tamsyn's hand and pulled her toward the room where the supper was now laid, as servants rushed to open champagne. The guests moved in that direction as well. Tamsyn was caught in a raging current, floating headlong toward unknown waters.

She wanted to stop them, say something, even scream. But an encouraged light had appeared in her father's eyes as he walked with Thatcher's father. Mr. Winslow had his arm around her father's shoulders. He even offered Angus a cigar.

No, Papa...no. Don't get drawn in.

But as Angus enthusiastically joined in the toast, she knew in her heart the situation had moved beyond her control.

And try as she might, she could see Drake Ashton nowhere.

The rest of the evening, once expected to be her crowning introduction to local society, passed in a blur. She managed to get through supper, picking bites from her plate as she'd totally lost her appetite. When the dancing began again after the meal, she pleaded a headache and asked her father to take her home.

Thatcher volunteered his carriage for Angus and Tamsyn to return and made a show of walking her out, lightly kissing her cheek before he handed her up. Without a shred of disappointment that she was leaving, he returned inside. The music struck up, and the party apparently continued on.

Angus boasted the whole way home, touting offers Mr. Winslow had made him. Tamsyn half listened, realizing these were more silk tendrils in the web Thatcher had constructed. *No. The web I constructed with my ridiculous dreams. Only a fool cannot see what's directly in front of her nose.*

Her father bid her good night at the bottom of the stairs. "You've done well, Tamsyn. I'll be thankin' the Almighty in my prayers tonight. Your mother is watching over you, I'll say that."

She murmured something noncommittal and hurried upstairs. Clara met her in her room.

"You home early, missy. The party was not all you desired?"

Tamsyn let the girl help her take off the lovely dress. Her reflection showed she'd reverted to the lowly servant maid once again. *No more Cinderella here, Master Ashton.* She pulled on her nightgown and dismissed Clara, rather more sharply than she'd meant to. Blowing out her oil lamp, she went to bed, hoping that maybe she could wake up in the morning and find it had all been a bad dream.

****

Of course, it was not.

Before she'd even had breakfast, Tamsyn was summoned to the Winslow home for wedding discussions with Edwina Winslow. Thatcher's mother had summoned Angus as well, but he laid it down in no uncertain terms that he had no time for such things.

"You'll do fine, daughter. I'm sure Mrs. Winslow will guide ye as your own mother would have. This is a subject for women, and I'll not interfere. Go on with ye, now."

He shooed her toward the door and retreated to his office.

The Winslows sent their carriage for her; apparently they didn't find her wandering the city on foot to be desirable. She dressed in her least-worn wear-at-home dress, knowing her father would want her to make the best impression possible.

If I went in rags, do you think Thatcher's mother would talk him out of this?

Tamsyn considered her situation on the way to the Winslows' home and found herself actually torn. On one hand, she was disillusioned at her experience of Thatcher on the night of the ball. He certainly was not the picture of the gentle lover she'd cobbled together from their brief meetings and her own imagination. On the other, she'd managed to catch one of the most eligible bachelors on the island—had apparently stolen him from the most eligible young woman, right under her own roof. She had to judge that some sort of accomplishment.

She wished for a rational, objective person with whom she could discuss her circumstances.

I do know what I want. I want to be loved. I want to be able to love my husband.

If she could love Thatcher enough…

I don't know how much I can love him at all, if he doesn't treat me as a person.

Then she arrived at the Winslows', and there was no more time for thinking. In fact, Mrs. Winslow didn't particularly want to hear her opinion at all.

"God knows why that boy chose you out of all the women available to him, but he has, and he's made it open and notorious. So we'll have to make the best of it."

Tamsyn stared at her hostess over her untouched teacup. "Mrs. Winslow, it's not my—"

"Oh, come now, you've been swishing your skirts after him for months. Do you think I'm blind, girl? Chasing round the docks watching for him, even coming into the office of the shipworks like you belonged there." The woman actually looked down her nose at Tamsyn through half-framed glasses.

Tamsyn's cheeks flushed hot. Yes, she'd done those things, but Thatcher had never discouraged her. How was she to know it was something that was inappropriate?

"Why are we even proceeding, then, if it's not something Thatcher—or you—even want? Let's pretend it was a bad jest, and I'll walk away."

Even as she said the words, she felt a weight come off her. Could she really escape that easily? Just refuse?

Her freedom was short-lived. Mrs. Winslow's voice came down on her like a judge giving a life sentence.

"My son wants this. And he shall have it."

Like any bad dream, the impending ceremony took on a life of its own, like a few small rocks gathering momentum toward an eventual avalanche. The next weeks were replete with terse meetings between Tamsyn and Edwina Winslow. Tamsyn had no stomach for arguing over the details, since most requests she made were met with an exasperated frown and an "I hardly think that will do!"

Tamsyn felt abandoned and desperate, left with all these decisions on her own. If only her mother was here to help plan this event, it would surely proceed more smoothly. Tamsyn, as always, missed her mother's calming voice and sure hand. A bastion of common sense, she would have been able to speak up to Mrs. Winslow and dictate terms of her own. Tamsyn found it too difficult. No matter how overwhelmed her mother had been by circumstances, she'd always had a strong center which allowed her to bend, not to break, in the face of adversity. Tamsyn hoped someday she would have the same fortitude to follow her heart and do what she knew was right.

But wouldn't "someday" be too late?

Another point of contention came when Thatcher wanted the wedding set as soon as possible, suggesting several dates in February. This led to Mrs. Winslow demanding to know if Tamsyn was in the family way. That accusation caused a complete shutdown of the process, as Tamsyn departed immediately, shocked and insulted. *Is that what Thatcher told his mother? What did he mean for her to think of me?*

For his part, Angus, as he realized that the projected expenses were mounting with every meeting, begged Tamsyn to delay the event as long as possible. Thatcher's mother constantly sent servants to the MacKiernan home with demands cloaked as "suggestions," such as how many were to be seated for the wedding dinner, or what style of invitations would be fitting.

As weary as Tamsyn became of the whole topic, Angus was fit to be tied when the hard figures were presented to him. "I know the Winslows expect a certain elegance, Tamsyn," he had said on one particularly difficult day, "but is it necessary to import four dozen white roses just for the tables?"

"Papa, it doesn't matter to me. It's Mrs. Winslow—" she'd protested.

"Aye, she'll be the death of me!" He'd grumbled off into his office, slamming the door behind him.

If the demands and the preparations for the ceremony weren't enough, the MacKiernan house was besieged for the first time with invitations to parties and soirees, Tamsyn's engagement apparently transforming her into someone welcome at the best tables in town. Tamsyn accompanied Thatcher and stayed on his arm for the duration of most events, as he fretted if she was out of his sight. He was, for the most part, the doting fiancé, charming and proud, and she drank it in.

Mrs. Thatcher Winslow had a nice sound. A nice, secure sound. Maybe he would come to love her in the way she wished. Tamsyn daydreamed about her future life as she stood by his side at these gatherings, since he scarcely included her in his conversations with people he'd known all his life.

He often discussed people she didn't know and places she'd never been, without any explanation. His friends quickly adopted the same tactics, seeming relieved not to have to start at the beginning of every familiar story.

Tamsyn tried not to mind. Thatcher and his friends had traveled extensively and been educated at the best schools. She was impressed, but intimidated when they talked about walking along the Champs-Élysées or visiting Buckingham Palace. It was easier to nod and smile and remind herself of the advantages she'd enjoy once she was married. She could finally be free of her father's Scottish penny-pinching. Miss Pearl could make her more than one or two dresses a year, and she could preside over wonderful dinners, where she could at last impress Thatcher's friends with her own abilities. She'd read all the books at her own home, and she would read every book in the Winslow home, if necessary, to come to understand the things her future husband knew.

He would see that marrying her had been the right thing to do. And he'd love her with that romantic, all-encompassing devotion she'd dreamed of.

She also thought occasionally of Drake Ashton, especially at the soirees she and Thatcher attended, wondering if he might suddenly appear, to be her knight in shining armor. He never did. As the nights continued without his sudden appearance, she realized with a pang of guilt that his absence made her sad.

Did his nonattendance at other than a masked gathering, and his comments about being most comfortable on his ship at sea, mean he really was a full-time sailor? A pirate? *How romantic that would be.* Had he been involved in many battles, shooting cannons broadside and boarding Spanish galleons to rob them of their gold and treasure? In her mind's eye, she could see him, brilliant scarf wrapped around his head, gold earring in place, brandishing a long sword, hanging from the rigging as he delicately but thoroughly insulted his adversary before robbing him...The thought brought a slight smile tugging at the corner of her lips.

"What is it, my love?" Thatcher said one evening, breaking off his conversation, suddenly noticing her distracted face.

"It's nothing, Thatcher, nothing at all." She bit her lip guiltily, not wanting to confess her true thoughts.

"Ecstatic about our upcoming wedding, no doubt," Thatcher said broadly to his gathered cronies. "It will be a wonderful occasion. I understand my mother has invited the governor."

"She has?" Tamsyn asked with dismay.

He looked at her with disdain. "Of course, Tamsyn. Mother and Father know *everyone*." Thatcher examined his fingernails, as he did several times a day, to make sure they were clean. He'd once remarked that his mother had told him unsoiled fingernails were the hallmark of a true gentleman. "Besides, you don't have much family, so Mother didn't think you would object to her inviting enough people to fill the church."

"Of course not," she quickly assured him. There was no harm in agreeing. It was true she had few family and friends, Angus and his clerks, and some girl friends from her classes. The church might as well be full. She just wished the ceremony would be done so she could get on with her life. Perhaps then, she'd be rid of the nagging doubts about Thatcher and his love for her and could put her strong attraction to the miscreant Drake Ashton from her mind.

The other point of contention was Edwina's insistent invitation that Tamsyn join her during the day to practice needlework and music and do good works with the Women's Assistance League.

Tamsyn always refused. "I still need to help my father," she'd explained. "He depends on me to justify the household and business accounts."

Mrs. Winslow had appeared shocked. "But, my dear Tamsyn, surely he will have to find someone else to perform that task in future?"

Tamsyn had never really considered how her marriage would influence her father's business. She spent time in his office every day except Sunday, helping organize the business paperwork and correspondence, though Angus' clerks did most of the serious accounting. She'd taken over this task when her mother died, and Angus seemed to think she was at least as apt a worker as Ellen MacKiernan had been. As the wedding approached, he seemed to use her more and more, as if reluctant to let her go, and she noticed she saw the clerks less.

"I suppose he shall," was all she said.

"The league will be expecting to meet you soon." Edwina plucked a loose thread from Tamsyn's dress. "Thatcher's wife will have a place in Key West society, and you must learn to fill it. No one expects much of you, so you don't have to worry. Hopefully, you can have some finer dresses made?"

"Miss Pearl has some silks in mind..." Stymied,

Tamsyn wasn't sure how to reply. She wore her best day dresses whenever she visited Thatcher's mother, and she used her best manners. But no matter how she tried, it seemed Mrs. Winslow always found fault.

"Oh, no, my dear!" Mrs. Winslow chortled. "You must have your dresses made by that new French seamstress who's just come from Marseilles...what was her name? Madame Duprès. She will guarantee you are wearing the latest fashions."

"But—"

There was no sense arguing with the woman. Tamsyn was perfectly happy with Miss Pearl, who instinctively knew what style would best suit her. Tamsyn trusted her judgment, as Ellen had. But this new madame? Would she dictate Tamsyn wear whatever ridiculous styles were all the rage, whether she liked them or not? Was that something else which came with Tamsyn's new role as Mrs. Thatcher Winslow?

Tamsyn had envisioned moving into the social commitments of Thatcher's wife with anticipation, seeing herself being a lady of bounty at the holiday, providing meals to the poor, playing whist with the ladies at the club. But now that she had met some of these ladies and felt their unspoken disapproval, she was reluctant to associate with them, sure she'd be found lacking. They would not share her love of wild things, botanical and animal, and the independence which she'd cultivated under the benign neglect of her single parent would be a detriment, not an asset.

We cannot change our natures. We must be true to our own selves. Drake Ashton's words haunted her at night in the dark before she fell asleep.

She had believed she wanted to marry Thatcher more than anything, but sometimes she felt she was being changed into someone she didn't want to be. *No, not sometimes. Often.* The feeling frightened her. Tamsyn had always imagined that somehow she would remain the same once she'd married. She'd have the responsibilities of her own household, of course, but her essential self would remain. She had never imagined that being married meant giving up one's own pursuits in order to maintain the image of a certain social class, or not being allowed to choose one's own seamstress or dishes or clothing or wedding guests…

Papa had never told her so. But then he was the husband. Husbands apparently didn't have to sublimate themselves to meet their wives' expectations; it was the other way around. *Mamma, I need your wisdom,* she'd prayed. Though the thought of her mother usually gave her comfort, on this issue, now she felt a great emptiness as she waited for guidance.

Maybe it is a mistake. Before this planning and expense goes too far, I could still forfeit my agreement…

But Papa seemed to want this marriage for her so badly. She smiled as she brushed her hair before the window one night, watching the last of the rosy, scarlet bands of clouds fade away at sunset. As ridiculous as the Winslows' demands might be, Angus seemed to find a way to accommodate them. He must be worried about what might happen to her when he passed on. The thought had warmed her, as Angus MacKiernan often went out of his way to avoid showing he was a sentimental man.

But a conversation one evening sent shocks of

alarm through her.

Angus had been working at his books, breaking one pencil after another in frustration. Tamsyn had brought him tea, trying to repay his patience in accommodating Thatcher's mother. The intense expression on her father's face as he paged through his ledgers concerned her. But the answer to her softly spoken query was shocking.

"I'm about to lose everything, Tamsyn." Hard lines were drawn on his face, and his gaze was joyless.

How had she not seen this in the accounts?

Surely, he was exaggerating. Or perhaps overreacting to the Winslow bridal demands. "What do you mean, Papa?"

"All the sabotage, the sponge boats, the theft from our stocks on the pier, and now this wedding. I'm so far in debt, I-I don't know how we can survive." He put his head in his hands.

She embraced him, desperate to alleviate his distress.

"Papa, what shall we do?" All those accidents and incidents which troubled her father, she'd thought those had come to an end. But "lose everything"? Those were words she'd never expected to hear.

He patted her hand and stood up, moving to take her in his arms instead. "At least I won't have to worry about you, my pretty girl. You'll be well taken care of, as a Winslow bride." He sighed, his chin over her dark head. "And maybe after you've been married, the Winslows will consider making me a small loan. We'd be family then, of course."

A loan? From the Winslows? Is that what all this was about? She began to shiver as she thought about all the implications. Was her father pushing her into Thatcher's arms to save his home and his business?

Nonsense, you originally wanted to marry the man. You loved him.

That was so, but the consequences were starting to sink in.

We must be true to our own selves...

Ashton! How she suddenly craved his directness, his chivalry, an escape from the horrible burden which had been laid on her. Her father had provided for all of her eighteen years; she owed him everything, including her life and loyalty. She had to save him if she could. That meant settling into the wedding plans with Thatcher Winslow. Her own happiness was not capable of being reduced to a financial cost, so it didn't matter.

The realization was too much for her to handle. "I have to go, Papa." She slipped from his arms. She ran upstairs to her room and closed the door. A few minutes later, she heard her father's footsteps on the stairs; he knocked once, half-heartedly. When she didn't answer, he went away. She stayed hidden for the rest of the evening.

Chapter Eight

She had the dream again that night.

She waited just inside the gate, the footsteps that followed her echoing in her head. *I love you...* whispered on the wind.

She snapped awake, then found herself disappointed.

A hail of hard taps hit her window. At first, she thought a bird must have crashed into the glass. But it happened again. And again.

"You're going to break the window," she muttered. She scooped her way out from under her netting and carried her oil lamp through the darkness to pull back the curtain. Her face lit by candlelight, Norah Brennan leaned out slightly over her windowsill some twenty feet away. Tamsyn rubbed the sleep from her eyes and opened the sash. "Norah?"

The red-haired girl, eldest of seven Irish children, leaned out of her corresponding window, still dressed in a white cotton nightgown with lace around the neck. She dropped the rest of the pebbles on the ground. Her eyes sparkled, and her smile told Tamsyn that Norah was full of gossip.

"So, you're to be married. I've heard some of the excitement from the kitchen girl."

Tamsyn pulled a chair up to the window and curled up on it. "Yes," was all she said, hugging her knees to her chest. They'd sat up many, many nights over their adolescence, darkened rooms leading parents to believe they were asleep, when in fact they were talking about all the things young girls gossip about as they grow up, about men and life and being adult.

Who knew being adult would be so hard?

"Thatcher Winslow! Quite a catch, me mum says."

"Jealous, Norah?" Tamsyn said, wondering if she'd be envious if she knew what was really going on.

"You know I've only wanted one man, ever," Norah said sadly.

"Brian Hamilton," Tamsyn said with a sigh. "I'm sure he'll be back soon, Norah."

"I begged him not to go into the naval service, you know. He's been gone now for two years. How long can he make me wait?" Norah's voice broke.

Tamsyn shook her head with sympathy. They'd had this discussion often, but it seemed the longer Brian was gone, the less hope Norah had that he would return to her as he'd promised. Norah's parents had refused Brian's offer of marriage before he left, as Norah was only sixteen, and there was no guarantee he'd return for her. "Where is he now?"

"I haven't received a letter for several months," Norah said, "but the last time I heard he was posted to the USS *Maine*."

"I heard…" Snippets of a conversation from the Pickhams' ball came back to her with the mention of the *Maine*. "I heard that the *Maine* was to be returned to these waters, to be posted here to be ready if there is war in Cuba."

Norah smiled brilliantly. "D'you really think so? That would be grand."

Tamsyn listened to the buzz of crickets and chirping of the night birds as she pondered the burden of Norah's loneliness. Even of her own loneliness, before she'd dug herself into a hole.

"Tell me all about the wedding," Norah said. "I want to hear all the details."

Tamsyn closed her eyes and shook her head. It was the last thing she wanted to talk about. "Norah, I always thought a wedding would be wonderful, you know, two people in love, learning to understand each other and share each other's joy."

Norah nodded, encouraging her.

"I hate everything about preparing for this wedding."

"Hate? How could you? You're marrying one of the island's most eligible bachelors, girl. I was told the president of the United States is expected to attend." Her eyes glowed with excitement.

"The president?" Tamsyn shook her head in dismay. "I heard the governor. But with Edwina Winslow compiling the guest list, all the crowned heads of Europe might be there."

"You don't like her?"

"I don't think she likes *me*, actually." Tamsyn watched as the half-moon appeared behind the poinciana in the courtyard. "So to compensate, she is making this *her* wedding."

Norah nodded. She reached up, took her brush from her dressing table, and began brushing her hair. "What does Thatcher say?"

"He says since my mother has passed away, someone ought to help me with the planning of the event. His mother is being ever so kind by putting herself in that place."

But it certainly didn't feel kind, the way that Mrs. Winslow spoke to her, or how she took over the event instead of helping Tamsyn make her own plans, and certainly without Tamsyn requesting her assistance.

They'd had one unforgettable scene in the front parlor of the Winslow home, when Thatcher had come to collect Tamsyn at his mother's bidding. Edwina Winslow had asked Tamsyn to sit down on the Chippendale sofa, and ordered the servant to bring a tea tray. The room was hung with heavy dark-red curtains, and the floor was nearly covered with a huge Persian rug which must have cost a fortune, Tamsyn guessed. She tried to avoid stepping on it, afraid she'd leave a speck of dirt. The room would have been entirely at home in Philadelphia or London. No effort had been made to take advantage of the local conditions and colors. It overwhelmed her.

While they waited and Thatcher paced by the thick-curtained window, Mrs. Winslow passed a paper with a long list of names to Tamsyn.

"These are a few more people to whom I have sent invitations," she explained with an apologetic smile.

"Thirty-five," Tamsyn said, dazed. *What would her father say?*

"My dear, we have already invited a number of persons who will speak with the persons on this list—if we don't invite them all, there will be hurt feelings." The older woman leaned back into her chaise, waving a Chinese fan.

"I don't know any of them," Tamsyn said without thinking.

"Are you saying my mother can't invite her

acquaintances to the wedding?" Thatcher looked on from the doorway, cheeks taking on an agitated red tinge.

"Of course not, Thatcher," she said quickly, but her heart pounded as she contemplated telling Angus.

The tray arrived, and Mrs. Winslow dismissed the girl, insisting instead that Tamsyn pour.

"If you're going to have a suitable household, you must be able to serve correctly," Mrs. Winslow said in a sweet conversational tone.

Tamsyn began to protest that of course she knew how to pour tea, that she had not been brought up by heathens, but Thatcher stood by, waiting for her to make a good impression on his mother. She began to pour the tea, but resentment, anger, and anxiety overcame her, and her hand shook, splashing a few drops onto Mrs. Winslow's rose satin.

"Oh, my Lord." Mrs. Winslow shrieked. "Bridget! Quickly!" She leapt up from the couch and swept from the room, calling for her personal maid. Tamsyn looked at Thatcher, who just shook his head and turned back to the window. Later, on the way home, though, he had kissed and cuddled her, so he must not be really angry. It was just so difficult to face each new demand from her future mother-in-law. She tried to shield her father as best she could, not wanting to hear objection from his quarter as well. She had promised her mother to take care of him, and now she was causing him heartache. It was not what she'd set out to do.

Norah said, "How kind of her to assist you." Tamsyn supposed it could be perceived in that way, though she knew better. "Do you have much time to spend with Thatcher?"

Tamsyn shrugged. "Not as much as I'd like. There's so much for me to do, and Thatcher leaves all our wedding plans to his mother. No one asks him his opinion, and he doesn't care." She thought a minute. "I wish someone would ask me."

"Ask you what?"

"What I'd like for my wedding."

Norah leaned forward, the sparkle in her eyes standing out from the shadow. "What would you like?"

Tamsyn considered for only a moment. "A small chapel with a few close friends, you, the parents. There would be no performing or show, just my beloved and myself, expressing our lifelong devotion to each other in the presence of people we care about." She pictured the ceremony in her mind's eye, brief but packed with meaning, perhaps with words they'd chosen themselves to declare their true feelings. "I'd have a bouquet with frangipani and vine leaves dangling, and the minister would know these were two people who loved and respected each other more than any others he'd seen." As she closed her eyes to envision this, she saw herself in a long white dress, thick with lace, moving slowly up the aisle toward the groom, who waited for her there in the front of the church, tall and dark...with a start, she realized her groom in the vision was Drake Ashton!

She shivered, feeling disoriented, and looked back across at Norah, her heart pounding. *Ridiculous! Marrying a pirate?*

"Did you ask your father for help?" Norah said.

Tamsyn sighed. "He and I agree on this subject," she said. "The requirements for pomp and circumstance are those of the Winslows."

Norah whispered conspiratorially, "Maybe you

could elope."

"Elope?" It was a possibility she hadn't considered. "Where would we go?"

"Arrange passage on a boat to the mainland. Thatcher should be able to find a captain willing to take you. It would take at least a day, and by the time you returned, if you couldn't find someone to marry you to each other there, Mrs. Winslow would certainly expedite matters to protect the reputations of all concerned."

Only Norah could think of such a devious plot, Tamsyn acknowledged with a smile, remembering various pranks her Irish neighbor had played over the years. A girl's reputation was all she had, particularly when one was not as well-endowed financially as Mary Elizabeth Pickham. To have spent the night with a man to whom one was not married was tantamount to walking down Duval Street peddling one's favors. A girl would be thought of as a scarlet woman indeed, unless of course she married the man directly in a quiet ceremony. And if he wouldn't marry her, she would be free to make other plans. Wouldn't she?

"Well?" Norah prodded.

"Thatcher would never agree to sneak around," Tamsyn said, her hopes falling. "He expects the fanfare." Her voice was sad as she wondered if the chance to be in the spotlight was quite as important to Thatcher as she was.

"You do love him, though?"

"I thought I did. Does that matter?"

She'd dreamed, as most little girls do, of having someone like Thatcher in her future, a shining knight who was good and true, with enough wealth to make her feel like a princess. She never would have guessed that a simple desire for a prince could become such a trap, entangled in issues of money and power and control, changing who she was as a person. "I just never thought it would be so difficult."

Norah giggled. "Well, if you're expectin' me to feel sorry for you, you can just forget that right now. I hope my name is on the guest list. I'm not sure Mrs. Winslow would have invited me."

Tamsyn frowned, trying to remember. "I'm sure I suggested that you and your family be invited, but I've long ago lost count of the guests. I will ask Mrs. Winslow tomorrow and make sure if it is not there already, that it is added immediately."

"I would hardly want to miss the wedding of the century," Norah teased.

"Please stop," Tamsyn begged, embarrassed. "I can always tell you the truth, can't I?"

Norah became more serious. "Of course you can, Tam." She leaned over the sill, her elbows square against it. Tamsyn moved up, too, so her head was out the window. From this vantage point, the girls could see the occasional person passing on the sidewalk in front of their homes, discover who else was up late by whose lights were on, but most importantly, see each other's face clearly in the moonlight.

Tamsyn took a deep breath. "I wish it was over," she said simply.

"You'll be fine. All this trouble will be worthwhile in the end, you'll see," Norah said, her wide face lit by an angelic smile.

"Someone told me in order to be happy, I had to be true to myself. None of these preparations feels 'true' to me, but there's nothing I can do to change them."

"Who told you that?"

Tamsyn was reluctant to reveal the identity of the pirate. What would Norah think? "Someone I spoke with at the Pickhams' masquerade."

"But if you love Thatcher, whatever it takes to marry him must be done. Once the wedding is over, the two of you can begin your lives together. I'm sure the feelings you have for each other will bloom and grow then."

"I hope you're right," she said.

Norah bade her good night and blew out her candle, closing her window. Tamsyn, restless, didn't go right back to bed, but just stared at the moon, wondering if anyone she knew might be sitting on the deck of his ship, watching it, too.

****

Later that week, Tamsyn found a need to get away from the frenzy of the house and the latest demands of the Winslow family, so she rode out with Clara to the cove once again. She wore her beach clothes under her "town" skirt, which she quickly removed once at the shore.

There was a strong easterly breeze, and she braided her hair at once before its length became tangled in knots she wouldn't be able to comb out. The water was cool on her bare feet, and she walked in to her knees, relishing its feel. They had come out the back road, so there were no passersby to frown on her, as they had when she had walked in town, and no strident voices to disturb her contemplation of the horizon. The rush of the surf whooshed as it rolled onto the sand, and the rustle of the wind whispered through the dried grasses along the dunes. The sky was clear azure, dotted with pure white fluffy clouds. Gulls glided along the wind currents, calling to each other. She closed her eyes, breathing in the salt-scented air quietly, absorbing the power of nature.

She stood there for some time, just breathing in and out, trying to banish the wedding from her thoughts. Something splashed near her toes, and her eyes snapped open, seeing a tiny fish swimming away, the water rippling from its passage.

Tamsyn suddenly realized that what she had hoped to see—or who—was Drake Ashton.

The two of them had made an instant connection through the touch of their dripping hands, when she'd removed the poisoned spine from his finger. Though she had not seen him since the New Year's ball at the Pickham house weeks before, she missed the sense of companionship he engendered in her. She felt his presence here, and there was a tingle of anticipation that she might see him again.

Scanning the horizon quickly, she was disappointed not to see the sails of a large ship anywhere in sight. *Why should I expect him? He has his own life. And you are trapped in yours.* Just the same, his absence drenched her with the surprising sadness of a personal loss.

Tamsyn had been still long enough that the small shallow-water fishes now moved around her feet, nipping at them. She watched them dart through the rippling currents, leaving a wake of bubbles. She looked for other creatures, on her guard for a spiny urchin or the flat shadow of a stingray, which could lash up and stab the unwary beachgoer with its weaponed tail. Fifteen feet into the water, she noticed a huge shell and carefully made her way out to pick it up. It was a queen conch, native to the island, pink-and-pearl shell easily ten inches long. As she held it up, the water drained from inside, and the snail-like foot slowly lengthened, hanging down, searching for solid ground. Tamsyn held it up to eye level to examine the small antennae which the animal extended, eyestalks waving in the unaccustomed air.

Conchs were a prime seafood source for the Bahamians and, as a result, those people had been called "Conchs" by the European immigrants who arrived in Key West after them. Once the meat was removed and the shell dried thoroughly in the sun, they blew into the shell as if it were a trumpet, producing a hollow horn-like sound which could be heard up to half a mile away. If several of different sizes were played at the same time, they could produce slightly different tones which became a natural symphony. Her father had told her how the wreckers had often used conchs to announce a wreck offshore. Tamsyn remembered hearing them from time to time as she was growing up, a plaintive moan in the night, sometimes answered, sometimes not.

"What that?" Tamsyn heard Clara call hopefully behind her. As she turned and held up the animal in its multi-shaded shell, Clara let out a squeal of excitement. "A conch!" She splashed into the water to get a closer look at the prize. "That be a goodly size—Juba make fritters tonight!"

Tamsyn looked down at the creature, feeling guilty for not returning it to its environment. But the thought of Juba's fritters, full of small bits of onion and celery and chopped conch, and the spicy red sauce which complemented their crunchy, finger-licking taste, made up her mind. She handed the shell to Clara. "There's one for the bucket," she said.

As the girl sloshed back to the shore, Tamsyn looked around once again for some sign Ashton had been here, but saw none. Saddened by his failure to appear, she lost a little of her enthusiasm for the cove and followed Clara back. She replaced her dry skirt and slipped the wet one out from under once again, and told their driver, one of the new boys, to take them home.

Tamsyn watched the horizon longingly as they pulled away, hoping to see white sails full of the wind, but saw nothing. She caught Clara looking at her speculatively as they came to the main road back into town. "What?"

"Nothin', missy," Clara said, but she continued to sneak a sidelong glance at her mistress.

"I've just seen enough of the sea for one day!" Tamsyn snapped, irritated that Clara could read her frustration so easily.

"Hmmm," Clara said softly. "Seems to me like you ain't seen enough of somethin'."

Was it so obvious? Tamsyn shook her head, unable to contain a tiny smile. "I'll just have to keep looking, then, Clara."

Clara smiled wider. "Don't worry, he'll be back."

"I'm not worried." *I shouldn't be thinking of him anyway*, she berated herself. *I shouldn't remember his eyes or the relaxed way he smiles, or...* She shook her head.

They listened to the wheels rattle down the road for a few moments, then Clara said, "Mmm, mmm. But he a fine-lookin' man." Tamsyn looked at her with a frown, but the dark-skinned girl was staring off at the passing scene, seemingly disinterested in Tamsyn's reaction.

He certainly was. She conjured up a picture in her mind of Drake Ashton's dark, flashing eyes, and how it seemed he had purposely set himself in her path at the Pickham house. They'd enjoyed each other's company immensely, as he stepped in when Thatcher had abandoned her once again to the company of his cronies, leaving her feeling most vulnerable.

She was always in hopes she'd see him again. It was, after all, a small island; she was certain to encounter him on another occasion.

****

As suddenly as it had begun, Tamsyn's social whirl stopped. Kenton Winslow had business dealings in New York and took Thatcher with him, as he'd be gone for several weeks. Thatcher explained he'd be meeting presidents of companies and other important people, making the connections which would allow him to work into a vice presidency in his father's business.

"Once I obtain contracts on my own, I will earn my own profits," he confided to Tamsyn as they held hands in her home's sitting room the evening before he left. It was one of the few concessions that had gone in her favor; she had made him agree to court her in a more usual way, in her home, where her father was in earshot.

"How long will you be gone?"

Knowing she wouldn't have to attend parties where no one spoke to her was a relief. The life of the Winslows was much different than she had expected it to be, the glamour of fancy balls and dress affairs tarnished by her observation of the behavior of the participants. They were shallow, full of themselves and what Tamsyn found to be meaningless pursuits, especially the women. Most had never worked a day in their pampered lives. While Tamsyn had dreamed of the luxury of a life of leisure, she'd expected she could spend it in her garden and at the shore, not wasting it in endless hours trying to retain her youth or gossiping with other women.

Perhaps once she and Thatcher were married, she thought, she would begin a new trend. It would become fashionable to devote oneself to nature, instead of solely to oneself.

The thought encouraged her. Thatcher asked if he could walk in the courtyard with her, and she agreed, feeling he'd been on his best behavior. Insects filled the air with their night song, and thick green foliage overhung the path as they walked away from the house to the small alcove where they'd shared many passionate moments.

Thatcher abruptly took her into his arms, covering her face and neck with warm kisses, which she dutifully returned. His kisses moved down her neck into her décolletage, and she felt his lips on the top of her breasts. Her immediate reaction was to pull away from him.

"Thatcher!" she whispered sharply, reaching to grab his wrist.

"What is it, my love?" Thatcher acted as though she hadn't touched him, ignoring her anxious grip and moving his hands downward to cup and squeeze her breasts. He leaned closer to her, sliding one arm behind her to pull her close.

"Thatcher, please!" Tamsyn squirmed back a few inches, trying to escape his questing hands, but was stopped by the white wood of the arbor.

"We're engaged to be married, Tamsyn. We're promised to each other." His eyes seemed soft at first, but in the reflected moonlight, she could detect a hard note within. "Why shouldn't we taste these forbidden fruits? After we're married—"

"I-I don't think it's proper—you shouldn't take such indecent liberties." She pushed him away. *Isn't that what her mother had always said? A well-brought-up young woman saves herself for marriage?*

"Stop being such a little girl!" Thatcher's demeanor underwent one of its quick changes. He moved away from her, seeming to grow taller in his rage, and his blue eyes now blazed with anger. "I thought you were a woman. Why shouldn't I treat you like one?"

"Is this what you did to Mary Elizabeth Pickham? Is that why she wouldn't marry you?"

She couldn't believe the words had come out of her mouth. She'd been so curious as to what had happened between those two, but she'd never been brave enough to say anything. The silence that followed was deafening.

Then he lashed out. "You leave her name out of this. We're talking about you. In a few short weeks, these will be mine," he said darkly, grabbing her breasts until she gasped with pain. "I will taste them if I choose."

He leaned forward and kissed her breasts, his hands all over her. Tamsyn felt a tug, heard fabric tear, and realized he had ripped her dress. Her breasts spilled forth as Thatcher made animal-like noises, feeling and nuzzling them.

Tamsyn's fear overcame her shock, and she pushed him away, then slapped his face. "Get out!" She waited, frozen, wondering how she'd get past her father to her room to change her ruined dress.

He turned away, and she wondered if she was in further danger now that she was cornered. His breathing slowed to a more normal pace, over the course of several minutes, during which she wanted nothing more than to shove him farther from her. But she was apprehensive what he might do then.

At last Thatcher turned to her once again. He leaned forward to kiss her lips.

"I must go, my darling. Miss me while I am gone. I shall certainly miss you." He surveyed her condition and sighed. "I am sorry," he said. "I can't imagine what came over me. Why do you make me into a madman?"

He stared at her bared breasts for a minute with pleasure, then reached into his pocket for his wallet. Removing several bills, he set them down on the nearby wooden bench. "Have the seamstress make you a pretty, new dress. I want to see you wearing it, waiting for me at the dock when I return." He left the garden, whistling, a bounce in his step.

It was several moments before Tamsyn could move, terrified by what had just occurred. She understood that marriage involved giving oneself to one's husband, but Thatcher's words brought home the meaning of that ceremony: *In a few short weeks, these will be mine*, he had said.

The recognition of what he was really saying made

her even more uneasy, especially because she knew she should expect no help or sympathy from Angus. His intentions in this matter clearly revolved around his bank account. Tamsyn was suddenly very relieved that Thatcher was going away.

Clutching the torn remnants of her dress together, she slipped in through the kitchen, where only Clara was still working. Issuing a silent prayer that she'd get upstairs unnoticed, she quietly but quickly passed through the foyer and ran up the stairs to her room, where she closed the door and leaned against it, breathing hard. She waited with her eyes closed, trying to gain control of her racing heart.

When she finally opened her eyes, the first thing she saw was her reflection in the mirror across her room, revealing her best silk dress torn nearly to her waist.

Tamsyn took off her dress as quickly as she could and shoved it deep into her closet, never wanting to see it again. She slammed the door shut. *How could he*? He said he loved her. Shouldn't a man treat the woman he loved with gentle respect? Taking her light cotton robe from a hook on the back of the door, Tamsyn put it on quickly, jangled nerves beginning to twitch. Her feet led her back and forth across her room as her agitated mind searched search for reason.

At last, her mother's deeply instilled common sense took over, and she reopened the closet and removed the dress. She didn't have many silk dresses, and her mother's teachings wouldn't allow her to waste this one. She set it out on the back of her vanity chair for one of the girls to take to Miss Pearl. Perhaps she could sew it together and place a cunning ribbon so the repair wouldn't be seen.

Reluctant to speak with anyone, even Norah, she blew out her light almost immediately and wrapped herself in a cool cotton sheet on her bed. She remained in her room undisturbed the rest of the night, beginning to put together the beginnings of an escape plan.

Chapter Nine

Knowing he could remain close to Key West, where his heart was currently more engaged than was good for him, Drake was comfortable investigating the rumors of a viable shipwreck off the reefs of the Dry Tortugas. One never knew what might come to light in such a venture, and he hoped to fill his pockets. For many in Key West, wrecking had made them rich and powerful, like Captain John Huling Geiger, who had practically ruled the island with his treasure sales earlier in the century.

"Won't be able to dive these wrecks much longer, Captain," Samuel said as they came in sight of the lighthouse at Loggerhead Key. It was the newer of the two on the seven islands, standing one hundred and fifty feet tall and fitted with an alternating red and white light to emphasize the danger of sailing too near the coast. "New steamships have steel hulls that make it unlikely they'll wreck on the rocks."

"True enough." Drake stood at the tiller, lackadaisically steering toward the island cluster some seventy miles west of the city. They were far enough away not to encounter the reefs; he'd sailed the area often over the years and knew the shoreline well.

When he and his brother had just started sailing on their own, they'd often sailed from Islamorada south around the island chain to the east coast of Florida and back. Each had accidents on the rocks. Drake's had caused mostly cosmetic damage to his boats. Freddie, who tended to sail faster and more recklessly, actually scuttled several rowboats, trying to get in too close.

Even as teenagers, they had landed often on the islands at the farthest end of the Florida Keys and investigated the old fort, its hexagonal structure standing three stories tall. Once an active military facility, now it served only as a coal depot for US military ships. Legend said that Ponce de Leon named the place Tortugas because the place was home to hundreds of sea turtles, and "Dry" was added because the coral rock islands had only salt water. When Drake and Freddie had camped on the island, they'd watched ships coming east from Gulf Coast ports, and those coming west from the Caribbean or even farther up the American East Coast. Nearly any ship passing through the Florida Straits would sail within range of the deadly reefs. Some came much too close.

While Drake had come in search of an Irish ship that had gone down, a brand-new wreck had been sighted this second week of January. A Norwegian barque, the *Osmond*, bound east from Pensacola, and reportedly carrying a cargo of lumber, had been caught in high winds and dashed on the rocks, its "back broken," according to the survivors when they reached land. Lumber wasn't what Drake wanted, precisely. He searched for items that would turn a quick and hefty profit. But there was always the chance that personal items of the crew could be worth something above and beyond.

Or that they are as crafty as I, and carry something of a different nature underneath all those logs.

He called up to the barrelman in the crow's nest. "Any sight of naval ships?"

The man surveyed in 360 degrees, then replied, "Just one ship, anchored at the fort, Cap'n!"

"Hmm." Drake cocked a brow and turned to his first mate, and his second, a burly fellow whose belt strained to hold up his breeches, by the name of Roderick Chaney. "Not that the navy particularly cares about who's wrecking, as long as it's Americans."

Chaney frowned and scratched his pocked arms. "Everyone's a little nervous these days, with the Spanish doing God above knows what. Maybe we should investigate the interest of this ship before we drop anchor."

Drake considered the advice, then nodded. "All right, let's make a pass. If they're at Fort Jefferson, they're likely refueling with coal. That should be the extent of their interest in the area. We'll hold off on hauling the diving equipment on deck until we make sure we'll be safe."

"Aye, aye, Captain," Chaney said. He marched off to tell the crew.

Samuel had his eye on the birds circling around the old brick fort. "Hand me that spyglass, will you?"

Drake chuckled as he passed it. "Still fancy yourself another Audubon, my friend?"

"Bird-watching is a perfectly respectable hobby," Samuel replied with a bit of heat. "Fort's always good for seeing something new, not just pelicans and cormorants." He took a peek through the glass. "Brown noddies." He pointed at the birds as he spied them. "Roseate terns."

Drake shook his head and clapped his first mate on

the shoulder. Birds didn't matter to him, unless they were fat chickens on a spit. "Carry on, Mister Johnston."

He stepped aside, giving Samuel the wheel, and walked to the bow, watching for the navy ship. It came into view as the *Raven* rounded an island archipelago. The silver-white plates on the side of the ship shone bright in the morning sun. Though the ship had masts, it was clearly a steam-powered vessel, more than three hundred feet long, by Drake's estimate. An armored cruiser, this close to the mainland? It could only be—

Chaney came up behind him. "Damn me, but I never thought I'd see that one, not here."

"It's the USS *Maine*." Drake pondered a moment what it might mean to his quest that one of the American Navy's newest battleships was this close to Cuba, and came to the obvious conclusion. "They're right," he said, referring to the cigar-puffing aristocrats on the Pickhams' porch. "America is about to join the war."

He turned around and waved to one of the crew. "Hoist the Stars and Stripes, José!"

It's not always wise to announce we're American, but this is one time we can do it comfortably and go on about our business. Those sailors have a lot more on their minds than a passing galleon catching turtles for lunch.

"Chaney, keep the turtle nets out. And have the diving equipment brought on deck."

"Aye, aye, Captain."

Drake leaned over the railing and peered down into the clear water. Most places along the shore, one could see through to the bottom, even as deep as fifteen or twenty feet. Here, in the vicinity of the recent wreck of the *Osmond*, the sand was stirred up below, and the water darkened from its usual sparkling aquamarine. Closer to shore, the water shaded greener; farther out into the Gulf, a deeper blue.

As the heavy equipment and the manual air pumps in their bulky wooden cabinets were brought up, several of the crew studied the copper helmets and heavy canvas suits with trepidation. Long rubber hoses trailed along the deck behind the men carrying them, each some fifty feet long. Only a few of the crew enjoyed the deeper dives. Sinking into the water with only a thin tube to provide air from the surface, weighted with heavy lead bars, wearing a suit that weighed more than one hundred and ninety pounds...

Drake could see why they were reluctant. He didn't do the deep dives, himself. Some of the men excelled at it. The policy of the *Raven* had been agreed among the crew. The job was strictly voluntary, with those who performed the dive receiving an extra share of the proceeds of whatever they recovered.

He checked again, finding the *Maine* comfortably remaining in port. *Can't help but be a little paranoid after what happened to Freddie... Best to know where all the ships are, all the time.*

He gave the high sign to begin. The ship's five suits were shared among the volunteers. Each diver needed the help of several other sailors to wriggle into the bulky suits, which were worn over their clothes. The lower portion was a solid sheet of rubber sealed between layers of canvas. The arms of each suit ended in gloves, and the legs of the suits ended in thick "socks," made extra sturdy to protect against puncturing the suit on barnacles or the jagged edges of the wreck. They wore shoes with metal toes to protect their feet.

The thick rubber collar was then clamped to the corselet making the joint waterproof. The inner bib, made of the same material as the suit, was pulled up inside the corselet and around the diver's neck. There were some controls on the suit that the diver could manipulate, but their main communication method was by pre-arranged signals of tugs on the hose.

Drake studied the operation, double-checking each diver's suit before they were ready to go overboard. Feeling personally responsible for each of them, he helped secure the bolts that attached the helmets to the corselets, then affixed weights to the helmets.

The men could see out the left, front, and right via tiny glass plates, and Drake made sure he saw the sparkle in their eyes to indicate they were set. He tightened the safety lock at the rear of the helmet that kept it from rotating loose. They were ready.

The divers waddled to the edge of the deck, where a piece of the railing had been retracted. There, they lined up, each receiving a handful of large canvas bags, which were already secured to a line that would be monitored by a sailor on board. When they'd filled it to their satisfaction—and most importantly, Drake's— they would tug on the line, and the sailor would haul up their treasures.

He gave the order for the divers to enter the water, and then stepped to the air pumps to supervise the turning of the large wheels that operated the cranked machines. The double-action cylinders were driven by the flywheels, turned by the sailor aboard the *Raven*. From personal experience, he knew that the constant motion of an arm, turning the wheel just so to provide a smooth airflow, wearied the participant; the men would rotate in and out of the job until the dive was complete.

When he was satisfied the dive was solidly underway, he left Chaney in charge and retreated to his cabin to get his personal binoculars. When he opened the door, he surprised Mateo, who whirled where he stood at the table, with a guilty look on his face.

All the sketches Drake had scribbled of Tamsyn were gone from the floor, and everywhere else for that matter. He raised an eyebrow and studied Mateo in silence.

"I cleaned up the cabin, *capitán.* I hung up your clothing, and the...drawings?" He swallowed hard. "I put them in here." He indicated a carved wooden box on the small table behind him.

Drake recognized the box. He'd brought it from the house at Islamorada. His mother had kept family photos in it at one time. Six months on the ship, and this was the first use someone had found for it.

Probably better that the crew doesn't see my useless obsession, right? They'll be thinking the captain has lost his mind.

He nodded to Mateo and crossed to peek inside the box. So many drawings. All a reminder of something else beyond his grasp.

"Ella es muy hermosa." Mateo smiled.

Drake nodded. "She is very beautiful indeed. Last I heard, though, she's marrying a man on the island." He closed the box and shrugged. *"Así es la vida."*

Mateo shook his head. His hands tightened to fists, and his eyes blazed with determination. "Do not give up hope, *capitán.* There is no one as brave and as deserving as you. She just needs to see you in the right light. She could never refuse you!"

Drake shook his head. "We'll see about it, *chico,* we'll see."

Mateo finished straightening up and grinned. "Cook says we shall have turtle soup tonight!"

"I expect we will. Let me make sure he's got his supplies." Drake tousled the boy's hair and went back up the steps to the deck, then made his way by three different sets of narrow stairs, to the bowels of the ship, just inside the front hull.

The ship's galley was a small room, perhaps twelve feet long and eight feet across. Its wooden floors were scrubbed clean. Two iron stoves stood at the far end of the room, both heating huge pots of water. The aromatic steam rose and swirled around the ceiling. From the scent of garlic and onion, Drake surmised that turtle soup was indeed on the menu.

The cook, Alvaro Diaz, had been employed aboard the *Valdinez* when Drake first met him; he'd stolen him for the *Raven* soon after. His sailors ate well, when they had fresh stores. It made up, mostly, for the times at sea when they had little left.

"So, the rumors are true," he said.

"*Sí, capitán.*" Alvaro had his back to the captain, and he half turned to reveal his work. The upper and lower halves of the yard-long shell lay on the narrow wooden table before him, the head and feet of the turtle in a waste bowl along with the bones. He continued to cut the remaining meat into cubes, which his apprentice scurried to add to the pot. He gestured to the large storage box under the row of myriad latched cabinets. "Got another one in there, waiting for his turn."

"Smells delicious. That's enough?"

"It should be. I'll have Juan take the leavings up for bait."

Nothing to waste. I've got to love that. "Good work. The crew will be happy tonight." He took in one last sniff of that tempting aroma, then made his way back up the stairs. If someone caught a swordfish or other large fish with a turtle head, they'd eat well for a week or more. Especially after a trip to Key West with whatever treasure his divers recovered.

A trip to Key West...what other treasures might he find there? Perhaps a glimpse of his lady.

He dashed that thought from his mind. More important considerations lay in front of him. Legally, when a man chose to dive a wreck for salvage, he was to take the accounting to the district court, where he'd be registered as the wreck master. He'd then be expected to complete the salvage of that vessel and bring the proceeds in to either be returned to the owner, with proper recompense to the wreck master for its value, or auctioned off and the money split between the master and the court. Either procedure would tie him up for weeks. He didn't have that kind of time.

He'd have to make a trip to Blackie's shop to sell his find. He wouldn't make as much in trade, but he'd be in and out of the city in a day and back to his real work.

Maybe that does make me a pirate.

The thought made him chuckle as he came out on deck. Several large canvas bags awaited his inspection. The crane dipped down in the water again, hopefully for more booty, if not, for the lead weights that held the divers down. They had sufficient air in their suits to be buoyant at this point, so they'd easily swim to the surface.

He checked the horizon and saw the *Maine* remained in port at Fort Jefferson. Then he strode to the mainmast and dug into a small leather bag tied to it. The map with the coordinates of the second wreck curled into his hand. Walking over to share the view with Samuel, he pointed out the expected area.

"Once the divers come up, we move on to this site. Seems to be in deeper water, but rumor has it we could find gold."

Samuel's eyes lit up. "Would make the dive worthwhile, Captain, aye."

"As long as no one asks questions, we'll be fine." He glanced again at the port. "No more than an hour or two, understood?"

"Aye, aye, Captain."

"Then quick as we can to Key West to make our sale. The rebels await."

Chapter Ten

Tamsyn had brooded too long about Thatcher's ugly behavior. It was time to cleanse it from her system with a long walk. When Angus discovered he needed some writing supplies for his accounts, and both clerks were busy preparing documents for upcoming contracts, Tamsyn volunteered to go to the dry goods store to get them.

She took a wide-brimmed hat from the coat stand in the foyer and tied the scarf under her chin. Heaven forbid Mrs. Winslow or one of her companions would find her baring her face to the sun. What public hysterics that might cause!

The regular business section down by the docks was not as colorful as La Africana, but the hubbub of people going about their daily errands was always exciting. The tropical breeze blew in from the ocean, rippling Tamsyn's pale blue skirt as she walked. She noticed one of her father's ships at the pier, as well as a couple of strange ships she'd never seen before. There were sailors and matrons, merchants and thieves, people of all kinds in the marketplace. Many greeted Tamsyn as they passed, recognizing her from either her father's office or the social circle she'd met as Thatcher's fiancée. She felt inadequate to have conversation with those, since Thatcher monopolized most of the discussions when she was around. She mostly nodded and smiled, using her father's errand as an excuse to avoid extended discourse.

Tamsyn escaped several ladies of Edwina's circle in that manner, ducking into the necessary shops, and likewise, detached herself from a couple of young men who seemed determined to make her acquaintance. She recalled seeing them at the Pickhams' ball, hardly a hair out of place and fashionably dressed from head to toe.

Now that Thatcher's out of town, perhaps he has set them to watch me—to test me. Well, that effort will fail. Despicable that he'd go so far.

"Really, I must go." She backed away. "So sorry." She continued to walk away from them. As she turned to make sure they stopped following her, she ran into someone on the sidewalk.

"I beg your pardon," she cried, spinning around to discover Drake Ashton's laughing eyes looking down at her. He wore a deep-blue long coat and dark trousers, with a bright yellow scarf tucked in the top of his white shirt. With him were several sun-browned men in colorful shirts and worn, dark pants. "Miss MacKiernan, honestly, you always seem to be in flight." Drake raised an eyebrow.

"Mr. Ashton?" Stifling a wave of guilt and disloyalty to Thatcher Winslow, the burst of joy she felt taught her that she'd been longing to see Ashton since she'd returned to the cove and found it empty without him. This day, he looked every bit the daring sea captain, jaunty scarf just as she had imagined.

He smiled at her. "How kind of you to remember." Turning to his companions, Drake said, "*Compadres*, I believe you know what we need to replenish ship's stores. Please carry on while I spend some time with this young lady."

Tamsyn noted the round of elbows in the ribs and winks among them, but they ambled onward to comply with Ashton's suggestions. If one looked beyond the unshaven faces and longish hair, she saw, they really weren't as unkempt as they first appeared. All their metal buckles were carefully shined, and their dungarees were worn but clean.

"So, how progress the plans for the wedding?" Ashton asked as they moved down the street together.

"Please, let's not talk about it!" Tamsyn said with more force than she intended. Her stomach fluttered as it did every time she thought about the date and the time ticking down toward it. Everyone else seemed to be much more excited for that day than she.

"My dear Miss MacKiernan, at your request, I shall ask nothing of the sort." As they walked, he looked over at her from time to time, a deep wrinkle between his eyebrows.

The silence grew long but not uncomfortable. Tamsyn occupied herself by looking in shop windows—and observing Ashton when she thought he wasn't watching her. *How pleasant to be able to share someone's company without constantly feeling inadequate.* She quickly sublimated the thought. *You made the bargain. Now you have to live up to your word.*

Finally, she spoke. "Your ship is in port, taking on stores?" She turned to survey the harbor. "Which one is it?"

Drake pointed to a small galleon flying a blue flag with a black bird on the tallest mast. "That's her, the *Raven*." Men scurried around the deck like beetles, and others climbing the webbed rigging looked like insects, too.

"She's very nice," Tamsyn said. The ship looked every bit as big as any of the Winslows' ships. She wondered what the *Raven* carried in her spacious cargo holds. "You...trade?"

He smiled and winked at her. "You could say I trade."

"Mr. Ashton, I believe you're avoiding my question," she said, emboldened by his smile.

"Please call me Drake." He stopped in mid-step to take her hand and kiss it. He released it at once this time but kept his eyes on hers.

Drake...how that suited him. Tamsyn felt the warmth in his eyes like the sun's rays, and she abandoned herself to their kindness.

"My father is in trade, also. He made his first income as a salvage master. Fifteen years ago, a ship ran aground nearly once a week, blown from its course in the Gulf Stream." Having found a safe topic, she babbled on, grateful to have someone listen to her, for once.

"He had partners at first, but he said after he salvaged a few particularly valuable wrecks, he bought out his partners' interests. He still dabbles in wrecking, but his money went into the sponging business. Now he has a whole crew of Cuban and Greek men working for him.

"Everything was going well...until recently..." She trailed off, realizing this was another sad story.

As suddenly as he'd stopped walking, he started again, taking her elbow and pulling her into the street, where he hailed a passing open carriage for hire. When the driver stopped, Drake turned to Tamsyn, fire in his eyes. "Are you interested in an adventure, my lady? Forget all that brings you sorrow. Come for a ride with me. Let me show you the island like you've never seen it before. Do you dare?"

Tamsyn was intrigued. She knew she shouldn't do it. Her father would be expecting her. And she was, after all, engaged to another man. Drake knew all this, too. But he still asked her. She could see the open invitation in his eyes.

Then she heard Thatcher's angry voice in her head, saying, *"In a few short months, these will be mine…"*

If all she had left was a few short months, Tamsyn decided to throw discretion to the wind and keep some dignity and memories for herself. Thatcher certainly seemed willing to indulge his own wishes and desires; why couldn't she? Could her mother have scolded her for something she needed so dearly?

It's something I must do, Mamma. Something for myself.

"I'd be delighted," she said, and he handed her up into the carriage.

"Where to, sir?" the driver asked.

"Continue up Duval Street and turn off onto Fleming." As it was an open carriage, clearly nothing inappropriate could happen—well, except the ride itself—and Tamsyn enjoyed the feeling of traveling in style. After she'd recognized some disapproving faces in those they passed, she stopped looking at the people and listened to the birds, observing the flowers and trees instead.

Several blocks down Fleming Street, Drake bid the driver stop. "I believe I can provide the tour from here."

"Sir?" the bewildered man said.

"Step down, my good man, and I'll return the cab to you in an hour. Here." He handed the man several bills from a wallet Tamsyn could see was stuffed with money. "You could take some luncheon while you're waiting."

The man looked confused, but more respectful at the show of wealth. He climbed reluctantly out of the driver's seat, clutching the money, and handed the reins to Drake. "In an hour? You promise?"

"On my honor as a gentleman," Drake said, sitting up straight. As the driver looked like he was convinced, Drake climbed over into the driver's seat, helping Tamsyn to sit directly beside him. He clicked his tongue, and the horse started up immediately.

"A gentleman, is it?" She didn't look at him. A little smile twisted on her lips.

"My dear Tamsyn, I must maintain my image, for what it's worth. There's no need for him to know this is the ship's money. I just sold a hold full of salvage to add to my purchasing power."

She grinned at his honest revelation. "I see."

Drake turned to her, his fervor for his tale bringing bright spots to his cheeks. "Let me return to your tour. Listen closely, and I'll tell you the real history of this island which used to be known as *Cayo Hueso*, the Island of Bones."

She shivered at the gory moniker.

Drake chuckled. He must have felt her slight movement. "You didn't know that? It's the old Spanish name, given to this island in the 1500s. It is said that when the Spanish explorers first found this island, it was strewn with bleached bones."

"Whose were they?" Hard to imagine, traveling down one of the most prosperous streets in the city, in the largest city in the state of Florida, that the paved street was once simple ground with bones scattered across it.

"Historians believe they may have belonged to the Caloosa Indians, who were the earlier inhabitants. Have you ever been to the northern islands?"

Tamsyn shook her head. "I've never been away since we arrived when I was two years old."

"You must go!" Drake said, waxing enthusiastic. "There are so many species of wildlife, flowers, and plants. Just thirty miles north of here are whole herds of small deer as tall as your waist, and north of that, pineapple plantations, thick with spiky leaves."

"Sounds wonderful," Tamsyn said, jealous he'd seen these things. She suddenly wished she could travel, see what else was happening in the world, even return to New York to see where her parents had lived. Escape had rested heavy on her mind of late. She might have begun life as the child of a merchant, but nothing held her to that life forever. She could work in Miami, in Philadelphia, in New York, even in a factory.

I could be free.

"You must sail from the Keys often. Have you been to the mainland?"

Drake nodded, pointing out a huge air plant, a parasite, clinging to a Spanish lime tree. It was a particularly magnificent specimen, living without roots in the ground as it anchored itself to its host, then waited for sunlight and water to nourish it.

"My ship sails the East Coast as far north as Washington, DC, and Baltimore. We often carry rum and cigars north from the islands and then bring root crops and other supplies from the mainland to sell here and around the Caribbean."

That sounded like the route of a genuine businessman. *Have I been mistaken about him? I hardly know him at all, really. Certainly less than I'd known Thatcher—and look how wrong I was about him.* "So you're not—" Tamsyn blurted out. She stopped before she offended him. He spoke to her as if she were intelligent, and she wanted to do the same, but it was still difficult to ask him what she really wanted to know.

"Not what?" He seemed amused at her discomfiture.

"Not engaged in anything..." Words which would be inoffensive, in the event she was wrong about him, just didn't come to her.

"Illegal?" he asked, finally.

When she looked up at him under lowered lids to see if he were angry, he laughed.

"Tamsyn, the Florida Keys' history is rich with pirate legends." He expertly guided the horse around the corner onto Margaret Street. "Piracy is a matter of definition, of course. Early wreckers plundered the ships which wrecked on the reef, and got rich, taking advantage of the lack of lighthouses which now warn passing ships. Some even put out false lights to lure the ships onto the reef." He shrugged. "But those were 'legitimate' businessmen, of course, so that line of work was perfectly acceptable."

"If they tricked the captains into foundering on the rocks, that would be just as bad as piracy." For the first time, she wondered about the gold jewelry or ornate carved wooden furniture her father brought home. Many other houses she knew in the city where she'd grown up held various treasures which must have come from wrecks as well. Had Angus MacKiernan been involved in a venture so underhanded? It shouldn't surprise her, particularly with his current interest in money. If wealth was what he loved, he might ruthlessly sacrifice the human element in any transaction.

"So, if what you are asking me is if I conduct all my business aboveboard, Miss MacKiernan, I would have to ask for an explicit definition." He winked at her as he turned the carriage onto the cemetery grounds. Amid the brilliant purple bougainvillea stood whitewashed tombs and attractive statuary, both of which made an appealing Sunday walk for many Key West residents.

"I believe, sir, you have answered my question, by not answering it." *So, I was right all along.*

"You're a clever girl. Thatcher Winslow is a lucky man." He flipped the reins across the back of the horse with a snap, and the carriage began to move again, on past the cemetery to the eastern part of the island.

Tamsyn worked hard at suppressing the black cloud which had arisen to hang over her at Ashton's mention of Thatcher Winslow. Why had he done that? Just when she had nearly concealed the impending disaster from her mind. She and Drake could speak about so many other fascinating topics, in a lighthearted way, history and science and current interests. *Please, leave Thatcher out of it.*

As they continued, Drake shared his historical and botanical knowledge of the island with Tamsyn. They stopped at the turtle kraals and played with some baby sea turtles. Their last drive was by the beach where the two of them had met. Drake was an excellent host, flirting shamelessly and making her feel beautiful. A light breeze blew off the ocean. Tears stung her eyes. She couldn't tell exactly why, but something in her was about to break.

He checked his pocket watch. "Sadly, our hour is up. Now that I've taken all your time for myself, you've missed your lunch," Drake said with mock regret. "I feel honor bound to feed you at least."

He rounded the corner onto the main road and returned to the tavern at Fleming Street, where they dismounted and returned control of the carriage to the waiting driver, who was visibly relieved to see them.

The thought of spending another hour with him was tantalizing. Tamsyn was disappointed to refuse but knew she'd been gone as long as she dared. Angus would need his pens and paper before the afternoon progressed much further. "Thank you for asking, but I shall have to decline. My father is awaiting my return." She held up her paper-wrapped bundle, and he nodded.

"Are you sure you've found everything you came for?"

"More than I expected, indeed," she said with a smile. "Thank you so much for your wonderful tour." She hated to take her leave of Drake Ashton, knowing she could easily have spent the rest of the day with him. What was his ship's name? The *Raven*. Thinking of its master's dark visage, she thought the title would fit him as well.

"Well, then." He scuffed his foot on the ground, obviously wanting to talk further.

"Thanks again." She found it as hard as he, apparently, to walk away.

"Of course." Taking a deep breath, he bowed with a flourish, bending to place a kiss on her hand, and then turned and walked briskly off to find his companions. Heads turned as he passed, especially the young women. He smiled and bowed at them also, greeting all with equal cheer.

Tamsyn smiled as she started home with her father's purchases, having thoroughly enjoyed the morning. The encounter had nearly banished the shadow of the wedding from her mind, and she felt happier than she had for weeks.

Chapter Eleven

"How could you do this? I never thought I would see the day a daughter of mine could bring such shame upon us."

Tamsyn could not remember when she'd seen her father so angry. Angus cornered her in the sitting room, the evening of the next day. He paced between her and the doorway which would allow her flight, reddened face and quivering voice betraying his feelings.

Hands shaking, she clutched the linen pillowcase she'd been embroidering, and accidentally stabbed her finger with the needle. With a hissing intake of breath, Tamsyn looked down to see a drop of crimson blood accumulate on her fingertip, which she quickly wiped on her lace-edged handkerchief before it could stain the linen.

"Papa, I—"

"No fewer than five customers stopped here to inform me they'd seen you riding in a carriage with a man, laughing and throwing yourself at him."

"I did no such thing!" Tamsyn burst out, frustrated by her embarrassment that Angus MacKiernan would upbraid her because of loose rumors from his cronies. When his face flushed with anger that she had interrupted, Tamsyn's throat closed. She was incapable of speech. She swallowed tightly, awaiting his next outburst.

It didn't come. Angus just stared at her, his heightened pulse evident in a vein throbbing in his temple.

Finally, she went on, just to fill the awful silence. "Papa, there was nothing inappropriate about my time with Mr. Ashton. We took a ride around the island in an open carriage. Anyone could have seen us. He told me about the history of the island. That's all."

Angus continued to glare.

"I'm sure you spoke with Mr. Ashton yourself at the Pickhams' ball, Papa. He's a-a gentleman." Silently she crossed her fingers under her abandoned sewing, protecting herself from what might not be true. *But it's not a lie. He certainly has more the character of a gentleman than Thatcher Winslow, who's been raised that way all his life.*

Her father's coloring faded back to normal, though he still said nothing. His eyes were hard as he stared, but then softened without warning, filling with tears. He sank to his knees.

Tears! From Angus MacKiernan? What would happen next? Tamsyn was alarmed by her father's swift change in demeanor. "Papa?" She rose to her feet and crossed to his side. She placed a hand on his shoulder, bewildered at the sight before her.

"I dinna know what will become of me if ye can't marry Winslow." His words came out between great hiccups of air. "If the Winslows hear what I heard, I don't know what they'll say, Tamsyn. It may have been the most innocent ride in t' world, but if the man willna marry ye…"

"Papa." The brogue was thick; the man was on the edge. *And it's my fault.*

"Tamsyn, dear daughter, I'm only thinkin' of you. If I lose everything, ye'd have to hire yourself out as a servant to live." His tears were falling fast. "I couldna bear the shame of people knowing I couldn't feed and clothe you. What would your dear mother think of the both of us?"

"Oh, Papa!" She bent down beside him, taking his hands. *Mamma, I didn't mean to hurt him,* she thought in anguish. *He seems so concerned about me…*

…and I'm not so sure I wouldn't rather hire out as a servant than marry that man.

Her hour with Drake had reminded her she could be a whole person. "Don't worry, Papa, everything will be fine. Just fine."

The door to the drawing room had been left open, and Clara stuck her head in as she passed. The dark-skinned girl gawked at the sight of the master weeping.

"Clara, bring some brandy for my father," Tamsyn called.

The girl complied, bringing a glass with amber liquid from the golden tray on the sideboard. "Want I should I call Old James?" she whispered.

Tamsyn hesitated, unclear what to do under these unfamiliar conditions, but Angus forestalled the discussion.

"No, girl, I'm fine." He took a deep breath and a gulp of the brandy, then rose to his feet. "Go on now." He waved his hand in the direction of the door. Clara obediently scooted away.

After she was gone, he took another long sip of the brandy, watching Tamsyn intently. "I thank the Lord your mother passed before she saw everything come to this."

Tamsyn had no reply. She returned to her seat, completely disoriented. Her father seemed to be twisting the focus of her pain to serve his own purposes. Even though he'd earlier broached the subject of his pending economic disaster, she still couldn't believe the business could be in such desperate straits. Surely the damage to the sponging boats wasn't enough to ruin her father's fortune. She hadn't felt strong enough to inquire further the last time. But her father seemed weaker, more vulnerable now. This was the time to ask for more details.

"Papa, how can this be true? Surely the sabotage of a few sponge boats can't be enough to bring your shipping business to a halt."

He shook his head. "There is much more than that, Tamsyn. The sponge boats have been scuttled on no fewer than six occasions this past season. With repairs, this means we lost five weeks of sponging. My other ships have been stopped by pirates and ruffians, and several cargoes lost. The Greeks who were the backbone of my business have moved on to begin their own operation in Tampa. And now it seems war in Cuba will erupt any day, and Lord knows what that will do to our ability to trade."

Pirates? She remembered the discussion she'd had with Drake about the definition of a pirate. It piqued her curiosity to hear her father use the term. Of course he wasn't referring to Drake. He wouldn't be doing this. "But these people who have injured you will be found and brought to justice, Papa. Surely you won't have to depend entirely on the Winslows for assistance."

Her mind sorted quickly through the possibilities. *Who would gain from destroying her father's business?*

Other local businessmen? Was her father still engaging in illegal activities and crossing people he should not cross? She was also wise enough to know that the Winslows would hardly choose to enter into an alliance with a family which found itself on the verge of financial ruin. *Were they aware of Angus MacKiernan's true situation? Wouldn't that be as large a detriment to any potential union between herself and Thatcher as an innocent jaunt about Key West with Drake Ashton?*

Confused, she wondered whether her father had already discussed loans or money with the Winslows, since he seemed sure the wedding was necessary to stabilize his personal empire. The belief she was being traded like a cargo of sponges again assailed her, and she felt sick to be reduced to a commodity.

But no matter what other considerations existed here, Angus was her father, and she owed him a duty of love and support as his only child. He had promised her mother he would look out for Tamsyn. The memory surfaced of her mother on her deathbed, wasted and pale, grabbing their hands with remarkable strength. "Promise me, Tamsyn, that you will love and care for your father. You must obey him as a good daughter should."

"Of course, Mother." Her tears fell as she realized her mother was failing.

"Swear it on my life." Ellen looked from one to the other of them. Her skin had blanched to nearly the same white as her cap and her nightgown, and the fever burned so fiercely she could hardly bear to keep a cover on. "You both must keep each other in the highest regard."

They had both agreed, a single look between them

sealing the bargain. They'd kept their promises...until now.

Angus straightened his shoulders. Strength seemed to return to him quickly. His shifting emotions seemed almost too mutable to be natural as a spark of stern determination grew in his eye. "It will stop, by God, at whatever cost. I haven't toiled these fifteen years to see everything I've worked for taken from me!"

He turned and threw his glass into the fireplace, an uncharacteristic action which shocked Tamsyn and sent shards of glass flying everywhere. Their eyes met, and her surprise must have been apparent.

"I have let this upset you, Tamsyn, and that was never my intention. I'd hoped to protect you from the whole bloody mess. My apologies." He abruptly left the room. His footsteps diminished up the polished wooden stairs. His door closed with a definitive slam as Old James entered the room.

The elderly man looked around the room, apparently seeking the evidence of broken glass. Tamsyn pointed at the fireplace, unable yet to move.

"Are you all right, Missy Tamsyn?" He came closer, his rheumy eyes examining her face. "Marse Angus, he be in quite a state!"

Tamsyn nodded. "I think I'll walk in the garden, thank you." She slipped through the French doors off the sitting room. A comfortable, perfumed breeze entered as she escaped to the fresh air. She walked down along the paths, moonlight showing her the way, revealing the familiar flora she loved.

What was her world coming to? A few short months before, she'd dreamed of marriage as the key to a romantic future. Thatcher was her prince, come to rescue the lonely daughter of a cold and dispassionate king and carry her away to a life of luxury. He wrote her poetry, he was physically affectionate—everything her father was not, all she'd lacked for so many years since her mother had died.

But something had changed. Thatcher had, at heart, never grown up. The same easily hurt child remained. Instead of being rescued by his mother on a regular basis, he'd developed a harder shell outside to protect himself, and just hidden that fragile adolescent inside.

The enormity of this revelation shook Tamsyn, and she knew immediately it was true. The difference was, of course, that a ten-year-old boy who was hurt could only sulk until he could play with his companions again. Now that Thatcher had grown up, he had the power of his parents' wealth at his disposal. He'd become much more dangerous to those who didn't play his games as he wanted them to.

And Angus? Her father had always been a rock, the most stable part of her life. Even when he hadn't provided her with all the affection she might have wished, she had always been able to count on his firm presence. Now, after the emotional display she'd just witnessed, her faith in his strength was shaken as well. If what he said was true, his business was failing because of malicious sabotage. If matters did not improve, they would both be much reduced in circumstances.

And what of Drake Ashton? The only warm, bright spot in her life intruded himself into her thoughts as well. There was a strong attraction between them she couldn't deny. Drake Ashton made her feel smart and appreciated for herself, not as others expected her to be.

He was gallant and caring and seemed to have all those fond characteristics she wanted in a companion. No one made her feel more capable and secure in his presence than Drake did. When he talked about the places he'd been or strange things he'd seen, it wasn't to make her feel inadequate, as Thatcher seemed to do. Drake told her things to share with her, to encourage her to do the same...

If only we'd met at a different time. Before Thatcher had turned his attention to me.

She had to shut her mind to her budding awareness that her feelings for Ashton were those of love. Her priority was her promise to her mother, her duty to her father.

Of course, as soon as she resolved not to consider that dark, handsome visage, his eyes, so full of life, his self-assuredness, he was all she could think about. He'd shared with her a beautiful part of the island's history, as one friend to another, excited to disclose his own passion.

Standing still in the garden, Tamsyn listened to the sounds from the homes of her neighbors that filled the cool night air. Norah Brennan's younger siblings were squabbling upstairs. The house behind her was dimly lit, and emanated sweet tones of harp strings being plucked. Birds twittered and insects sang from their safe places curled in the leaves of trees. From her vantage point in the garden, life seemed perfectly normal.

She headed for her usual seat in the alcove, a favorite refuge of hers since she was a child. But as she entered it, the memory of her last encounter with Thatcher filled the space, and she withdrew hastily.

He's even poisoned this place!

Choosing instead to walk along the perimeter of the garden, she reached for a peach-colored hibiscus flower and bumped her finger on the branch. Pain assailed her, as she hit the same point she'd just stuck with a needle. She gasped and held it up to the dim light from the open French door to see if it was still bleeding. It was too dark to tell, so she moved closer to the street where the light was stronger. *No, it had stopped.* She hadn't thought it would hurt so much.

She closed her eyes and leaned back against a palm tree trunk, wishing she could be at the shore, listening to the night sounds and the soft rush of the waves.

When she'd nearly calmed herself and was ready to return to the house, she started for the French doors but stopped as a carriage pulled up sharply out front. Thatcher's raised voice demanded her father's presence—again. What was his fascination with commanding Angus MacKiernan? And why—

Well, she didn't really wonder why he was here. Her father's prediction had come true. Thatcher had heard the same rumors as had her father, and he'd come to wreak vengeance.

Was it possible he'd call off the engagement?

Perhaps I have never prayed to my mother's God before, but I humbly beseech His help now. I don't care if I spend the rest of my life scrubbing floors. If Thatcher releases me from this dreaded obligation, I'll do what it takes to prove my gratitude...

She inched as close to the open doors as she dared, and settled in to listen.

****

Moonlight fell on the woman's face, creating

shadow which only accentuated her wide eyes, there as she leaned against the tree. Drake was not the type to stalk women like a Spanish ship seeking vengeance, but he found himself spying on Tamsyn through the hedge which surrounded her courtyard.

His ship remained docked at Mallory Square. While others of his crew frequented drinking establishments in town, he had opted for a stroll through the residential section where he'd discovered, through discreet inquiry, that she lived. He should have been planning his upcoming voyage north to purchase another round of supplies for his compatriots. But every time he tried to concentrate, he was haunted by the sound of Tamsyn's laughter and her voice. Finally, he'd made his inquiries, hoping he could exorcise himself of her if she was perfectly happy, planning her impending nuptials, the ubiquitous Thatcher close by her side. He'd seen little enough of that when they'd ridden together. If she truly loathed the idea of the marriage, did that mean she would consider him as a suitor?

And why do I keep returning to that impossible idea?

Drake had seen her draw back after touching the hibiscus. *No thorns on a hibiscus,* he thought, wondering what had occasioned her injury. He'd been tempted to speak then, to announce his presence, but held back. She was almost close enough to reach out and touch her, and he wanted nothing more than to be with her. But she looked troubled and distracted, and the French doors to the house remained open. It was more prudent to watch.

Particularly when the hubbub began in front of the house and Winslow's unmistakable injured bellow rang out.

Drake's head swung around in time to observe Tamsyn had heard them as well. She took a step forward, then hesitated, alarm crossing her face. She hid behind a tree to listen.

After several minutes, Winslow appeared in the room with the open doors. Angus MacKiernan entered a few moments later.

"Have you heard—?" Winslow burst out.

"I'm well aware of the situation," Angus said. "I've spoken to my daughter, and I'm satisfied she did nothing to compromise her integrity. She assures me it willna happen again."

"Why did you allow her to do it in the first place?" Winslow demanded. "Riding around town, bold as brass, under the midday sun with that-that—mercenary?"

Drake knew they meant him and the time he'd spent with Tamsyn the day before. *Mercenary? All too close to the truth.* He noticed Tamsyn had frozen in her forward motion. She focused very intently on the two men inside, her palms pressed together as if in prayer.

"She's a young girl, with her own mind," Angus said. Drake thought his voice was tight, almost frightened. Remembering Tamsyn's eyes at the Pickham ball after Winslow's outburst on the veranda, he realized she was frightened of the man as well.

What kind of man was this? How have I never noticed anything in his countenance which would strike fear into someone?

Ashton maneuvered slightly forward so he could see in the door. The tableau was almost theatrical. Young, strong Thatcher, dressed immaculately in an obviously brand-new suit, towered over Tamsyn's father by some six inches. The old man almost cowered, backed up against the sofa, appearing pathetic in his worn shirt and pants and his stocking feet. Winslow's hands opened and closed into fists, agitation obvious.

"If she's going to be my bride," Winslow said, his bluntness chilling, "I require she behave with a certain propriety."

MacKiernan shifted uncomfortably. "If you're suggesting I don't maintain the same standards, then you know nothing about me."

"I don't need to know anything about you. Tamsyn is my only interest. I told the community I would marry her, and I shall. Nothing you say will keep her from me."

"But I am doing nothing to—"

"I know more about you than you think." Winslow's eyes blazed, and he took a step closer to MacKiernan, who tripped and fell back onto the sofa. *Dead end.*

Winslow pressed his advantage. "D'you think I don't hear the stories along the dock, how you've lost money gambling on ventures that don't pay off? Shipping treasures off the reef to the Caribbean, trying to make the Spanish pay to regain their own possessions? And the mockery of the sponging operation! How many weeks were you unable to harvest because your boats were not fit for duty? You can't even provide for your own daughter." He strutted back to lean against the fireplace, a foppish pose which looked practiced to Drake's eye, quite the "lord of the manor." "You'd better tell her—"

151

"You'd better tell her yourself." The old man spoke wearily, the lines in his face conceding defeat. "She doesn't always choose to listen to me."

Winslow laughed coldly and turned away. "Very well, MacKiernan. I'll take that as your permission to do what's necessary to keep her in line."

Drake saw Angus reach out as if to stop the man, then draw his hand back, with a defeated, horrified look.

"She will appear on Friday night at my home for our engagement party," Winslow said. "Tell her to dress appropriately. If she doesn't have something good enough to wear, have her ask my mother. We'll add the bill to the cost of the wedding."

Angus sputtered but didn't protest.

"I want no more of these incidents to dampen the plans for our party. Until then, I suggest you keep her inside this house, since she's not to be trusted in public."

Footsteps stalked away, and the front door closed with a bang. A few moments later, the carriage out front drove away with the snap of a whip and a loud whinny.

Almost without volition, Drake stepped, outraged, toward the hedge, ready to take action to defend this woman against something that was likely his fault. Sure, his impulsive offer to take her for a ride on the streets when Winslow's people were such snobbish and cruel hypocrites was probably ill-advised. He just couldn't help himself when he saw her. Something drew him to her, stronger than any magnet, overrunning his common sense.

He glanced over to discover Tamsyn's reaction, only to find his sudden movement had attracted her attention. She stared at him as if he were a ghost or spirit that had inexplicably materialized out of thin air.

She didn't move toward him or toward the house. She froze, there in the shadows.

Drake's heart ached for her. *Who did Thatcher Winslow think he was? Dictating orders to Angus MacKiernan about his daughter? And what did he mean by "permission to do what's necessary to keep her in line"? If he touched one hair on that girl's head...*

There was nothing he could do, but so many things that he wanted to. He couldn't remain here and take no action, however. His long legs moved him forward, away from the house, briskly, anger fueling his motion. He'd believed when he came ashore earlier in the day that she was engaged and busy, happily diverted by an association with the spoiled son of the Winslow shipping empire.

He'd wanted to reassure himself she was not a woman who should occupy his thoughts hour upon hour, diverting him from his chosen course and devotion to his vow of revenge. He'd even made the excuse that Winslow would be better situated financially and able to provide her with so much more than he. As long as she'd been happy, he couldn't interfere.

But to the best of his knowledge, she wasn't happy. She didn't even want to discuss the upcoming wedding. Her face had shown distress, but she had maintained her dignity.

Not like her retreat to the shadows under the palm tree he had just witnessed a short time ago.

Drake thought back to her look of shock at the

Pickhams' home when the engagement had been announced. He should have realized there was something seriously wrong even then. Now what to do?

He was a man of action, so he felt he should do something. *But what?* He didn't know the history between them. Obviously there had once been an attraction. But it was clear that at least for Tamsyn, the fascination was gone, and her father would be of no help in the event she wished to change her mind and break the engagement.

And what was that Winslow had said about an engagement party? Friday night, at the Winslow home, no doubt. Drake smiled speculatively. Now, there was the possibility of skirmish, just waiting to be taken. If he was to be accused of being a mercenary and a pirate, perhaps he should behave like it. He should set his sights on the most valuable prize of all.

A plan forming in his mind, his steps slowed to a saunter, and he whistled his way onto the dock. The moon shone full upon the waters as he approached the *Raven.* Its light illuminated the crew at work on board.

Aye, there was action to be had, and he knew the members of his crew would enthusiastically respond to his suggestion. Friday night, they'd lay out a surprise to leave the townspeople speechless. *Then what would Winslow do?*

Chapter Twelve

Tamsyn woke early from a dreamless sleep, the thought of the shadowy Drake Ashton the one bright spot in her worldview. *Had he been real, standing there outside her house?* Distracted by her lack of control and revulsion toward Thatcher, hating the argument she'd overheard and its implications, she could hardly trust the evidence of her own eyes.

But she had a way to discover whether he was still in Key West.

She quickly dressed in a simple, dark cotton blouse and skirt and slipped from her room without stockings or shoes. Noises rose from the kitchen downstairs, pots clanking and the laughter of women, but she stayed along the upstairs hall, the polished wood slick under her bare feet. At the end stood a large door. She tried to open it, but the wood had expanded in the humidity to fit the frame rather tightly. Her shoulder up against the door, she shoved, and it screeched ajar. The door reverberated, and she froze, clutching the handle for support, afraid she'd be discovered. When no one came to investigate, she pushed it open all the way.

Inside, a narrow set of stairs led upward. A trapdoor was latched in place at the top of the stairs, but beyond that was the roof where she'd find the widow's walk. She fumbled with the latch in the shadows at the top of the steps. The hinged door swung upward and over. A burst of bright sunlight nearly blinded her after the darkness inside, but she shut her eyes and then opened them slowly under the shade of one hand to readjust.

Many houses in Key West had the small fenced space on the very top, a place where those left behind when the master of the house went out with his sailing ship could watch for his return. It was a small area, some five-foot square, but it commanded a view of the port and dock area, so the watcher could see incoming vessels and recognize, by a brightly colored flag or distinctive sail, that loved ones had come home.

Coming out onto the walk, she found it was another beautiful day in Key West. The breeze was stronger here than on the ground, and the smells and sounds of the neighborhood passed around her with a wispy touch. She paused and looked to the west first, wishing she could see her precious cove, but too many trees blocked the view. Afraid he was gone, she delayed looking to the harbor until the last, scanning the tops of the dozens of masts for the bright blue flag which belonged to the *Raven*. She spied it at once and was filled with relief.

He was here.

Her pulse rushed, and her knees went weak. Perhaps it had really been him last night, outside her hedge. But why would he have been there? *Unless to see me.* And why wouldn't he have announced himself? *The answer was obvious: Why would anyone have spoken in the wake of the horrible confrontation between Thatcher and my father?*

Her face blushed red with shame, recalling the demeaning tone Thatcher had taken to her father, and the way he had spoken of her. If Drake maintained any illusions about the state of the wedding and the relationship she had with Thatcher, this would have dispelled them. It was clear from Thatcher's tone that he thought of her as his property, his straying pet, and he intended to treat her accordingly.

Tamsyn looked out, the tiny blue flag catching her eye once again as it rippled in the sea wind. What was he doing, there on his ship? As captain, did he have his own cabin, or did he share in one big room with his sailors, rollicking through port after port of the Caribbean and the East Coast?

His easy laugh echoed in her mind. He'd traveled widely, according to his stories, seen pineapple plantations, walked on countless beaches, met probably hundreds of women. Perhaps he was one of those sailors who lived to travel from one tropical city to another, a lonely woman in each waiting impatiently for him to return...

But Tamsyn didn't think so.

He seemed too intense in his attention to her. Even the story of his discussion over a smoky fire with an old Cuban obeah woman, listening for clues to his future, sounded more sensitive and imaginative than the life of a hard-boiled seafarer. The exchange between the two men last night had been painful to her and must have been offensive to Drake's ears as well. His swift disappearance afterward must mean he believed himself well quit of her, and left her to deal with the results of her own bad choices.

Knowing she shouldn't remain too long, not wanting to attract attention, she stole a last glimpse of the *Raven* and noticed for the first time the excitement which seemed to possess the harbor area. Men ran and shouted, accosted each other waving large papers. She couldn't hear their words. *What could have happened?*

She returned down the steps. Her sun-filled eyes went completely dark once she put the door in place, so she felt her way down the stairs by a hand firmly anchored on the wall on each side until the light from the bottom of the stairs showed her the faint way. She then returned to her room, satisfied no one had noticed her, and finished getting herself dressed. She was determined not to let her father know she'd heard a word of his degradation, and pinned her hair up severely so he'd have no reason to feel she was acting irresponsibly in any way.

When she appeared downstairs, she found the household caught up in the same excitement she'd seen at the waterfront. "They've sunk the *Maine*!" Timothy eagerly cried when she looked into her father's office.

"Who has?"

"The Spanish, of course, as it was anchored in Havana harbor." Timothy's eyes positively glowed with excitement. "Now we'll have to go to war."

Tamsyn tried to remember the vague bits of conversation she'd heard about the Spanish and Cuba and the war. The *Maine*? Wasn't that the ship Norah's beau was on? Though she'd heard forerunners of war, Tamsyn hadn't paid much attention to those rumormongers who whipped up sentiment, nor to the newspapers bent on raising bloodthirsty excitement to a peak. So far, she'd been sufficiently occupied with her own drama to avoid contemplation of the subject at all.

"How awful!" she said. "Poor Norah."

"I think I'll volunteer." The passion in the skinny

clerk's eyes brought a warm smile to her lips. She'd never thought dour Timothy capable of such emotion about anything except his balance sheet.

"Please, think about it awhile first." *What does my father believe?* Probably didn't worry about the loss of life, as long as his business didn't lose a dollar. *He wouldn't be happy to lose his clerks to war fever, either.* She continued on to get her usual tea and toast from Juba in the kitchen, determined to ignore the war until it landed in her lap.

****

Friday evening came at last, and Tamsyn was thrilled to be allowed to leave the house, even if it was only to the Winslows' for the engagement party. Thatcher's mother had insisted Tamsyn arrive several hours early to dress under her guiding hand, to make sure she was "presentable." She had dispatched Thatcher to fetch his fiancée, and they'd made the fifteen-minute ride back to the Winslows' without exchanging a word.

Now, as guests arrived downstairs, Edwina Winslow stood behind Tamsyn, a critical eye scrutinizing the new, emerald silk dress as Tamsyn posed in front of the mirror. It was the most beautiful dress she'd ever worn, fabric shot through with small gold threads that shimmered when she moved. The neckline was cut low, a gentle slope from her outer shoulder. The bodice curved softly at her waist, then flared in draped folds to the floor. Reluctantly, Tamsyn admitted that the madame had made a wonderful creation with the money Thatcher had so callously thrown at her.

She tried her best to hold still while Mrs. Winslow

spit orders to her thin and angular French maid. It was hard to allow the fussing to continue. Two hours of pinning and sewing and curling was just about more than Tamsyn could stand. The girl obliged her mistress by making minute adjustments to the dress or to Tamsyn's carefully coifed hair, which was a shower of ringlets leading down from a knot at the top of her head. Tamsyn sighed at last, and the elder woman looked away in frustration.

"Tamsyn, I am only trying to help you make a good impression. This is *your* party. Will you stop fidgeting?"

Tamsyn looked up apologetically, finding the older woman's eyes on her in the mirror. "I'm sorry, Mrs. Winslow. I am afraid I'm nervous."

Her future mother-in-law stepped up close behind her and put a hand on her bare arm. "My dear, we've talked about this gathering for weeks. I have corrected your table manners, shown you how to stand properly, and hopefully discussed topics with you which should provide you with adequate conversation." She shook her head and took a moment to straighten her own silver gown as she caught sight of herself in the mirror. "Thatcher says when you are in a group, you're positively tongue-tied."

Tamsyn's eyes burned, as she was stung by the words. *Tongue-tied? He hardly lets me get a word in!* But there was no sense arguing with the Winslow chatelaine. The woman would always believe her son could do no wrong. "I'll try, ma'am."

"Do better than that." The music was already playing below. With the point of a bejeweled finger, Mrs. Winslow directed the maid to adjust some strands of gently graying hair that had come loose. The girl quickly responded without a word, apparently able to read her mistress' mind after their long association.

The thought of Drake tightened Tamsyn's throat. She would much prefer spending this time with him, laughing together, sharing some adventurous experience. Would he be a true companion if they spent time together? A day? A week? A month? A lifetime?

Realistically, he had nothing to offer her, no security, no future. But she had the opportunity to have all that with Thatcher, and she considered walking away. Was she ready for an adventure instead?

"I'll be along in just a moment," Tamsyn said timidly.

The older woman sighed and capitulated, moving toward the door. "A moment only," she warned. "Thatcher will be anxious to introduce you to our guests from out of town."

Tamsyn nodded. She waited while Mrs. Winslow and the girl left, then she turned back to the mirror, looking deep into her own green eyes, searching them for some assurance this was really happening. She would be married to Thatcher sometime within the next several months. Three different dates had been set and later changed, as Mrs. Winslow tried to accommodate the schedule of one important guest after another.

But as she stood very still and closed her eyes, she could imagine the sea breeze at her cove, and the touch of Ashton's hand in hers…

Enough!

She shook off her longings. She had to deal with the trial at hand. Thatcher was waiting. *Mamma, give me strength.* She took a deep breath and walked slowly out the door.

Mrs. Winslow had insisted on the best of everything for this party. Fifty people had been invited, most of them friends of the Winslows. The thought was intimidating to Tamsyn. She would be on parade the entire evening.

She paused at the top of the back stairs, sorely tempted to sneak down and escape out the kitchen door. As her circumstances stood at the moment, however, that would likely cause heartache rather than solve anything. Instead she squared her shoulders, taking confidence in knowing she was pretty in her new dress, and moved down the hall to the front stairs, taking them slowly, hand on the banister, pausing just a beat after each step.

All eyes turned to see her.

Even Thatcher looked genuinely pleased. He crossed the room to the bottom stair, where he took her hand and kissed it delicately. She could almost believe he was the gentleman she'd thought he was. But in the burning glance they exchanged, she realized they both knew better.

The next hour passed in a blur of faces as she was introduced to one couple after another, old, young, some with thick English accents, others with Southern, all expensively dressed. They greeted her politely. Tamsyn felt their gazes like little spyglasses, examining her for flaws. The only blessing was that before she could say something more than a simple acknowledgment, Thatcher whisked her away to meet someone else.

The topic of discussion on every man's tongue was the tale of Spanish atrocities in Cuba and the horror of the 266 dead sailors of the USS *Maine*. Most seemed concerned from the point of business losses occasioned by the impending hostilities. Some of the younger men more enthusiastically cursed the Spaniards with much braggadocio, and vowed to take up arms.

The women, on the other hand, were more reserved, eyes wary, as their husbands and sons debated the issues. It wasn't so much what they said as the rattled nerves betrayed by the twitch of a finger or the surreptitious removal of a tear. Norah's beau Brian gone, just like that. *She must be devastated.* The fact that war had touched so close to people she knew saddened her. Worse, this celebration in the face of so much loss was monstrous.

As the evening passed, she received many compliments on her gown, and Thatcher positively glowed with the pride of his possession. His affected smile sickened her, and she wished it could all be over.

Just as the guests were being summoned to dinner, a commotion disturbed the front entryway. Tamsyn had slipped away from Thatcher's grasping hand and was talking quietly with a couple of women who were neighbors from her childhood, when they heard loud voices raised and what sounded like the clash of steel. *Sword fighting? Here? Had the war intruded on their little party?*

The people in front of her were too tall for her to see what was happening, so she climbed up the stairs to see over their heads. What she discovered were men, half a dozen of them, armed to the teeth and dressed all in black, their faces covered by masks. They swarmed into the room once they had gained entrance, backing those at the door away at swordpoint. The masked men spread out through the guests, searching for something—or someone.

"Good evening, ladies and gentlemen." One of the men stepped to the center of the room. "I apologize for disturbing your soiree, but we come on a mission, a mission of the heart." As he surveyed the room, Tamsyn recognized the voice. His roving gaze met hers, and she saw the fire flare in his eyes. The contact sent a thrill of delight through her.

"We shall be leaving you at once when our task is accomplished so you may return to the festivities. Although, it pains us to go…the ladies are so beautiful." He cast an appreciative eye at the women nearest him, and they blushed with pleasure. *That man could charm the peel off an orange.* She stifled a smile. *What was he doing here?*

Ashton turned back to her, then smiled and raised one arm. He held it up for a few moments, then suddenly dropped it. As he did, the lights went out. In the rush and babble of terrified voices which began there in the dark, Tamsyn was grabbed by someone she couldn't see. Her captor pulled her forward down the stairs, then tossed her over someone's shoulder. She was carried down toward the side door, which opened onto a veranda. Tamsyn thought belatedly she should have screamed to let someone know she was being taken, but the sheer adventure of the moment and the knowledge that Drake was involved exhilarated her more than frightened her. He would not allow her to come to harm, and she was much too curious what he had planned. Could this be the escape she'd longed for?

The man carried her outside and around the corner of the house, where an old buggy waited. She was handed up into the buggy and set down on the floor of its back seat. Two men sat down quickly, one on either side of her, and removed their dark overshirts, revealing light-colored shirts. Their legs filled the space on either side of her, so she could not be seen from the street, especially in the dark. She regretted any damage to her dress, but everything was happening so fast, she couldn't worry about it.

Tamsyn heard feet running away in the opposite direction, and shouts following the footsteps. *Fools, it's a false trail!* She giggled in spite of herself and felt the men jerk at the sudden sound.

"Keep your head down, miss." The man spoke in a squeaky Spanish-accented voice which led Tamsyn to believe he wasn't as old as she'd thought.

The buggy rocked suddenly as someone leaped into the driver's seat, also shedding a dark jacket, tossed to the men in the back. They concealed it on the floor by Tamsyn. "Quite an adventure, eh, boys?" came Drake's voice, followed by a deep chuckle. He chirped to the horse to start the buggy. Tamsyn was caught off guard, and banged her head on the seat behind her. It didn't hurt, thanks to the adrenaline rushing through her system. *What was Drake thinking? This was crazy!*

"Now, let's see," Drake said, "we should dispel any thought that we have just come from the Winslows' home, while making our way to the harbor as quickly as possible." There was a pause while he obviously considered the alternatives. "Perhaps La Africana?"

The men beside Tamsyn grunted in assent, and the buggy took a turn. As it rolled on, Tamsyn thought about what she'd heard. *The harbor? He means to take me on his ship, then.* Her heart beat faster as her excitement grew. From her spot, scrunched on the floor, she couldn't see much but the moon overhead, nearly full. She watched it as the buggy gently swayed, traveling over the cobbled street. The sound of island music grew louder as they continued, so she knew they must be approaching the Bahamian neighborhood.

Drake never stopped, though he called out greetings as they passed, and received many from those in the neighborhood. Soon, the music receded. Sounds of the harbor took their place.

The buggy came to a stop, and Drake turned to lean over the seat. "This is the difficult part. Look sharp, now!" As the men jumped down from the buggy, he leaned over and grabbed Tamsyn's hand. "Are you unharmed?" he asked softly. His face, lit with excitement, was split with a wide smile.

"Quite," she said.

"This has been more fun than I anticipated."

Tamsyn laughed, shaking her head. "You're mad!"

"Emotions drive a man to terrible lengths." He was suddenly serious. "But not far enough to ignore the risks. We'll have to conceal you for a moment." His voice was apologetic. One of the boys climbed back up into the buggy, standing very near her.

She nodded and took a deep breath.

Without warning, two things happened simultaneously. Drake lifted her to a standing position by grasping her waist, and a grain sack was pulled down over her head, totally covering her to her feet. She heard the others step down off the conveyance, then she was laid over a shoulder once again, her ribs pained by the pressure, and carried a short distance, first on level ground, then slightly uphill. She could tell thereafter, by the gentle rocking, that she was on board a sea vessel.

Men's voices called out as she passed. She heard the music of a harmonica, and voices raised in a sea shanty, and she wished she could see what was happening. Her thrill turned to fright as the rough strands of the sack rubbed against her skin, and she suddenly considered the consequences of being on a ship full of sailors, out at sea, the only woman among the men.

Whoever carried her wore heavy boots that stomped across a wide wooden deck and now down some stairs. The passage down them was narrow, and Tamsyn bumped into walls as they moved ahead, but not hard enough to cause any damage. At the bottom of the stairs, they went forward a short distance, and she felt the man breathing hard as he struggled. At last, he paused before a door and opened it, then set her down on her feet, still covered by the sack.

"*El capitán* will come. Wait," he gasped, then he was gone.

Chapter Thirteen

"Just another moment, Tamsyn," Drake said in the same soft tone with which he'd caressed her before. He removed the sack very carefully, so as not to tear her dress. She had looked so beautiful at the Winslows', and he wanted to recapture that.

At last, she stood revealed before him. "Are you all right? You're not hurt, are you?" He reached out to wipe a smear of dirt from her forehead.

She smiled shyly, and it was all he could do not to pull her into his arms. "No, I think I find myself complete and unharmed," she said.

"Let me give you a moment to compose yourself." He gestured to a table under the mirror, where he'd laid out combs and a bowl of bay-scented water.

"But—"

He shook his head and stepped outside the door. Once out of her sight, he leaned against the wall, astounded his reckless plan had succeeded. Winslow's own words had put the idea in his head, so concerned he was nothing more than a mercenary. *Might as well steal something valuable, right?*

He had presumed Tamsyn felt the same way he did. Every time Drake had been with her, she'd seemed happy. *But circumstances change.* After he'd seen her in the garden, knowing from the conversation inside that she'd be forced to marry Winslow, it was possible she'd put him from her mind.

What if I have misinterpreted her feelings?

Surely if she had objected, she would have called out and had them all captured before they left the Winslow premises. So she was at least willing to go along with the outrageous stunt.

Satisfied that he hadn't been totally mistaken, he let himself wonder what other risks he had exposed himself to. Had he been recognized? Would Winslow and the others know immediately where to search?

If they tried to find the *Raven*, of course, they'd have to launch their own ships in the middle of the night. Not always the wisest course of action, even with lighthouses to mark the reefs. No, he should have a clear shot to escape, here on the ocean they both loved.

His door creaked open a few inches. "Drake?" Tamsyn asked.

"Here." He anxiously examined her dress, her hair, her expression. She had survived the caper with very little harm. And her face! It was radiant. The unexpected joy there grabbed at the strings of his soul. "You are fit for company?"

"I'm fine," she said.

"Shall I come in?"

"It's your room. You hardly need permission."

She stepped back, and he entered, hoping belatedly she wouldn't find the captain's cabin too rough and utilitarian. It wasn't designed for social encounters. "So."

"So." She cocked one eyebrow. Her amusement was clear. "It would seem I am at the mercy of a pirate."

"It would." He smiled. "I trust that does not cause

you distress?"

He listened for the thunk of heavy boots outside the door. His crew awaited orders. While they had, in fact, set sail, they had no heading yet. He'd waited to see how Tamsyn would react to the "kidnapping," knowing it might all have been a blunder.

But she seemed content.

"No." She gave a tiny, self-deprecating laugh. "I was desperately hoping the evening at the Winslows' would end. But this was hardly the conclusion I had foreseen."

"I had to do something, after that night... Winslow's threats to your father." His voice trailed off, as she looked oddly at him.

"You heard him? You were really there?" she asked, emotion softening her voice.

He nodded. "You looked right at me. Didn't you see me?"

Her eyes filled with tears. "I couldn't believe it was really you. I had hoped you would come, and then what Thatcher said made everything go from bad to worse." She dissolved into sobs.

Drake took her in his arms, holding her tightly to him, kissing her hair as she shook. "Shh, hush, *querida*, everything will be well now." He was overcome by a feeling of inadequacy, chills running through him. His heart went out to her in her need. If there was any question of his serious intentions about this woman, his visceral reaction to her pain convinced him.

Tamsyn soon regained control, and her crying stopped with a final shudder. She nestled against Drake's chest in a familiar way. He suddenly realized he wanted to enjoy this every day of his life. He closed his eyes and just held her, savoring the sensation.

A sharp rap at the door jerked them apart. Tamsyn turned away, wiping her cheeks. Drake reluctantly answered the knock.

"Yes?" He opened the door to discover young Mateo, hesitation written across his face. The boy nervously smoothed his shock of shiny dark hair.

"*Señor*, where are we bound?" Mateo asked.

Drake smiled at the boy's nervous bearing. Samuel must have sent him down, knowing he was the only member of the crew who wouldn't get chewed out for disturbing the captain. Mateo reminded Drake very much of himself at the same age—curious about new things and always ready for an adventure, despite his handicap. He often escaped sharp words which might be heaped on another.

"Very well, Mateo. Tell Samuel to follow the wind, for now." As the boy sighed with relief and started away, Drake called him back. "And tell him, next time he should be man enough to come down himself."

The boy grinned. "*Sí*, señor!" He limped away toward the stairs.

By the time Drake turned back to Tamsyn, she'd dried her face and was calm once again. "I'm sorry," she said. "I hadn't let myself feel that. It truly takes the soul from me."

"No need to apologize. We don't have to discuss it."

He was more interested in the depth of her sincerity when she knew he'd really been there. *She wanted me to help her. She wanted me.* The ship moved under his feet, Samuel moving her offshore as he'd asked. "Once we're well away from the dock, we can go up on deck. I don't want anyone to spy you from shore."

"Should you go up now? Will your crew need you?"

He shook his head. "We've been together a long time. They know what I want, and could probably manage it all without me. But they expect to consult with me, at least." He gestured toward the table. "Shall we sit down? I can get you some juice or a glass of wine."

"Juice would be nice, thank you." She looked around as if noticing her surroundings for the first time, then took a seat at the table. "This is your cabin?"

He nodded. "It's probably not what you're used to. But when I'm out at sea, I spend most of my time on deck." He crossed to the oaken dresser, where a tray with the pitcher of fresh fruit juice awaited, and poured some of the orange and mango mixture into a golden goblet. The cup was one of his personal favorites, found on the scene of a wreck during his youth. The juice he'd prepared himself in those anxious hours before going to the Winslows', when his nerves demanded that he find something constructive to do. While this caper was pending, all attempts to think about his shipments were futile.

She sipped it with a satisfied sigh. "This is wonderful."

He thanked her and stood observing the woman as she rested, here in his private space. He was pleased she was on his ship. Other men, perhaps, would feel the shift of power and might take advantage of a lady in such a position. But he had no such designs.

Actually, he hadn't thought much beyond the initial stages of this adventure. *First, he would capture her, then he would...what?* Her glittery dress was obviously unsuited for time at sea, and he had no other proper women's clothing for her. *But she was here, now.* Time to think of that later. He'd judged the speed of the ship from its movement across the waves, and he deemed it now safe for them to go up into the open air.

"I believe we are far enough from the island not to be seen," he said. "Shall we?"

She agreed readily. "It's been some time since I've been on the ocean, and I've never been after dark."

"On a night like this, with the moon hanging low over the water, it promises to be stunning." Drake extended his hand. Her soft fingers slid into his, and he cherished the very texture of her skin.

"Where are we going?" She stood still as he moved forward, so he was forced to stop and turn back to her. Her eyes were bright with excitement, but he could see concern as well.

"Just on deck." He knew that wasn't what she asked.

"I mean—"

"I know what you mean." He smiled again to reassure her. "I honestly don't know. I wanted some time alone with you, far from the eyes of those who judged our time the other day. This was my chosen alternative."

"There are attendant risks," she warned him. "If they find you have engineered this abduction, a bounty will be placed on your head, and they will arrest you on sight."

"It's worth it."

Her lip trembled, and she bit it. "Not if I can never see you again."

"Nothing will ever keep me away," he promised. Not wanting to dwell on the consequences of his actions, he took her arm and led her up the stairs into the fresh air. She leaned gently on the wall as they went up, still working to acquire her sea legs.

The moon shone brightly enough to light up the whole deck, and Drake glanced around to find his men, each in his appointed place. They looked up as their captain passed, curious to see what sort of woman had captured his heart. After all, he'd risked their futures, too, in this mad escapade. They'd established unquestioning trust, but such risks were only justified if the woman was worth that effort. Tamsyn spoke to some of them as they passed on the way to the prow, and they responded by doffing their hat or nodding in greeting, a word or two exchanged.

The moon's glow was reflected on the water, too, the whitecaps shimmering as they rippled past. The sky was clear, and the dome of heaven was filled with sparkling stars. A moderately strong, warm breeze moved the ship along, and the sound of the gurgling water as the prow cut through the waves filled the air. Drake could think of nothing which could make his night more perfect.

****

As she surveyed the scene before her, the night wind and the moon sparkling on the water, Tamsyn thought she'd never been anywhere more beautiful. She walked forward to the bowsprit, until she felt like she herself was leading the ship on its journey. The wind dragged at her coiffure, so she reached up and began pulling pins out, throwing them over the side, releasing her curls to fall down around her shoulders. Once they were all out, she shook her head, combing her fingers through her hair until it hung loose. *Thank you, Mrs. Winslow, but this is much more the hairstyle I prefer.* The simple thought set her laughing, as heady freedom filled her being.

"I like that sound." Drake waited a few steps behind her.

"What sound?"

"Your laughter. I haven't had much opportunity to hear it."

She grinned at him. "I haven't felt much like laughing, except when you—"

She fell silent, afraid to say too much. As impulsive and exciting as this adventure was, she couldn't put from her mind the reality that she must return to the island and her life there. Her father would suffer, both financially and emotionally, if she simply disappeared. She expected as well that Thatcher would know exactly who was responsible, and he would have Drake hunted down and jailed or even executed for his "crime." Better that she return and distract him from vengeance.

But for now, in this dazzling place, she could exist for the moment. Time enough to deal with consequences in a few minutes or a few hours...

He moved close behind her as she looked out over the water. Tentatively, he slid his arms around her in a way that felt completely natural and protective. She leaned back against his broad chest and placed her arms on top of his. They stayed like that for a time which seemed endless, breathing in the salt air and looking at the stars. It seemed like heaven.

This was how it should be. Not vicious pawing and

coerced kisses, not threats and blandishments, but two people relaxed and comfortable with each other. She recalled her fantasy wedding and smiled at the thought of walking up the aisle to find Drake waiting there for her.

"Señor?" asked a young voice from behind them.

Drake reluctantly released her, and they found the cabin boy waiting with glasses of red wine on a tray. She took one, thanking the boy, and Drake took the other. The boy smiled at her, and she recognized the voice as her companion in the wild buggy ride to the dock. He wasn't very old, in his teens at most. He bit his lip with embarrassment under her gaze.

"Dinner?" his captain asked.

"It shall be prepared shortly, señor. Where shall you dine?"

"In my cabin, I think—"

Tamsyn interrupted him. "I hate to leave this sky, this moon. Could we stay right here?" She looked up at the celestial lights, trying to fix all these new sensations in her memory forever.

"Very well, Mateo." Drake sent the boy on his way. To Tamsyn, he said, "I realized I kept you from your supper at the Winslows', so I felt obligated to provide."

"The least you could do." The wine would go straight to her head soon, she knew from previous, infrequent consumption, so she must sip it slowly. One of them had to keep their wits.

She felt the curious eyes of the crew, some shy, others bolder in their observation. Tamsyn smiled at them all. One broad, bullish man came forward with a blanket, which he spread on the deck. Drake clapped the man on the shoulder.

"Good thinking, Chaney. A picnic it will be!" He gestured to Tamsyn that she should seat herself, which she did without hesitation.

Within a few minutes, trays of food came up from belowdecks, chicken spit broiled with crispy skins, fruits and cheeses, Bahamian bread with a thick slab of butter. The men vied for the opportunity to serve her until Drake finally dismissed them with a laugh.

"Cook has enough for all below. Go take your supper. We may have some business awaiting us yet tonight."

The men cheered and noisily went down to eat. The skinny cabin boy remained to serve his captain. Drake saw that the boy got a plate of food, then sent him away. "A few moments alone," he whispered conspiratorially.

"Just a few," she said with a sad smile. "Then I must—"

Drake held up a finger, silencing her. "Not a word of that now."

Tamsyn started to argue, then realized he would just cut her off again. It was right. What might happen in a minute, in an hour, would not be changed if she took the time to immerse herself in the joy and comfort of this time with Drake.

The food smelled so good in the fresh night air, and Drake urged her to taste everything, from sweet melons to spicy chicken. It was simple fare, but it satisfied her more than any of the expensive delicacies that had been served at the Pickhams' buffet. *Surely it is the company which has improved my appetite.* Drake's dark eyes danced in the moonlight, and he often turned to her with a smile, perhaps wanting to say something but reluctant to break the spell they seemed to be under.

But not yet, Mamma, not yet...Can you see me, Mamma? Tamsyn wondered silently. *Can you see how happy I am?*

When she'd eaten her fill, Drake helped her to her feet, and they strolled around the deck, her arm through his, their bodies close. It seemed to be a fine ship. Drake talked to her about the *Raven*, how it had survived battles and storms at sea, the loyalty of her crew. The tone of his words demonstrated his passion for his chosen vocation. Pirate or shipper, mercenary or merchant, he obviously cared for these men and felt his efforts mattered.

"Is it true you're a gunrunner?" she asked.

He glanced at her, assessing her question, then nodded. "I sell guns to the Cuban people, insurgents who want to rid themselves of the tyrannical rule of the Spanish."

"So you are helping bring the war to a head." She watched his face closely, admiring the shadows in the hollows of his cheekbones as the moonlight angled across his face.

"No, I'd say I'm just evening the odds a little." He explained how the Spanish had tightened the grip on the people to the point they had nearly choked. "The sinking of the *Maine* is just the beginning. The United States government will soon send ships in retaliation, and the Cuban people will have the opportunity at last to free themselves, with the Americans' help. But they need to be able to defend themselves." He paused. "Besides, the Spaniards and I have a debt to settle. They killed my brother."

Tamsyn saw his eyes, first hard, then soft with unshed tears. The sight tore at her heartstrings. She moved closer and took a firm grip on his arm. Her small movement sparked him to sweep her into his arms, holding her tightly to him. She held his shaking body, comforting him as she would a beloved child, as he had her earlier, waiting for him to continue his tale.

Haltingly, Drake told Tamsyn the story. His voice was tight with hate, showing a bloodthirsty drive for vengeance. She could see where others might have judged him poorly to have such thoughts at all, but the love this man had held for his lost sibling shone through. She could not blame him in the least.

"My dear Drake." She leaned back to see his face. "You have suffered enough for one lifetime." She caressed his cheek. His face was open, his eyes vulnerable. It was only natural for him to bend forward and kiss her softly, feathery touches which gently grazed her lips.

She reached an arm around his neck, as if to make sure he did not escape from her, and let a hand slide up his neck to gently smooth his hair, then her finger ran along the edge of his ear. He gasped, and she did it again, causing a shudder the length of his spine. A warmth rushed up through her body, making her fear she'd lose control. She knew she couldn't cross the line. She could not be with Drake until she'd settled her obligations on land.

She broke away from him, pushing him back with both hands firmly against his chest. "If we don't stop now, it will be too late." Her breath came hard and fast. Her head was light from the wine, and her face felt fevered. She turned away into the breeze, hoping it would cool her passions.

"What's wrong with that?" Drake reached out to her.

She stepped back reluctantly. Her heart pounded so fast, she could hardly think. She had lost herself in his touch, so different from Thatcher's grasping, controlling behavior. Drake was considerate, proceeding at her pace. It would have been easy to continue. But if she did, she would lose the opportunity to save him.

"You must take me home."

He looked stunned. "Why? You're not happy here?"

"That's not it at all."

"You'd prefer to be in the city, safe with Winslow, then." His voice was chill and dark.

She tried to match her tone to his. "If you believed that, you would never have brought me here tonight."

He finally looked down at the floor, his face grim. She moved close to him again, venturing a soft kiss. "It is for your own good, Drake. Do you not realize what's happening back on the island? Thatcher probably has the police on guard at the port, awaiting your return. He may already have launched ships in pursuit."

"I'm not afraid of him."

She smiled at his petulant tone. "My love…" *It felt so odd to say it. But somehow she knew it was true.* "I will not be the weapon which destroys you. Please don't set that burden on my conscience."

"Tamsyn!" He held her chin lightly in his hand and looked into her eyes. "I would never hurt you in any way."

She smiled. "I know. This was a brave adventure,

and I wouldn't have missed it." She turned away and looked out with longing at the sea, light still glinting off the tops of the swells, salt breezes filling her senses. *No, I wouldn't have missed it...but how could I stay?*

"So," he said, the sparkle in his eyes a clue that he was not angry, "I go to all the trouble to help you escape, and now you want me to find a way to take you back into the lion's den. A challenge worthy of the mind of a pirate."

"I would expect no less of you. Perhaps a sail into the cove?"

"No way to convey you home from there, my dear." He scratched his head, thinking of alternatives.

"You can't just sweep into the port."

"No, of course not." Moving slowly back and forth, he paced, breathing deeply. "They'll be watching at the Winslows'."

She nodded, pushing herself for a solution as well. The breeze rippled across her skin, and she felt chilled, now that she was out of his arms. She wanted nothing more than to slide back against his chest, safe with her protector. But she felt more strongly that if anything happened to him as a result of this night's work, she'd never forgive herself. *Better to deal with Thatcher and hope for a different resolution.*

"There's a small dock by the Pickhams'. It would only be a short walk from there. You could send a small boat into the shore. They would probably never notice at this time of night."

"You may have something." He returned to take her hand. "I can walk you home to make sure no harm comes to you."

"Too dangerous," she said. "I'll be fine. The only

one who's caused trouble has been you." When he started to protest, she silenced him with a finger against his lips. "I insist. It's the only way. For now."

"For now?" Something in his eyes lit up as he realized what she'd said.

"Yes. This will not be the end." *I hope I can keep that promise. It is where my heart lies.*

Finally, he agreed, and gave the order to turn the ship back toward the island. Just as she was wondering how they could make headway against the wind, she felt the breeze come about. Drake felt it, too.

"It seems even the gods agree with you." Disappointed, he put his arm around her shoulders and walked with her to the bowsprit, where they could watch as shore approached. In the background, she could see and hear the crew jump to comply with their captain's orders, letting out the sail, making preparations for shore. As they were well underway, still a good distance out, they began to sing, a melancholy sea shanty Tamsyn had not heard before, but it was clearly the song of a lost love.

Please, dear God, not lost, just…delayed.

She couldn't worry about it now. She had too much to think about. What would she say when she returned? She must have a good story to throw the focus off Drake. Staring across the waves, she felt Drake come up behind her once again and slip his arms around, bracing her. She closed her eyes, feeling as safe and loved as she'd ever felt in her life, and thought about the hours to come.

When they were near enough to launch their small boat, Drake stirred at last. He took her hand and held it up before her in the moonlight, looking over her shoulder to examine the lines in it. His deep sigh provoked her to ask a question. She felt stronger in asking him since her back was to him. She couldn't read his thoughts in his eyes, as he couldn't see hers.

"You told me, the day we first met, about an old Cuban woman and a prediction," she said. "You said she foretold that a woman would rescue you. Was that all?"

"She said the woman who came to help me would mean more to me than life itself." After a pause, he added in a whisper, "I have come to realize that is true, Tamsyn."

"I know it is." *Why else would he have risked everything to appear at the Winslows' and steal me away?* His tenderness and generosity here on the ship reinforced what she already knew in her heart. He was that one true love she'd been awaiting her whole life. "Is that all?"

Voices called out for Drake on the rear deck, and he slid away and went to help make preparations. Tamsyn couldn't help but feel he was hiding something. As she considered his reticence, she realized the island had grown much closer. She mentally rehearsed her story, reluctantly distancing herself from this evening and the memories she would treasure forever.

Drake insisted on rowing her in himself, Mateo tagging along at Tamsyn's insistence to make sure Drake remained behind. The boy steadied the boat along the rough wood of the dock as Tamsyn alighted. When she would have hurried away, Drake caught her to him and kissed her.

"I'll come to see you soon," he promised.

"Don't come!" she cried. "They'll be after you." Catching herself, she brought her voice down, despite her dismay. "Mateo, he must not come until it is safe. Don't let him."

"*Sí*, señorita, I understand." His dark eyes were wide with excitement.

"But if I don't see you…" Drake held her tightly.

"I'll send word when it's safe," she assured him. "Now go." She stepped away, nodding to the boy to shove off. Drake hurried to the boat, watching her every step of the way. Her eyes burned with tears, and she turned away before he could see them. She knew that would be all he needed to encourage him to take her back with him. *And I'd want to go.* That would be impossible.

She turned her quick steps toward home.

Chapter Fourteen

As Tamsyn crept up through the shadowy trees of the neighboring yards, she found all the lamps at her home were lit. *So much for avoiding an open confrontation.*

Her story would be that she'd been kidnapped and held somewhere on the island. When her captors became inattentive, she'd managed to escape. She could say she'd been blindfolded and had no idea who the criminals might have been. She couldn't say anything about a ship, as that clue would inevitably lead to Drake.

Then she had to pray that Thatcher hadn't recognized Drake and his men.

But she'd hoped she could quietly come in and find her father alone. Now, with uniformed people hurrying in and out the front door, anything connected with Tamsyn's arrival would be an immediate crisis.

She waited under a banyan tree for some time, trying to decide what to do. The heart-pounding excitement of her moonlight sail faded, as it was early morning. *Do I look like someone who's been taken against her will?* Though her hair was loose and windblown, was she too composed to look as if she'd struggled with kidnappers?

Sad for the unnecessary destruction, she tore the stitching of her dress in several places, places she hoped would be easy to mend. She debated bruising her skin to demonstrate force had been used, but couldn't bring herself to do it. But to claim she'd been confined by ropes would leave traces, so she took a broken stick nearby and rubbed her wrists and ankles until they were slightly abraded, biting her lip to keep from crying out at the pain. The tears on her face were real. *What I do for you, Drake Ashton...* Then she watched her front door and waited for a moment when the activity seemed to slow down. *There...it was time.*

Tamsyn hurried through the trees into the courtyard behind her house. The thought of facing her father, Thatcher, and the constabulary at the same time was too unsettling. She'd come in through the kitchen, perhaps enlist the help of the women there before she dealt with the men.

The door was closed and locked for the first time Tamsyn could remember. *Papa, how could you? Not tonight!* Seeing light inside, she peeked in through the window screen. Clara and Juba scrubbed tables that looked very clean already. Those who really cared about her were obviously worried, and she regretted causing them heartache. Tamsyn moved back to the door and knocked softly.

"Who there?" Juba's contralto voice dripped with suspicion.

"I-It's m-m-me." Tamsyn's nerves made it difficult for her words to escape her lips. "Juba, open the door."

"Missy Tamsyn?" There was a scrabbling at the lock, and then the door flew open. Tamsyn smiled wearily, and Juba moved to take the girl in her substantial arms. "You come in here right now, girl!" she scolded. "What mischief you been up to?"

"Mischief?" Tamsyn allowed the women to guide her to a stool, onto which she gratefully melted. The thought of facing her father and Thatcher made her legs weak.

Juba stood before her, Clara behind her right shoulder. "Clara be talkin' 'bout this pirate man, say he the one took you away." She narrowed her eyes as she examined her young lady's face.

"P-Pirate?" she stammered.

Clara added, "I told her all about him, how he look so fine and speak like de gentleman."

Tamsyn focused hard. "Don't speak of him again, Clara. If you care for me at all, you will not mention him." She leaned forward, nearer to Juba's shocked face, and spoke softly to them. "I came back here tonight to protect him, and I would defend his life with my own. My father and Thatcher must not suspect—"

"Then it *was* mischief," Juba interrupted. "I shoulda known. But look at you." She shook her head and started to laugh, covering her mouth. Her body continued to shake, but she controlled herself under Tamsyn's deadly serious gaze.

"Please, you must help me." She looked back and forth between them until they nodded. Once she knew they would keep her secret, she took a deep, relieved breath. "Is my father here?"

Juba nodded. "Marse Thatcher was here earlier. He and Marse Angus had a terrible fight."

"About what?"

Juba shook her head. "We couldn't hear what they say, but they was yellin', and things was flyin' around Marse Angus' office."

"Somethin' 'bout a bargain," Clara said suddenly.

As the two women turned to her, she said, "I be cleanin' in the front room when Marse Thatcher arrive. So I listen."

"Go on," Tamsyn urged.

"Marse Thatcher, he say Marse Angus gave his word you would marry him, and he expect Marse Angus to keep his word. Marse Angus say he not know where you are, that you at Marse Thatcher's house. He ask what happened, and Marse Thatcher tell him dark men came to the party and take you away." She gulped. "Marse Angus must have jump up then, 'cause I hear his chair fall over and he demand to know more."

Tamsyn noticed her hands were shaking. "He was frightened?"

Clara shook her head. "More angry-like. He shout back at Marse Thatcher that he s'pposed take care o' you now. That that's what he wanted."

Why should I have expected more? The revelation stabbed her in the heart. *Mamma, he lied to you...* "Then what?" Wearily, she watched Juba's face as she too digested the true feelings at work.

"Marse Thatcher say he gonna marry you, and if he don't, that Marse Angus will keep having accidents at the harbor."

"What?" Tamsyn demanded. *How did Thatcher know about the sabotage? And how would he know the "accidents" would continue, unless...* The realization left her breathless. "It's not me he wants at all, is it? It's all about who's in control." Her eyes filled with tears as she looked at the old cook, the woman who'd been confidante for a lonely little girl who had grown into a lonely young woman.

"Now, honey." Juba took her hand and squeezed it

188

warmly.

"What did my father say then?"

"He didn't say nothin' for a long time, then he was mad enough to spit. He musta flew cross the room, 'cause I hear Marse Thatcher say to stay 'way from him."

Clara paused, remembering the scene. "Marse Angus was cursin' Marse Thatcher, callin' him everythin' but a white boy, and then..." The girl shivered. "Then Marse Thatcher started to laugh. It was a real scary laugh, sent chills down me." She shivered again.

He'd really lost his sanity if he thought he could tell my father he was committing these crimes and ruining his business, and not expect some kind of reprisals. "Surely he'll change his mind about the marriage now. My father will never allow it," Tamsyn whispered.

"Marse Thatcher say that if Marse Angus say one word to keep you from marryin' him, that something would happen to you. He say, 'See how easy it is to make her disappear?'"

Clara's eyes were huge with horror that Tamsyn knew echoed her own. How could Thatcher even threaten such a thing? It was even more imperative that she carry on as if nothing had changed between them... but how could she bring herself to do it?

Before the conversation could continue, loud voices echoed outside the kitchen door. "I've got to move," Tamsyn said. *Move? Out the kitchen door? You can't. Finish what you've started.* Feeling a part of herself, a part drenched in youth and innocence, had just died, she stood up. "We've got to get through this.

Let's go."

Tamsyn sent Clara through the swinging door first, instructing her to call for Angus MacKiernan. She followed, Juba lending physical support, her motherly tendencies in full bloom. She put her arm around Tamsyn, who was feeling the very real effects of shock setting in.

"Marse Angus, it's Missy Tamsyn! She's back," the girl cried.

Tamsyn made it as far as the office door before her father reached her. Her jaded mind noticed his face was blotchy and his hair uncombed. He really looked like a parent distraught over the kidnapping of his only daughter. She wondered how much of it was an act and how much was real. *And how much was due to Thatcher's behavior instead of any real worry about the kidnapping.*

"Tamsyn." He reached out for her. As much as she doubted him, she went into his embrace. It would be a stressful evening. Sometimes, only a father's magical touch could help make things feel all right again.

"Are you all right, girl?" He extricated himself from her grip and looked closely at her. "You're not hurt, are ye?" As he saw her exposed wrists, he gasped. "Have you been molested? Defiled? Girl, ye better tell me."

"No, Papa."

He reached out and touched her torn dress, one he'd never seen. "This was your party dress?" His tone was softer than any he'd used with her for many weeks.

"Yes, Papa. Mrs. Winslow had it made up." Her throat caught with tears at the feeling in his voice. For the first time, she wondered if he still loved her as he always had. Unlike the night they'd quarreled, his emotion seemed genuine.

"I was so worried." He grabbed her hands and held them.

She shook her head. "I'll be fine, Papa."

He pulled her into the office, exhorting Juba to send a boy down to the Winslows' to tell Thatcher she'd returned.

"Papa, there's no need to call him." She wanted nothing less than to deal with Thatcher, too.

"I must, Tamsyn. He's left me no choice." Angus' face was resigned and as blackly sad as she'd ever seen it.

Tamsyn felt her breath escape when she saw two uniformed men waiting in her father's office. "This is my daughter, Tamsyn," Angus said to them.

"Miss?" The taller one bowed slightly. "I am Captain Gray of the city constabulary, investigating your disappearance." She had time to notice his gray hair and kindly blue eyes before her head got all swimmy, and she swayed on her feet. "Please, miss, sit down." He and Angus helped her to the desk chair. "Are you quite all right?"

She nodded slowly, worried, disappointed, and frightened all at once. "Papa, please."

"Nonsense. It was Winslow's demand that he be notified should you be found." Angus stood uncomfortably, arms crossed. "And where ha'e ye been? Settin' half the town out lookin' for ye."

Captain Gray, a pad and pencil in hand, straightened his jacket and looked askance at Tamsyn's father. "Can't you see the girl's had a shock, sir?"

"Well, of course I can, she's my daughter, isn't

she?" Angus blustered. Tamsyn could tell he wasn't angry at her, that he was just lashing out at the nearest available person. "I just wanted to know what she'd been up to."

" 'Up to'? Sir, we have the statements of a dozen witnesses, upstanding residents of this city, that she was kidnapped from the Winslows' home by a bunch of men, bold as brass, who walked in and walked out without anyone so much as lifting a finger. Are you suggesting your daughter was a participant in something nefarious?"

Tamsyn suddenly wished she were anywhere else. Memories of her evening snaked across the palette of her mind, and she longed with such intensity to be back on the deck of the *Raven*, free, her hair blowing, breathing the fresh air, that she burst into tears.

"See, now, you've upset her," the captain said. "Would you please step out?"

"This is my office," Angus roared, stamping his foot. "Ye can't ask a man to leave his own office!"

Captain Gray straightened up to stand even taller. "I most certainly can, and I just have."

The whole scene was taking on the look of a bad comic opera, Tamsyn thought. *Better to let them fight it out among themselves than draw their attention.* From her seat, she noticed that Juba and Clara had withdrawn, awaiting Angus' inevitable explosion. The second officer waited too, a thin, little man meekly standing by for orders. She breathed deeply, trying to control her urge to cry.

Angus was eventually ushered out, strongly protesting all the while. The captain then sent his minion for a glass of brandy for Tamsyn and settled into a chair across the desk.

"Miss MacKiernan, you've obviously had an eventful evening. Could you please tell me what happened, to the best of your recall?"

Tamsyn took a sip of the brandy when it was offered to her, a sharp intake of breath marking the burn as it went down her throat. She then described her fictional kidnapping in as much detail as she dared, how she'd been carried down an alley and locked in a warehouse of some sort, tied to a chair and her eyes covered. The captain nodded, saying he'd noticed her wrists had been injured. Tamsyn modestly showed him her ankles as well. No, she had no idea who the men were. No, none of the voices had sounded familiar. No, she had no idea what they wanted, but it seemed it was something about her father's shipping. They'd been lax in watching her, and she'd slipped her bonds and scurried home.

"You're a brave girl, Miss MacKiernan." The captain smiled and gave her a pat on the hand.

Tamsyn might have thought he was flirting with her, if he hadn't been her father's age. "I just kept my eyes and ears open for opportunities, Captain."

Loud voices sounded outside the office, and Thatcher burst in, disheveled and without a jacket.

"My love!" he cried. He rushed to her, grabbing her up in his arms.

Tamsyn protested, the rush of activity making her dizzy. "Thatcher, please let me go." She felt faint as he set her back into the chair.

"Tamsyn?" His look was stern. The constables might not notice his change in demeanor, but she certainly recognized it.

I don't want to talk to him now. She closed her eyes to make him go away. Still dizzy, she started to slide from the chair.

"Call a doctor!" Thatcher ordered. He reached under her chin and grabbed it, tipping her face upward. When she didn't open her eyes, he squeezed until it pinched. The pain brought her fully to her senses. "What sort of act is this?" he demanded. "Where have you been?"

Captain Gray intervened. "This poor young woman has had a traumatic evening. She's asked you to let her go. You're certainly obstructing our investigation. Please step out."

Thatcher ignored him and continued to address Tamsyn. "Was it Ashton? Would he dare come into my house and steal you from under my nose?"

She heard him, but it sounded like it was from a long distance. *Ashton…Drake, I wish you were here…*

Thatcher grabbed her by the shoulders and shook her. As her head snapped back, she came fully awake and looked at him with terror. This was a man who'd threatened her life, in so many words, holding her father hostage to his wishes. She had to get away from him.

"Captain?" she said weakly.

The officer was ahead of her.

"Mr. Winslow, I'll have to ask you to remain outside, sir, since you cannot control yourself." The captain took Thatcher by the arm and steered him out the door, ignoring his struggles as if he were a small boy.

The second officer stepped quickly forward to assist Tamsyn back into the chair. "You drink the rest of the brandy, miss."

The two men stopped directly outside the door, where Tamsyn could hear every word. The captain asked Thatcher, "Now, who is this Ashton character to whom you referred?"

"He's a brigand of the worst sort, Captain, running guns to Cuba, arming those filthy rebels to revolt against their Spanish masters. The man has stalked my dear wife-to-be repeatedly. He won't leave her alone." Thatcher's voice broke. "You must stop him!"

What a liar. Light-headed, she didn't know how much longer she could remain functional. Being in the center of this maelstrom of tension absorbed her energy as fast as she could produce it.

"What makes you think this man is the culprit?"

"Why? What did she say? She's protecting him, no doubt. She'll tell me what's happened, if you let me have time alone—"

"Sir, if you'll just calm down, I'd be glad to share the report she gave me. It would be better not to make her relive the experience again, don't you think?"

"Ridiculous."

Tamsyn could almost feel his frustration as palpable. Knowing him as she did now, she guessed he wanted the satisfaction of hearing the words from her lips. Yet to maintain his public persona, he did not want to appear a thoughtless ogre before the captain.

"Yes, Captain, I'd like to hear, too," Angus said.

Tamsyn listened anxiously as the officer read back the story she'd told. It seemed sound enough to her, in the retelling, realistic enough to have happened, vague enough that it would be difficult to pinpoint where the "captivity" could actually have occurred.

"She thinks it had something t' do with the shipping company?" Angus asked when he was finished.

"She didn't know, sir," the captain replied. "She escaped before she could learn much."

"Someone goin' t' hold her for ransom, then?" A note of suspicion rang in her father's voice. "What do you know about that, Winslow?"

Tamsyn held her breath, praying her father would seize the opportunity to tell the police about Thatcher Winslow's threats, to remove him permanently from their lives. But he said nothing of Thatcher's treachery. Her heart sank.

"Balderdash!" Thatcher bellowed. Tamsyn steeled herself for his return. As she expected, he burst back into the office to confront her. "I know as well as you, it was your lover Ashton who threw down this gauntlet. Where did he take you? Did you make love to him?"

Feeling the alcohol hit her on a nervous stomach, Tamsyn said feebly, "Thatcher, I never—"

"Has the doctor been called?" he asked.

"Yes, Marse Thatcher," Old James said from the door.

"Very well." Thatcher spun around to face Angus, and his face was deadly serious. "When the doctor comes, I want to make sure she is perfectly unharmed. Perfectly. Do you understand?"

"I think she's not been hurt, Winslow, other than the bruises on her wrists," Angus said.

"I mean *intact*, you old fool. I'll not be wedding someone who's not a virgin."

The rush of infuriated emotion which rose in Tamsyn as she heard his words quickly dissolved in a wave of dizziness which overtook her senses completely. She slid to the floor in a pile of green silk.

****

She woke sometime later as the sun streamed in her window. Her eyes opened to her familiar bedroom. The sight of her white lace curtains, her paintings, and girlish toys reassured her that she was safe, at least temporarily.

Someone had undressed her and tucked her into bed. *Was it the same morning? Or later than that?* There was no way to tell from her timepiece. She could just go downstairs and—

The sound of a man clearing his throat made her gasp. She pivoted to find her doctor seated at the head of her bed. He wore his customary black suit and thick spectacles, and his elderly face was solemn. "I am sorry I frightened you, child." He spoke in his usual mournful tone. "How are you feeling?"

She hesitated before she answered. Her self-inflicted wounds were sore, and there was a feeling in her private parts that was uncomfortable...*oh yes, Thatcher's demand.* "Very tired," she whispered. *There, that was safe.*

He nodded wisely, gray goatee bobbing up and down. "You seem to be in good physical condition." He couldn't meet her eyes.

"What does that mean, Doctor?" She believed she knew what he meant, as Thatcher's words came back to her, but she wanted perversely to hear him say it.

"That means," he said in clipped words, "that you seem to have suffered no harm from your abduction."

"Have you shared that information with Thatcher Winslow?" A bitter note crept into her voice. "He was *so* anxious to know."

"Miss MacKiernan," he said, with a matter-of-fact attitude, "I have been your doctor for a number of years and certainly have had the opportunity to examine you on many occasions. This was just another routine examination, particularly in light of the events which took place. I was at the Winslow home during the abduction, you know."

She shook her head. "I didn't know. My memory of what happened is unclear."

"Hmmm." He reached out to touch her head. "Did you receive any injuries to your head in your struggles?"

What do I say? Would a cloudy memory serve me well? It would certainly explain any inconsistencies. "I may have. I tried to get away from these men whenever I had the chance, and I may have hit my head, because it aches now."

"I see. That would correspond with Mr. Winslow's version of the facts."

Thatcher? He wasn't even there. "I beg your pardon?"

The doctor cleared his throat, as if he was delaying some unpleasant news. "Mr. Winslow seems to believe you received some sort of brain injury, resulting in your mental instability."

"What?" Tamsyn's mind raced along the path of absurdity, and she nearly burst out laughing. *Now, that would convince them I was crazy...* "He thinks I'm unstable?" She tried to sit up, but the doctor laid his hand on her shoulder.

"You must rest so that any further damage may be avoided." His tone was grim.

She looked up at the doctor with her most winning smile. "Exactly what makes Mr. Winslow believe that I may be...unstable?"

He smiled back. "You should save your energy for your recovery, Miss MacKiernan." He patted her hand where it lay on top of the covers.

"I want to know." *This coddling attitude is irritating.*

"There's no reason for you to become upset," he soothed. "I stayed until you regained consciousness. I'll go now and let you rest."

She grabbed his wrist. "I'm no more unstable than you are, Doctor," she said in the most convincing voice she could muster.

His face as he peeled her fingers away from his arm failed to reveal his beliefs about her mental condition. "I'm sure you'll be better soon," he said firmly. "I've given orders you should remain in bed for the next two to four weeks." As she started to protest, he held up a finger in warning. "If you remove yourself from this bed, I cannot be responsible for the consequences."

"Consequences?" Now what silliness was afoot?

He leaned close and looked her right in the eye. "Mr. Winslow believed it was best to remove you to an institution in Jacksonville or Charleston for proper treatment for your mental condition, until you could make a full recovery. As your father was persuaded to agree with him, it was all I could do to convince them you should remain here."

"An institution?" she whispered in horror. *Her father had agreed to send her away? Whatever had Thatcher threatened now...*

199

The doctor nodded, sympathy obvious in his eyes. "Now that I've spoken with you, it confirms my opinion that you have no need for such treatment, and it is my desire to keep you from such a fate." He shook his head. "Those places can be quite horrible, and scarcely the best situation for healing, if you ask me."

"Oh, no, I—"

He cut her off with a raised finger. "I've instructed Mr. Winslow and your father that it would be dangerous to move you any great distance at this time. Rest here in your own bed would be superior to any treatment you'd receive elsewhere." He leaned close. "But you must promise to carry out your half of the bargain. Stay in bed, as I direct, so that they have no excuse to send you away."

Tears rolled down her cheeks as the doctor spoke. The more she learned of Thatcher's true nature, the more she despised him. An institution? Not because he was concerned over her health, but because he felt her slipping away from him. She could hear him now. *If she doesn't want me, she must be insane.* So she was trapped in her room by Thatcher's command.

"Tamsyn?" The doctor waited for her agreement.

She nodded at last, too weary to consider further options. "I understand."

"Very well." He bowed his head in farewell. "I'll be here often to make sure your recovery continues."

"Yes, Doctor."

He left her room, closing the door behind him.

Finally, a voice of reason. Someone in this place who did not follow the orders of Thatcher Winslow. Tamsyn smiled with genuine pleasure at finding an unexpected co-conspirator. It was wonderful to find someone willing to help her, as it had become more than apparent Angus MacKiernan could not.

Agreeing to send her to an institution on the mainland? What was her father thinking? And was Clara's report to be believed? Was Thatcher behind all those acts of sabotage? Thatcher had done everything possible to place Angus in such a precarious position; he had no choice but to do whatever Thatcher told him. The extent of Thatcher's grip on her life was just now becoming clear, as if there was a huge net hanging over her, becoming visible at last as it drew closer and closer.

She had to escape from him, somehow, and for now, this plan gave her some time to consider her options. There were certainly worse things than being in this room for several weeks.

But Drake...

She'd have to send word to Drake, warn him to stay away for her sake as well as his. Clara would carry a note for her, she was sure. Weeks with nothing to do but think. And that she would do, until she could find a way out of this horrible bargain she'd made. Her concerns about her responsibility to her father were slowly slipping away, however, now that she realized he was no better than Thatcher's lap puppy.

If you lie with dogs... They could both be damned!

Her willingness to adhere to the strict letter of her promise to her mother was beginning to slip as well. After all, she and her father had agreed to take care *of each other*. Angus was not living up to his promise. If it had been a shipper client of his not living up to his agreement, Angus would have cried, "Breach of contract," and abandoned his own duties under that worthless piece of paper. Surely he would expect no more duty from her.

Tamsyn rifled through the drawer of her nightstand until she found a calendar. Three weeks. The date was February 28, 1898, and Key West boiled with excitement. The time would go by quickly. She'd just have to entertain herself by gathering information about the battles the newspapers promised, in the waters off Cuba. That was where Drake's heart would be, and she at least could follow along.

Newspapers would also hold advertisements for young women ready to strike out on their own. Anything was possible.

Chapter Fifteen

Drake sat in the stern of the dinghy, trailing his fingers in the warm water of the aquamarine bay. The *Raven* lay anchored off the east coast of the Yucatán, and he, Samuel, and two other sailors were bound for the mainland, rowing through a chain of emerald islands to get to the main village of Rio Lagartos.

The small fishing village would be perfect for his planned rendezvous. Not only was it out of the way of curious eyes on the sea, it actually provided some wonderful native hospitality. One of Freddie's favorite "hidden treasures," the raggedy community of Rio Lagartos, or River of Crocodiles, was comprised of twenty or thirty huts where the residents lived and several concrete block buildings which housed their various homegrown industries. Closest to the beach was a ramshackle cantina that served a passable homemade ale and the freshest shrimp empanadas on the coast, fried by a rail-thin octogenarian who was seldom seen. Patrons, however, were often astonished by her screaming obscenities from the kitchen.

Freddie used to say you couldn't trust a thin cook; I prefer to let my stomach make the rules. Delicious.

When they'd reached the shore, the three paused to let Drake disembark near the bar. The others intended to go farther along the river-like estuary to the small lake where literally thousands of gorgeous pink flamingos made their habitation. Various egrets, ibis, and other birds would also be there, Samuel had said when pleading his case to visit. Drake had lost track of all the species Samuel spouted. He just agreed that his first mate's fascination with birds would be well-fed this trip.

"No more than an hour spent wandering through the *guano*," he cautioned them. "You come back and retrieve me regardless of Samuel's obsession. We have things to do."

"Don't you worry, Captain, we'll be here." Samuel grinned. "Thanks to you for the opportunity to stop."

Drake helped them shove off, for several minutes, watching as they rowed away. *Important to keep the crew happy, and here, we're killing two birds with one stone.* He turned to go inside. *Maybe killing birds is a bad metaphor. No dead birds.*

He chuckled to himself, then walked up the sandy path to the open door of the cantina. The transition from sunny skies outside to shadowed cavern inside blinded him for a moment. He paused to adapt his vision.

"*Capitán* Ashton." A rough voice emanated from the far corner where a dim figure sat alone at a table.

Drake nodded in the speaker's direction and went to join him. The bartender brought Drake an ale in a tall glass. The one-room bar held a dusty collection of mismatched tables and chairs, decorated with a few rough-sewn curtains on the open windows. Flies buzzed lazily through the air. Three other men sat, scattered through the place. None of them even bothered to look up.

A quickly exchanged conversation in Spanish revealed that the speaker, Manuel Ortiz of Merida,

Mexico, had brought a cache of guns, ammunition, and medical supplies that Freddie had requested some months before. He was ready to be paid.

"*Cuanto?*"

The man just shrugged instead of stating how much. "It was difficult to obtain what your brother asked for. Is it true he's dead?"

"It is."

He studied the man, trying to guess if sympathy might buy him a lower quote, or if the fact no one could contradict him would drive the price even higher. *I wish Freddie had kept better records so I knew what in blazes I would obtain from his suppliers.* It wasn't an option to quibble with the man; Drake's camp needed the cache.

Drake withdrew his wallet, the one he'd replenished since his ride with Tamsyn MacKiernan in Key West, and removed several bills from it, placing them on the table. "*Es suficiente?*"

Ortiz shrugged again.

Drake laid two more bills down. He also waved a bill in the direction of the casually dressed bartender. "*Señor, dos cervezas más?*"

Ortiz relented and smiled. He laid a hand atop the bills and slid them off into his pocket.

"Where are my crates?" Drake asked.

The man pointed to the floor behind the thatched bar.

Drake stood and went to examine them. Several smaller ones were stacked atop a long, rectangular one that held the rifles and shotguns. It was a good cache. The fighters of Matanzas would be pleased. He resealed the lids and straightened up.

A jolly laugh boomed from the doorway. "Have you taken to serving ale and rum to fund your little insurrection, Ashton?" The heavyset, sandy-haired man wearing a bright red shirt, dark pants, and a rakish hat ducked inside, barely avoiding knocking the hat off.

"Surely you jest." Drake stepped out from behind the bar. He laughed and embraced the man who'd been one of his and Freddie's heroes since they'd learned to sail. "What hells have you been traversing, Gavril? Clearly, they are filled with trays of food. I can't even reach around you any longer!"

"A long time without companionship of the female persuasion, Ashton. I must indulge my carnal lusts in some manner, true?" He chuckled.

Drake led the newcomer to the table where Ortiz remained, drinking his second ale. "Manuel Ortiz, Captain Gavril Rupert, skipper of the *Hawk.*"

"Señor," Ortiz mumbled. He gulped down the rest of his drink and excused himself, double-checking his pocket to make sure his money was still there.

Gavril raised an eyebrow. "Didn't mean to frighten away your drinking companion, my friend."

Drake shook his head. "Our business was concluded. Or rather, Freddie's business." He gestured to the bartender, holding up his glass and nodding to Gavril. The bartender took his time bringing the ale.

"Ah, yes, Freddie." Gavril's pale blue eyes moistened with tears. "I was so sorry to hear what happened to your brother, Drake. He was a good man."

Drake nodded. "I miss him every day. I also renew my vow to skewer the Spanish at any turn. Every day."

"Good. So your hold will be loaded?" Gavril asked.

"I've made two stops plus this one. We should be welcomed in Matanzas, that is for certain." He finished the liquid in his own glass, regretting the quality of the home brew. *Still, it's better than the local water.* "I trust you've been equally successful?"

"Indeed we have. And is it true what I hear about imminent American involvement in the war effort?"

"From all I can see." Drake shared his sighting of the USS *Maine*, and other bits of fact and rumor he'd gathered in Key West. "Certainly, it makes our effort less central to the removal of the Spanish from the island. Let them take the heavy hits. We can assist on the ground."

Gavril took a swig of ale. "Every bit will help. What have you done to replace the *Blackbird* in your plans?"

"That's where I hoped you'd come in. The *Hawk* is a sturdy clipper. We could use your support."

Two of the other patrons left without acknowledging them.

Gavril studied the room. "Haven't been here before. It's a damn sight better than trekking all the way inland to Merida."

"Exactly."

The important items checked off his to-do list, Drake let his mind wander a bit. He didn't have to watch and worry, like he did in some Mexican ports, that someone would rob him. These honest, hardworking people. Both he and Freddie had experienced this. Of course, when his thoughts were released from tight control, they went the one place they'd always gone of late: Tamsyn. He replayed their carriage ride through the cemetery in his mind, enjoying every expression on her face.

Some time later, Gavril elbowed him in the ribs. "Drake. Where are you, man?"

"My apologies." Embarrassed, he fumbled with his glass.

Gavril eyed him for a long moment, then chuckled. "No. It's not possible. Is it? Can it be that a woman has snaked her way into that well-protected heart?"

"Gavril, please—"

"It is." The two words were underlined with ironic import. "Who is she? Where is she? Is she one of your Matanzas rebels?"

Drake's jaw tightened. *So what now? Gavril's going to take over Freddie's brotherly derision of any potential relationship?* "It doesn't matter. She's engaged to marry. So how I think about her is irrelevant."

Gavril's grin spread wider. "She's a society lass, then? Surely you wouldn't be so complacent about a Cuban village woman. You'd persuade her with just a flash of those sparkling eyes, a flex of those manly muscles. No, this one really does matter. Tell me why?"

Drake growled and concentrated on the view out the open window. "Can we not discuss my love life, please?" He eyed his companion. "Are you so starved for female company that you have to listen to the details of others' conquests? Loving only vicariously through the lives of others?"

"Alas, 'tis true." Gavril laughed, not insulted in the least. "Besides, I have experienced considerably less heartache remaining at a distance from love. It makes sailing away from so many ports a joyous occasion, rather than a sad one."

"Better to have loved and lost?"

"We're not talking about me, Drake. We're talking about you."

"I told you, she's engaged. There are obstacles—"

"Boy, there is nothing that you ever truly desired that you let get away. Not one thing." He studied Drake thoughtfully. "You're the one who must take action. Your life is in your hands."

My hands? Ha!

Right now, I'm responsible for and to so many other people, my friends in Matanzas, my crew, Freddie's crew, my brother's memory. Adding Tamsyn to the list feels cruel. If she had anyone else who would stand up to protect her, perhaps I could avoid that duty right now. But she doesn't.

I've got to save her, too, somehow. She deserves it.

But more than that pulls me to her. She doesn't seem right in that society, like she's born into the wrong place or time. She's well-read, she loves to study nature, she loves the sea—all the things I enjoy. We are destined to be together; I can feel it.

I just have to find the correct path to make it happen.

Gavril cleared his throat. "I envy you, my friend." He left the table in search of *los baños,* stopping to order a steaming plate of empanadas from the cook in the back of the hut on his way. Even listening to New Englander Gavril totally mutilate his conversation in Spanish failed to cheer Drake.

First, I must get to Matanzas and deliver this shipment, to make sure my people are safe. What the Spanish will do to them is worse than Tamsyn's semi-protected life. Winslow is a bastard, but he won't hurt her openly with the eyes of the upper class on him as this wedding closes in. I have a small amount of leeway. Very small.

Then I'll come for her.

By the time Gavril and the meat pies arrived, Drake had set his plan in his mind. It might just be possible to have everything he wanted.

Maybe.

Moving on, he grinned at Gavril, then picked up one of the crusty pastries, pausing to inhale its spicy aroma before he sank his teeth into it. "So, Gavril, let's make it our mission to get you a woman!"

Chapter Sixteen

Tamsyn experienced the buildup of the Cuba theater of the Spanish-American War secondhand, as she kept her promise to the doctor to remain in her room. Daily reports filled the newspapers, sharing the wrath and fury of the American people at the senseless deaths of the sailors aboard the *Maine*, and more about the atrocious deeds of the Spanish on land and sea, and these Tamsyn devoured with great fervor. She felt almost as if she had a personal stake in the matter because of the story Drake had shared with her, and her knowledge of his contribution to the revolution of the Cuban people.

The US plan, according to various reports in Key West's five newspapers, was to blockade the island of Cuba, cutting off the Spanish ships which would supply them with guns and food. Cuban nationals, with the support of American troops, the papers said, would then rally and free themselves of Spanish tyranny. It was likened to the American fight for independence, which spurred people further in their patriotic support.

For days at a time, nothing seemed to advance the conflict, with troop departures repeatedly delayed from the swarming ports. As forces began to collect in Key West, the fresh water supply dwindled. Fresh water had always been a problem on the island, surrounded as it was by salt water, which is why most houses had a complicated system of gutters and downspouts which saved rainwater and sent it underground to cisterns. But the overuse took everything from the wells.

The navy finally arranged to send in barges full of water from the North, which was shared between soldiers and townspeople.

News reports were supplemented by intercepted telegraph messages from the Spanish on Cuba to their homeland and replies to those desperate missives, and the press reported various orders given to the navy to cut those telegraph cables, further hampering the Spaniards' efforts.

"What can the Papists expect, when their supply base is four thousand miles away?" Thatcher gloated during one of his first daily visits. "They are sitting ducks without the direct support of their *amigos.*"

Tamsyn wished she could just ignore him, but it didn't seem to matter how she reacted. He made a pointed effort to visit each day, taking the opportunity to interrogate her further about her whereabouts the night of the engagement celebration. She declined to answer any further, which just infuriated him.

Maybe if I upset him enough, he'll let go.

But he never did.

He also hated when she offered her opinion of the political situation, so she contributed it freely. "Cuba may be four thousand miles from Spain, but it's only eighty miles from here. It is no wonder the government will use Key West as a launching point."

"Regardless of what the overcrowding at the port does to our businesses!" Thatcher complained, frowning.

Despite Thatcher's grumbles, the news came that

volunteers wanting to fight had signed up with such keen enthusiasm, that their numbers had been underestimated. Early regiments were quartered in Key West and the Dry Tortugas to the southwest, but more came still. So many came, that the navy was forced to hire transport ships to bring the troops to Key West for assignment.

Angus MacKiernan was one of the shipowners who reaped a temporary golden harvest, as some of his inactive ships were commandeered for use by the navy, at a handsome fee. Thatcher Winslow went so far as to say that the war was the best investment his father's company had made, as they managed to lease half a dozen ships to transport troops to their destinations.

Everyone who stopped by Tamsyn's room was questioned for any bit of news: Had more troops arrived? Were there new ships in the harbor? Had anyone else they knew joined up?

Thatcher was, sadly, her most frequent guest, and Tamsyn suspected her father was being forced to keep others away. Her fiancé sang the praises of the war to such an extent that, one day, Tamsyn flatly asked him why he didn't join one of the regiments drilling by the harbor.

"A regiment?" he asked incredulously. "My dear Tamsyn, I could never consider such a thing. Business is booming. My father needs me to help him manage the shipping company." He squeezed her hand and leaned over to steal a sloppy kiss before she could avoid him. "Besides, I wouldn't want to leave you alone. That Ashton fellow might spirit you away while I was off liberating Cuban peasants."

She didn't respond, thinking what she knew of

Drake dictated he would be doing what he could to liberate the Cubans, whether there was a profit involved or not.

After the initial hubbub about her disappearance and return, Tamsyn had attempted to send a note via Clara to Drake on the *Raven*. The girl had gone to the harbor three days in a row and finally returned with the gloomy news that the *Raven* had left the harbor several days after that glorious sail under the full moon. No one knew, or at least no one would tell Clara, why he'd gone so suddenly or when he might be back.

So, Tamsyn was relegated to her confinement without hope of Drake Ashton appearing to brighten her day or help her escape from her prison.

After she'd been bedridden for nearly a week, Clara popped her head around the door one afternoon to see if she was sleeping. When she saw that Tamsyn was not, she stepped out, and Norah Brennan came in.

"Norah!" Tamsyn was so glad to see a friendly face, she leapt out of bed and hugged her neighbor until Norah had to wiggle away to catch a breath.

Clara held her finger to her lips as she tucked Tamsyn back under her light sheets, then slipped away. "What's the mystery about?" Tamsyn asked Norah.

"I made Clara sneak me up when no one was looking. I'm just dying to know what really happened to you. The neighborhood is buzzing, what with the constabulary here until nearly midnight the other night, and Thatcher Winslow talking all over town about your delusions." Norah peered closely at Tamsyn. "You look all right to me."

"There's nothing wrong with me that—" She was about to say, "that an ocean cruise wouldn't cure," but realized it was not something which should be openly discussed. "There's nothing wrong with me. Thatcher is the one with delusions." *There, that should add fuel to the rumor fires...*

Norah raised an eyebrow. "So, were you really kidnapped?"

Tamsyn nodded. Seeing the sparkle in the Irish girl's eye, she almost told her the truth, knowing she'd appreciate the lark. But concern for Drake made her hold her tongue. Instead, she shared the tale she'd told the constable.

Norah's eyes grew wide as she listened. "And you managed to escape and just walk back home, willy-nilly as you please? They must have been stupid kidnappers!"

Tamsyn sighed. Norah knew her too well. "Maybe it was their first time. I don't know. I'm just glad to be home. Even if I have to stay in my room."

"I wish I could stay alone in my room." Norah smoothed her gray skirt under her as she sat in a chair near Tamsyn's bed. "Pleading a visit to you was the only way Mamma would let me leave the children for an hour. I swear they're making me crazy."

"Do you hear anything new of the war?" Too late, she remembered that Brian Hamilton had been assigned to the *Maine*—he had probably been lost. She hadn't intended to bring up any bad memories for her friend, who'd been kind enough to come cheer her. "I'm sorry about Brian."

"Brian?" Norah looked puzzled for a moment, then shook her head as her face broke into a smile. "Brian wasn't on the ship."

"What? I thought you said—"

Norah's eyes sparkled as she pulled a sheaf of papers from her black, knitted reticule. "I received several letters from Brian, all at once. He'd remained behind in Washington as assistant to a navy officer who was ill and unable to travel on the *Maine*." She leafed through the papers, her red head bent over the worn pages and smeared ink that Norah must have read many times. "He says he loves me, and he wants me to marry him when he returns!"

"Norah, how wonderful." She reached for her friend's hand. "When will he be here? Does he say?"

"He plans to return by midsummer."

The happy silence they shared, buoyed by the glow reflected in each other's eyes at the thought of Norah's joy, was broken by the sound of the streetcar passing outside and the cries of Norah's siblings as they waved and called to those riding in it.

"I trust you shall invite me to your wedding," Tamsyn teased.

"Of course, I will, dear one." Norah settled back into her chair comfortably.

"What does your mother say of his request?"

Norah shrugged. "I think she is of divided mind. I believe she thinks it time I married, but she is reluctant to lose the second mother for the children."

"She'll learn to live with it. How old is Bridget now?" Tamsyn tried to remember all the Brennan children in order. All she could remember was that Bridget was the next in line.

"She's twelve. High time for her to take on some more responsibility." Norah smiled. "What about your wedding, Tamsyn? When does the doctor believe you will be well enough to have the ceremony?"

Never! was the retort that came to mind. But that answer would hardly be appropriate under her circumstances. "He hasn't said," she replied. *Well, that's true at least. I can still hope it will never come to pass...*

Clara, eyes wide, suddenly flew in the door and tugged at Norah's arm. "Please, Missy Norah, you must go. Marse Thatcher is comin'!"

Tamsyn echoed Clara's concern. "Oh, thank you so much for visiting. Please try to come again." They exchanged a quick, sisterly kiss and hug, and then Clara spirited Norah away. Thatcher entered several minutes later without remarking on Tamsyn's prior visitor, so Tamsyn had to assume Clara had been successful.

Thatcher had a small basket filled to the brim with fresh fruits, golden pears, ripe oranges, and even several polished red apples. "How is my girl today?" he asked. "Some color in your cheeks, I see." His eyes narrowed. "Have you been out of bed? You know what the doctor said."

"No, Thatcher. Actually, I've been reading for quite a while, and I'm very sleepy just now." She snuggled down into her pillow. "You wouldn't mind, would you?" She allowed her eyes to close, listening intently to make sure he didn't approach her. He didn't. After a few minutes, as she slowed her breathing as if she'd fallen asleep, he snorted and left the room without saying anything further.

As her door closed behind him, she allowed herself a tiny smile.

She had other sources of information in the days that came and went. As her father's clerk Timothy heard snippets of news, he'd run upstairs and share them with her, as socially inappropriate as it might be for a man to be in a girl's bedroom. She'd insisted she wanted him to come; he just had to avoid Thatcher and Angus. One such afternoon as March continued, he popped in with the news that Congress was discussing the possibility of officially declaring war on Spain.

"Finally, some real action!" Enthusiasm overcame his normal reticence.

"Aren't you worried about being killed?" she asked. "What do you know about war, Timothy Franklin?" All she could envision was his lifeless body on a field in Cuba as the battle raged around him, hardly taking notice of his noble sacrifice.

Or anyone else I know who's involved...

"We're not going to be earnestly fighting, Tamsyn," he said, blue eyes suddenly serious. "The Cubans are revolting against the oppression of the Spanish. The bloody Papists control everything! They sit as the judges of the courts, they make every government decision—the Cubans are taxed much more harshly than our colonies were a hundred years ago. They should be throwing tobacco over the sides of the boats in the harbor and declaring themselves independent, as we did." He strutted around the room as he spoke, waving his hands for emphasis. "We'll just be there to inspire them, as the French came to help us during our own revolution."

"I hope you're right," she said. As the days passed, she watched from her window, and as the activity increased, she found it hard to believe any good would come of the war.

As the city became overwhelmed by the influx of soldiers and sailors preparing to ship out for Cuba, the residents found their businesses slowing to a crawl. Army traffic congested the streets, and soldiers with nothing but time on their hands accosted women around town and spent much too much time in the taverns.

Angus spent much of each day raving at anyone who happened to cross his path, having exhausted the money he'd taken in from the navy in short shrift. It was the end of April, and President McKinley had finally declared war on the Spanish.

These had been long, sad weeks for Tamsyn, too, as she went without word of Drake Ashton. If it had been frustrating to be bedridden for three weeks, unable to gather information except through the bits and pieces received from visitors, it was ten times so to be able to go out (when Angus wasn't watching her like a hawk) and still not receive the slightest bit of information. The port was packed with soldiers and sailors coming in, purchasing and storing supplies, and taking up space with their cannon, horses, mules, and camp equipment, causing shortages which made the residents unhappy.

Finally, those ready for war began to receive orders to Tampa, Mobile, and Jacksonville. Timothy Franklin and the other 125,000 volunteers who were part of the patriotic frenzy born of the *Maine*'s demise were assigned to their ships, many of them having never fired a weapon in their lives. The newspapers, however, inspired by William Randolph Hearst and Joseph Pulitzer, continued to blare jingoistic headlines, seeming to try to outdo each other's sensationalism.

The advent of the uniformed men who seemed to have such a heroic purpose galvanized others on the island to enlist on the spot, anxious to demonstrate the new American enthusiasm for the Monroe Doctrine:

that Europeans would not hold land in the Americas against the will of the natives, and that "our boys" would teach them a thing or two if they didn't abdicate their holdings.

By mid-May, the forces congregated from the alternative sites and prepared to sail for Cuba, satisfied with blockading no longer.

For the most part, Tamsyn stayed at home and worried about the lack of news. Knowing Drake Ashton's strong feelings about the Spanish, she couldn't imagine he had stayed out of the conflict. He had been aware of his chances if he was captured by the Spaniards, but she was sure those odds had not kept him from his revenge. The thought of losing him stabbed her, sharp as any knife, whenever she thought of it. As the days passed, her heart ached at the possibility that he had been captured or killed, and she would never see him again.

As her hope for Drake's safety died, she found it harder to combat the pressure Thatcher exerted to set a date for the wedding once again. At least when she'd had the happy thought that she might see her beloved Drake in a day or a week, she could deal with the despair of being trapped into a loveless marriage.

Finally, Thatcher asked one too many times as they strolled in the courtyard, and Tamsyn shot back an angry answer. "No, Thatcher, I do not want to set a date for the wedding!"

Thatcher scowled. "Please, my dear, lower your voice. What will the neighbors think?"

"They'll think that I am distraught over the advent of the war, and all our friends who have gone to fight and die for others' freedom!"

Thatcher stared at her. "I suppose you mean Ashton." The frozen temperature of his voice snapped in sharp contrast to the summer breeze.

She stopped and turned to look at him. "I can't believe you're still obsessed with this subject. What is the matter with *you*?" Backing several steps away, she continued, "I mean Timothy, and Brian Hamilton, and Francis from the meat market, and the thousands of others. I'm sure none of your vaunted friends are put out in the least, but other men, men I know, are jumping into this fight, and they'll die! As long as this war is being fought, I find I have no enthusiasm for my own petty frivolity."

Thatcher was struck dumb. He took several steps away from her, shaking his head. At last, he said, "Frivolity? That's what you call our vows, the words which will seal you to me until death parts us?" Tamsyn couldn't suppress the shiver that ran down her spine at the tone he imparted to the word "death."

"Frankly, I think it's just what the town needs, a little distraction to remind us that there is more to life than just this cursed war," he finished.

She stalked away from him. His footsteps hurried up behind her. He grabbed her arm. "I'll tell my mother we wish to set the date as soon as possible," he hissed. "I don't like the look in your eyes, my dear. Even if all the guests she invited cannot come, I think we do not dare delay the ceremony more than a week or two." He reached around and tipped her chin up so she had to look at him. "Then you shall be mine."

Tamsyn fought to keep her expression frozen, not to betray her revulsion at his touch. When she didn't reply, he dropped his hands and walked away. He

221

barked orders to his carriage driver, and the wheels rattled on the cobbled street as they drove away. From that moment, she knew the time remaining for her freedom was limited.

Chapter Seventeen

At the time of Timothy's flag-waving speech, Drake wasn't worried about inspiration. He was dashing through the humid jungle on the outskirts of Matanzas, Cuba, carrying a small boy, dragging his wailing mother by the hand, taking them to the safety of a waiting boat.

Others dashed before him and after him, crashing through the deep, green underbrush. Some uttered prayers under their breaths, as Drake did, that they could save these families from the Spaniards. No shots pursued them so far; that was the first good thing that had happened the whole day.

The woman tripped and fell. As he helped her up, Drake regretted that the sinking of the *Maine* had precipitated events here much more quickly than he had anticipated.

He'd waited several days after leaving Tamsyn off on shore—*against my better judgment*—to hear she'd returned home safely. As the *Raven* prepared to lift anchor, a battered ship limped into port, crewed mostly by Cuban sailors. It was the *Mariposa*, captained by Franco Ordonez, a man with whom Drake had done business for many years, supplying his constituents with the needs of war.

Drake, with the rest of his crew, solemnly took note as the *Mariposa* docked, its wooden sides splintered by cannon fire, one mast snapped in half, hanging pitifully on the lines. Even the townspeople conducting business along the waterfront stopped to look at the wounded ship, as stretchers started coming off the gangplank.

José de la Tierra, one of Drake's most trusted officers, was a distant cousin of Ordonez and was the first to reach the ship when it docked. Drake found him in the spartan captain's cabin speaking with a bedridden, blood-spattered Ordonez. Both men were white-faced with anger.

"Captain, we must go to Matanzas immediately," José said. "The Spanish have gathered outside Havana and plan to sweep through the countryside."

"Your wife and children are in danger," Drake said. "They all are. It doesn't make sense, though. Why would the Spanish attack Matanzas instead of engaging the Americans?"

Ordonez sat forward on his bed. "Word traveled through the city that the rebels have gathered there, ready to launch a wave of the insurrection." He shrugged. "In reality, the men have left the camp to join freedom fighters in Santiago. The families are alone and defenseless, except for some older boys and *los viejos*."

"What of the weapons we brought?"

"Some remain," Ordonez admitted, in a gravelly voice. "Most of them the rebels took as their contribution to the cause."

Drake's heart told him he must go immediately. But his head intervened. *We can't take on the whole Spanish Army to maintain a single village. What can we do?* "We could evacuate the families," he said at last.

"Our two or three ships could hardly defeat a whole battalion. If we go quickly, perhaps we can arrive before the Spanish."

Ordonez nodded, his hatred evident in the dark of his eyes. "My ship will be of little worth as it sails this day. But any of my men or supplies that can help are yours."

"Thank you, Captain. We will do you proud."

Drake and José returned to the *Raven*, where he gave orders to be underway in an hour. The crew went through normal pre-sailing routine, checking supplies, fastening loose objects in place, and making room for a dozen or more sailors from the *Mariposa*. As those sailors spread word about the attack on their ship, Drake's own men pitched in with a sense of urgency.

At the last minute, he fought with a small voice nagging him. *What about Tamsyn?* He had no time to do more than send her a message. She'd understand. After all, she was the one who'd insisted on going home; she must have anticipated she would be welcomed back by her father, no worse for the wear. He couldn't prioritize her now. She would understand that, too.

Unable to spare a member of his crew to take a letter to her, he ran down the gangplank and grabbed the shoulder of a boy who was admiring the ships at anchor.

"I have a very important task for you, young man," Drake said, squatting down so he was eye level with the towheaded child, who must have been ten or eleven years old. "Can you carry a note for me to an address in town?"

The boy, thin and not often included in exciting

events, was thrilled to help a dashing, young sea captain. "Certainly, sir!" He grabbed the proffered note and the coin in the other hand and rushed down the street toward the destination the captain had requested.

Drake, relieved he'd had the opportunity to warn Tamsyn he'd be gone, climbed back up onto the *Raven* and made his final launch. The ship sailed away from the port in midafternoon, bound for Matanzas.

What he did not know was that as the messenger boy rushed along his way, he ran in front of a carriage traveling at a high rate of speed. The horses shied, and the boy fell, being struck in the head by a flailing hoof. The message he had clutched in his hand flew into the air and floated down into a sewer grate. The boy would recover, but his memory of the message and the handsome man sending it never returned.

****

The heat was oppressive under the trees where the air didn't move. Drake wiped sweat from his brow. The child held tight to Drake's neck, huge dark eyes ever watchful, as if he knew something unusual and important was happening. Drake urged the woman onward. They'd come farther than he expected, and they soon burst from the tree line onto the beach, where the scene was mass confusion.

Whatever belongings the villagers had been able to carry were loaded onto the *Raven*, including food and some water in sacks. Baskets filled with clothing sat beside crying infants and tubs of papayas. Women milled around the bottom of the gangplank and clutched each other for support. *Los viejos*, the old men, valiantly strove to carry loads as they would have in their younger years, their pride stung by the strong young sailors working around them. Mateo organized stacks of provisions to be loaded, Drake noticed, but also took time to comfort some of the smaller children who were obviously overwhelmed, silent tears running down their cheeks.

"Mateo!" Drake gestured to the cabin boy. When the boy came, eyes alert and stance ready, Drake handed him the child and put him in charge of the woman as well. *That boy is an angel in disguise.* He then turned to supervising the loading, knowing they had limited time. José and some others had scouted out the other side of the hill beyond the camp. The Spanish were coming.

"*Andale, amigos!*" Drake called to his mixed crew, a wary eye on the edge of the jungle, expecting to be attacked at any moment. He'd noticed the sudden silence of the birds, most likely disturbed by some further movement yet to be discovered behind them. As the provisions were finally stowed, he set his sailors to herd the women forward, keeping children and mothers together. The old men followed the women.

About half the refugees had been safely hunkered down below deck when the tree line lit up with guns blazing.

Drake cursed his luck. "*Vamos! Adelante!*" he shouted, but the remaining people didn't need his encouragement. Their panic was obvious, as they shoved and clawed at each other trying to board.

"Mamma!" came a clear voice from the deck. Drake looked up and spotted Mateo, face anguished. He spun around to spy Mateo's mother, Leta, running back toward the camp. *Now what was she thinking?* Satisfied the refugees were nearly loaded, Drake ran after the woman.

"*Mammacita!*" he cried. He ran in a zigzag path, trying to dodge bullets which whistled past him. "Senora! *Por favor!*" The woman ignored him, and just as he reached her, she was hit, tumbling to the ground. Fire stabbed between his left ribs and his underarm.

He fell to the sand and crawled to her side. "Senora!" He shook her, but she was clearly dead. *Damnation...* What could have been so important she had to run back for it?

Not that I'll find out, considering...

He tried to sit up, and found his shirtfront soaked in blood. Muttering apologies, he took Leta's shawl and wound it tightly around his ribs. His side stabbed with pain at each breath. He struggled to his knees. Mateo ran toward him, followed by five men.

"Go back!" Drake cried. "Get ready to sail!"

But they were nearly to him before they realized he hadn't been killed and Leta had. By then, a burst of Spanish fire had taken out two of the *Mariposa*'s men and Alberto, the *Raven*'s assistant purser. Their staring dead eyes accused him as they hit the ground. The other men collapsed as well, but only to avoid bullets as they crawled forward on their elbows to reach their fallen captain. The boy embraced Leta's corpse, sobbing.

Wrenching himself up with a supreme effort, Drake got woozily to his feet and grabbed the boy's arm. "Come on, Mateo, *querido.* We can do nothing more for her."

When the youth would not move, Drake growled at the men to bring him along, knowing his own strength was ebbing. "Boy, I'm saving your life whether you want me to or not."

Two men pulled the youth away, practically dragging him back to the *Raven*. Drake followed, staggering several paces behind, leaning on the last man's shoulder, scanning the shore to see if they'd left anyone else. As the rescuers hit the gangplank, Drake felt a sharp punch to his left leg just above the ankle, and it gave out beneath him, pitching him into the sand.

A cry came from the ship, and footsteps thunked down the wooden gangplank. He was unceremoniously hauled up onto the deck and propped, at his unsteady direction, against the mainmast. The sounds of the battle faded. The pain made it difficult to focus, so he was glad to see the crew pull up the plank and get underway without his direct command.

Despite the men's efforts to stay low, several were wounded by Spanish bullets as they raised the sails, none seriously, if his eye was accurate. The sails snapped to in the wind, and the ship moved away from shore briskly. While the shooting continued, it soon became clear they were out of range, and no ships had appeared to follow them. They were safe.

Samuel, José, and others who were unharmed moved among the injured, assessing the severity and extent of damage. The old men and some of the women who had experience treating injuries came up from belowdecks to cleanse and bandage wounds.

Though Samuel had come to Drake first, the captain had ordered his men be treated before himself, accepting some bandage material to tend his injuries. The bullet to his left side had apparently scored both his arm and chest, causing two wounds. By squeezing some clean linen between them, he could effect direct pressure on both. The leg—that was another matter.

Blood gushed over the top of his boot, and he could feel nothing.

"How do we stand?" he called to Samuel as the first mate finished his round of the deck.

Samuel shrugged and nodded, counting off on his fingers as he spoke. "Could be worse. We lost seven men—six on the beach and one on board." Looking over his shoulder, he verified his count. "Half a dozen with bullet wounds, some bruises, but I think the rest will live." Samuel's hazel eyes narrowed. "Now, you need help."

Drake nodded, reluctantly gesturing toward his left boot. A huge gash had been ripped in it by the bullet that hit him, and blood continued to dribble, pooling on the deck under his ankle. "Let's get it off."

Samuel waved Chaney over with some fresh bandages. "All right, Drake, hold on." He eased the boot off, and Drake saw his face freeze in consternation. "Mary, Mother of God," he said.

"What?" Chaney leaned forward to get a better look, then paled and closed his eyes.

Mateo appeared, alerted from wherever he'd been by their tone. *That boy has a sixth sense for danger.* The boy knelt down near Drake and took his hand. *Must be bad...*

Samuel's Adam's apple convulsed before he spoke. The motion seemed slower than normal, and as he looked around, Drake felt like everything seemed to be off-kilter. He realized he was drifting into unconsciousness. He slapped himself on the cheek, the sound surprising the others. *I've got to get control...*

"The bullet's still in your leg," Samuel said.

"Well, we'll have to take it out," Drake replied. He

was distracted and confused by the sight of the women on deck. *When had they picked up women as crew? No. That wasn't right.* "Wait a minute," he said. "Where are we taking these people?"

"To Andros Island." Samuel looked at him curiously. "As we planned."

Drake nodded. "Good." Samuel and Chaney exchanged a glance, then Samuel stood up.

"Let's get him below," he said.

Even with a fourth man helping, it was difficult to descend the narrow steps when one of his legs was useless. The space was too constricted, one body passing at a time, so it was impossible to prop him up under the one shoulder. Drake faded in and out during the process, cursing inwardly at his lack of fortitude.

The next hour was a blur of excruciating pain. The men held him still while Samuel worked. Rum flowed freely, which dulled agony's edge after a while. In his mind's eye, he was in the cove at Key West, an extremity injured by a foreign object, and gentle hands held his to remove a sea urchin's spine. "Bring Tamsyn," he mumbled, liquor fully taking effect. "I need her."

"What in blazes for? No time for lollygagging with the ladies now. We're in enough trouble, Captain." Samuel, hands shaking, wiped the blood from his fingers and climbed off the bed. "It's the best I can do. You need a doctor."

"No," he said. "No doctor. Looking for me. Fool stunt, bringing her on board." He chuckled, his tongue tripping over his words. "It was fun, though, wa'nt it?"

Samuel couldn't smile. "I hope it was worth it." His face was nearly drained of blood.

Mateo pulled at Samuel's sleeve. "Please, what is 'nurse'?"

" 'Nurse'? A nurse is a medical person. Someone who's trained to…oh." He eyed Mateo.

"*El capitán,* he say this woman is nurse. If no doctor can come, maybe she would."

Drake half listened, the pain blotting out some of the words. But it sounded promising. "Yes. Send for her."

Samuel's face took on a grim aspect. "I suppose it can't hurt. Mateo, you stay with the captain and let me know if he needs anything."

The boy nodded and took up a position next to the bed. He fussed over Drake, making him take sips of lukewarm water and asking him every few minutes if there was anything he needed. Drake asked for a pen and paper, intending to write a note to be sent to Tamsyn, but he was too drunk and light-headed to complete it. The trauma and the alcohol combined to overcome his will, and his consciousness mercifully faded to black.

Chapter Eighteen

Despite Thatcher's impatience to get the wedding over with, Mrs. Winslow was in no hurry to inconvenience those for whom she'd planned such a show, so life continued as it had, though in a more strained mode.

Tamsyn was in the kitchen one day in late May with the servants, preparing baskets of food and medical supplies to send down to the docks, when Clara came rushing in the back door. When the dark-skinned girl saw others present, she skidded to a halt. The sudden movement and sudden stop caught Tamsyn's eye, as did Clara's obvious agitation.

Curious, Tamsyn quickly finished packing the last items in the baskets directly in front of her and sent the waiting boys on their way. As soon as they were gone, Tamsyn turned to a fidgeting Clara. "What is it?"

Clara took several steps forward, drew out a crumpled paper from her pocket, and handed it to Tamsyn. Clara's eyes were huge in her face, and she was obviously terrified.

Tamsyn, further alarmed by Clara's reaction, grabbed the paper and laid it on the table in front of her, smoothing it until it could be read. The sun shone through the kitchen window, brightly illuminating the note. The ink was faded and smeared, but the message was readable. The words made her heart skip several beats:

> *You must come to the cove at once. The captain*
> *has been badly wounded and needs your help.*
> *Samuel*

Trembling so hard she had to clutch the edge of the table for stability, she asked, "Where did you get this?"

Clara backed away and burst into tears. "I sorry, Missy Tamsyn! The man say give it to you, but I don't know what it say. I don't want to hurt you."

Tamsyn turned to the girl and smiled as warmly as she could manage. "Clara, I'm not angry. It is very important that I know who sent this message."

The girl calmed herself and said, "A man came to me when I was coming up de street. He ask me to give this paper to you and not to no one else. He say it a matter of life and death. Be you going to die, Missy Tamsyn?" Clara wiped her face as more tears threatened.

"No, not at all!" Tamsyn reassured the girl with a quick hug while her thoughts leaped ahead. *When had the message been written? Was Drake still alive? How could she slip away?* For there was no question she would go. She'd been waiting to make an escape—here was her golden opportunity.

"Clara, listen to me very carefully." She looked closely at the girl to make sure she heard every word. "It's my captain. He's been hurt and may die." The girl nodded, biting her lip as she tried hard to concentrate on Tamsyn's words. "I must go to him now. Have someone bring a carriage around to the alley. Call Old James, and tell him not to speak to anyone about it."

The girl smiled and scampered out the door. Tamsyn bolted for the stairs, mentally composing what she would need. In her room, she took a carpetbag from her closet and rummaged through her drawers, packing as many ordinary, useful clothes as she could fit. She also packed various medicinal remedies which were kept in a lockbox in her room, including a bottle of laudanum, and some carbolic spray her mother had stored in the medicine box. From the terse language of the note, she had no idea how severe the wounds might be or how long it might take Drake to recover, but she intended to stay as long as she was needed, without regard for the consequences.

As she packed brushes and lotions, stockings and shoes, she knew if she were gone more than a day, her reputation would be forfeit. Thatcher would break the engagement in a scandalous burst of temper, and her father would—what? Go bankrupt? Disown her?

It was disarming to suddenly realize she didn't care. She'd tried to be dutiful, just as long as she could. But his behavior in light of her horrible relationship with Thatcher had not reciprocated that duty, and he'd passed up any opportunity to report Thatcher's illegal acts to the police. She'd tried to discuss the situation with him, but he refused to take a position contrary to Thatcher's.

"I canna take the risk he'll carry through on his threats to harm ye, girl," he'd said the first time she asked.

"Papa, how can you let me marry him, knowing that he doesn't care for me at all?"

She could see his helplessness in his slumped shoulders and the shaking head. "I canna interfere," he said, and he refused any attempt to make him change his mind over the weeks that followed.

Tamsyn couldn't continue as a virtual prisoner in her own house, Thatcher controlling her every move. Angus had become Thatcher Winslow's puppet. Once a marriage took place, it would be the end of her.

No. I'm sorry, Mamma, but I can't do it.

As she sat for a final moment of meditation before she left, she felt a note of warmth inside and suddenly knew her mother would approve her escape.

Surveying her room one last time, she saw nothing she couldn't live without. She'd had a good life in this house, but she was ready to give it up.

Not wanting to alert her father, Tamsyn removed her shoes and quietly slipped down the stairs past his office. She hesitated for only a moment, listening to that once-loved voice give a tirade about Thatcher's interference in some shipping transaction, then she moved on through the kitchen and the courtyard to the alley, where Old James was waiting as she'd instructed.

He looked at her bag and back to her face, concern for her evident among his worn wrinkles. "Missy Tamsyn, you sho' you know what you doin'?"

She smiled. "I've never been more sure of anything in my life." She looked back at the house, at Clara standing nervously nearby. "Clara, you didn't see anything."

"No, ma'am." The girl appeared to be unsure whether she should laugh or cry.

Tamsyn took a deep breath. "Let's go."

His constant grumble a clear revelation of his disapproval, Old James took her to the cove. Tamsyn ignored him, her mind racing. *When had the note been written?* Tears caught in her throat. *Would the* Raven *still be there? Would Drake still be alive?* Her hands twisted in her lap as they rode down backstreets to avoid being seen.

It was an interminable twenty minutes to the beach, during which time all sorts of scenarios went through Tamsyn's head. The ship could be gone, Drake lost at sea by now. She could be followed by Thatcher's minions. Just the thought made her whip around in her seat to make sure no one was coming. She could arrive too late. *Please, not that,* she begged silently. *After I made him bring me home that night, he has to be all right...*

When they pulled up at the cove, Tamsyn jumped down from the carriage almost before it came to a stop. Kicking off her shoes, she ran out to the water. No one was on the beach as far as she could see. "Samuel!" Maybe he was just hidden for safety. "Samuel, I'm here!"

Old James, his arthritis giving him slow and deliberate movement, hobbled to the edge of the water after her, shaking his head. "Missy Tamsyn, what you be looking for out here?"

"He's got to be here," she muttered.

"Who dat?" he persisted.

She turned to the old man. "Do you see a ship?" she demanded.

He dutifully looked along the horizon, then shook his head. "Don't see nothin'."

Tamsyn shook her fists in frustration. *She couldn't have missed them!* Cursing fate, her father, and a number of other handy targets, she ran to the north, toward the place she'd first met Drake. Not watching where she was treading, she felt fleeting pain as she stepped on a shell or sharp-edged rock, but it didn't slow her down. "Samuel!" she called again. When there was no answer, she felt her throat constrict with tears.

She rounded the big rock, praying she'd find someone there, but the water and beach were unoccupied. Dejected, she stood leaning against the sharp-edged coral, feeling sick and empty.

Drake called for me, and I wasn't even able to help him.

As she turned to go back to the carriage, her fingers brushed against an object propped on a chink in the coral, knocking it into the water. It was an empty sea urchin shell.

Tamsyn bent to pick it up, wondering how it came to be on the rock. *The tide doesn't come that high.* Then she saw the note inside. Scrambling to remove the small paper before the ink faded in the water, she could barely make out the message.

We are watching for you. Wait there, and we shall come.

A wave of relief overcame her, and she nearly fell. *Thank the stars.* "Old James! Old James! They're coming." She returned to the puzzled coachman, giggling with glee. She took his arm, shaking it. "They're coming."

"Who coming?" His forehead wrinkled. He removed her hand from his arm and looked at her as if she were a lunatic. "What you doing out here, Missy Tamsyn?"

"He's called me," she said. "He's been hurt in the war and needs me."

"That…pirate?" His eyes opened wide with sudden realization. "Your father—"

"My father will hear nothing of this," she said,

voice sharp. She realized, at the look on his face, it couldn't have hurt him more if she'd slapped him. "Old James, please. You all know how unhappy I've been, the way Thatcher has behaved. My father..." She shrugged. *What was the use of trying to explain?*

"Marse Angus been worried 'bout his boats and his buildings," Old James said. "He don't take time to worry 'bout anything else."

"I don't think he does care about anything else," she said sadly.

Old James looked at her a minute, then shrugged. "Mayhap not, missy, mayhap not." He jerked his head toward the open sea. "You love this man?"

She nodded. "He loves me, too. He treats me well. I'm never as happy as when I'm with him."

The old man pursed his lips as he considered all she'd said. "Then it must be meant to be." He nodded and smiled in understanding. His gaze was caught by something over her shoulder. "Here they come."

Tamsyn turned around to see a small boat, some ten or twelve feet long, rowing along the shore toward them. *They must be anchored up the coast, waiting out of sight.* She waved, then ran back to the carriage to get her bag and her shoes, returning before Old James could get back to assist her. Anxiously, she waited for the boat to pull ashore.

"Remember, not a word, James." She nervously shifted from one foot to the other. Worries about Drake were foremost, but the hard reality of her decision and its consequences were beginning to sink in. Butterflies crept into her stomach at the thought of boldly leaving her home for the *Raven*.

"Yes'm," he said.

The boat keel dragged in the sand. The two men in it jumped out to hold it steady. James stepped in front of her slightly. "You be all right with dese men?"

Tamsyn smiled. "I'll be fine. Don't worry. Tell Juba—" Her throat caught at the realization she hadn't bid her "second mother" goodbye. *Well, I won't be gone forever.* "Tell Juba not to worry. She knows I'll be happy."

Old James nodded and stepped back as the swarthy men beckoned her forward. The ties to her former life slipped away with each step, as she ran forward, her skirt dripping with salt water, to climb into the boat.

Neither of the men were familiar; her stomach did a little hip-hop. The first handed her into the boat and secured her bag. The second launched the boat and jumped in as they cleared the sand. As he caught his balance, he spoke to her in Spanish.

"I'm sorry, I don't understand." She raised her hand to shade her eyes from the sun's reflection on the water. *"No comprendez."*

"I say, don't worry, pretty lady." The man smiled wide, and she smiled back, her fears dissolving.

"How is Drake?" she asked.

The man looked over her shoulder at his companion, his face solemn. When he didn't answer, she turned around so quickly the boat rocked. The men jerked sideways to try to compensate for her motion.

"How is he?" she asked the second sailor. "Is he dead?"

"Muerte? No, no, he's not dead," said the first man. "But he is very ill."

Then I'm not too late. "Where is the *Raven*?"

The first sailor jerked his head toward the north.

"There. Not far." They didn't speak further as the sailors' powerfully muscled arms pulled the oars and set them gently into the water. The current seemed to be with them. The little boat moved quickly through the waves. Tamsyn turned slightly just in time to spot the sails of the *Raven*.

When they came alongside, she saw the boy Mateo leaning over the side, waving at her. "Señorita, you came, you came!" He tossed a rope ladder down to the rocking boat. The two men in the boat held the trailing ends steady so she could climb up.

As the wind whipped her skirt, she hesitated, conscious of her modesty, but then realized the ladder was the only way to the deck where she'd find Drake. *Well, needs must...*

She'd never climbed a ladder like this before and found it a nerve-wracking experience. The "rungs" slid and folded under her feet as she stepped from one to another, making her footing tenuous. As the ship rocked, the ladder swayed, too. The rope was rough on her uncalloused hands. But she fired her determination and clambered steadily to the top, where hands reached to help her over the edge onto the deck.

Sailors dropped ropes with great hooks on the ends to retrieve the skiff as well. The men who had brought her climbed up a good deal quicker than she had, one carrying the handle of her bag across his shoulder. The men gathered around them, waiting for something to happen.

"Where's Drake?" Tamsyn asked Mateo, who had been waiting for her.

"This way, señorita." He took her hand and led her to the captain's quarters. The way was not as foreign as

Tamsyn remembered; she recalled making the trip up to the deck the night of the moonlight cruise.

Mateo knocked softly on Drake's door, without answer. He opened the door anyway, and Tamsyn was greeted with a stench of unwashed linens and foul air.

"This won't do," she said at once. "Open a window and let some air into this room!"

The boy hurried to do her bidding. Sunlight streamed in, allowing her to see the pale, white face like a cloud in a dark sky of hair spread out on the pillow. The man in the bed looked like death itself. "Drake," she whispered in horror.

She crossed the room and sat next to him on the bed, clutching his hand. *His skin was hot, so hot...* Some new bed linens would go far toward improving the smell and, likely, the cleanliness of Drake and his wounds.

"Mateo, I need clean water and fresh linens as soon as I can have them, please?"

The boy nodded gratefully. "He knew you would know what to do, señorita. I shall bring these things to you." He scurried away.

Tamsyn noted with approval he'd left the door open. A breeze passedthrough, dislodging the fetid air. *How long has he been shut up in here?*

Tamsyn had no formal medical training, but one of her household duties, taught to her by her mother, was the care of the servants. If there were any injuries or illnesses, it was the duty of the woman of the house to treat them, Ellen had always said. Tamsyn had grown up able to stomach the sight of blood, and not be overcome by the sight or smell of human waste products or vomit. She felt she was ready to deal with whatever injuries Drake may have suffered.

When she gently pulled down the sweat-drenched sheets, however, and saw the bloody wounds, her nerve deserted her. She gasped and turned away. *It was different when it was someone you loved. How can I...but who else will?*

Reluctantly, she assessed the damage, sending her consciousness into the same crisis mode which had possessed her the first day she'd met Drake. Delicate sensibilities had no place in nursing; the welfare of the patient came first.

Locating the several bandages which either Drake or his crew had placed, she found a wound on the underside of the left arm, and a corresponding laceration along the skin of the left rib. *Had Drake been shot?* She'd never seen a bullet wound before. If it was, the bullet must have come in at an angle between the two, tearing the skin in both places. Tamsyn winced at the amount of blood and effluvia soaked into the bandages. They needed changing badly. *Where was that boy?*

Pulling the sheet up from the foot of the bed, careful to avoid exposing any private parts, she saw the shin had taken a bullet as well. It was no longer lodged in his leg, but whoever had removed it had done a rough job. It was hard to tell now what had been original damage and what added on. Other bruises and scratches covered what she could see of his body, but those looked like the extent of the injuries.

It could be worse. The leg would take some time to recover, and certainly force a rehabilitation period. But the other wounds were less serious. A determined effort to keep them all clean would contribute much toward healing. She covered him with the sheet once again and leaned down close to his face.

"Drake?" she said softly. "Drake, it's Tamsyn. I'm here, love."

She watched for some sign he'd heard her. He stirred but didn't wake. She reached down and found his forehead as hot as his hand. He needed to be bathed in cool water, as soon as Mateo brought her supplies. *My dearest love, please don't leave me.*

Just as her patience was about to give out, the skinny boy limped back through the door, his arms full of cloth, followed by two other sailors carrying buckets. Tamsyn looked up in surprise.

"I didn't know if you'd need to hold him." The boy said it as if it were an apology. "When Samuel took the bullet from his leg, it took four of us."

She nodded. "First, I need the bed linens changed. Can they move him while you do that?"

The boy agreed, speaking to them in Spanish. They lifted Drake while the boy pulled away the squalid sheets on the bed, then Tamsyn took the new sheets he'd brought and smoothed them out on the bed, tucking the edges in swiftly. The captain was reinstalled in bed, groaning as he was laid back down.

"Where can I find a clean shirt?" she asked.

The boy took one from a drawer in the oaken dresser. "*Hermanos?*" he asked the men. They hurried to assist him, carefully removing the bloodstained shirt Drake had been wearing.

"Wait—don't put the new one on just yet," Tamsyn interjected. She folded the old shirt and laid it under the arm and rib wounds in preparation for changing the bandage. "A basin?"

Mateo had to think about that for a few moments, then ran out of the room, returning shortly with a shallow metal pan.

Now, to clean the wound, she told herself. Taking a deep, ragged breath, she moved in close, sitting on the edge of the bed again, and gingerly peeled back the blood-encrusted bandage on his side. "Water?" She clenched her teeth to avoid crying out in sympathy.

"Here, señorita," the boy said, handing her a cup.

Tamsyn poured a small amount of the water over the laceration, watching as layers of blood, scab, and pus were rinsed away. She used the whole cup, then handed it back to Mateo for more. The next time, she used a bit of cloth to delicately brush away some of the scabbing. This must have been painful, because Drake groaned and moved.

"Drake, I must see the extent of the damage, dear one. Please know that I love you and won't harm you." She went on talking in a soothing voice, not as concerned with what she said as the tone. Drake settled back into sleep, and she continued debriding the wound. When she was satisfied with the state of the first injury, she moved to the underarm and repeated her steps.

As she continued, working past her dismay at the torn flesh, she became aware that the body next to her was nearly naked. She'd never seen a man's bare body before. How beautiful Drake Ashton was! His skin smooth and evenly tanned, for the most part, muscles rippling under the skin when he moved, and his chest thinly covered with soft, dark hair…She couldn't help stealing a glance every opportunity she had, as she watched his beloved face sleep peacefully under her ministrations.

Once the arm was re-bandaged, she instructed them to leave his shirt at the foot of the bed until he'd been thoroughly dried. She sent away the basin with the bloody water and asked for a refill. She took the next cloth with clean water and washed his face and neck and hands as a matter of principle. That cloth she rinsed out and left on his forehead to help lower his temperature. Then she turned to the leg.

Tamsyn set the basin under the leg so she could rinse enough away to see what was needed. Her skin crawled. *Just work, don't think about it, pretend it's a stranger.* She washed the wound and saw that while the skin had been torn considerably, the laceration was not as deep as she'd believed at first glance. The infection, however, caused her concern.

"Why didn't you take him to a doctor?" She eyed the botched job with disgust.

"Señor el capitán, he say no," one of the men said.

"He thought they would be looking for him," Mateo explained more gently.

Of course. Thatcher had alerted all the authorities to bring Drake in for questioning. "But not in one of the islands," she scolded. "Look at this!"

As the men leaned in to look at the wound, beginning to form nasty green pus pockets, the shorter of the sailors keeled over in a faint. Tamsyn turned and looked at him in exasperation. "Get him out of here," she muttered.

The boy and the other sailor dragged the unconscious man from the cabin. As Tamsyn tended the injury, Mateo came back alone, looking mortified. "I am sorry, señorita." He shrugged, and she was quick to reassure him.

"Just because he's a big, strong man doesn't mean he likes to look at blood," she said. "Come sit down."

The boy pulled a chair close to the bed so he could speak to her while she worked. "Will he be well soon?"

The tremble, quickly controlled, in the boy's voice tugged at Tamsyn's heartstrings. He obviously cared for his *capitán*. "I think he'll be well, Mateo. Maybe not soon, but he will survive, with the proper care."

He looked at the floor, but she still saw the tears in his eyes.

She turned back to her patient, using a little of the carbolics she'd brought to cleanse the wound. "Tell me what happened." She would have listened to any story that might distract her from the vision before her.

Mateo told her, in detail, the story of how the *Raven* crew and its foolhardy captain had saved the entire village of women and children, after their men had gone to Santiago to fight the Spanish. Tamsyn winced as the boy told her about the last stand on the beach, as his mother died, despite Drake's attempt to rescue her.

"I'm so sorry, Mateo, *chico*. Drake told me she has done so well for you, despite her hard life."

He hung his head. "I not know what made her run back. But he try to save her. He saved many people."

"You think a lot of him, then?"

"He has always been a hero in my eyes, since he came to the village when I was young. I will never leave him."

So this is your worthless mercenary, Thatcher. Tamsyn looked down at the unconscious man, with pride. *He's a man of valor, a champion.*

"Were other members of your crew injured as

well?"

He nodded, sorrow moving across his face. "We lost several men. Others bled but have survived." He looked at Drake. "The captain did not rest until all were tended."

"I would expect no less," she said. Finished cleaning and wrapping his injured leg, she covered him with the clean sheet. Now, he seemed not to look so pale. "He needs to rest now. We shall see what ground we have won when he wakes. I have some laudanum that I can give him for pain, if he needs it."

She examined Mateo's face closely. "When was the last time you slept?"

"Me, señorita? I…" Under her steady gaze, she could tell whatever placating lie he had been about to manufacture dissolved. "Yesterday? The day before?"

"I thought as much. Go, now. I will keep watch over your captain."

"But—"

"Go." Her tone brooked no refusal. The boy stood up to leave the room. To her surprise and gratification, he leaned down and pecked her on the cheek before he hurried out. Her smile was spontaneous and lasted for some time. Loyalty earned was a sweet reward. Drake Ashton had plenty of it here.

She realized with a twinge of alarm that the ship was moving. Crossing to the window, she saw that the *Raven* was bound away over the waves. *What did you expect?* The authorities were on the lookout for Drake; he was in no condition to deal with them at present. *Best away from shore.*

When she looked back at Drake and contemplated the last hour's work, she began to shiver as shock set in.

The crisis and action had passed, and the implications of the blood and infection and ruptured skin, and the battle, and the war, hit her all at once. She'd had no idea, in her safe bedroom, what was really happening to these soldiers and sailors, despite her angry words to Thatcher.

These men Thatcher had casually characterized as lowlifes and scoundrels were the ones who had helped rescue the Cuban people from a life of virtual slavery. They were freedom fighters, liberating the people. And her own dear Drake had placed himself and his shipmates in danger to save a village of women and children from the Spanish!

She finished rinsing her own hands in the remaining clean water, then set the buckets outside the cabin door in the hallway. She'd done her best. Now it was up to Drake's own strength and God's hand.

With a sigh, Tamsyn returned to Drake's bedside, forcing her trembling away. The fever must be brought down if his pain-wracked body was to heal, this she knew. She took the cloth she'd left on his forehead, now warm to the touch, and shook it out, cooling it by its damp contact with the air. She then wiped his cheeks and forehead, allowing the dampness to evaporate from his burning skin.

She continued to stroke his exposed skin with the cloth for some time, until she noticed the light dimming. The sun must be going down. She wondered briefly where they were, but realized it didn't matter. Her stomach growled, almost simultaneously with Mateo sticking his head in the door with a tray for her supper.

"Thank you, *chico.*" She was grateful he'd thought

about her without her having to ask.

He broke into a smile. "*De nada.*"

"You've eaten?"

"I will." He stepped close to the bed. "How is the captain? Does he require food?"

"Not yet. He hasn't regained consciousness." She came to stand next to the boy. She wanted to put her arm around his shoulders. "We must rid him of the fever."

"First, you eat." He placed his hands firmly on her shoulders and guided her to the table. "Tell me what I can do for him." As she started to get up from the chair where he'd put her, he pointed to the table with such a serious face, she was compelled to laugh. "Tell me."

His gaze was stern, and she agreed. As she turned to the simple fare, the soup and dry bread, she realized she was hungry. *When had she last eaten? Breakfast, maybe?* She quickly ate her portion, watching Drake rest, lying still, so still.

Around bites of a seafood chowder that might have been better, more buttery, and creamier than any she'd had on land, Tamsyn explained that he had to continue wiping down Drake's limbs and face to cool him. "We'll need more water." A sudden inspiration came to her. "Do you have rum?"

He nodded slowly. "Yes. Shall I bring you a glass?"

"Not for me. For him. I remember reading that alcohol evaporates faster than water. Let's mix the two and see if that is more effective."

"Very well," he said. "You eat, and I will gather these things."

Mateo returned as she finished, and she helped him

blend water and rum. She demonstrated how she wanted Drake tended, and watched until the boy's technique was satisfactory. "I'd like to go up on deck, just for a few minutes," she said.

"Of course, señorita," he said. "I will continue here." He went at his work with an enthusiastic but tender touch.

Tamsyn pushed herself along the hallway, one hand on each wall, trying to accustom herself to the swaying of the ship as it sailed. On deck, she found the men gathered in small groups of twos and threes, most of them diligently working, even without the active supervision of their captain.

She walked along the outside of the deck, where she could watch the water. The moon played hide-and-seek behind clouds this night, and for the most part, it was becoming dark. The fresh air was bracing; wind rattled the rope netting which climbed to the masts.

The men smiled and nodded when she passed them. Several asked about the well-being of their captain, but most watched her with such trust she knew they simply believed she'd heal him by being here. *I wish I had such confidence in myself. But I've seen the wounds, and they likely haven't.* She knew it would be some time, perhaps weeks, before Drake would be able to command on deck once again.

Tamsyn paused at the bow, feeling as if she were flying as she leaned over, spray splashing up in her face as the *Raven* cut through the water. The water reminded her she was really here, out in the ocean, running away from her father, her fiancé, her home, in search of...*what?* Her dream? Her life? Her love? Perhaps all of these. All she knew, as she stood on the ship which carried Drake Ashton, is that she was in the place where her heart lived.

Half an hour later, having breathed the sea air and calmed herself, Tamsyn returned to Drake's cabin to relieve Mateo. The boy assiduously mopped his captain's brow. Tamsyn lit the lamp on the table, turning it up so she could see even into the corners, and then came around to the head of the bed to feel Drake's forehead. It seemed cooler. She told the boy so, and his joy was hard to contain.

"Jesu!" he whispered. "*Madre de Dios*! I will go tell the others." He jumped up, and Tamsyn laid her hand on his arm to quell his excitement.

"Let's wait, just a while," she said. "Let's make sure before we share the news."

Dismayed by the negative implication of her request, Mateo seemed to shrink in stature. "But you said—"

She nodded. "I'm optimistic. He's not out of danger yet, however. If he continues to improve through morning…" Her voice drifted off, and she took a deep breath as she thought a tiny prayer. "Now off with you."

"I can stay and help you," he insisted.

"I think it would be better for you to get some sleep." She placed a hand on his left shoulder. "Tomorrow there will be more to do, and you will be my right-hand man. Are you up to it?"

He straightened immediately. "I will be here."

"Very well. Go on now." She ushered him out of the room and closed the door. The room smelled better than when she'd arrived, and she felt safe in leaving the window open to continue that improvement. She gathered her skirt and moved to the edge of the bed to pick up where Mateo had left off. Her fingers grazed Drake's cheek as she made a pass with the cloth, and she still believed the fever had lessened. Maybe it was wishful thinking on her part, but she had to hope.

Soon the motions became monotonous, and the high excitement of the day and the rocking of the ship combined to make her sleepy. She had not discussed with anyone where she was to stay, but at least for this night, she did not intend to leave Drake's side. One more pass with the damp cloth, then she came around to Drake's uninjured side and slid on top of the sheet next to him, laying her head on his chest. There, she could feel his heart beating, hear him breathing—the two most reassuring sounds she wanted to hear.

It wasn't long before she drifted off to sleep holding the hand of the man she loved.

Chapter Nineteen

Drake struggled his way to consciousness, aware that the atmosphere had changed. He had no idea how long he'd been asleep, but the extent of his disorientation convinced him it had been many days. His eyes flickered open and closed again quickly, faced with unaccustomed light coming in the open window.

He felt more like himself. His leg hurt; as he moved it gingerly, pain shot up his shin. *Not long enough to be recovered...* He tried not to move it again.

In the next few seconds, he noticed many things. The *Raven* was underway, at a fairly good pace. The air was fresher than it had been. And there was a weight on his mattress...*someone in bed with him.* Barely turning his head, he smelled perfume, one he recognized immediately.

Tamsyn!

So the men had summoned her. And she had come. She had left her life to join him. He suddenly realized the implications of this thought. *That's what the obeah meant—not that she would die, but that she would give up her old life for a new one.*

The revelation and rush of love he felt shook him so deeply he spun back into sleep, fighting uselessly against the currents of unconsciousness.

****

Tamsyn woke as she felt movement under her

head. Stiff from the unaccustomed cramped quarters, she recalled with a start she was sleeping in Drake's bed. His motion had alerted her. Her cheek lay against his chest's bare skin, sensing his heartbeat, strong and regular. He was still too warm, but she was sure he'd lost the searing heat his skin had held the day before. She sat up quickly, hopeful by his stirring that he was awake. "Drake?"

But her patient slept peacefully, the hint of a smile on his lips.

With a sigh, she rose from the bed. Tamsyn splashed water on her face and hands, finding it refreshing despite being lukewarm after a night in the tropical air. Perspiration caused her blouse to stick to her. *I'll need my bag.* In the meantime, her priority was keeping Drake's fever down and fighting the infection poisoning his body.

She did stop by the dresser and brush her hair out before pinning it up off her face and neck in a twist. *Much too hot to leave it down. Besides, I'll want to look attractive if Drake wakes up.*

Samuel came in a few minutes later, giving her a shy bow as he asked about his captain's condition. "I'm sorry I couldn't visit you last night," he said, scratching his russet sideburns. "I had too many duties around the ship. How is Drake?"

She turned back to her patient. "He seems less fevered."

Samuel approached the bed, rolling a little as the ship took a wave. "Storm's coming up. You'll probably want to stay belowdecks." He examined the face of his captain and laid a hand on his forehead. "I think you're right." A hopeful note lit his voice.

"I'm glad you sent for me," she said quietly. Mateo had told her the surgery was Samuel's handiwork. The concern on the first mate's face quashed any desire to scold him for any mistakes he'd made.

"The first few days of the fever," Samuel said, not looking at her, "he was delirious. All he spoke of was you. He was certain some disaster had befallen you, and he berated himself for allowing you to leave."

She nodded. "Then the war came."

He grabbed the bedpost as the ship swayed again. "As soon as Drake heard about the troops heading for Matanzas, he knew he had to help the village he'd been supplying. As it turned out, we arrived just in time."

Samuel sighed deeply. "Bullets were flying, but he would not leave the shore until all of us were safely on the ship, the villagers, too. I saw him hit, then hit again, but he continued to stand there until we dragged him into the boat."

The lines of the lanky sailor's face shared his pain, but it was the admiration in his voice which impressed her. Just like the boy Mateo, Samuel shared that near-worship of a man who gave himself over to his passion for life. The way his men spoke of him dashed any last doubts she might have had about not knowing him well. Her intuition had been right. He was a good man.

"I have to be back at the wheel," Samuel said. "Do you need anything?"

Tamsyn smiled and asked for her carpetbag, as well as more clean water and rum. "It seemed to work last night."

He nodded sharply. "Send Mateo for me if there's anything I can do." Turning to his captain, he said with approval, "He seems to have regained some color. I think you're right about his recovery." He reached for Tamsyn's hand and bowed low over it. "Thank you, from all of us." He left the cabin.

Sustained by his words, she returned to her nursing.

In the next several hours, she found that existence on a ship in foul weather was an adventure in itself. In addition to the incessant rocking of the *Raven* as it traveled through what seemed like towering waves, she learned from Mateo how to secure everything, or lose it sliding to the floor. Fortunately, those who lived aboard ship were prepared for such events, with cunning fasteners for the lamps and other items which must be set out. "Anything you don't need should be put away in a drawer," he advised.

She agreed, tired of scrambling to grab whatever slid out of her reach. "How long will this go on?"

The boy shrugged. "Usually a few hours. Will it affect him, do you think?" His troubled glance at the captain showed her again where the boy's heart lay.

"I doubt it. Just like rocking a baby," she said with a smile.

"Can I bring you something before I go on deck?" Mateo asked. "Some fruit or other breakfast?"

Tamsyn considered it and then shook her head. "I'm afraid I haven't been much of a sailor in my life. I'm fine right now, but I'm afraid if I were to eat something..." Her voice trailed off, and he gave a sympathetic nod.

"I understand, señorita. Perhaps after the storm passes." He left the cabin.

The ship dipped sideways, and she grabbed the table. *I can handle anything for a few hours, right?* She had her day's work set out before her, with Drake's constant care. Tamsyn returned to his bedside and began her routine once again.

The next week's days followed the same pattern. Drake's temperature would spike and plunge as his body shivered with chills or burned with fever. Tamsyn spent hours changing bandages, cleaning the wounds with first water, then conservatively using the small amount of carbolic spray she had to help sterilize the incessant infections. At times when she most felt lost and incapable, she cleared her mind and asked herself what Ellen MacKiernan would have done. The answer would come to her, after a time, and she'd move on.

Members of the crew would relieve her at watch several times a day. She escaped to walk on deck, relishing the warm sun on her skin. Often she'd assist with simple tasks like swabbing the splintery wooden deck, for a change of activity. She learned the names of all the men of the *Raven*'s complement and shared her meals with them. Many of them were shy at first, but seemed to appreciate her quick wit and thoughtfulness and treat her as one of them.

Drake's weary flesh finally beat the infection, and on the morning of the seventh day, his eyes fluttered open and remained so. Tamsyn had been cleaning, sorting through his things, dusting the dresser, when she found him staring at her.

"Drake?" she asked. "How are you, my dear?" She crossed immediately to hold his hand, finding his skin the same temperature as her own.

"You came," he said weakly.

She nodded. "Of course I did." Her other hand felt his forehead, reluctant to believe what her eyes were telling her. "Let me get you some water."

As she moved away, he refused to let go of her hand. "I don't want you to ever leave my side," he said.

"You *need* water," she snapped, and extricated herself from his grasp. She poured the clear liquid into a wooden cup and handed it to him. He drank it eagerly, and she refilled it three times before his thirst was satisfied. "You must continue to drink plenty of water. It will replenish the blood you've lost."

"How long have you been here?" he asked.

"Seven days."

The look they exchanged was electrically charged with innuendo. "What will the neighbors think?" Drake asked, amusement thick in his voice.

"I suppose they'll consider me an amoral strumpet," Tamsyn said reflectively. She twisted a piece of loose hair around her finger, feeling its softness and resilience. It was a combination she felt within herself as well. It would hurt that Norah's family and others would think poorly of her, but she had done what, to her instinct, seemed right. Inner strength would sustain her.

Too late to change things now.

"They'd be wrong." Drake wore a ghost of his former smile. "A lady of love and mercy, beyond reproach, is how I'd see it." He turned slightly, grunting as he jarred his arm and leg.

She moved back to the bedside. "You've made great progress. I have laudanum for pain."

He jerked his head toward the bottle of rum on the table. "That'll do."

Tamsyn poured a small amount in the cup and took it to him. The alcoholic smell didn't even bother her anymore after all the days she'd used it medicinally. He gulped it down and held the cup out for more. She shook her head. "First, something to eat."

She went to the door and called for Mateo, who had never been far from the cabin since she'd arrived. When the boy appeared, his face broke into a smile, and a stream of excited Spanish left his lips as he came in to stand near his captain.

Drake smiled back and clapped the boy on the shoulder with his good arm. "*Bueno, muchacho. Gracias!*"

Tamsyn touched the boy's arm. Drake had lost weight over the week he'd survived without eating, and she knew from her mother's teachings that it had to be restored.

"Mateo, *chico*, bring the captain something to eat." As the boy started off, she added, "Nothing too heavy now. Some broth and soft fruit. Maybe some juice."

"*Sí*, señorita, I shall bring it all." He scooted out the door.

"He's full of gunpowder, isn't he?" Drake asked with a mocking grin.

She nodded. "He's been a godsend. More water?"

"Yes, thank you." He reached eagerly for the cup she poured, and drank several more. She was not surprised. He'd certainly been dehydrated over the days he'd been unconscious, between his inability to take in sustenance and his loss of blood. But the upper wounds were nearly healed over now, and the leg…well, he'd likely have a limp for life, but she thought his leg would eventually heal, given plenty of exercise and fresh air.

"Have you been here the whole time?" He stirred restlessly. "I somewhat remember you wiping my forehead or attending the bandages…or lying here holding me."

She blushed at the reminder of their nights together. No more had happened than a casual touch, but that contact had bonded them as surely as any marriage vow.

"I've mostly been here," she said. "But the others have been some help as well."

He tried to sit up, and she stood before him, forcing him to stay on the bed. "Not yet, Drake." She distracted him with stories of the men. Samuel had given her his traditional chair in the galley. Curly haired José had refused to come on deck when she was there, because his pants were worn through, so she'd gotten one of the others to bring a pair to her while she sat in the cabin so she could sew a patch on them. She embellished her tales, a modern Scheherazade, to keep him occupied until Mateo could return.

And return he did, with a tray full of delicacies to tempt his captain's appetite. Close on his heels were Samuel and Diaz, the cook, both anxious to see for themselves. Drake assured them, as much by his ready smile as by the spoonfuls he was coaxed to swallow between his demands for the status of the ship.

"Where are we exactly?" he wanted to know. He overrode Tamsyn's faint protests and ordered Samuel to fetch the maps and show him their course.

Franz, satisfied by his captain's appetite, faded away from the door and apparently went on deck to spread the word. Tamsyn sat in a chair near the head of the bed, observing that faces came and went at the door, often just remaining long enough to light up with hope and joy. Mateo planted himself at the foot, his back against the wall, trying to make himself as small as possible, probably hoping no one would notice he was there and ask him to leave. The boy hung on every word Drake said.

Tamsyn was just as glad not to be the center of attention for a change. Drake would occasionally reach for her, as if to reassure himself she was still there, and touch her hand or leg, whatever he could reach. As the ship's bell rang the noon hour, Tamsyn found herself drowsing, now that her goal had been achieved.

She was roused by Samuel gently shaking her shoulder. "Tamsyn, come to bed," he said.

She allowed him to help her from the room to the cabin next door, his own cabin which he'd now vacated for her use since she didn't need to monitor Drake so closely. She fell asleep almost immediately and didn't wake again for nearly forty-eight hours.

****

Drake was at Tamsyn's bedside when she woke.

At first she was alarmed at her bed swaying, but within a few seconds, she remembered she was on the *Raven* and how she'd gotten there.

"So, now you in turn must sit in vigil at my bedside?"

"I wanted to be here," Drake said. "It seems lonely on deck, knowing you are here but not with me." He stacked makeshift crutches against the foot of the bed.

"You shouldn't be on your feet yet. The leg should not bear weight. You will damage it further!" She sat up, reaching for his leg.

"Leave it." He barely concealed agitation in his voice. "Mateo changed the dressings for me, as you taught him. I've got something more important to tell you."

Her heart skipped a beat, and a thrill of tension ran through her. *Something was very wrong indeed.* She pulled her legs up and sat, arms wrapped around her knees, hugging them, her back against the headboard as she waited for him to speak. He got up instead and went to the port to look out.

"For pity's sake, Drake!" she cried. "Delaying the news only frightens me more. Is it Thatcher?"

He didn't turn back to her. "No. The ship has somehow come far off the original course I had intended. We have drifted into the Spanish shipping lanes. We are becalmed in waters which are at war."

The implications of his statement set her trembling. The Spanish were no doubt aware of not only Drake's illicit support of the Cuban people before the war, but probably of his activities since the war had begun. If they were to intercept the *Raven*, its captain and crew would no doubt suffer. She'd heard such terrible tales of the Spanish atrocities during her confinement. What might happen to a young American woman who fell into their hands?

A whimper escaped her. Drake came to her side immediately to take her in his arms.

"You must be my brave girl now," he said. "We have been here already for a day, and we've seen no other ships. Our intelligence indicated the Spanish fleet is currently split into a dozen forces, fighting American regiments and Cuban people on a number of fronts. The Spanish should have more to do at present than scour the seas for intruding ships this far from Cuba."

Tamsyn prayed he was right. Luck and timing

hadn't played a great part in their lives together to date; she didn't trust that would change a great deal. If only Drake wasn't so troubled, she would find it easier to be confident of their safety.

"How long must we stay here?" She straightened her shoulders in an effort to feel brave. She hoped the answer would be the same as the length of the storm. Didn't the winds and weather change nearly as one watched in Key West? It wasn't unusual for torrential rains to last for ten minutes, then blow past, or for rain to fall on one side of the street but not on the other. Surely this situation could not be prolonged.

Drake returned to the port. "I see no motion in the sky, no clouds. Without some indication of movement, I've no way of knowing when the wind will return."

She rose from the bed and went to his side. "Drake, your injuries could well have killed you. It is obvious you were spared for some reason. Heaven is not finished with you yet. That must mean you will survive past this day."

His right arm slid around her shoulders. "Your faith in me sustains me, Tamsyn. We must believe in the best possible outcome."

A cry from abovedeck snatched their attention, and they turned as one as Samuel knocked at the open cabin door. As they listened to his report, the pain returned to Drake's dark eyes, and his lips pulled into a tight line.

The Spanish battleship *Vizcaya* had been sighted some distance off the port side of the ship. Captain Guillermo de la Jolla had signaled his intent to board the *Raven* immediately.

****

Drake silently berated his fate for bringing them to

this state of affairs. But there was nothing his crew could have done. A ship becalmed was the fault of no one but the weather gods.

He'd been in tight spots before, and this would no doubt prove to be one of the worst, mostly because the life of his beloved Tamsyn was at risk as well as those of his men. "How long?" he asked Samuel.

"Fifteen or twenty minutes is as long as we can hold them off," Samuel said in a grave voice. "They're rowing over, but the *Vizcaya* is in firing range, and the cannons are—" He glanced at Tamsyn's wide eyes, then choked off the remainder of what he was going to say. Drake well understood the situation.

Drake nodded. He saw Tamsyn's eyes turn to him, wild with fear, though bless her brave heart, she'd not uttered a word. He held her, his mouth close to her ear as he said quietly, "We'll get through this. Let's see what Heaven has spared us for."

Another part of his brain was clicking through strategies he'd learned through years of experience on the high seas. If the ship was that close, the Spanish had had an opportunity to spy out the goings-on on ship for the past day. They would have noted the ship's notorious captain had not appeared on deck much. Would that be a problem? Showing that he was crippled and powerless would certainly compromise their position.

But how can I avoid that appearance?

I need time I haven't got. I need…I need…

"I need you on deck," he said to Tamsyn, as a ridiculous plan came to him.

"What?" Her first reaction was incredulous, but she suppressed it immediately. "Yes, Captain."

"Wear something pretty." He gave her a lingering kiss, then took the crutches and limped after Samuel, calling for Mateo. Drake nearly collided with the boy, who barreled out of the captain's cabin. The boy, too, looked anxious, but as Drake began to lay out the scheme coming together in his head, Mateo nodded and even smiled as he turned to dash off down the corridor.

"Take a gun," Drake admonished, "and all the ammunition you need. Let me know at the first sign!"

Samuel's face twisted into a scarab of confusion. "We have a plan, I take it?" he asked in a voice tinged with cynicism.

Drake smiled. "My man, these are Spanish whores we are talking about. We should hardly have to defend ourselves." His eyes were serious, however, and Samuel listened closely as Drake instructed him to have the sails fully unfurled, even though there was no wind. Each man on deck was also to conceal a firearm near him, in his bucket, under a coil of rope, or anywhere he'd have easy access. "Bring the rest of the weapons belowdecks and meet me here."

"And the lady?" Samuel asked as Tamsyn appeared behind Drake, pale but ready.

"The lady has nothing to do but be herself," he said with a cheery smile. "That should be more than enough."

"Anything else?" the first mate asked.

Drake's attention to the horizon had not been casual, looking out the port while talking to Tamsyn. He'd finally spotted some clouds moving in the distance. *If we can only hold out...*

"Pray for wind."

Chapter Twenty

Tamsyn shivered though the sun blazed down on the deck. The boarding party was arriving. She wished Drake could have refused to admit the Spanish, but they were in gunning range with a full battery of weapons trained on the ship. For all intents and purposes, they were probably safer with the four Spanish officers on board. The *Vizcaya* surely wouldn't fire on its own captain.

Mateo shimmied up the rigging to the crow's nest, loaded down with a burlap sack which looked extremely heavy. His actions looked so exaggerated and clown-like, at first she wondered if he was trying to provide a bit of comic relief. But her glimpse of his expression before he tucked himself down inside was dreadfully serious.

The small transport boat carrying the Spanish officers bumped against the *Raven*, a thick sound of wood against wood, and Roderick Chaney, second mate and suddenly commander on deck, ordered the ladder ropes to be dropped.

Tamsyn, on the other hand, was armed with only a lacy white blouse and navy-blue skirt, the prettiest clothes she'd brought in her mad dash to escape home. *Not that I would have known how to fire a gun, of course, but I would feel safer holding one. I could at least throw it at someone.*

The first man aboard had to be the commander of the *Vizcaya*. His hair was long and black under a wide, gold-trimmed hat, and his mustache curled with a precision which told Tamsyn he was quite vain about it. He was a tall man, and looked even larger because of the gold-embroidered layers of clothing he wore. They no doubt proclaimed his rank and authority, but Tamsyn couldn't understand how any human could survive in such clothing on a windless sea under the May sun of the Caribbean.

He surveyed those on deck. "*Soy capitán* Guillermo de la Jolla."

Three sailors followed. One of them was a lean, hungry-looking man with a scar bisecting an entire cheek. From the look of the barely healed tissue, Tamsyn guessed his sword fight hadn't been more than a week earlier. He and the others stood in a little clump on the deck as the captain glared at those watching him, trying to determine who was in charge. The captain's eye fell on Tamsyn, and his face lit up with pleasure.

"*Hola!*" he said, coming forward with a grin. "*Que linda!*" The men behind him turned to see what the captain was seeing, and there was a hurried exchange in Spanish.

Tamsyn's heart raced. *What is it Drake thinks I can do to dissuade these men?* She looked around at the men of the *Raven*, who stood by in a manner which was deceptively casual. Their faces showed concern for her. She took a deep breath, straightened her spine, and followed the Spanish captain with her gaze.

"*Hola, guapa! Como te llamas?*" he asked her.

"I'm sorry, I-I don't speak Spanish."

The man continued to smile. His teeth were brown

and his face pockmarked. She crossed her arms to keep her hands from trembling.

The captain raised an eyebrow. "You are...ship's, ah, woman?" he asked haltingly.

"Ship's woman?" She didn't like the sound of the phrase. She caught José's eye. He gave her an encouraging nod.

"Woman," he said, stepping closer and gesturing around at the crew, "for ship's men?" When she continued to stare at him blankly, he made an obscene gesture which clarified his meaning. Several of the *Raven*'s men cried out, indignant on her behalf.

"Certainly not!" she said.

He stepped back at the blaze of anger in her eyes.

He inspected her again, obviously concerned he misunderstood the situation. His fingers touched the fine lace on her blouse, and he lifted her skirt ever so slightly to see she wore stylish leather shoes. *"Mira!"* he called over his shoulder to his officers. They came close and stood around her, listening as their captain spoke quick Spanish.

Tamsyn's apprehension grew. She wished she had a clue what they were discussing. As he spoke, they scrutinized different parts of her body or clothes in a possessive way which made her very uneasy. *Did Drake know they would do this? What am I supposed to do?*

This seems a lot more like bargaining at the market than diplomatic negotiating.

She looked over her shoulder and saw that shy José was closest to her. "What are they saying?" she whispered.

He replied in English, "They cannot understand

why a lady of wealth would be aboard the ship. Women are not usually allowed aboard—bad luck, you know. At first, they thought—"

"I know what they thought," she snapped, turning away to face José.

One of the Spanish sailors, the one with the scar, grabbed her when she turned away. His fingers squeezing her arm, he began to berate her in Spanish.

Tamsyn struggled, guessing the diatribe was a string of threats, simply from the tone. "José?" she cried, unable to see him.

"He says you should not be rude to his captain, who will decide what should happen with you," José replied. His voice had acquired a husky edge of anger.

"What should happen with me? What do you mean?" She stopped squirming, and Scarface let go of her. Tamsyn took a step forward and looked the captain right in the eye, planting her feet square on the deck and her hands on her hips. "Nothing is going to happen 'with' me. I'm a passenger on this ship, and I intend to stay that way. Now leave me alone!"

The captain recognized her tone, if not her words. One of the officers translated for him. His eyes grew wide, then he began to laugh heartily. He patted her on the head, as one would a spoiled child. He then spoke to the translating officer, one who looked softer and more educated than the others. The officer turned to her with a speculative expression.

"My captain wishes to thank you for providing him some much-needed amusement on his long voyage to rendezvous with Admiral Cervera," the man said in a well-modulated voice. "He admires your spirit."

Tamsyn looked from him to the captain, noticing

the leader's eyes were hard, not complimentary. "I see." She was sure that wasn't the last word.

It wasn't.

"However, he cannot afford to tolerate insolence from mere women. He is prepared to take you aboard his ship and teach you the proper place of a *puta*."

"That won't be necessary." Tamsyn's heart pounded in her chest. Was Drake even watching? Surely he wasn't hiding belowdecks until the captain left. He wasn't that kind of man. *I wish he'd let me in on his plan.* "I have no intention—"

Scarface grabbed her right arm again. Their serious faces convincing her she could be in danger, she began to fight him off in earnest. She swung on him. One of the others took her left arm, preventing her from moving. When several of the crew stepped forward, yelling at her captors, Scarface shifted behind her and drew a short dagger from his boot, holding it to her throat, his words foreign but definitely a warning. She froze, then gently slid her hands to her sides, no longer combative. There was no point in losing her life, if she had a chance to escape.

The Spanish captain strutted around the deck, giving the crew a perfunctory examination. Though his own men were armed, the *Raven*'s crew apparently were not. It had to puzzle him that they would allow themselves to be taken. He fired questions at several crew members. He was apparently not getting the answers he expected, because after the fourth man, his questions became short, staccato bursts, followed by a backhanded slap.

How long will Drake let this go on? Tamsyn anguished over the senseless violence. Drake had ordered everyone to have a weapon in reach, and surely they could overpower the four officers. *But what would they gain if they attacked?* The *Vizcaya* would blast them, and without any way for them to sail…

She heard the cry of a seagull overhead and felt the breath of a breeze on her face soon afterward. *Wind!* She kept her face impassive as she was dragged side to side as Scarface turned to keep an interested eye on his captain. He took advantage of his movements to lean close to Tamsyn, whispering, hot breath in her ears. She shrank away from him the best she could, to his amusement. He probably expected to have his turn with her back on the Spanish ship.

Finally the captain grew weary of whatever game he believed the crew was playing with him. Summoning his officer who spoke English, he gave him a series of commands, which the man translated.

"El capitán says he has never seen a crew so undisciplined and without honor. When he asks to speak to the captain of the vessel, all lie to protect the coward!" He paused, and the captain barked out another string of words. "The captain and crew of this vessel have been providing guns and supplies to the rebels, and should be punished accordingly, but we are on our way to meet Admiral Cervera, and have no time to conduct a thorough investigation."

He and the captain eyed the crew, who managed to keep their faces impassive. The captain spat out more vitriolic words, practically foaming at the mouth with frustration.

"If he will not show himself voluntarily, perhaps we should just scuttle the ship." When no one moved or spoke, the captain pulled his sword from his scabbard and surveyed those on the deck, obviously choosing a victim.

The seagull overhead called twice, and Tamsyn heard the flap of sails filling with air. She looked up and saw Mateo peek over the edge of the crow's nest, catching her eye. He made the seagull call again, drawing the attention of the Spanish officers.

"*Mira! En alto!*" the captain bellowed, pointing upward as the ship lurched forward, the sails billowing.

Scarface, distracted by the boy's appearance, loosened his grip for a crucial moment. Tamsyn stamped on his instep and launched herself away, landing on the floor behind a barrel. As he lunged after her, a bullet from the firearm which had appeared in José's hand caught him in the face.

A flurry of heavy footsteps came from the open hatch to the captain's chamber. Drake and Samuel burst from the hole, guns blazing. Another Spanish officer was hit. The rest of the men on deck snatched their concealed weapons.

"Who are you calling a coward?" Drake stood tall facing the captain.

How is Drake even walking without his crutches? He'll destroy his leg. What is he thinking? Tamsyn was dismayed at the paleness of his face, but the devil-may-care grin plastered across it seemed to raise the spirits of the watching crew.

The Spanish captain's vicious smile replaced his alarm that he was outgunned on deck. He twirled the tip of his drawn sword in Drake's direction, speaking in Spanish. Drake only laughed. His gaze scanned quickly as he noted the positions of his crew and Tamsyn.

"My friend, I don't believe she'd have you if you

were the last man on earth." He winked at Tamsyn where she huddled behind the water barrel.

The scar-faced man lay near her, half his face blown away. Her stomach turned, and she tried very hard not to stare. How could Drake be so cheerful? His display of confidence seemed very near the edge of delusion.

The Spaniard made another comment, and Drake looked as though he was considering whatever the man had said. At last he nodded. "I accept your challenge," he said in English, then Spanish. Drake tossed his pistol to Samuel and picked up the sword from one of the fallen Spanish officers.

What did he mean to do? This was no swashbuckling lark! People's lives were at stake. And Drake is only two days out of bed. This could be a disaster.

Tamsyn redoubled her prayers and studied him as he slowly moved toward the fight. His injured leg was very thick, tight in his boot. Had they bolstered his leg with wood? How else could he walk so steadily?

The two men circled warily, each apparently waiting for the other to make a move. *Why didn't Drake just finish him when he'd had the chance?* José and Chaney held the remaining officer at gunpoint, to prevent him from interfering in the fight between the two ships' masters.

Drake called to his first mate casually, over his shoulder, never taking his eyes off the captain as their swords clashed with a grating edge. "Samuel, do take the helm, will you?" It was said in English and in such a nonchalant tone, the opposing captain didn't bat an eye.

"Aye, aye, sir." Samuel strolled to his place at the ship's wheel, with a smile, taking advantage of the rising winds. He steered the ship away from the *Vizcaya*. It took only a few minutes to substantially widen the distance between them.

As the Spanish captain was distracted by his ship's predicament, Drake inched forward, slashing and cutting at the front of his uniform. The captain parried Drake's onslaught as best he could, forced into a defensive position, backing up until he was leaning against the side of the ship. With a flash of his sword upward, Drake sent de la Jolla's blade sailing over the side.

Drake glanced around and called to the men closest to him. "I think we've had enough of Captain de la Jolla, gentlemen. He smells like shark bait now."

Four men converged immediately on the captain and, before he could fight them off, tumbled him over the side of the ship. Drake spun around and, with a wave of the sword, indicated the same treatment should be provided for the remaining officers, dead and alive. They were tossed overboard with a rousing cheer.

As they continued on, the *Vizcaya* was forced to stop and retrieve its fallen officers as the *Raven* flew on ahead, steering back into safer waters.

Pandemonium reigned on deck as Mateo plummeted down, hanging by a rope, impelled by the weight of his weaponry. "I didn't get to fire a shot!" he protested.

"You'll have plenty of chances, *niño*." Drake crossed the deck to congratulate the boy. "Your signal as the wind came through was perfect."

The boy beamed and joined the men in their

cheering and bragging. "Did you see me?" they said, one to the other. "I was the one who…"

Drake left them to it and came to take Tamsyn's hand, pulling her into his arms. "You were magnificent," he said, after he kissed her. He reeked of rum.

"You knew he'd behave like a lout?" she asked, still shaken. Death had been much too close for her to calmly accept it.

"I knew no man in his right mind could take his eyes off you when you put your mind to it." He chuckled.

She wasn't finished with this discussion, her heart still racing. "I don't like being used as bait."

He went on, more quietly, "I could see everything. If the circumstances had gotten uglier…" He held her tighter. "But they didn't, and you saved the *Raven* almost single-handedly."

He turned to the crew, still busy slapping each other on the shoulders and swaggering about. "What about it, *mis compadres*? Shall we make Tamsyn one of us?"

Amidst a roar of acclaim, Mateo disappeared belowdecks. José's warm tenor led a song about men of the sea, and Tamsyn was bound at last to join into the victory celebration. The crew returned to their posts, Samuel steering the ship toward the horizon, while others climbed the rigging, adjusting the sails to provide maximum speed. It seemed like a well-oiled machine under the direction of its true captain, and this experience made her feel a part of it. As she relaxed, Drake let go and sat on a nearby tall barrel, brandishing his new sword.

"It's quite an instrument, is it not?" he asked. "Very fine craftsmanship. Of course, the Spaniards pride themselves on such work."

"You look very much like a pirate I once met."

"Madam? A pirate?" he said. "Even without an eyepatch?"

"Even though you've set your recovery back a week or more by your bravado."

"Hush, woman. I'll be fine." He raised his pant leg to display a metal brace wrapped around his shin. "I'll deal with it when the rum wears off."

Mateo returned, bearing a mug full to the brim with some sort of ale. Eyes turned expectantly toward Tamsyn.

What now? Am I expected to drink that in one session?

Drake took the mug with a grin. "As you all know, there is a tradition on board this ship each time we recruit a new member." His grin widened as he looked at Tamsyn, and she began to squirm inwardly. But all she saw in the faces around her was excitement and affection. *Whatever it was, it would be worth the opportunity to become one of these...*

"As in the church, when a man first comes to God, he is baptized, so shall you be as you first come to us." With a sober face, he held the mug high in the air and dumped it over her head.

Sputtering, she wiped her face clean as the men laughed and applauded her. "I hope I really deserve this," she said ruefully.

"Ale for everyone, Diaz," Drake called. The men hurried to bring the barrel up the steps and pour cups for all. Even Tamsyn had a small cup, though she found the drink bitter and not to her taste.

Drake drew her aside a few minutes later, leaving the men to their revelry. They met up with Samuel in the stern, where he surveyed the horizon behind them with a spyglass.

"Anything?" Drake said.

Samuel shook his head. "We got clean away, Captain. Some plan you concocted."

"I do my best." Drake's smile was becoming worn. He stumbled, and both of them reached to steady him and help him to sit against the aft rail.

"You may have been up and around yesterday, but that's hardly enough to decide you're recovered," Tamsyn scolded. "You've probably used all your energy for the day in that one burst of silliness." She leaned close, feeling his forehead for a return of the fever, muttering about men and their need to strut and swagger to impress each other.

"Isn't she endearing?" Drake whispered, winking at Samuel.

"Shut up before I punch you myself," Tamsyn warned. To Samuel, she said, "Isn't there somewhere we can anchor for the next several days to avoid any more encounters like that one?"

"We could be at Nassau by tomorrow, if the wind holds," Samuel said.

Drake nodded wearily. "It will be a good place to gather news and learn when it might be safe to return across the lanes," he said. "Perhaps we can anchor in that cove just west of the harbor." As Samuel nodded, Drake turned to Tamsyn. "You'll like this place, dear one. There is a white, sandy beach where you can hunt sea creatures to your heart's content."

She smiled in encouragement. "Fine. If you've made up your mind, you should return to your bed now." She looked at Samuel, beseeching his help, which he offered immediately.

"The wind will be at our backs, Drake. We shall arrive in good time."

Drake shook his head. "I will not put Tamsyn in peril again by being in the wrong place. I should stay on deck and watch our course."

Samuel got down on one knee before his captain. "I swear to you on my mother's life I will personally watch until we arrive safely."

The two men gazed in silence for several moments, then Drake acquiesced. "You're a fine man, Samuel Johnston." He used his first mate's shoulder to heave himself to a standing position.

Tamsyn signaled to Mateo, who waited nearby. The boy limped over, and he allowed Drake to wrap an arm around his shoulders for support. Tamsyn slipped under the other arm, and the two guided him toward the steps to go below. Before they'd gone ten feet, Drake stopped.

"What is it?" Tamsyn asked.

"Samuel," he said in a mocking tone, "I know your mother's been dead these fifteen years."

Samuel, behind them, had risen to his feet, and broke into a loud guffaw. "Drake, man, I've always said you can be too clever for your own good."

Drake smiled faintly, distressing Tamsyn by his failing strength. He whispered, "As long as I'm always one step ahead of you, me boy." He kissed Tamsyn on the cheek nearest him. "Take me to bed, woman, before I fall down right here in front of the crew."

****

It was Drake's turn to sleep long and hard, and he found they'd been anchored nearly ten hours before he came out on deck. Tamsyn, as he'd expected, ambled through the water just offshore, her gray skirt cut off at the knees. As he watched through a spyglass, she would lean down to pick up a shell or observe something closely, then walk on to discover more wonders. The wind on the water carried the sound of her quiet singing to his ear.

Many men were engaged in activities which would sustain them for the next several days—gathering firewood and food, hanging tarpaulins from trees as shelter from the sun and rain. While they were at sea, the breezes managed to keep mosquitoes and other flying pests away, but they'd have to contend with them now that they were on land. There was some netting stored below; the rest would have to sleep in the ship's hold or take their chances.

Drake turned back to see Tamsyn, now down on her knees, digging in the sand. She seemed perfectly content, a childlike smile on her face, as she came up with a large shell which must have been buried.

He knew then he had to join her. "Samuel!" he bellowed. He stumped with his crutches back toward the bow, strength returning to him with the sun. "Mateo? Who's on board?"

The only one he could find was Diaz, who was busy packing items he'd need for cooking into a big sack. "Captain?" the cook said as he entered the darkened galley. "Come to assist me, have you?"

Drake grinned. "Actually, I was looking for someone to row me to shore."

"They'll be back soon," Diaz said. "They carried our water barrels on land for refilling."

"Very well." Since there'd be a delay, Drake decided to wash up and get dressed in some old clothes so he could share a water adventure with Tamsyn.

Before long, the skiff arrived back at the *Raven*, and Drake helped load as he could, careful not to overtax himself before he could even disembark. He intended to have plenty of time to lie in the healing warm waters and enjoy the wind and waves.

As the small boat grounded on the sand of the beach, Tamsyn ran to meet it. "Drake! How are you feeling?"

He just looked at her, her dress soaked, her hair loose and curling in the humidity, sand crystals sparkling on her face. He thought he'd never seen anything so beautiful in his life. "I feel fine, now that I've seen you," he said. "Help me out."

As the crew finished their chores and piled a huge stack of firewood for the evening's bonfire, Drake sat on the sand, his legs soaking in the water, and Tamsyn brought a small stack of treasures she'd found, a couple of pearly pink shells, a dried starfish, and some sort of dark-brown, shiny seeds which were wonderfully smooth to the touch. He admired them and placed them in his pocket so they would not be lost. He added a bright-coral crab claw which had become separated from its owner, and some sets of lavender angel wing shells which were still attached in pairs.

They didn't have much conversation. Drake sensed Tamsyn was still recovering slowly from the skirmish with the Spanish. The past week had been an unusual one for her, staying on a ship with thirty-six men, doctoring him, trading words with a Spanish commander. He was willing to provide her with the time she needed. Himself? He was happy just to be with her, to be alive, after the frightening period of half wakefulness and pain following Matanzas.

After his skin felt sizzled by the sun, Drake asked Tamsyn to help him up, and he walked all the way into the water, stripping off his shirt and the bandages along his ribs, allowing the salt water to bathe his wounds. After the first lip-biting seconds, it didn't sting nearly as badly as he'd expected; he must really be healing.

Most of all, Drake wasn't ready to think beyond the next several days. Any conversation between them must involve what was to happen farther in the future. He'd sent for Tamsyn in a moment of desperation, just as his mental faculties had begun to slip, knowing his wounds were serious. He'd had no idea if she would actually come, but he knew he needed her.

As amusing as it had been to "christen" her as a member of the crew, he could hardly ask her to remain on the ship. His work for the liberation of the Cuban people had not been completed. As long as the war continued, Tamsyn's presence on the *Raven* would dull his instincts, as he thought first to protect her, instead of about his mission. And his mission would be dangerous.

But could he send her home? After she'd been with him, although nothing untoward had happened, her reputation would be in tatters. She'd run from Key West—and Thatcher Winslow—too fast to make him think she was anxious to return.

You could marry her.

The thought shocked him, not because he didn't

love her enough, but because he had no time to consider his path so far into the future. There was no question she'd stolen his heart, having rescued him several times now, as the Cuban obeah woman had predicted. But marriage? He'd never planned his life beyond revenge against the Spanish. His promise to Freddie's ghost had driven him through many waters and skirmishes. What would be left for him to do with his life once the Spanish were gone, truly punished for their marauding ways?

The question stopped him where he stood in the water. It was one he obviously had to consider, and soon, if the Cubans were successful in their rebellion in the next several months. He would have to move on.

He was gratefully distracted from his sudden insecurity about his future, as Mateo shyly interrupted their walk with a small wreath of pink and white hibiscus flowers he'd wound together for Tamsyn. Her laughter tinkled like falling water as she set the "crown" on her head and began to pose regally.

"It's splendid." Tamsyn gave the boy a kiss on the cheek. He blushed nearly as pink as the flowers she wore, and backed away, loping down the beach toward the others, silly grin pasted on his face. The teasing started as he joined the other men, but the gibes were friendly and even a little jealous.

Drake basked in the glow which radiated from her face. She'd tanned while she was on the ship the last several days; her cheeks were rosy from the sun. *What an angel she was...*

She turned to him suddenly and squeezed his hand. "I just wanted you to know I've never been happier, never in my life." Her eyes, full of emotion, were unreserved in their openness to him. "No matter what happens, I wanted you to know."

No matter what happens? Her words wrung his heart. Her thoughts must have paralleled his, wondering what the future held. She'd obviously made the decision to follow her heart and leave her previous life. Could he do the same? But he, too, was happier than he could remember. "I share your joy, Tamsyn," he agreed, voice solemn. "No matter what happens."

As they walked, hand in hand, back down the beach toward the rest of the crew now gathering for an informal supper, he wondered about his unwillingness to commit himself further than he could speculate. *No matter what happens...* What could lie ahead for them?

Later that evening, the fire leapt high into the Bahamian night, showers of sparks competing with the stars to sparkle in the sky. As the remnants of the evening meal were cleared away, the men, laughing and telling stories, gradually congregated around the fire. Tamsyn had stymied anyone who wanted Drake to help. Instead, she laid a blanket on the sand, near a thick log to serve as a backrest, and invited him to sit there with her near the fire.

"You wouldn't leave a lady alone, would you?" Her eyes offered a challenge.

"Go on, *capitán*!" José passed on the way to the trees, his encouragement echoed by several of the other men. "We will manage here."

Mateo, never far from his captain, brought him a cool drink with rum. "What else shall I fetch for you?" he asked as Drake seated himself awkwardly.

"I wish all of you would stop treating me like an old *abuela*," Drake groused. "Mateo, enjoy yourself tonight, would you? Don't worry about me. I'm here in the company of a lovely lady, on a night of a thousand stars, with open water and all the beauties of an island retreat. I need nothing else."

Tamsyn settled back into the crook of his arm, relaxing at last. Drake pulled her close, and she nestled her head under his chin.

The blaze climbed through the dried wood until it stood seven or eight feet high. The smell of the woodsmoke blended with the more pungent odor of cigars, which many of the crew lit from small sticks taken from the fire. Drake was pleased to see them loosen up after some genuinely stressful days.

The past week had been a tense one, between Drake's recovery and the incidents of the day before. But now, a bottle of rum was passed around, and the men were practically boisterous. It was an occasion akin to the Pickham ball, as those of a certain social group gathered to celebrate—but how different the group, and how much more Drake felt at home.

****

Tamsyn, too, felt blessed to be surrounded by these valiant companions. *How strange my life has become. Less than two weeks ago, I hadn't slept anywhere but my own bed...and tonight I'll sleep in the open, a ragged piece of net all that stands between me and the elements.*

A tiny voice from the Thatcher-time protested at the scandalous thought, but she shoved it aside as a new excitement overtook her. *How free this life is.* No prying eyes, no critical tongues, just the opportunity to do what felt right, living in the moment day-to-day without conscious regard for the consequences.

Mamma, I'm so happy. She hoped Ellen would understand that constricted life under Angus' stern hand and Thatcher's greedy, selfish hand would never be for her.

The sounds of guitars being tuned drew her attention to the far side of the fire, where several of the men had seated themselves on rocks or sand, with a number of instruments, from guitars to flute. One drummer began a Latin beat, followed by a second playing counterpoint. The drums and guitar were joined by what sounded like a cowbell, maracas swishing their seeds inside, and a clear, sweet flute. The fire seemed to crackle in rhythm.

After the musicians had played for a time, voices began to blend in, singing some song of the islands, the tune of which was familiar to Tamsyn from the blacks working at her home. She listened closely, picking out familiar voices, José, Charlie, a bass that had to be Diaz, and then a high, clear tenor which could belong to no one but the cabin boy. The music, the open air, the smoke, the wonder of it all brought tears of joy and awe to her eyes.

She heard, too, Drake's strong heartbeat and steady breathing, as her head lay on his chest. It reassured her further, and she snuggled close.

A short while later, she realized she was dozing. Listening, she guessed from Drake's breath sounds that he was asleep as well. "Come, my dear, you need to rest in a comfortable place."

Drake muttered, "Quit mollycoddling me." He stood slowly, allowing himself to lean on Tamsyn slightly, wrapping his arm around her shoulders. She propelled him to the makeshift bed set up for him by the crew. In consideration of his injuries, they'd brought Drake an actual mattress from the ship, unlike their hammocks and blankets. A tarp hung over part of the mattress, which was situated behind a large rock for privacy. He sat down, light flickering across his face in the fire's reflection. As she would have left him to his sleep, he grabbed her hand. "Come, sit with me."

"You need your rest," she protested. She tried to pull away, but he held her tightly.

"I need my nurse," he said, voice thick with longing. "Come sit with me."

Tamsyn knelt down next to Drake, willing to indulge him for a few moments, expecting him to fall asleep as soon as he relaxed. The air was full of night insects, keening in the trees behind them. The gentle lapping of the waves as they hit the shore soothed her. "I'm here."

His arms slid around her, and he pulled her to face him. "This is where you belong."

It felt so good to be held. She realized she was very close to him, their faces nearly touching. It seemed natural to place her arms around his neck and lift her lips to his. He kissed her back, feather-like touches of warm skin to warm skin, which gradually changed to heated, firm touch of lips. His fingers slid up and down her back, stimulating her to the core.

They kissed, tasting each other, breath coming hot as their excitement increased. The slow buildup seemed to heighten all her senses. She lifted her chin in ecstasy as his mouth moved in tiny kisses down her neck, leisurely, deliberately. She welcomed his hands as they caressed her breasts. Mindful of his injured left side, she slid her left hand around to his back, pulling herself closer and kissing every part of his beloved face.

Tamsyn knew from eavesdropping on a number of persons that in order to truly excite a man, they liked it when a woman touched his private parts. Having never done it, the thought unnerved her. Trembling as she reached a hand out to his lap, she was amazed to find a lump hard as a stone there. *That must be it*, she thought with a little thrill. She stroked her hand lightly along its length and was jarred by his quick movement away from her.

"Tamsyn, my beloved, you don't know how I wish we could pursue your warm and, ah, stimulating thought." He shivered and pulled her to him again. When he spoke, his voice was ragged. "I love you so much. But I want to love you as a whole man."

He set aside her protests. "I mean this. The time will come when I can share with you an evening of passion we will both remember, and not for its inadequacies."

"I love you, too, Drake," she said, eyes closed, secure in his arms. "I will be ready when you are." She breathed in his scent and enjoyed the thrill which traversed her body as it continued to excite her. "Now, shall I leave you to rest?"

He hesitated. "I don't want you to leave. Will you stay with me?"

She assented in a split second, waiting while he arranged himself to be comfortable, then curling up beside him, her head on his chest, arm draped across his body.

"Good night, my sweet love," he whispered as he closed his eyes.

"Sleep well."

Her heart gradually slowed, and she thought about the wondrous sensations her body had experienced. It amazed her, thinking back on it, that she never stopped to compare Drake's approach to Thatcher's. She had often noted the differences, even only so long as to be pleased by them. But for the first time, she was thoroughly engrossed in her desire. Perhaps it was the beautiful setting or the cherished man beside her. Or it might be part of that aura of freedom which she now enjoyed, liberating her to be herself, act as she really felt, say what she meant.

For the first time in many months, she believed herself totally at ease.

****

As the idyll continued, various members of the crew took turns sailing into the city with their small boats to get fresh supplies and catch up on the news. With time, they were apparently accepted as regular visitors. They found the coffeehouses and taverns where the fishermen congregated, and tapped into information about the war and also what was happening back on the mainland. After they'd been in their little cove outside Nassau nearly three weeks, Tamsyn and Drake were surprised, as the latest team to go to the city returned with a bit of excitement.

"We saw some familiar faces in the marketplace," Chaney reported with a wide grin. "I expect we'll have some visitors soon."

Chapter Twenty-One

Tamsyn spent many hours during the weeks on the island in joyous solitude, spending time in nature. Marvelous parrots and other singing birds nested in the tops of trees in the jungle, and she could sit for hours to observe them. Thick, mottled snakes oozed along the tree branches, and small fish of rainbow tones swam in the warm, shallow waters. She loved them all.

The best part was that Drake cherished her enjoyment of these things and never criticized her for leaving him to explore. He turned his attention to his recovery or planning the next mission, once they received reliable news from Cuba about the current situation. They each had their occupations, which never seemed to infringe on time they wanted to spend together.

Living life with him was as close to heaven as Tamsyn had ever hoped she'd be.

Even if she had wanted to return to her life in Key West, she knew now it would strangle her. The constant responsibility for others and the mandate to keep up appearances as a MacKiernan would be bad enough, far worse, compared to Winslow standards. Here, she didn't even bother to wear stockings. What was the point, when there was water and sand and soft grass among the trees? Bare feet were much more comfortable.

Bare skin, too, was prevalent on the island, as its residents worshiped the warm summer sun. Drake was deeply tanned and spent most of the days shirtless, adding to the wonderful sights available to her. She, of course, remained as modest as a sleeveless blouse and shortened skirt could make her.

The men of the *Raven* teased her and looked out for her and vied for her attention just like siblings. Their antics made Drake laugh. He wanted them to like her. He was never jealous in the least. *Thatcher would have—*

Tamsyn nipped that thought before it reached completion. She didn't run her life by Thatcher Winslow's standards any longer. Drake had rescued her from a life of desperate affluence, trapped behind fans and under high collars and long skirts, trying to impress high society with the way she poured tea for her guests. The thought made her shudder.

But the time was coming when she'd have to decide what her future held. Having escaped from society, she now hovered in limbo, savoring every drop of her new freedom. What would come next?

The war in Cuba was in full flare, and she understood Drake's deep commitment to see the Spanish leave the Caribbean. She couldn't stand between him and his promise to his dead brother. Of all people, she understood the importance of promises and the damage caused when they were broken.

If Drake returned to Cuba, once he was whole, what would she do? It would be difficult to remain on board the *Raven* in time of war. She wouldn't want to distract anyone from their duty. Though she had no wish to leave him, Tamsyn believed it would be better for her to remain on land somewhere and await his return.

Where that might be was the next puzzle. Drake had spoken to her often of his home in the northern islands, even hinted he'd like to show it to her sometime. But he'd issued no explicit invitation nor offered to allow her to stay there until his return. Until he did, she had to wonder what his intentions for her future might be.

If he never asked her to stay…what could she do? Her throat caught. She could travel to the mainland to find employment. Maybe she'd even board a ship to New York, see the place her father and mother had lived, as she'd always wanted to. There had to be positions available for young women there. She could put her nursing experience to use, or become a nanny for a huge family of children.

But begin again, in a strange place, knowing no one? The prospect is terrifying. Even though it may be the best choice available to me.

As she sat on the branch of a huge tree, watching small animals on the ground below and listening to the insects' chorus, however, she thought of her beloved ocean and her life here. *I don't want to give this up. I just want to stay right here forever.*

She put her head back against the tree trunk and closed her eyes, listening. Gradually, she heard happy cries from the beach, men calling out to one another. *What now?*

Tamsyn climbed down, then ran lightly on her bare feet to the edge of the jungle to see what was causing all the fuss.

She gasped as she saw the tall ship, white sails full

with wind, plow into the cove and come to a halt near the *Raven*. She didn't recognize the flags. At least they didn't look Spanish. But her heart beat faster with panic at the intrusion of any stranger into their little paradise.

Reluctant to step out of the tree line until she was sure it was safe, Tamsyn watched as her sailors waved at those on the ship and ran out to greet the small launches rowing in. *It must be someone familiar.* Her feet still felt buried in the sand.

Using only one crutch now, Drake limped to the edge of the water, beaming in welcome. A heavyset, sandy-haired man wearing a bright yellow shirt, dark pants, and a rakish hat crawled over the side of his little boat, falling in the water with a huge splash. Both crews roared with laughter, pointing at the dripping man, who stumbled out of the water and walked right up to Drake, wrapping him in a huge bear hug.

Drake winced as the big man squeezed his ribs. Tamsyn flinched along with him, imagining how that pressure must feel on his healing wounds. The men clapped each other on the back, talking nonstop, and walked to the area under the big tarpaulin, which was coolest in midday. Drake scanned the jungle and beach, looking for something.

Probably me. She ran her fingers through her hair, making an attempt to look like a lady instead of a hoyden. Her good shoes were on the ship. She sighed. *So be it.* She finally came out to meet their guest.

"Tamsyn!" Drake called as he saw her, voice tinged with relief. "Woman, don't vanish without telling me where you'll be. I want you to meet someone."

Tamsyn made a face at Drake to offset his nagging.

In return, he swatted her gently on the behind. *That,* the man turned and saw.

"Oh, ho, Drake. What is this?" The big man's infectious smile was shared with Tamsyn, and she recognized a New England accent. "A young lady in the midst of these rowdy sea dogs?" He looked at her, head to foot, grinning as she curled her toes under the sand.

"Miss Tamsyn MacKiernan, may I present to you Captain Gavril Rupert, skipper of the *Hawk.*" Drake gestured toward the ship now anchored near the *Raven,* its sails being furled and secured. "Gavril has been a hero of mine ever since I can remember. He took Freddie and me on some of the wildest sails of my life."

"Captain." She inclined her head, trying to keep a blush from her cheeks at his frank look.

"Madam," the captain said, bowing deeply. "You are surely a rose among all these thorns." His eyes twinkled as he raised an eyebrow at Drake. "I can see why he found it hard to keep you off his mind."

The obvious flattery made her smile. "Captain Ashton may well feel I am the one who is a thorn," she said. "You and your men should join us for lunch."

"I would lay good odds Rupert has never missed a meal." Drake slapped the man on his ample belly. "I hope you brought some provisions. You can't expect us to keep you fed."

"Unloading them now." Rupert took off his hat, wiping sweat from his brow, and gestured at the boxes and sacks being passed down a row of men from ship to shore.

"I'll go make sure all is in preparation," Tamsyn said. Rupert seemed larger than life. Drake claimed the man had been a "hero" to him, so he must be important indeed. There were not that many men for whom Drake felt respect.

At the cooking site, however, she was not needed. Men from both crews put a goat on a spit and lit a blazing fire beneath it. Potatoes were buried in the hot embers around the fire, while other men brought fruits in from the jungle, and others gathered wide leaves to use for plates. Ale and rum flowed like water. It would be a wild day—and night, Tamsyn thought, observing their good spirits.

When they sat down to eat at a large table constructed of tree trunks lashed together with rope and covered with palm fronds, Tamsyn and Drake sat on either side of Rupert, eagerly listening as he gave them the latest news on the war.

"Well, the American blockade of the Cuban ports has been successful. Once the choke hold of the Spanish was loosened, the Cuban people rose in force to take back their country. The Spanish on the island, most of them military, are in retreat.

"The battles at sea aren't going much better." He speared a hunk of blackened meat, waving it for emphasis as he spoke. "Admiral Cervera's fleet, in just one battle, was hit by nearly ten thousand shells. But only one American died, while countless Spaniards perished."

Drake and Tamsyn exchanged looks. He remembered the pompous Spanish captain of the *Vizcaya*, who had said he was on his way to meet Cervera. *Had he made it? Or had he been destroyed as well?*

"Are the Americans proving to be of any use?"

As several of the *Hawk*'s American crew protested

Drake's cynical question, he shook his head. "I saw them as they left Key West. Most of them hardly knew how to hold a firearm," he said. "They have a lot of heart but not much training."

Tamsyn thought of her father's clerk, Timothy, and his burning passion to teach the Spanish a thing or two. He'd be a prime example of the poorly trained men who volunteered for the romance of it all. There was more to war than the drumbeating.

Rupert nodded as he stabbed a piece of fruit with a long dagger. "Come, Drake, give them some credit. They're trying hard enough, and what they don't know, they will learn."

One of Rupert's men, a short, thick Irishman, added, "But they're droppin' like flies. After they took Santiago, probably two-thirds of the men were sick with every rotting disease you could name—malaria, yellow fever, dysentery, and typhoid. And you know why?" He shook his head in disbelief. "Because they were ignorant sonsabitches. Beggin' your pardon, ma'am," he said with a nod to Tamsyn. "What I mean to say is they have no training about proper disposal of wastes and keeping theirselves clean. So they spread the disease through the whole camps in no time a-tall!"

"Sad commentary when more men are killed by disease than by bullets," Samuel grumbled. Agreement was murmured around the table.

Tamsyn caught Rupert's eyes on her several times during the meal, particularly when the war was being discussed, and she was relieved when he suggested they change the subject. The part of the war she'd been most worried about was sitting across from her. As far as she was concerned, the rest of them could blow each other to bits as long as Drake was safe.

The conversation segued into an exchange of tall tales, each crew trying to outdo the other with stories of their prowess. Tamsyn was giggling by the conclusion of the meal, as it became obvious they were all trying to impress her. "No woman has ever been so lucky as to be surrounded by as many heroes as we have on this island," she said at last.

This brought on a round of cheers. "Hurrah for us!" shouted one of the *Hawk*'s crew. The men, still laughing, left the table, tossing their eating instruments into a pot near the fire pit. Their "dishes" were discarded, and the crews went off to take some rest and relaxation.

****

Drake poured a shot of rum for himself and Gavril, as Tamsyn wanted none, and the three of them sat on crudely fashioned stools the men had hacked out of driftwood.

"What do you hear from the Keys?" Drake's gaze flicked to Tamsyn and back to Gavril.

The big man tossed the alcohol to the back of his throat in a single gulp, his eyes watering from the burn. "I haven't been back that way for several months, boy. Profit is much higher in the islands, you know."

"I see." Drake had hoped for news of the reaction to Tamsyn's second disappearance. He had no doubt there was a bounty on his own head, and he had not been oblivious to Gavril's interest in Tamsyn. It was not attraction to a pretty girl. *I wonder if he knows more than he's telling…*

"Besides, there's too much military presence, with troops shuttling between Fort Jefferson, the mainland,

and Cuba. Eager lieutenants with not enough to do could be bad for business." Rupert broke into a raucous laugh, and Drake joined in, remembering past exploits.

Tamsyn smiled politely, but Drake could see she was uncomfortable. *She must have noticed him watching her.* Tamsyn was not stupid; she'd guess something was up.

"When are you coming back to sea?" Rupert held out his glass for another.

Drake shrugged. "I have no specific plan right now. I'd been waiting for accurate information." He reached for the bottle, which he'd twisted into a depression in the pale sand. "Which I have now, thanks to you."

"Seems to me you have everything you'd want right here," the *Hawk*'s captain said. Drake looked up sharply, but Rupert was staring off into the distance. Tamsyn was, too, and a longing in her eyes told him she agreed with his friend.

"It's a temporary stay, Gavril. I couldn't have remained at sea in that condition."

"I think he would be entitled to recover as he sees fit," Tamsyn said in a tight little voice.

"Tamsyn's right." Drake smiled. "She was my angel of mercy."

She reached out and caressed his arm. "It must be my destiny," she said. "He seems to need rescuing often."

Rupert cleared his throat. "The guns you left at Matanzas were put to good use."

"I hope they were worth the cost." Drake frowned, remembering those of his crew killed and the mother of his cabin boy. "The Spanish left me no choice but to remove those who the rebels left behind."

"Where'd you send them?" Rupert looked down the beach. "I didn't see them here."

"Samuel said he took them to Andros Island. They'd find support there, people to care for them until the fighting is done at home."

Rupert nodded. "That's sound. And you? She indicates you needed to recover?"

Drake pulled off his shirt, the dark-red scars beginning to fade, pale against the rest of his tanned skin. Rupert leaned forward to examine the healing wound. "And the leg."

"The leg? I'd noticed you limping." A fatherly concern shone on Rupert's face.

Drake slowly pulled up the pant leg to display the twisted flesh which covered his lower limb. Rupert winced. Drake briefly shared the tale of the villagers' rescue. "If it hadn't been for Tamsyn, I would probably have died. That's what Samuel says."

"Really?" The grizzled captain looked at the girl with new appreciation. "Then I'm grateful, miss. This boy—hah!" he said. "This *man*, I should say, he's been a special interest of mine since his parents died. It would grieve me sorely to lose him." He stood up and formally bowed to Tamsyn, then tumbled into the sand.

She blushed and tried not to laugh. "I'm afraid my interest was entirely self-motivated."

Rupert studied her face. "I would believe that to be true, my dear Miss MacKiernan." He seemed to carry the name on his tongue for a long minute.

"What is it, Gavril?" Drake demanded, curious about his friend's interest in Tamsyn. "You look like the cat who's swallowed the canary every time you look at her. What do you know that you haven't told us?"

"I've heard the name MacKiernan recently, and I've been trying to remember where." With a gasp of remembrance, the big man turned his pale green eyes on Tamsyn. "There's word out around Nassau Harbor that you must be found."

****

Tamsyn's heart felt as though it would stop. "Found?" She turned to Drake with a forced smile. "Am I lost?"

Drake was more direct. "Who wants to know?"

"As Angus MacKiernan's ships have come to the harbor, the captains have inquired to see if anyone has seen his missing daughter." He looked from one to the other of them speculatively. "I'd have to say, miss, the picture I saw did you no justice."

Tamsyn's first instinct was to wonder how long it actually took for her father to notice she was gone. Then she conceded if he was looking for her, he must care to some extent. Perhaps. She looked at Drake, whose face was solemn. *What was he thinking? Was he glad my father wants me back?* "Is that all?" she asked Rupert.

"The message was passed that he had fallen very ill and wanted her to come home as soon as possible." Rupert pulled a small piece of wood from his pocket, and a knife, and began to whittle.

"Ill?" Tamsyn was skeptical. *He seemed fine before I left, other than being beside himself at the thought of his lost fortune. Was he up to something to aid Thatcher Winslow in finding me?* "He's going to be all right?"

Rupert shrugged, not taking his attention from his creation. "I didn't ask too many questions, since I didn't suppose I'd ever come across this wayward daughter." He stopped carving and stared at her. "I take it that is your father?"

Tamsyn nodded. Her head was awhirl with possibilities. *Could it be true that he really cares? Or perhaps he is dying and wants to make amends. Or is it Thatcher who's pushing?*

"The message seemed sincere enough," Rupert said. "A father whose only child has left him surely doesn't deserve to die alone."

"He should have thought of that before he—" She bit her lip, holding back tears.

Rupert nodded solemnly. There followed an awkward silence, broken when Mateo came running toward their tent, blood dripping from a cut on his forehead.

"Señorita, help me!" he called.

"Mateo, what have you done?" Tamsyn rose quickly and went to meet him. He said he and some of the others had been up to a bit of horseplay, and he'd been smacked in the head by a dried branch. She got up to clean and bandage his wound. As Drake rose to come with them, she waved him back.

"It looks worse than it really is," she told him. "Facial cuts always bleed more than others." She took Mateo's arm, and they walked back toward the main camp.

She'd need some time to think about this new information. Whatever else was true, if her father was ill and wanted her to return to Key West, Winslow would have his chance to get her into his clutches once again. That was the last thing she wanted.

But could she honestly ignore the plea of a dying father?

****

The *Hawk* stayed in or near the cove most of the next week, with sailors making occasional forays off to Nassau and other places around the islands for supplies. Drake and Captain Rupert both took some time to give their respective ships a good shakedown cruise, testing their equipment, mending their sails, and trading skills with each other.

Drake was pleased to find that even though he'd been out of commission for the last several weeks, the crew had maintained the ship in reasonably good condition. The rudder needed some adjustment, but other than that, the decks and sails were well-kept, the wheel thoroughly oiled, and everything was squared away, right down to the galley spoons.

Tamsyn seemed preoccupied with the news but said nothing about her desires in the matter. Drake didn't think she'd choose to return. He couldn't imagine she'd want to go, not after all she'd been put through by Winslow.

Instead, she sailed with them on these cruises, and she insisted on having something to do. She borrowed a shirt and pants from Mateo and reported for duty.

"I'm no longer someone's ornament!" She scolded Drake when he told the men to bring her a chair on deck. "I have to earn my keep now. Give me a job."

When Drake demurred, Tamsyn swung over the side of the ship and climbed nimbly down the rope ladder. Then she marched up the beach to Captain Rupert and made the same demand. "Captain Ashton apparently has enough help." She shot a wicked glance over her shoulder at Drake, who watched with his mouth open.

Rupert tried to keep from smiling, forcing his features into a pose of serious consideration. "Well, now, I think we could use another boy to climb the rigging and secure the mast, if you're interested."

"Aye, aye, Captain," she said pertly and climbed aboard the *Hawk*.

The rest of the day, as the ships sailed in tandem, Drake glared over at the other ship, watching helplessly as Rupert and the others taught Tamsyn how to trim sails, and a dozen other skills. When Rupert caught him spying with the glass, he broke into laughter Drake could hear all the way across the water. It was the last time Drake didn't find something for her to do.

After being on the island over a month, Drake at last was ready to take on more than day sails around the Bahamas. First, he wanted to know more about the situation in Key West. He cornered Rupert and asked him to sit down on some high rocks, where they'd have a clear view of anyone approaching.

"Gavril, when the news was passed about MacKiernan, was anything said about the circumstances of Tamsyn's disappearance? Are they looking for me?"

"Should they be?" Rupert blinked, then his eyes narrowed. "What did you do?"

Drake flushed. "Exercising my excellent judgment." He followed with an explanation of his abducting Tamsyn from under Thatcher Winslow's nose, on the night of the engagement party, for their romantic moonlight cruise.

"Ho, ho!" Rupert chortled. "What a pirate you are. They ought to be scouring the seven seas for such a reprobate." He offered Drake a cigar; when he refused, Rupert lit his own, puffing out clouds of odorous smoke.

"I don't know about that," Drake said. "It sounded like such a lark when I conceived it. But in the end, Tamsyn suffered mightily at the hands of that blackguard Winslow as a result."

"Was she sorry you'd taken her?"

Drake shook his head. "No. She was ecstatic. We both were. She was concerned that harm would come to me. She insisted on returning so she could allay suspicion."

"Then no real harm was done. How long has she been with you now?" Rupert took a deep drag on his cigar, blowing the smoke out slowly, in the form of rings which vanished as the breeze hit them.

"Four weeks. No, five." Drake thought back on the moments he and Tamsyn had shared on the peaceful island, surrounded by friends and companions. It had hardly seemed so long.

"Five weeks traveling with an unmarried lady?" Rupert asked. "And from what I can tell, you're not doing more than sleeping together."

"Gavril!"

Rupert raised his hands. "All I hear, all I see tells me this, boy." He pointed the cigar at Drake, his face serious. "You love her."

Drake realized if Rupert saw it, his feelings must be that transparent. "I do. She's wonderful. She's the reason I want to get out of bed in the morning—and one day, she'll be the reason I go to bed." He looked down the beach where she'd been walking with Samuel and Chaney to find shellfish. "But I don't know what to do."

"About what?" The older captain winced and shifted on the large boulder, stone solid and rough under them. "What is to do?"

"Look at me," Drake said, pulling up his pant leg. "I've nearly gotten myself blown up, playing the hero. That business with the *Vizcaya* could have turned out very nasty. I still have nightmares about her throat being slit because I was not quick enough to save her." He shook his head. "This is no life for a lady."

Rupert agreed with a sage nod. "My lad, you may have to settle down. You have your house up in Plantation. It would be comfortable enough." He shrugged. "I would even agree to come visit you there when I retire from the sea."

"It's not that easy, Gavril. If what you've told us about the situation in Cuba is true, there's months more fighting ahead for the *Raven*. Freddie's spirit cries out for vengeance." Drake's voice diminished, and he put his head in his hands.

"You promised to avenge your brother's death," Rupert said. "Haven't you fulfilled that promise by now?"

"The Spanish remain here." Drake frowned, not looking up.

"How many guns have you brought to Cuba over the past four years, my boy? A hundred? A thousand? Ten thousand?"

Drake just shrugged.

"If each one of those weapons kills only one Spaniard, you've more than repaid them."

Rupert went on. "But of course, anyone could ship guns. Your real achievement, and what makes me most proud, is the spirit you've imparted to these oppressed people. The peasants of Matanzas were always good people, but it wasn't until you helped them that I saw hope in their eyes again. They began to talk like men, to take their own destiny in their hands, and incite others to do the same." He reached for Drake's shoulder and held on until he made eye contact. "Drake, you've achieved your goal. Losing this mainstay of the Spanish holdings in the New World will hurt them economically far worse than the loss of individual Spanish lives."

He was right. "I hadn't thought of it that way," Drake conceded. "But there's more to be done. I don't think I should rest until the Spanish blight is wiped from the Caribbean." *Isn't that what I meant? Or is it?* "Gavril, I hoped speaking with you would clear my mind. Instead, I think you've clouded it more."

"Why is it you won't take the evidence of your eyes into account?"

"I don't understand." *Where was the old sailor going now?*

"I think you're using Freddie as an excuse not to confront decisions you need to make about that pretty girl. I saw your eyes light fire when I said they wanted her at home. If you don't want to be with her, you should tell her. It would be the honorable thing to do."

Drake sighed. "That's not it at all! I want her here, safe, with me. They don't deserve her back in Key West. She can't possibly choose to return. I'll never be without her in my soul." As he spoke, he realized deep within the truth of his words. *I could lose her if she returns to Florida.*

"She apparently feels the same. Anyone looking at her when she watches you would know that. She made her choice when she came to nurse you. Isn't it about time you made up your mind as well?"

"I don't know how to make those choices," Drake said quietly. "If she goes back, it may change our lives beyond reconciliation. There are too many forks in the road to see clearly."

The elder captain smoked some more until his roll of tobacco was half-burnt, then ground the red tip out to save it for later. He finally stretched his neck from side to side and stood up. "Then perhaps this summons back to Key West is a test for both of you. During the time she's home, taking care of her obligations to her father, perhaps then you can settle your own score with the Spanish. Once you've both laid your ghosts to rest, then you'll be free to come together."

"But if she thinks I'm sending her home—" Would she believe he didn't want her? Nothing was further from the truth.

"Lad, did you see her face when she heard the news? She was stricken with guilt. She'll want to go back of her own accord, mark my words. Then you're off the hook."

Drake worried that Tamsyn would take his silence as an indication he wanted her to return to that old life. But he'd watched her bloom on the island. They'd had time to talk and explore so many different aspects of themselves and each other. Away from her confining life at home, he found her to be creative and joyful, bursting with enthusiasm for freedom. She would discuss the war, politics, the weather, religion, love— all with the same intense interest. The trading of one life for another had served her well. *How can I return her to that other place, which only dragged her down, even for a short time?*

Rupert patted him on the shoulder and chuckled. "You've got it bad, boyo," he said. "I wish it were me. She's a beautiful and generous lady." Seeing Tamsyn walking toward them, bucket in hand, he excused himself to run to the *Hawk* and check on the preparations for his sail the next day. "I'll be waiting to hear from you."

Drake nodded, then walked out to meet Tamsyn. Her bucket was full of crabs, pinching each other as mistaken enemies in an effort to escape their captivity. Drake sensed her heart was full, too. "What is it, love?" he asked.

"I'm sorry, Drake. I must go to my father." Her sad eyes showed the inner battle she must have endured. "I believed he would deny me once I left his home. Perhaps his illness has made him more forgiving, and he wants to make amends." She wiped a tear from her cheek and looked up at him. "Can you transport me, or shall I ask Captain Rupert?"

He smiled half-heartedly. His good humor sank. How could he let her go? "Of course I shall take you. We can go in a day or two."

"Thank you," she said.

"Do you want me to go with you?"

She looked as if she wanted to say yes, but shook her head. "My father is my problem. You have many more souls to care for." She turned away and carried the bucket to that day's cook, who stood by a huge pot on the beach over an open fire.

Rupert was right. How did he know? Drake

wondered. He felt a sense of relief that she'd made the decision for him. But the thought of Tamsyn in Thatcher Winslow's sphere of influence was an unsettling one. He wished she had invited him to go along.

Two days later, Rupert sailed into Nassau Harbor for a final opportunity to scavenge for fresh produce and news of the situation at sea, before they returned to Key West. When he came back to the cove, his eyes danced with amusement.

"What have you to say now, Gavril?" Drake asked when he saw the other captain's face.

"I asked around about you, my boy. I figured it was time to hear the worst so you'd know what you faced."

"And?" Tamsyn asked. She stopped near Drake's elbow, hair braided tightly around her head, her overlarge shirt blousing over Mateo's trousers as she struggled with a load of wood bound for the ship. "What did you hear?"

"A news reporter was asking if anyone knew where you could be found, in connection with your rescue at Matanzas."

"Really? Why would that come to a reporter's attention?"

"Someone came across the families you'd evacuated to Andros, and they apparently sang your praises."

"I find that hard to believe. I hope they are all well," he said slowly.

"Apparently they are. You did a fine thing by saving them," Rupert said. He pulled out a copy of a newspaper with a front-page story about the hero of Matanzas.

"Me?" Drake couldn't believe it.

"Someone who knows our association found me at the dock and asked if I'd seen you. Apparently, the mayor of Key West wants to decorate you himself. For the publicity, of course."

"Drake, if you're considered a hero by the mayor, surely any charges Thatcher will have made against you will disappear like smoke in the wind!" Tamsyn cried, dropping the wood. "You will be free to travel wherever you choose without fear of reprisal." She hugged him, covering his cheek with kisses of joy.

"Might it not be a trap?" Drake asked, still unsure of his good fortune. "Perhaps if I appear there, lured by the temptation of these rewards, then the authorities will be waiting to take me into custody." While he played devil's advocate, his heart grew lighter by the minute. No more fears about going home! While Tamsyn was at her father's house, he could visit her with impunity. *Unless Winslow takes her...* He shoved that thought from him.

Rupert shook his head enthusiastically. "I don't think so, Drake. Everything I heard sounded sincere. At last you're being recognized by your peers for the honorable and courageous young man I've always known you are." He clapped the young man on the back. "You're taking Tamsyn there. You might as well test the waters then."

Drake felt his life was moving fast, like river waters toward the rapids of change, twisting him this way and that as he tried to survive. Tamsyn's excitement was infectious.

"Then what are we waiting for?" He turned to the remaining crew on the beach. "Let's sail!"

****

Drake insisted on openly dropping anchor in the harbor at Key West, in full defiance of any possible consequences. None of Tamsyn's words urging caution could dissuade him. The irony of the situation was still difficult to grasp. Three months ago, he'd been a wanted man. Now he would be toasted and celebrated in salons where he would never have been received before the war.

Tamsyn had changed, too, following her decision to come back to her father's house. She'd changed into more formal dress the second day out from shore, squirming in unaccustomed shoes. Also, she'd felt withdrawn the closer they came to land. But she was fully supportive of his approaching reward. "I'm so happy for you," she said. "It was a heroic rescue. You deserve some respect for all you've done."

"Tamsyn, are you sure you want to return?" He'd asked her a dozen times, not liking the pall that had fallen over her since they'd left the Bahamas.

"My father has sent for me. Like Captain Rupert said, I'm his only child. I owe my duty in the time of his illness." She shrugged, her eyes downcast. "My choices are…limited. I can't stay here." She hesitated, and he felt she had something important to say. But she only shook her head. "I must see to him, that's all. You know I promised my mother to—"

"But your father broke his promise first." Drake had never forgiven Angus for failing to protect her, especially once Winslow's treachery had been revealed.

Tamsyn just shrugged. It was, in recent days, all too often her response to his questions about her return home.

"And Winslow?" he asked.

For the first time, she smiled. "I'll handle Thatcher Winslow."

Chapter Twenty-Two

After they'd docked at Key West Harbor, it was easy enough for Tamsyn to gather her things and slip away from the ship before Drake could follow, since a captain had pressing priorities at landing.

As she passed each familiar shop, she realized how much she'd missed the home of her childhood. Her eyes filled with tears as her heart overbrimmed with longing for the security this place had once represented. That safety was destroyed now, replaced by frightening scenes with Thatcher, and Angus at his angry worst. For most intents and purposes, she was alone.

She was greeted as a stranger by those passing by, even those she recognized. Her hair had taken on quite a red tint during her days in the sun, and she wore it long, loose, and curly in the humidity. Her skin was darkly tanned, and she looked healthy, she'd noticed in Drake's mirror. The young woman reflected there was anxious yet expecting good things. She had to keep her focus positive. Too much could go wrong.

Her steps quickened as she rounded the corner of Duval Street and thought of all the familiar faces she would soon encounter: Juba, Old James, Clara…the ghost of her mother, who'd been noticeably absent during these weeks she'd been on the island. *Perhaps she knows I'm happy, and I don't need her constantly watching over me.*

It wasn't until she put her booted foot on the bottom step of her front porch that her father's face appeared before her mind's eye.

It gave her a chill.

But Angus had wanted her to come. Filial duty required that she appear, as Rupert had reminded her, as little as she'd wanted to hear it then. Her father must have gone to some effort to get word to her, as far as the *Raven* had traveled, sending his ships out to search even during the worst throes of the war. *How had he known I'd gone so far?*

Perhaps Thatcher had forced the information from Clara or Old James that she'd left by sea. But from what Rupert said, they hadn't been looking for Drake Ashton. So it could have been chance encounter.

She was hesitating on the front steps, steeling herself to go in, when the front door of the Brennan house burst open. Norah came flying out and across the yard. "Tamsyn?"

"Norah," Tamsyn whispered, holding her dear friend tightly in her arms, eyes squeezed shut with the force of her embrace.

"Is that really you? What have you done with your hair?" Norah held her at arm's length, examining her. "You've been out without a hat."

Without a hat? Tamsyn laughed out loud. *If Norah only knew how many things I have been out "without" in the last month.* "So I have."

Inspection complete, Norah smiled widely. "You look wonderful."

"Thank you. I feel wonderful."

"Thatcher Winslow is beside himself. Where have you been?" Norah's eyes sparkled.

"Can I tell you later?" she asked. "I heard my father was ill. That's why I came home."

Norah's face grew serious at once. "Of course, dear friend."

"Norah?"

As the male voice called, both young women turned to the Brennan porch. Tamsyn recognized the young Navy man at once. "Brian?" she whispered to Norah.

Her friend positively beamed. "We're to be married a week from Saturday before he is sent out to sea again. Tamsyn, I just can't stop smiling." She looked up at the MacKiernans' door. "You'd better go. Come see me later."

"I will," Tamsyn promised. With a deep breath, she turned and continued up the steps, walking in without knocking. She couldn't stand to be turned away, especially in front of Norah.

The house was very still, except for some noise in the kitchen. Peeking in the sitting room, she saw nothing had changed since she had gone. Even her sewing still graced the basket beside her favorite chair. She could have just stepped out for a walk to the market. Her breath caught, and she moved on before she began to cry.

Tamsyn looked up the stairs, guessing, since her father wasn't established in the sitting room, he must be in bed. *Should I see him immediately?* Her stomach sank. She decided she could delay that confrontation a little longer. She passed by the polished wooden stairs, slipping down the hall toward the kitchen.

Her father's office door stood open, and she went in quietly. The room felt empty without the constant activity she remembered, Papa shouting at his clerks the way Drake called orders to the crew. The inkwell on the desk had been left open, and she crossed the room to cap it before the ink dried up and was wasted. Her father's presence was strong there, but so were the memories of the last weeks before she left, the angry argument with Thatcher the night she returned from her adventure on shipboard, as he demanded to have her virginity checked.

No, I can't stay in this room, either.

Tamsyn went on to the kitchen. As the wooden door swung open, all eyes turned. There was a moment of silent astonishment, then dawning delight.

"Missy Tamsyn!" Clara came forward impulsively, then restrained herself, as if she wasn't quite sure what she was seeing was real. Old James, too, just stared as if he'd seen a ghost. It was Juba who finally came to her, folding her in pudgy arms, cuddling her against an ample bosom that smelled of cinnamon and vanilla and other wonderful aromas. *Now it feels like I belong*, Tamsyn thought.

"Tamsyn, child," the woman said. "'Bout time you come home. We've been missin' you."

"I'm glad to see you, too, Juba," Tamsyn said. She looked around the kitchen, familiar smells and sights filling her senses. These people loved her, and she'd missed them, too.

"When de last time you eat?" Juba demanded. When Tamsyn didn't immediately answer her, she set right to making iced tea for her young lady. "Clara, you get ham from de icebox and make Missy Tamsyn a sandwich, right quick."

"Juba, you don't have to—" But watching the

woman in action, she realized she might as well be talking to the wind. Once Juba had made up her mind that Tamsyn needed nourishment, she would not rest until her girl ate.

Clara stared at her. "Your hair," she said at last, her voice thick with wonder.

"Yes." Juba narrowed her eyes at her young charge. "What 'bout that hair? And I know you been out without a hat in the sun." She shook her head, stirring sugar into the tea furiously. "What does Miss Ellen always tell you? People know a lady by the whiteness of her skin and hands." As she handed Tamsyn the cool glass, Juba gasped as she saw the calluses on Tamsyn's palms. "Girl, what you been doing with these hands? Miss Ellen will curse me from Heaven."

Old James moved closer to see what had horrified Juba so, and Tamsyn quickly put her hands flat against her sides. "You all look fine." Tamsyn took her usual seat on a stool next to the stove.

"Don't think you can escape me, missy," Juba warned. "Let me see those hands now." With a sigh, Tamsyn put her hands in the large dark ones. "Well?"

"I've learned to sail, Juba. I've pulled lines and trimmed sails. I've steered a ship with a huge, splintery wheel," she confessed. "I've been climbing trees and picking coconuts and building shelters on a beach." She smiled contentedly. "And I've never been happier."

"Lordy, Lordy," Juba said, shaking her head. She dropped the offending hands and chose Tamsyn a pear from a bowl on the counter. Clara brought the sandwich, and Tamsyn took a few bites, but the nagging reminder that Angus awaited taxed her appetite.

She settled into her surroundings, feeling she was in the real heart of her home, almost as if the last several weeks had not happened at all. Memories flooded over her, of Thanksgiving turkeys and midnight toast and Juba as a younger woman, teasing the daughter of the house into eating her vegetables.

Old James asked, "You still wit' dat man? Dat pirate?"

She nodded. "We've been all around the Caribbean. We encountered a Spanish battleship—"

Clara let out a peep, quickly cut off by her hand across her mouth. "They didn't kill and eat you?"

Tamsyn chuckled. "Obviously not. But Drake saved us all by tricking them into letting their guard down when they came to take the ship." She told them the whole story, leaving out the part about herself as bait. She was still squeamish about death happening around her so fast, well aware her own capture could have ended her life just as quickly.

"Lordy!" Juba moved to her own chair, where she sat down heavily, fanning herself to release her excitement. "I always think Missy Tamsyn be de death of me."

"What about my father? Word came to us from Nassau that he was ill, maybe dying, and needed me to come home."

The three looked at each other, then Old James nodded. "He been abed some three weeks now. Doctor been here every day or two, but he say nothing about dying." The old black man shrugged his wiry shoulders. "If someone ask me, I say he just letting his anger eat him up."

"Anger...at me?" Tamsyn asked, dreading the answer.

Old James looked at the floor. It was Juba who finally spoke. "He was hurt when you left. Spent a whole morning throwing things in de office."

Clara glared at Juba. "Tell de truth!" she cried. She turned to Tamsyn, eyes flashing. "He mad because de people come to him and say dey use Winslow ships now, not his! Marse Thatcher be all over town, talkin' 'bout how you be possessed by devils or just plain crazy, and soon no one come around here to send ships. *That* why he take to de bed." Her final words were bitter, and she backed out of Juba's reach, her arms crossed and foot tapping in frustration.

Tamsyn shook her head. "Thank you, Clara. It's better to know." She struggled to keep in the tears she felt dripping into her throat. "I'm sure he's not letting on that he's upset about his loss of business." The tale the captains were passing on could be no more than a cover story, she realized. Her father probably didn't want her here at all.

So what was she to do?

They all sat comfortably for several minutes, while she nibbled at her food. Finally, Juba nodded and winked at Tamsyn with her old, warm eyes. "I can see dat man make you happy. It's written all over you."

Tamsyn nodded. "Very happy," she said. She launched into a distracting tale of the sail home, talking about the different members of the crew and how well they had treated her. Clara's brown eyes got even wider as she listened to the adventure.

"Well, Missy Tamsyn, I never thought you be a pirate at heart," Clara said at last.

Tamsyn laughed as heartily as the rest. She'd not thought of herself as a pirate, either. Well, maybe not until the last few days, as she became a regular crew member, working in the sun with the other men. It had been hard work, as her palms reflected, but certainly some of the most satisfactory hours she'd ever invested. She'd come home in a huge burst of naivete. What if she'd lost her chance to spend another hour with those beloved faces? Was she wanted or not?

A furious bell-ringing sounded from upstairs, and they all jumped at the sudden noise. "You been up yet?" Old James said.

She shook her head. "I wanted to see you first. I knew that would give me strength."

The bell rang again. "Marse Angus know somepin' goan on," he said ominously.

She rolled her eyes. "You're probably right. I'd better go on. Shall I take anything?"

Old James handed her a medicine bottle and a spoon, and the three servants watched silently as she gathered her wits and left the kitchen.

Each step seemed taller than the one before, like one of those dreams where the hall lengthened as one tried to reach the end. *Maybe all I need to do to save myself is wake up...*

As she entered her father's room, she smelled a faint trace of his cologne, and it immediately took her back to girlhood. It was some occasion when he and her mother were planning an evening out. He'd smelled of spices and looked handsome as she'd ever seen him, dressed in a dark suit coat, and her mother in some sort of long blue dress. The memory was a faded one, fed by that one scent.

Wrapped in her nostalgia, it took her a minute to realize Angus MacKiernan sat and glared at her. "Papa." She froze, the spoon quivering in her hand. "I heard you wanted me."

"You did, eh? You rushed home to see if your father was really dying." His skin was pale, and she was sure he compared it to her own sun-drenched tone. "How devoted a daughter you are."

She steeled herself to deflect his sarcasm. "Yes, Papa. I came as soon as I heard." The room was darkened by drawn curtains. She approached the bed to pass him the medicine and spoon, which he snatched from her hand. Glancing around, she saw everything was just as it had been when she left. *Can I be the only thing that has changed?*

He poured some foul, brown syrup into the spoon and swallowed it, then shoved the bottle back at her. He stared off toward the window, in the opposite direction from his daughter. When he didn't speak further, Tamsyn came up to the bed and took his hand.

"Are you feeling better? Why did you send for me?" she asked, determined to break through the bitterness. *Surely these deep ties run both ways, Papa. Please remember you loved me once.*

"I'm as well as can be expected." Angus appraised her, eyes sorrowful. "Ye've obviously been out raisin' Cain. Did ye nae think what would happen to me when ye disappeared?"

"Of course I thought." Mimicking his Scottish burr, she replied, "Did ye nae think how I'd feel knowing ye were tradin' me like a cord o' wood?"

"Child, I thought ye loved Thatcher Winslow." Heightened color appeared in her father's cheeks. He didn't seem ill at all. "I only did what it took to get ye what ye wanted."

"Oh, Papa." She knew he'd never understand, but she tried to explain it anyway, just once. She might never have the opportunity again. "I thought I was in love with Thatcher. I believed I really knew him." She leaned closer, willing him to comprehend her story. "But the Thatcher I loved never existed—the gentle, thoughtful man with a broad education who cared for and respected me."

Her eyes burned with tears. "Once he got control of me and then you, he only thought I was a prize to be won, by destroying anyone who disputed his right to have everything his own way."

"Control of me? How d'you come to that conclusion?" Angus barked.

"They t-told me what he'd s-said," she stammered. "Thatcher confessed to the sabotage of your sponging boats. Didn't he?" He said nothing. "And he threatened to harm me?"

Angus shook his head. Tamsyn was confused. She'd believed even then concern for her could be her father's motive for compliance with Thatcher's wishes. But from his blank look, she had to conclude that her first instinct had been right. Money was the only thing he worshiped. Disappointment stabbed through her like hot lightning.

How could I still be so stupid?

"I thought you cared for me," she whispered. "You still haven't said why you sent word for me to come home."

"I wanted to see your face when you explained how you justify ruining me. Why could ye not think o' someone else besides yourself, just for once? Do ye have any idea what damage ye've done here?"

She nodded slowly. "I do, Papa. I'm truly sorry that you've suffered any consequences because I left. But you've got to remember that you made bad business choices even before Thatcher came into our lives."

"And who says this is true?" Each word spit from his wizened mouth.

"I worked on your books. And I heard Thatcher confront you right in your office. You know your own decisions."

"You're awfully sassy, young lady. How dare you accuse me? I've fed you and raised you with as many advantages as I could provide. And what can you say you've done to help me?"

"What's important is the fact that I've been saved from a life of misery with a man who didn't love me, Papa. Doesn't that mean anything to you?"

"I'm sure it will keep me warm at night," he said, his voice chill as ice.

If he expected an apology, he was sadly mistaken. She'd tried. It was time to leave before she'd say something truly horrible which would haunt her in the days to come, because she did still care, in spite of it all. "Is there something else I can get for you? Some soup, perhaps?"

"No, I need no more help from you. You've done enough."

She found it painful, as Angus wouldn't look her in the eye. She brought him a glass of water, setting it on the bedside table when he refused to take it, and adjusted the netting around his bed, trying not to take her discomfort to heart.

"The peculiar thing is, Thatcher never even wanted me, not really. He wanted Miss Pickham. I suppose they'll get together now."

"They can marry on my grave," he grumbled. Then he closed his eyes and ignored her.

The old man, lying there, pitifully clutching his covers in wrinkled fingers, seemed like a stranger. She felt closer to Mateo or Samuel or the other members of the *Raven*'s crew; they certainly cared more about her well-being and happiness. Angus would be well when he chose to rise from his sickbed. She had no obligation to nurse him back to health.

Just as she turned to go, thinking he'd fallen asleep, Angus murmured, "What will ye do now, girl?"

She stepped closer to him, glad the curtains were closed. Her grief was easier to hide in this dim light. "I don't know, Papa. Perhaps travel north and hire myself out as a servant." She remembered, once, he had threatened her with that possibility when she expressed doubts about the wedding. She hoped the statement would disturb him, to rattle him as she'd been shaken by her discovery of his true feelings.

He grunted. "Ye'd be worthless around here."

His biting words cut through her tenuous resolve to maintain the semblance of family. Perhaps she hadn't heard him right. "Papa?"

"Bad enough I've lost business over your willy-nilly, irresponsible behavior. If you were t' remain in the office, there'd be more leavin', nae doubt. I think you'd better plan on making those arrangements to take care o' yourself." He looked away.

Tamsyn had taken all the hurt she could bear. "I

shall, Papa. I trust you will allow me a few days to make preparations, then I shall leave you to your self-pity. But remember, my departure has been your choice, not mine."

He continued to ignore her. Soon his eyes closed again.

Humiliated, she left the room, her facial muscles trembling with her effort not to let him see her cry. She managed to contain her anguish at his callous treatment until she got behind her closed bedroom door and threw herself on the bed. Then her frustration and hurt burst forth in tears, then moans, then screams of grief, muffled thoroughly in her feather pillows.

I should never have come home, she thought, curled around her pillow, holding on to it for dear life. *Drake, bless him, knew I shouldn't come, but he never challenged my decision. He trusted me to make the right choice. How could I have been so mistaken?*

It was the last time she would cry for her lost childhood, and when she had no more tears left, she sat up and wiped her face as a different woman, a woman now on her own. Even her white, lacy bedroom she'd furnished herself seemed a foreign place. There were familiar items, of course, like the long-dried flower she'd received from some forgotten beau of her youth, and the seagull feather she'd found in the cove, nearly a foot long, soft, silver and white. Her writing table remained as she'd left it, pink paper laid out as if she'd simply stepped out for the afternoon. Everything seemed to be the same—except Tamsyn herself.

Cuddled with her pillow, she closed her eyes, thinking about the decision she had to make. Before she knew it, she'd fallen asleep. Her dreams began with a series of Spanish battleships full of angry captains, all of whom wore the face of Angus MacKiernan.

Soon the pictures segued into the shadowy recurrent dream that had troubled her for so long. *As she ran through the jungle, vines caught her arms, slowing her down. Footsteps sounded behind her, inexplicably loud, like boots on polished floor. Ahead, she saw the gate to her father's courtyard—safety!— and inside it, Drake Ashton.*

"Drake!" she called, reaching for the metal bars, but no matter how hard she pulled, she couldn't open the gate.

She looked over her shoulder. Thatcher appeared from the shadows, hands grasping for her. She turned back to the gate, but Drake was gone. Thatcher grabbed her shoulders and—

She screamed and woke to Clara's insistent shaking of her shoulder.

Startled, the girl jumped back. "Missy Tamsyn, Juba say it time to eat."

Tamsyn rubbed her eyes, her breath still coming in fits and starts. "What time is it?"

"Suppertime, she say." Clara picked at her skirt anxiously.

"All right." Tamsyn stretched and sat up. Her bedclothes were completely loose and disordered, though she'd slept on top of them. *Those dreams…*

"I bring your tray—"

"No, I'll come down to the kitchen. I'll be there in a few minutes after I freshen myself." Clara nodded and disappeared. Tamsyn got up and washed her face, still terrified of what her mind had shown her. She needed reassurance and warmth. She'd find it in the kitchen.

She ate good Bahamian bread and roast beef with potatoes simmered in its gravy, and Juba's special chocolate cake, two helpings of each, until she thought she'd explode. "Everything tastes so good," Tamsyn told the amazed servants as they watched her pack the meal into her once-delicate frame. "Diaz is a wonderful cook, but he just can't make this kind of feast."

Juba offered to get her a third plate, but she shook her head. "Maybe later, just one more piece of cake. Thank you so much." She jumped from her chair and hugged Juba. "I'm so glad to see you. I'm sorry I left without saying goodbye."

The older woman nodded. "When Clara come back and say you gone, I not believe you could go wit'out seein' me. She says it a matter of life and death, so I understand." She smiled at Tamsyn. "But I'm glad you're back."

Tamsyn's face grew long, and she walked around the table. "I'm not back."

"Where you go now?" Juba demanded. Old James paused in his trek to the basin with his soiled dishes. "Sailing away again with your pirate?"

Tamsyn shook her head. "I don't know. He hasn't asked me. But Papa made it clear he wants me under this roof no longer than it takes to make other arrangements."

Juba cast a malicious look toward the ceiling, and Tamsyn had to laugh. "Don't blame him. He's right, you know. I ran from responsibility, my engagement to Thatcher, and I knew when I did, it would have repercussions on this house. I was thinking only about myself."

"And about *him*," Clara added.

"And about him," Tamsyn conceded.

"He be back," Clara said solemnly, rising to take the rest of the dishes from the table.

Tamsyn smiled but said no more, helping wash the dishes as Juba prepared for the next day's baking. They all chattered about local gossip, people in the neighborhood, deaths and births, and events that had happened in Tamsyn's absence. The biggest news, of course, was the engagement of Norah and Brian Hamilton.

"I wanted to speak to her this evening," Tamsyn said. "Perhaps they're finished with supper now." She dried her hands on a linen cloth by the stove and slipped out the kitchen door.

The courtyard awaited and called to her, and she took time to walk its well-loved paths, even sitting in the alcove, remembering the first days of Thatcher's courtship, when he'd quote poetry and bring her pretty flowers. *I've had a good life. I've had food and shelter, never had an enemy overrun my city, as those women and children did at Matanzas, had a loving mother and a father. I've been asked to marry. I've found real love and adventure. There's no reason for me to complain. I just need to decide what I want to challenge me next.*

Norah's voice penetrated Tamsyn's thoughts, and she left the alcove seat. But Norah was not alone. In the light which shone from the rear of the Brennan house, she spied Norah, with her long hair down, wrapped in Brian's arms. He'd taken off his military jacket, but still stood straight as he leaned down to kiss his intended.

Tamsyn turned away, not wanting to interrupt, and returned to the alcove, where she sat and listened to the evening sounds. She was suddenly possessed by a haunting sadness that she was alone. A hundred images came to her of her own closeness with Drake, sitting together on the warm sand, their feet side by side in the water, sun blazing down on them...the scented tropical nights under a sky full of stars, brilliant as his eyes... She wanted nothing more at this moment than to be in his arms, to let him kiss all the hurt away.

He's not far, came a thought unbidden.

She considered the possibility. The *Raven* was anchored less than a mile from her home. She could sneak down and...

But she couldn't do it. Not here. No matter how often she strolled the Bahamian beach alone, unescorted ladies couldn't walk the streets of Key West after dark.

Perhaps more important, she wondered why Drake hadn't visited, now that he was safe from apprehension by the authorities. The ship needed to restock its supplies, of course, but he had others who could do this task. Maybe he had friends to see, since it had been months since he could show his face here.

But she'd hoped he'd miss her and want to come to her.

The fact he had not, strengthened her belief he wasn't ready to commit, though she knew to the depth of her soul that he loved her. She had to seriously consider other possibilities for her life's path.

She tucked her skirt up around her legs and leaned back into the wooden support. It would be late that evening before she went back inside, a plan finally forming in her head.

The next morning, Tamsyn received another unpleasant surprise when Clara came to announce that Thatcher Winslow had discovered her return.

"Marse Winslow be here," the girl said in a tight voice. "Shall I tell him go?"

Tamsyn turned from her mirrored vanity, where she was brushing her hair. Despite the critical looks she'd received, she was pleased with the red streaks. She wound the curly ends into a bun on the top of her head, wrestling with her hairpins from unaccustomed use.

She sighed. "I suppose he was bound to come." Strength and resignation warmed her blood. *He'll not dominate me again.* "Please show him into the sitting room and see if he'd like some brandy. I'll be down shortly."

"Yes'm." The girl respectfully nodded and left the room.

Tamsyn checked her reflection, then let her hair down. *If he wants to see me, by the gods, then he can see the real me.* It would be an unpleasant confrontation; this she knew. She went through her wardrobe, knowing her former dresses would pinch and be uncomfortable compared to the clothing she'd worn on the *Raven*. She chose the pink dress she'd worn to the Pickhams' ball, wondering if Thatcher would even remember. As far as she was concerned, it reminded her of Drake Ashton. That helped.

The pale tone of the dress set off the tawny tone of her skin. She looked like an Indian princess. She set about adding a touch of cosmetics to give her strength, and tried to relax.

Thatcher could do nothing to hurt her.

The realization made her marvel at how strong she had become. Had she really believed, just a few months before, that she was obliged to marry an abusive man, simply because she'd given her word? She'd learned much about love from Drake, though they had yet to fully know each other as man and woman. His love supported her decisions, not undermined them. Drake must realize that only by allowing her to be herself would he experience the fullness of her love.

When Tamsyn had delayed as long as was appropriate for a lady receiving an uninvited caller, she stood before the mirror and straightened her silk gown. She proceeded downstairs slowly, clutching the rail, unused to the heels on her dress shoes.

As she stepped into the doorway of the sitting room, Thatcher gaped at her in horror. "Why, you're nearly as dark as a nigra!"

Tamsyn smiled, a cynical eye evaluating the man she once had loved. He was still as handsome as ever, dapperly dressed in a white suit, but his usually smooth edges seemed jagged as he looked at her. The spoiled little boy he'd always been watched from his man's eyes. "I have spent some time in the sun," she admitted.

"Where have you been?" He crossed the room, standing close to her so she had to look up at him. His agitation was apparent. He'd given up all pretense of social convention, even failing to greet her. He obviously wanted to intimidate her, as he had often done in the past.

There was no need to play his game. She stepped away to stand by the fireplace. "I've been many places," she said. "I've been discovering myself. Most importantly, I've been learning what love is—what it *really* is."

"Love? You don't know what the word means." Thatcher scoffed, face beginning to flush. "You left me…to find love…for Drake Ashton," he cried with dawning realization. "You slut!" He positively quivered in his anger.

Tamsyn was glad she'd moved out of his reach, as his control began to slip. "You can believe what you choose, Thatcher."

"You're a coward, just like your father. You can't handle the true light of day to shine upon your life and face your failure."

"I see you're still using my father against me, and me against him. When will you grow tired of this manipulation?" She knew she was strong on the outside, but hoped the inside, which trembled with the weight of the emotion she felt, remained well hidden. *Betrayed, betrayed on all sides…*

He turned away from her, walking to the French door. When he swiveled back to the room, he switched tactics abruptly. His face was stricken as he spoke warmly, softly to her. "Tamsyn, my darling, you know how I care for you. I'm not sure what madness has possessed you, but if you will only let me arrange to put you under a doctor's care, I'm sure you will remember your true feelings." He stepped forward, caught up in his plan. "We can send you away for several months until this—this blackness"—he gestured to her face—"fades, and you can return to Key West, in triumph as my wife."

It was easier to deal with Thatcher when he was being ridiculous. She thanked Heaven for his change of style and stated her feelings in the most formal tone she could muster. "Thank you, but Mr. Winslow, I don't believe it appropriate to continue our engagement, as I don't intend to marry you."

"What?" he sputtered, in an instant back to his Mr. Hyde personality. "I'll ruin your father. I'll tear you down and leave you lying in the sewer." As he must have realized in the face of her implacable calm that she was very serious, his confusion mounted, demonstrated in the wildness taken on by his blue eyes. "Tamsyn, I'll not let you go!" Menacing, he took a step toward her.

"My dear Thatcher, I'm already gone," she said, composure not a whit disturbed by his raving. "Good day." She left the room, moving up the stairs toward her bedroom.

She heard a noise behind her as she ascended, a strange, feral sound. It sent a chill up her spine. Thatcher came to the foot of the staircase, obviously losing mastery of his emotions. His voice was cold. "Then it is I who shall break the engagement, you adulterous bitch."

"As you wish," she replied, not even turning around, then continued up. Old James came out of her father's room, and as she passed, she said loudly, "Please see Mr. Winslow to the door."

The old man nodded and meandered down toward the furious Winslow. "This way, please—"

"I know the way," Thatcher snarled. His footsteps echoed through the foyer. The subsequent slam of the door sounded like a cannon's fire. Tamsyn heaved a sigh of relief and continued to her sanctuary.

She knew it would only be a matter of hours before he spread more gossip and lies. Poor, wronged Thatcher! Sympathy would run high among the eligible young ladies; Mary Elizabeth Pickham would probably swoon from the excitement of it all. Tamsyn smiled, just thinking of it.

Having severed that connection, her thoughts turned to her next decision. What was she to do? Drake was involved today in all his pomp and ceremony. Before they left the *Raven*, he'd asked her to come to city hall with him, but she'd declined, sure her father would need her. It wasn't too late to go, she saw by the timepiece in her room; the event was scheduled for noon. But Thatcher would taint the crowd with his blatherings, and Drake deserved better. Let him have his spotlight and adulation. He'd earned it.

Tamsyn could slip away quietly, leaving her father to his fate. Whether Thatcher's threats would come to anything, she didn't know. Once he found he couldn't coerce the MacKiernans, he'd turn his attentions elsewhere and find another, more worthy bride for his mother to dress up and correct and hound. Or he might destroy Angus, just out of spite. She shrugged at her reflection in the mirror. It was no longer her concern.

What to do now?

The past few weeks with Drake had been wonderful, despite the drama, and she yearned for them to continue. But they couldn't. She'd realized that on the return to Key West. She and Drake had grown more distant on their last sail, each with a history to face when they returned from the idyllic sailing around the Caribbean. From the moment she'd fled to the *Raven*, Tamsyn knew she could never marry Thatcher. That decision made, it was easy to tell him so. But beyond that, it was much harder to decide.

She couldn't stay here. The humiliation she'd suffered at the hands of Thatcher and her father working in collaboration was still too painful, and her father had made his position clear. Even if she tried to stay elsewhere in the city, these events would haunt her. She had to move on.

Drake hadn't asked her to travel with him, and she'd noticed his growing excitement as they'd approached familiar ground. He'd finally won a little of the honor and respect he'd struggled for all his orphaned life, and it was obvious he planned to enjoy that recognition among his former peers. Tamsyn had told him she was happy for him, and she was. Finally all those society girls would appreciate the man Drake had become. Since he hadn't spoken to her about the future in other than vague, romantic terms, she assumed he had plans but was reluctant to say so, to avoid hurting her. He knew she'd suffered enough.

As a result, her decision would forestall any sort of unpleasantness with Drake. She'd book passage on a ship leaving for Miami. She'd see some of those things Drake had always talked about, and perhaps catch a train from there to New York or Boston or Chicago. A new life awaited her.

Even as she thought of leaving her beloved Drake, it felt like her heart was tearing itself open, hemorrhaging drops of her spirit. She'd felt loved and appreciated in his presence, for the first time since her mother had died. His constant faith in her had restored her self-esteem so that she could stand up to those who would reduce her to the status of a possession.

Once Drake's commitment to appear before the mayor was satisfied, she hoped he would come share it with her so she could see his proud face, eyes sparkling as he felt redeemed. She'd visit Norah Brennan and her fiancé and spend some time with Juba and the others.

Then she would pack what she'd brought from the

Raven and what she wanted from here, and have them sent ahead to whatever ship would take her north to her new life.

Chapter Twenty-Three

At city hall, the atmosphere was festive, scent of the colorful flowers both in and outside mixing with the odor of locally rolled cigars. Women, young and old, beautifully dressed, watched Drake with admiration as the mayor and his cronies toasted his heroism in the war.

The celebration followed music, speeches, and the reading of a proclamation in Drake Ashton's honor. The subject of the city's adoration, taking in the sunlit scene, reflected scornfully (but silently) on the hypocrisy of it all. Four months ago, he'd been a hunted man. Now he was the hero of the hour. The chamber was filled with people, and the attendees overflowed into the street outside. Drake noted the distinct absence of the Winslows. He hoped that didn't mean Thatcher was planning trouble.

While he drank champagne with the suit-coated gathering, his thoughts were on the woman he loved. She'd left the ship before he could say goodbye and wish her luck. He wondered how the reunion with her sick father had gone, hoping they'd reconciled their differences. As someone who found himself now without a family, he understood how important those ties could be.

He'd been tempted to go see her, but had been reluctant to disturb whatever peace she'd been able to create. She wanted to come to terms with the promise she'd made to her mother; she'd said so. He knew she didn't regret her decision to leave Winslow for a life at sea. But he wondered that she'd decided to return to Key West to be at Angus MacKiernan's side rather quickly. Did she miss her life here? More than that paradise they'd had together?

As he shook hands with congratulatory well-wishers, Drake questioned again whether he had the right to expect her to give up her home and her father permanently for an uncertain future with him. She'd certainly been brave enough to embrace that future by coming in his hour of need. If she believed so strongly in him, why shouldn't he believe in her?

Many of the words Gavril Rupert had thrown at him in their last conversation began to crystallize into a coherent pattern. Perhaps they meant he'd done enough. Freddie's revenge may have been satisfied by providing of guns and supplies, and the deliverance of the families of Matanzas. It was time to stop living for others, and to live for himself.

Himself...and Tamsyn.

But Tamsyn's bag had been packed and left by his door that morning. Everything she'd brought on the ship and accumulated while she was there must have been tucked into the bag, because when he'd returned to the room, it was scoured of all signs of her presence, other than a trace of her scent.

Why had she taken her things with her? Surely she had belongings, clothing at home to wear, so she was not in need of them. *But if she intended to return, why hadn't she left her things where they were?*

She was planning to leave him.

His heart sank. He couldn't let her go. He couldn't...

Time to set his course for a permanent arrangement, and always have her by his side. He had to marry her. Even if he had to leave her to return for the final battles of the war, it would be no great hardship. He'd know she would be waiting for his return. She'd be safe at his home, and she'd have access to beaches and mangrove jungles, all these for her to explore.

As he fully digested this revelation, Drake excused himself to the sixth eligible young woman introduced by her hovering and anxious mamma. He had to escape into the open air. He had to find Tamsyn before she disappeared.

He crossed the room, ladies trailing in his wake, to find the mayor, now speaking with various government officials. "Your Honor," he said, "I thank you for the recognition of my humble acts. Unfortunately, I find I have business I must attend to immediately."

"Must you go?" the mayor asked, dismayed. "A moment, please, sir. It is so seldom we have the opportunity to meet a real hero." He summoned a photographer who had been taking pictures of the extravagant social festivities. "One picture, if you would, Mr. Ashton."

"Certainly," Drake said, struggling to remain civil. Agitation at the thought of losing Tamsyn ate at him. The more he studied the clues in his mind, the more convinced he became that he was correct. *I have to stop her.*

Once the photographer was set up, others insisted on having pictures made with the famous man. He didn't dare to be rude, but when the cameraman stopped to unload a box of new photographic plates, he finally seized his opportunity and bolted.

Samuel waited outside the venue, and Drake sent him to hire a carriage. "Something expensive." What would impress Angus MacKiernan? He'd only seen the man once, at the Pickhams', and he hadn't seemed noteworthy in any particular way. *Perhaps a good bottle of alcohol*, he thought. *And flowers for Tamsyn.* He searched out a merchant who carried top-of-the-line liquor, then found a flower seller in the market who had long stems of perfumed frangipani. He bought an armful, because he knew they were Tamsyn's favorites. As he ran to meet Samuel, his bouquet caught the eye of most passersby. "I'm in love!" he shouted as the curious looks continued. His confession produced smiles from all.

Samuel appeared, driving a black enclosed carriage, rich with large windows, gold embellishments, and velvety seats. Nodding with satisfaction, Drake laid the flowers carefully on the seat opposite and climbed in, commanding Samuel to conduct him to Tamsyn's home.

His bravado wavered as he considered what to say to her father. The dour Scotsman wouldn't be easily disposed toward the man who had spirited away his daughter. What Drake said had to be brilliant.

Sir, I love your daughter. What an understatement. She was his breath, his heart, his life.

I don't have as much to offer as Winslow, but I promise your daughter will be happy. Surely any father would be concerned for his daughter's economic well-being. But what could he possibly offer that would compete with the Winslow fortune?

Tamsyn will never want for anything, as long as I live. In his business, as they'd seen quite recently, the length of his life was always a matter which was of variable duration.

Impossible.

When they arrived at the MacKiernan home, he still hadn't come up with a solid plan. He'd have to think on his feet.

Samuel grinned like a fool as he leapt down from the driver's seat, and slapped him on the shoulder. "*Vaya con Dios, amigo.*"

"Thank you, my friend." Drake looked at the door, then back at Samuel with a sigh. *What if MacKiernan said no? What if Tamsyn wouldn't have him?*

The first mate shook his head in disbelief. "What makes you hesitate? You're crazy in love with her, she's crazy in love with you—"

Drake grabbed his arm. "Is she? Are you sure?" he demanded, heart pounding.

Samuel laughed. "I take that back. You're just crazy. If you can't see how she feels every time she looks at you, touches you. All those days she tended you on the ship, every drop of blood, cry of pain, was as if it was hers." His eyes were moist with the fond remembrance. "I envy you," he said softly.

Drake nodded, feeling his shoulders snap a little straighter. "You're a companion of great worth, Samuel." He turned toward the steps. "I'm off."

Hearing Samuel's chuckles behind him, Drake rang the bell. The door was answered shortly by the elderly black man who'd driven Tamsyn to the shore the day of his first meeting with her. "Captain Drake Ashton for

Angus MacKiernan," Drake said.

"Marse Angus be indisposed," the man said, examining Drake suspiciously. "You'll have to come back." He peered past Drake to the street, his face a little more friendly upon spying the fine carriage and attendant waiting.

"It's very important I see him immediately," Drake said. *Before I lose my nerve…*

Someone gasped in the hall behind the old servant. Drake saw the dark-skinned girl who'd been with Tamsyn the same day. He winked at her. "I need to see Master MacKiernan," he said again. "Isn't there something that can be arranged?"

The girl ran back to the kitchen and was soon followed to the door by a large black woman, who must be the cook, judging from the flour across the wide apron she wore. The girl murmured to the older woman at great speed, and Drake could see her examining him. *So this is the first hurdle I must cross, is it?* "Ma'am," he said solemnly, inclining his head in greeting. She did the same and smiled.

"Take the man to Marse Angus," she said to the old man, in a stage whisper.

The old man hesitated, frowning, but seemed to reconsider as he looked over his shoulder at the women. "This way," he said at last.

Drake followed him inside. The girl smiled so widely it seemed her face would split.

"Is Tamsyn here?" he asked softly. She nodded. "Thank Heaven. I'm not too late." He followed the servant up the polished stairs and down a hall with several doors, wondering if behind any of them he'd find his love. He couldn't stop and search; for an elderly person, the grizzled attendant kept up a good pace.

The servant stopped before the last door on the left and announced loudly, "Marse Angus, Captain Ashton to see you."

"Ashton? Here?" Drake heard from inside the room. "What business does that mercenary have with me?" The tone was an angry one. Drake swallowed hard. Knees that stood firm in the face of many Spanish blasts and bullets trembled.

"He didn't say." The old man moved aside to allow Drake to pass. As he turned so his master couldn't see him, he smiled at Drake, teeth huge and white in his dark face. It was the boost Drake needed. He nodded to the servant and stepped boldly forward.

He entered the bedroom, which was musty and piled with papers and books, the center taken up with a white-sheeted bed covered with mosquito netting, which was parted on the side nearest the door. In the bed was a man who seemed to have aged years since Drake had seen him the night of the ball six months before. His temples were graying, and his skin pale and lifeless. Only his eyes held passion, burning blue with barely restrained fury.

"What do you want? Haven't you already done all you could to ruin this household?" Angus said.

"That was never my intent." Drake handed Angus the bottle he'd brought, feeling indignation rise at Angus' petulance. "I've come to ask for your daughter's hand in marriage."

"Hah!" That brought a bitter laugh. "If you think you're getting your hands on some rich dowry, you're greatly mistaken. All your shenanigans have nearly ruined me. I've lost most of my customers. They've all hired Winslow to handle their business concerns."

"I have no need of your money," Drake said. "I have my own land and household which are more than adequate to provide for Tamsyn."

Angus pulled his sheets closer to his chest, as if he were cold. "The girl doesn't want you, you know. She told me she's goin' north to hire herself out as a servant." His smile dripped malice. "She's leaving as soon as she can pack."

What? His determination wavered. He'd been right. He was going to lose her. "She can't—"

A voice said from the door, "Papa, you didn't want me here. What choice did I have?"

Drake turned to see Tamsyn, face drawn, observing the two of them. She wore the pink silk dress she'd worn the night of the Pickham ball, with her hair curling around her shoulders. Drake thought she looked like a goddess.

****

Tamsyn's packing had proceeded apace. She'd had time to be a little more reflective than the day she'd hurriedly stuffed her carpetbag to fly to the *Raven*. Several sentimental items she placed in a second bag, which waited now, ready for her departure.

When the bell rang, she had wondered idly who it might be, but she was expecting no one. It came as a shock when Clara burst into the room for the second time that day. *Not Thatcher again. Please, anything but that.*

"It him! Come quick!" Clara cried. She practically danced, pulling at Tamsyn's hand.

"What are you talking about?" Tamsyn retrieved

her hand and went to the window, where she saw the expensive equipage. "Who's here?" As Samuel came around from behind the carriage, she knew, just as Clara told her. *Drake had come for her.* A warmth rushed up from her toes, relief and love overwhelming her.

"The captain! He's wit' Marse Angus." The girl's excitement was so high, she could hardly speak. She opened the door to the hallway, obviously wanting to drag Tamsyn bodily across the hall.

Taking just a second to look in the mirror and smooth her hair, Tamsyn, delighted, slipped quietly down the hall to her father's room. Pausing on the threshold, she overheard Drake ask her father for her hand, and her father's harsh response. Her heart fluttered as the meaning of his words settled into her brain, that Drake wanted them to be together—he wanted to be her husband. He wanted her for her.

Moving into the doorway, she saw her father angrily clutching a bottle of some sort, and Drake, in an impeccable, dark suit which made him a stranger, holding an armful of her favorite frangipani. Her father had just told Drake she was leaving; from the anguished expression on Drake's face as he turned to face her, she had no further doubts about his feelings for her.

Oh, Mamma, finally I have found the love I've wanted...

After she spoke, she stepped into the room, and Drake handed the flowers to her, his arms open. "I have come to ask your father for permission to marry you," he said. "But...I didn't know you'd made other plans." He hesitated, studying her face.

"It didn't seem I had another choice. There's

nothing for me here in Key West, not anymore."

"But, Tamsyn…you and I. I thought we had an understanding. You…" He floundered.

"You never said you wanted to marry me."

"Well. I do," he said awkwardly. "That is, if you'll have me."

"Since you finally decided to ask me…" She paused, teasing him for a few moments, then said simply, "Yes."

She came into his arms gladly, and the flowers, pressed closely between them, loosed their sweet fragrance. It was a heavenly moment, and Tamsyn tried to make it last as long as possible.

"So?" Drake asked the man in the bed.

He looked from one to the other of them with disgust. Finally Angus snapped, "Fine. Take the wench. Just get her and yourself out of my house." He turned away and stared out the window, jaw clenched angrily.

Delighted, Tamsyn giggled and led Drake out by the hand before Angus could change his mind. "You heard what the man commanded." She ducked into her room quickly and handed him the bag she'd set aside.

"Is that everything?" Drake asked in amazement.

"The most important possession I'll have is you," she said, heart full to bursting. She stopped in her tracks as he kissed her deeply. Juba cleared her throat at the foot of the stairs, and she knew her second mother would want to meet the man with whom she'd spend the rest of her life. They scrambled down the stairs, both delirious with excitement.

"This is Captain Drake Ashton," Tamsyn said. "My father has just given us permission to marry."

"I'm happy for you, missy," Juba said, wrapping

her in a huge hug. She then turned to Drake. "You best take care of my girl."

"I will, I will, I promise." He shook their hands and was persuaded to come into the kitchen for a glass of tea. Old James went out to invite Samuel in as well, and they all sat around the kitchen table and chatted like old friends. Tamsyn glowed in the presence of her "real" family and Drake, finally here among them.

Drake said at last, "Tamsyn, we'd better go. I promised Gavril I'd meet him by midafternoon to plan our next voyage."

Tamsyn came to her feet immediately. As her dear friends gathered, she passed before them, hugging each, wondering when she'd see them again.

"I'll be back," she said. "I could never forget you."

"You better not forget me, girl," Juba cautioned, wagging a plump finger. "I expect you be callin' me when de babies start arrivin'. Marse Angus can find his own cook."

Clara laughed and clapped her hands. Tamsyn scolded, "Juba, there's plenty of time for that. You'll be the first person to know." She gathered up her flowers as Drake passed her bag to Samuel. "I love you all."

Clara followed them down the hall and whispered in her ear, "See, I told you that fine-looking man be back."

Tamsyn grinned. "I think it's forever this time."

They paused in the foyer, the six of them taking up the limited space. The front door flew open, and Thatcher stood there, jacketless and breathless, a sword in his hand.

Clara squeaked and withdrew into the kitchen, taking Juba with her. Drake pushed Tamsyn behind him with one arm.

"What in blazes are you doing, Winslow?" Drake asked.

Tamsyn peered around Drake's shoulder, seeing a mad light in Thatcher's eyes. *This is dangerous. What was Thatcher thinking? Does he really believe he can best a real-life swordsman?*

Thatcher surveyed them, waving his sword from side to side. "I don't like to lose. Especially to some criminal upstart who calls himself a hero." He gestured to Old James and Samuel. "The two of you, out. This doesn't concern you."

Samuel protested, but Drake agreed. "Go on outside. I'll be there shortly."

"Flat on his back," Thatcher added.

The two left, and Drake moved into the middle of the small room, his empty hands held out at his sides. "Let me send Tamsyn out, too, Winslow. She doesn't need to see this."

"I disagree. I think she has every right to learn who's the better man." Thatcher moved aside to let Samuel out, then closed the door.

Drake's gaze swept around the room and fixated on the pair of swords hung over the mirror. Tamsyn followed his gaze and moved in front of him to distract Thatcher.

"You're wasting your time," she told him. "I told you I wouldn't marry you. I thought you'd broken the engagement and moved on. What are you doing now? Asking for a death sentence?"

Drake moved as she spoke, lightning quick, and launched upward off a stool along the wall. He knocked the swords from their brackets, quickly retrieving the one that fell closest to him. He stood and tapped the tip of the sword against Thatcher's. "If this is what you want, let's go."

Tamsyn retreated to the stairs, going up five to give the men space. *What can I do to stop this? There's no sense to it. And it's not like I can depend on my father to come lay down some law in his own house.*

Thatcher smiled slowly. "A death sentence? Seems appropriate for a pirate." He jabbed his sword at Drake's midsection.

Drake parried and turned, coming back with a stronger attack, stroke after stroke backing Thatcher toward the door.

Tamsyn gasped as one of Drake's swipes laid Thatcher's cheek open. It only maddened him. He came back at Drake, chaotically thrusting and waving the sword, and kept up a string of invective about Drake, his probable parentage, his nature as scum of the sea, and more.

Tamsyn could hardly breathe as she watched, sure one or the other would end up dead. They continued to battle, knocking over the coatrack and the small table by the door. At one point their swords connected, and Thatcher's blade slid along the old Spanish sword to the hilt, with an awful screech. Their faces were inches apart, and they glared at one another.

"I don't want to kill you," Drake said. "We're leaving. We'll be off the island and out of your social circle, and you can marry whoever you choose. Probably that young lady in the magenta dress. She deserves you."

An inner burst of warmth penetrated her fear. *Just what I thought. Even in this, we think alike.*

"I can't let her be happy. She's ruined me." Thatcher jumped back out of reach, keeping his sword raised in front of him.

"Well, I've promised her she will be happy. So I'll have to disappoint you."

Drake stepped forward and held his sword out to the side, looking for all the world like he was giving Thatcher an opening to stab him through the chest. Thatcher took the bait.

Drake kicked the oncoming sword aside and placed a hand between Thatcher's shoulders as he passed, shoving him hard toward the wall. He crashed into the wood, then stood, weaving and trying to focus.

"Open the door," Drake told Tamsyn.

She raised an eyebrow in curiosity but did as he asked.

Thatcher, recovered, roared and rushed at Drake. He caught Drake's sleeve with the tip of his sword and stabbed, connecting with his arm.

Drake growled and let Thatcher's impetus drive him past where Drake stood, then he shoved him on out the door. Thatcher tumbled down the front steps and landed in the street. Samuel pulled the carriage out of the way. Tamsyn followed them out onto the front stoop. Startled passersby stopped to stare.

"That's not fair!" Thatcher scrambled to his feet, his white shirt thoroughly covered in dust.

"You name me pirate, yet expect me to play by gentlemen's rules?" Drake laughed and kept high ground on the steps, sword ready.

Several young ladies Tamsyn knew walked by and gave Thatcher a withering look.

"Go on, now. I have no wish to hurt you, despite

all you've done to Tamsyn. She's my responsibility now."

Thatcher looked as though he intended to charge again, but surveyed the street and saw the crowd gathering.

Surely he won't let himself be shamed before the whole town. Please, just let him give up.

They could rescind that hero status quite quickly if Drake has to kill him.

Drake took one step down. "Well?"

Thatcher's red face fell, and he skulked away. Tamsyn sighed with relief.

Drake examined the sword. "This is a very nice piece. I wonder what ship your father took it from."

"I have no idea." She retrieved the matching sword and handed it to him. "Here. It's my dowry. Now we must go, before Thatcher regains his courage and tries again."

"Agreed, love." He kissed her, picked up her bags, and took her out the door to the waiting carriage.

She took one last look at the home of her childhood and said goodbye. Time to begin her new life.

****

Tamsyn and Drake married on board the *Raven* that afternoon, as it sailed up the west coast of Florida, on a course for Drake's home at Plantation Key. The *Hawk* followed close behind. Captain Rupert came aboard to perform the ceremony as the crews of the two vessels gathered around. Tamsyn carried the pink-and-white bouquet of flowers Drake had brought her, wearing the rose-colored dress, which conjured up good memories all around. When they stood before Rupert at last, the chubby captain seemed overwhelmed by the requirement for formal ceremony, explaining he had misplaced the book he normally used for such occasions.

"Gentlemen—and lady," he added hurriedly. "We're gathered here, on board this ship, to conduct the marriage of, um, this man and this woman, in wedded bliss. Marriage is a very…lucky state, entered into by, ah, people who…" He shook his head, face turning red. "Drake, I can't remember the words. Why don't you tell each other your vows? You know what promises you wish to make to each other."

Amidst the chuckles of the men, Drake smiled and turned to Tamsyn. "That I shall find the easiest task in the world." Holding her free hand tightly, he said, "Tamsyn MacKiernan, I promise to love, honor, and cherish you all the days of this life and the next. You mean more to me than life itself, and this has been foretold. I would be honored beyond words if you would agree to be my wife."

Tamsyn felt like her soul would explode with pleasure as she suddenly recognized the ceremony she had wished for many months before, whispered in that midnight conversation with Norah Brennan, a ceremony where her own feelings and words would bind her. "Drake Ashton, I will love, honor, and cherish you all the days of this life and the next, forsaking my home and family to cleave to you, as has been foretold. I take you for my husband."

Their hearts full, they looked into each other's eyes in silence as those gathered waited and waited…

Finally, Rupert broke in. "I've remembered the end! I pronounce you man and wife." Mopping his forehead in the bright summer sun, he called, "Who's pouring the wine?"

Drake and Tamsyn shared a long, sweet kiss, their first as a married couple, then joined their friends as the ship sailed on. She held his hand, afraid if she let go he'd slip away into the shadows, as he'd done so many times in her life already.

Toasts were proposed to the happy pair, so often that Tamsyn felt quite light-headed as they arrived in the inlet which led to Drake's house. She believed it was the champagne, which Captain Rupert assured her was taken from a fine French ship in the name of diplomacy. But it could well be the giddiness of her joy, a joy she saw reflected in Drake's face, as their two halves had joined to become a whole.

The *Hawk* and the *Raven* anchored in the deeper water of Florida Bay, then the men quarreled over who should have the right to row them to shore. Finally Tamsyn selected Mateo, who'd only had a token glass of wine, pronouncing him the most sober. He rowed them in, then prepared to take the dinghy back to the ships, where the celebrating would probably go on most of the night. The boy smiled as they stood on the sand at last.

"This has been the happiest day of my life," he said to them, tears springing to his eyes.

"Mine, too." Drake leaned back to wrap the boy in a rough embrace.

"Thank you for everything, Mateo." Tamsyn kissed the boy on the cheek. "Thank you for being our friend."

They watched as the boy rowed back out the inlet, then Drake took her hand and turned her around. "Let's go home, my love."

The sunset was painted with coral, orange, and red

tones, spectacular over the Gulf of Mexico as they walked on the path of coral rocks which led to the house. The building itself was of rock and wood construction, a one-story house that spread low and wide across the yard, surrounded in tall grasses. A wide porch with thick wooden supports looked out toward the western horizon over the water, which captured the scarlet and golden reflections of the sun. As she turned to the east, the same colors shone in the glass of the sea-facing windows, painting the world in a rosy glow. Farther afield, she could see the shadowed, pointy plants which had to be the pineapples of which he'd spoken.

"This is beautiful," she said in awe.

"Not as beautiful as you," he replied, pulling her close. He kissed her thoroughly, then swung her up into his arms. "Across the threshold, milady."

She held on tight around his neck as he took her through the darkening house to the bedroom. "The lady and the pirate. It has a nice ring to it, don't you think?"

"I promise not to act too much like a pirate, if you won't act too much like a lady," he said gruffly, tossing her onto the bed.

Amid peals of laughter, they embraced as day faded to night, consummating their long journey to have and hold each other, discovering the promise of the years to come.

A word about the author...

Alana Lorens dreamed for many years of finding her very own knight on a white steed, or perhaps being one herself. Instead, she settles for flights of fancy, inspired excursions into fictional places with fascinating companions from her imagination that she likes to share with others.

She has been a published writer for over thirty years, including seven years as a reporter and editor at a newspaper in Homestead, Florida. Her list of publications is eclectic, from science fiction to romance to horror, from tech reporting to television reviews, and a blog about autism, a journey she shares with other parents of special needs children.

Alana has retired from her life as a family law attorney, and now lives as a post-modern hippie in Asheville, North Carolina.

www.alana-lorens.com

Thank you for purchasing
this publication of The Wild Rose Press, Inc.

For questions or more information
contact us at
info@thewildrosepress.com.

The Wild Rose Press, Inc.
www.thewildrosepress.com